IN DEATH'S COMPANY

SCYTHES & SOULS
BOOK ONE

NATALIE JOHANSON

First published by Tea and Dagger Publishing 2025

Copyright © 2025 by Natalie Johanson

All rights reserved.

All rights reserved. No part of this publication may be reproduced, stored, or transmitted in any form or by any means, electronic, mechanical, photocopying, recording, scanning, or otherwise without written permission from the publisher. It is illegal to copy this book, post it to a website, or distribute it by any other means without permission.

This novel is entirely a work of fiction. The names, characters, and incidents portrayed in it are the work of the author's imagination. Any resemblance to actual persons, living or dead, events, or localities is entirely coincidental.

Designations used by companies to distinguish their products are often claimed as trademarks. All brand names and product names used in this book and on its cover are trade names, service marks, trademarks, and registered trademarks of their respective owners. The publishers and the book are not associated with any product or vendor mentioned in this book. None of the companies referenced within the book have endorsed the book.

First edition

Editing by The Wallflower Editing

Editing by Dee's Notes: Editing Services

IN DEATH'S COMPANY

ALSO BY NATALIE JOHANSON

SHADOWSTALKER SERIES

Shadow's Voice

Shadow's Past

Shadow's Fall

CHAPTER ONE
I AM DEATH

The dead were rarely on time. Lady Death observed the funeral goers as they drifted away from the grave. Pulling out a small silver watch attached to a delicate chain at her waist, she checked the time. Soon. The rain was a soft drizzle, misting her face and sticking to the strands of her hair as it fell. Leaning with her shoulder against the tree, one of the few in this cemetery, she turned her attention back to the fresh grave with a lazy blink. The mourners had been few, the service short and quiet; simple words whispered in the night. They hadn't the money, it seemed, for a proper plot in the cemetery—or perhaps there wasn't the space—and so the family had hastily dug a shallow grave on top of the current inhabitant. With the cemetery quiet on the hill overlooking the harbor, they chiseled the man's name, small and without flourish, into the corner of the headstone above whoever he now rested on.

How he was buried didn't matter to Lady Death. It wasn't his body she was here for.

Looking around the dark space, she saw the faint glow of

the lingering souls. Many tended to do so in places with history and age. Some had faded with time to be simple spots of energy, but a few with forms wandered aimlessly around their stones.

She turned her attention back to the fresh mound of earth. This soul had clung onto the body and this world with a ferocity that had surprised Harper. Even still, it lingered. A foghorn blared from the harbor, its alarm a low warning through the night air.

Death sniffed the air and detected the ozone in the rain and a strange metallic taste of old magic. It tasted like the history you find in forests or bogs—ancient and forgotten. She couldn't place the magic, but it had a tang of familiarity to it that gave her pause. Tilting her head, she pulled the smell deeper, taking a larger breath. Some deep, forgotten memory knew this smell, but she couldn't put a name to it. Like a dream you forget upon waking.

With a frown, she shook herself and returned to her vigilance in the cemetery. Magic didn't just appear. It was summoned. Conjured. Woken. Something ancient and powerful was moving about the land of men again, but she relaxed her shoulders. Those were issues for the living.

As she glanced around the cemetery again, only the dead remained, and she checked the watch once more. The soul had some time still.

A shimmer of silver from the grave caught her eye. "Finally," she muttered, pushing away from the tree and slipping her watch back into her pocket.

The ghost of the man rose from the casket and glowered at her, then huffed a sigh and dropped his shoulders. Death stepped softly toward the soul and held out her hand to him.

"I didn't want to go."

"I know," she murmured, hand still held out to him, waiting.

"B-but..." His form flickered. "Who are you?"

She smiled softly. "I am Death. But you can call me Harper."

The man reluctantly took her hand. "Harper?"

She extended her free hand, fingers tipped with black claws, and split the air. The air shimmered and flashed, then a bright-silver crack appeared. With a wave of her hand, the crack widened to a fissure. Silver strands hung from the edges of the tear, reaching for each other in their desperate attempt to close the hole. She grabbed the edge with her hand and pulled the hole wider, her will stronger than the nature of the world.

"A friend gave me the name a long time ago. I liked it."

Then she pulled him into the Underworld. The split in the layers of the world closed behind her as she stepped into the snowy, silent Underworld. Upon letting go of her hold on the boundaries between worlds, between life and death, the opening snapped shut. In the hush that followed, she glanced around the gloom of the Underworld. Her eyes adjusted to the new dimness—a haze that doesn't quite exist in the human world. Glancing up through the barren branches of the trees, the slight orange glow of the overcast sky welcomed her. The trees and silence of the Forgotten Forest was an eerie shock after the noise and life and energy of the human world.

"Is this hell?" the soul next to her asked.

His face was sullen as she released his hand. "This is the next step in your journey. Hell is a place of your own making."

He looked around the silent trees, snow falling gently around them.

"When your business is complete, you will move on, wherever that is for you," she said. "Until then, you will walk the Forest."

His shoulders sagged at her words, hands hanging limp at his sides, before he floated away to join the other souls among the trees. The silence was deafening as she walked among their ghostly forms. A couple had enough presence of mind to look up from their gloom and nod at her. Most were still lost to themselves. While the Underworld served as the prison for the damned, it was also a way station for the dead. People who came to peace with their death and had no unfinished business moved on quicker. Those who couldn't... well, they lingered. Not all moved on.

She thought of those who never moved on and were stuck here as wraiths in a hell of their own making. Wraiths had little humanity left and needed to be banished to the other side of the Maw lest their malevolence corrupt the other souls.

Harper moved through the trees until they faded in the distance and the snowy plain opened up. A giant gorge scarred the land, splitting it down the middle. The Maw. A deep, unending chasm filled with lost and damned souls—the demons and monsters of the world. The other side was an area of flat, treeless expanse where the wraiths wandered.

Standing at the edge, Harper looked down into the darkness of the Maw. Wisps floated and flitted near the top—little ghosts of beings filled with hate and malevolence. The farther down you went, the worse the denizens. That was Death's true purpose. Her most sacred duty. Guardian of the Maw.

The thin shimmering magic that was woven across the surface of the canyon was the barrier she maintained. It glinted and flexed against the beings beneath it, and she felt it as tugs on her soul. Not often, but occasionally, one of the mid-level demons would get an idea in its tiny brain and hatch an escape. They never made it far. Harper's hounds were fine hunters and had quite a taste for demons.

Stretching her hand out, she sent a query of magic over the barrier, testing for weak spots or holes. Her lips curved in a small smile of pride when none were found. This barrier must hold until the End of Days. Only then would the damned and cursed be allowed to leave.

A Grim Reaper passed and nodded his hooded head to her. She returned the greeting. Once, so long ago she tried not to think of it, Harper had been alone in the duty of gathering souls. Alone... and lonely. She'd been constantly surrounded by the souls of the dead, but they were too lost in their sorrow, or memories, and were not companions for Death. They did not speak or engage with the living. When the Nephilim first appeared on Earth, Harper thought she had at last found companions. The rejected offspring of the angels and demons; they'd been scorned and hunted. Perhaps they could find peace and company in a land between with her. But Harper had eventually learned even offering her home to the Nephilim and having them join her as Grim Reapers had not gained her the companionship she sought. They were, in the end, often as silent as the souls they ferried. But she had opened up her home to them, taking them in and offering protection against those who would hunt them, and so they remain.

"Lady Death," a voice, crisp like angel bells, greeted her.

Armeal, the most beautiful of the Nephilim, standing nearly a head taller than Harper, blinked at her. As an Old One, Armeal was one of the eldest Nephilim that had survived the Great Hunt. Armeal's wings were folded close to his body, the edges of his white feathers tinged black and gold. Not every Nephilim inherited wings from their angel heritage, but Armeal had, and he made sure they were visible every single day. Angels were prideful creatures, and demons were arrogant beasts, but they had nothing on the pride and arrogance of a Nephilim. And Armeal was the worst of the Nephilim. The black at the edges of his beautiful wings was a sign of his time in the Underworld, but he resisted the contamination, fought against it. One day, however, despite his efforts, the black would overtake the white. It was a sign of his strength, his power, to be able to fight off the touches of the Underworld and retain his identity when most others couldn't.

"Still in white, I see," she said, eyes narrowing on the Reaper.

Armeal ran a hand down his pristine white suit. The beautiful three-piece suit and golden tie were not the standard attire of the Grim Reapers. It irritated her, his insistence to wear his white suit over the Reaper cloak, but she had told herself long ago she would not impose her will on the Nephilim.

"What do you think will happen when the mortals tell their stories of near-death experiences with being dressed in a white suit, when others have all seen the one figure dressed in a black robe before?"

Armeal shifted his wings, feathers rustling softly in the still air. "I think I will have given the mortals something new to ponder before their memory fades."

She clucked her tongue. Armeal nodded once more to her, then continued on his way. He was a complicated one. His resistance to the ways of the Underworld and his determination to be singular set him apart. He was arrogant and short, though he was the only one who spoke with her in any kind of regularity. So she tolerated his rough edges, his gruffness, his defiance. She huffed again and turned to collect her next soul.

CHAPTER TWO
BROKEN HEARTS

May Haines clamped her lips shut against the flies in the room—the smell and the flies. Mostly the flies.

Shallow breaths, she told herself as she bent over the heavily decomposed body.

As an investigator for Arizona's Medical Examiner's Office, this wasn't that strange of a day. Dead bodies were the job description. That didn't mean she enjoyed the smell. Or the fat flies buzzing too close to her face. May wrinkled her nose as she continued to take photos of the—probably male—body on the bed. Decomps, though... those sucked no matter how many years she'd been doing this.

As a daughter of Green Witches, her parents had been appalled when she took this job after finishing her degree in biology. *"Green Witches don't work in death fields,"* her mother had said. Well, since she couldn't even keep house plants alive, it had felt like the perfect job to her. She'd always been more interested in solving puzzles than making things grow, anyway.

A detective stood in the doorway looking as grim as she felt.

"You said he was last seen when?" she muttered, trying to keep her lips as closed as possible.

If a fly gets in my mouth, I will barf.

The detective cleared his throat as he checked his small notebook. "Family said they last talked to him on the phone four weeks ago."

May gingerly walked around to the other side of the bed, careful to avoid the piles of maggots and... sludge. "Sounds right."

"I checked the thermostat when I got here. Looks like the AC's been off and he was only using the pedestal fans."

The two pedestal fans stood in the corners of the room. "In this heat!" She scoffed and slung her camera over her shoulder to bend down to the floor. A pair of pants laid near the foot of the bed, and she hoped there was a wallet with an ID in the pockets. "No wonder he's so bad."

The detective just grunted and shuffled on his feet, and May grinned at him. "First decomp?"

"No," he said with heat in his voice. "But it is my first bug one. I don't do bugs."

She twitched and threw her hand over her head as a fly buzzed too close for comfort. Riffling through the pants, she found the man's ID. After snapping photos, she tucked the driver's license into a small baggie and stood, only to wobble and sink back to her knees. A hand landed on her elbow and another hand gripped her shirt to keep her from tipping face-first into what was left of Mr. Rayes. Her vision went white with static, like an old nineties TV that the cute detective holding her upright had probably never experienced.

"Hey, hey. Are you okay? Do you need medical?"

"No-no-no-no," she muttered, pulling air into her

suddenly starved lungs. The last thing she wanted was her mother finding out she'd passed out at work. Her mom was already pitching an adult fit about her working as much as she still was.

Stupid heart.

"Just stood up too fast."

"Ma'am, you went as white as a sheet. Are you sure?"

She waved him off even though she needed his help to get to her feet. "I'm good. Just... I'm good."

He held onto her, anyway, as she blinked her eyes clear and sucked down air. "I better not swallow a fly."

He chuckled and slowly stepped away.

"I'm good," she insisted. "Just... you know, a pesky heart that doesn't always work."

The detective watched her in that silent way cops did when they put together what you said with what you didn't. She waved him off again and pulled her phone from her pocket, not wanting to talk about her failing heart or the too long of a transplant list.

"Transport is here."

He nodded and went to the front to escort them in, and May stood in silence with the buzzing flies—and her dying heart pounding uselessly in her chest. Her head hurt from the drop in blood pressure, and her hands shook. All of which pissed her off more. She should've known better than to stand up so fast, but she also should do what her mom says and take the medical leave.

She pulled her camera back around with an angry tug; she also just didn't want to be dying all the time. Not yet.

The transport team, two men who got paid far too little to pick up dead bodies for a living, came trudging in. Mike, her favorite body snatcher, snorted at the scene. "You weren't kidding."

She shook her head. "Do I ever lie to you?"

He chuckled and laid out the body bag, lining it with the plastic bag. "One day, I wish you would."

"Never."

In the end, they rolled poor Mr. Rayes up in the sheet he was lying on and put the whole thing in the body bag as is. May finished her photos, then followed the detective and body snatchers outside into the blessedly fresh air.

The crickets chirped in the cool night. Cooler, anyway. It was still summer in Arizona.

"Well," the detective said as he walked up next to her, snapping off his gloves, "thanks for coming out."

"Any time," she said. "He's technically going in as a John Doe until we can confirm his ID. He's too decomposed to make an ID off his photo."

"Yeah, I figured," he said, and raked his hand through his sandy hair, turning his dimpled face toward her. "Let me know if it's a surprise and not who we think it is?"

May gasped a laugh. "Yeah. I'll be sure to let you know."

"You're gonna do DNA?"

May shrugged as the transport van drove off. "His one hand looked decent enough we might be able to get fingerprints."

"For real?" he asked. "Off that?"

"Oh yeah, we're gonna do cool science shit," she said with a grin, and started walking toward her beat-up Beetle. "Have a good night."

Finally in her car, she collapsed in the seat, panting to pull air into her overworked lungs with too little blood from a shitty heart. Digging around in her purse, she pulled out her bottle of Digoxin and swallowed one. Supposedly, it helped with her heart rate. It was the newest on the long list of meds her docs have tried, and they were getting into the we-don't-use-it-much-anymore list.

Her last appointment hadn't gone well, and she could read the news the doc didn't want to say in his eyes, in her mom's shoulders, in her dad's stillness. Unfortunately, May would have to face the fact she was probably going to die before a new heart was found.

She took a deep breath and wiped the sweat gathering at her hairline, then started her car. A flicker of movement, a haze in the air, made her turn and squint at the dark street. She could've sworn someone was standing on the front lawn, but the longer she looked, the more foolish she felt. No one was there. Not even the dead anymore.

Nearly two weeks later, May sat panting on her couch. Her vision swarmed and flickered, warning her she was about to pass out. These attacks were becoming more and more frequent. She took deep breaths, trying to avoid hyperventilating as she shakily pushed herself to her feet. Her meds. She needed her meds, but they were in her purse in the kitchen. Which was, unfortunately, too many steps away as she sank ungracefully to her knees. She barely managed to catch herself before her face ate carpet.

This one felt bad. Worse.

She tried crawling to the kitchen, but her vision went black, and she felt herself falling. A surreal fall that didn't seem real as she seemed to fall too far for too long. But the thud sounded very real when her shoulder hit the ground. Panic, true unadulterated panic, settled into her blood, and she knew death was coming this time. She wouldn't get up this time. That terror, the knowledge it was for real this time, had May blinking against tears as she forced her eyes open. Her breath was shallow and quick, basically useless, when she tried to lift her head, move her arms, *anything*.

A shimmer in the air caught her attention even though her vision had started to fade at the edges again. It hovered just outside of her ability to understand what it was. She had the impression it was watching her. Waiting. Judging.

But she wasn't ready to die yet.

Tears leaked from her failing eyes and down her cold cheeks. She wasn't going to die like this. Not alone on her apartment floor. It'd be at least three days before anyone came looking for her. She was off for the weekend, and she ignored her parents' phone calls enough already that it'd be Monday before anyone from work thought to look for her.

She wheezed a laugh, a guttural sound, at the thought that ignoring her helicopter mother would be what did her in.

"Not like this," she huffed, coughing, chest burning and heart failing.

She searched for her magic, the useless Green Witch magic her mother always yelled at her for not practicing more, and reached for the shimmering, hazy thing staring at her. She didn't know what it was. Or if it was even real, but it was her last chance, and she wasn't going to die without trying.

Her magic stuttered and failed. Like it always did.

That only angered her. She was already dying, dammit, and now her magic was giving up on her too! First her heart, and now this? Something warmed in her chest, a hot, burning spot, and it *reached* for the shimmering thing. Then something snapped.

With a gasp, May forcefully sucked air into her starving lungs, with her broken, weak heart puttering in a sad attempt at a heartbeat. The shimmering thing had left, if it was ever even there, and May rolled to her hands and knees. She didn't know what had given her this last little bit of life, but she wouldn't waste it.

It took all over her strength to climb up the cabinet to reach her purse on the countertop. With weak, shaky hands, she pulled it down, collapsing onto the floor again. She searched blindly for her phone and held down the side button until she heard the little ding.

"Siri," she wheezed, "call 9-1-1."

CHAPTER THREE
DELAYING DEATH

Harper sighed as the soul floated way. It was a bitter soul, filled with hate and anger and entitlement. In her eons of ferrying souls to the Underworld, she'd gotten quite good at picking which ones would move on and which would haunt the endless Wasteland across the Maw. That soul would fester. Without a doubt, Harper would be moving her to the Wasteland.

She tsked and turned away to where her next soul waited. Slicing through the air, the layers shimmered and weaved before rending beneath her claws. Striding through the opening, Harper's booted feet stepped silently into a dark room. The smell of sickness was thick in the air. The woman lay in her bed and her painful, wheezing breathing was a soft sound in the stillness. The shroud of death hung on her, dark and heavy across her shoulders. Her time was soon.

Harper stopped at the woman's bed and looked down at her drawn form. The cancer had eaten her, taken everything from her, and she was barely a husk of what she'd once been. On the bedside table sat a collection of empty pill bottles and needles. Harper tilted her head at the baggie of black substance next to the needles and stained spoon.

"Don't judge me." The man stood at the bedroom's door, and Harper lifted a lip at him. *Necromancer.* No wonder he could see her. His magic was slimy and thick around him, heavy in her throat as she smelled it.

"I do not judge the dying," she said.

He jutted his chin toward the table. "Heroin is easier to get than oxy, and it dulls the pain the same."

"I do not judge the dying," she said again, looking down at the woman. Her breathing had slowed and grown shallower with each pained effort.

"You can't have her." He rushed up to the bed and grabbed the woman's arm like he would hold her back from death.

Harper tilted her head again. "Victoria Thormunt's name is written in my Book of Souls. If it is her time, then I will take her, Necromancer."

"No," he protested. "No, I can raise her."

Her lips peeled back from her teeth in a silent snarl at the abomination he was suggesting. "Her soul," she growled, "will still be mine. What you do with her body is the living's business."

Harper pulled her watch from her pocket and flicked the lid open with the small button. Victoria's window of death was closing. Perhaps tonight would not be her time.

"But she told me," the man said, straining over the bed toward Harper. "She told me there was a way."

Harper resisted rolling her eyes at the ignorant man. Necromancers always thought they would cheat death. As if raising the body from the ground and reuniting it with a soul were the same things. With her watch cradled in her pale hand, she checked it again. Close.

Looking back at Victoria, she was surprised to see the

woman's eyes open, watching her. They were glazed with drugs and pain, her brow slicked with sweat, but she watched Harper.

"Are you ready?" she asked.

"No!" the man shouted.

Harper turned on him with a growl and waved her fingers at him. Her magic knocked him back against the wall. "This does not concern you, Necromancer."

"It does," Victoria whispered faintly.

Harper smiled gently at her. "He has no say in your death. Only the Fates do."

"Not yet," she wheezed, pleaded. Harper could feel the resistance in Victoria's soul and the fight she managed to muster against her death. "Not yet. He's not ready."

"They never are."

Victoria shook her head against her pillow. "No. No, he'll do something rash. Not yet."

Harper grunted and checked her watch again, and the window ticked by. Snapping her clock shut, she slipped it back into her pocket.

"It appears the Fates agree," she said as Victoria blinked at her.

She stepped away and over to Victoria's husband to glare down at him where he stayed on the floor. "You cannot stop death."

"But she said there was a way."

She ground her teeth. "All you Necromancers are alike. I will come, and when it is time, she will come with me."

She turned, but a scent caught her attention. One she had forgotten about, but that unnamed familiarity gave her pause again. Studying the room, she sniffed the air, but it was gone.

Angrily, she sliced the world apart and stepped away.

Her next stop was a room of beeping and hissing of machines keeping a woman alive. It was cold and sterile, a stark contrast to the home she had come from. This was the second time this month she had visited this woman. Harper stared down at May Haines with a frown. The last time Harper had visited the woman, she'd done something... unexplainable with her magic. Harper still wasn't sure what it had been, but she'd felt the witch's magic reaching for her. It had felt... Harper frowned again. She wasn't sure what she'd felt, but the human had found a last burst of life. For a moment, at least. May was once again perched on the precipice of life and death. Her heart was failing, and if the speed and tone of the beeps were any indication, failing quickly. But this was a world of artificial limbs and organ swaps. Her future was far from written yet.

Harper leaned against the wall and waited. May had resisted the pull of death many times before. Each time, the Fates waffled on her future. It was strange. The Fates rarely allowed so many chances.

Harper rolled her eyes. The Fates were fickle things, and trying to understand why they did what they did was beyond even Harper's abilities. She eyed May, pallid and weak, surrounded by tubing and wires. What was different about this one?

Suddenly, the beeping was replaced by alarm sounds and a long, solid tone. A flurry of doctors and nurses rushed around the woman. Harsh voices and barely controlled shouting filled the room over the din of the alarm bells. Harper remained unseen by the mortals, as she was on a different plane. A plane between life and death.

A shimmer of light rose from the bed, and May's soul drifted up from her still body. She remained tethered, not quite dead yet, and the bright-silvery thread linked her ghostly form to her physical. Harper squinted at May's soul, trying to see what was special about her. She felt a pull of familiarity, like a lost friend, but nothing that would explain the Fates' attention.

"Oh…" May said, glancing from the bed surrounded by doctors and then to Harper. "Am I dead, then?"

Harper smiled gently at her and pushed away from the wall to stand next to her. "Not yet. Not quite."

"Huh," she grunted, looking again at the doctors, and worried her lip between her teeth before turning again to Harper. "So, are you the Angel of Death?"

Harper tilted her head. "I am Death."

May squinted at Harper. "Have I seen you before?"

Harper smiled a close-lipped smile. "Who could say?"

May frowned, her eyes crinkling at the edges, then huffed a breath and turned away with a nod. "So, what now?"

Harper tilted her head at the soft-spoken woman. "Now we wait." She checked her watch, and May leaned around to try to see the watch face as well, but Harper grinned and tucked it away before she could.

"Just like that?"

"Just like that," Harper murmured.

May turned away, and they silently watched as the doctors continued to push medications through the IV lines and placed an intubation tube. Her soul was bright and vibrant, holding all the life her body struggled with. Bright-blue eyes crinkled at the corners when she smiled. It was a sharp contrast to the drawn and pale husk on the bed, with her cheeks sunken and hollow.

"Can we talk?" May suddenly asked, and continued to watch the doctors work around her body.

"We may," Harper said, amused. Rarely were souls this chatty, especially if the fate of their life sat before them still.

"So you're... Lady Death?" May asked, and Harper nodded. "And... does Lady Death like coffee?"

A laugh burst from Harper, harsh and loud and unexpected. "What?"

"Coffee? Do you like coffee?"

She laughed and shoved her hands into her pockets. "What a question to ask."

"What am I supposed to ask?" May asked with a smile.

Harper shrugged and folded her arms, only to unfold them and shove her hands back into her pockets. "I have had souls beg for their life, barter. I have had them try to fight and run but never ask if I like coffee."

"Well—" May giggled. "Maybe I'm just not as rude as the others, then."

"Are you not worried about your life?" Harper gestured to the doctors frantically working, one on her knees on the slim bed while rhythmically pressing May's thin chest.

"I've known my heart would give out eventually since I was twelve. The chances of a heart replacement were so low..." She shrugged and turned back to Harper. "I knew this was coming. At least I tried."

"Clear!" someone shouted from the bed, and the herd of doctors stepped back.

The buzz and clap of the defibrillator broke through the chatter and noise of the doctors into a now-eerily silent room as they watched the monitors.

"Push another epinephrine."

The Tether between May and her body blazed white, then slowly, she was pulled back.

"Oh." May frowned. "What's—"

Harper smiled. "Today is not your day."

"But you never answered my question," she said, voice hollow as it drifted through the planes.

Harper grinned. The human likely wouldn't remember this moment, this conversation, or Harper, but she answered anyway. "I love a good cup of coffee."

May smiled as her soul settled into her body just as a beep broke through the room. Then another. The doctors exclaimed in relief, and one clapped.

Harper checked her slim silver watch once more before splitting the veils of the world with her claw-tipped finger. The layers of the world bled a bright, blinding light. The opening widened, and Harper gripped the edge, pulling it wider still, before stepping through into the Underworld, into her castle, her room of the dead.

Blinking, Harper let out a breath and walked to her chair set behind a desk. The walls surrounding her simple desk were filled with rows upon rows of books. Books of the Dead with lists upon lists of names of each soul that had passed through her domain. Even the ones that refused to leave and lingered on Earth.

Armeal stalked into her office from the doorway, stretching his beautiful wings as he did. She raised an eyebrow at him, and he tucked them back again. "The human witch delayed you again, it seems."

"Yes," she finally said, flipping open the large leather-bound book in front of her. May's name had previously been inscribed in flowing golden script at the end of the list, but now, her name was gone. "Seems today was not her day."

Had she collected her soul, it would settle into a black ink, unchangeable and permanent. Above her name, Victoria Thormunt's name still glimmered gold. Her time was still soon. She had not escaped death, only delayed.

"The Fates must have something planned for that human, to save her so many times from you."

Harper silently let out a breath. "That is not how the Fates work. You know this."

Armeal shrugged, his feathers rustling in the deathly silent room. "They are fickle things."

Yes, she thought. *They are that.* She ran her finger down the faintly glowing golden names on the paper. Today may still be the day for these souls. She leaned back in her chair and magicked a cup of coffee into existance.

"Are you going out again, Lady Death?"

"No," she said with a sigh, and clasped her hands around her cup. She couldn't feel the warmth but knew it was there. "The Reapers can attend to these without me."

Something felt odd since she had left the witch and her failing heart. She rubbed her fingers to her sternum—like she had an ache, though she felt no pain. There was a yearning, a missing sensation at the back of her mind, and it left her feeling off balance. She couldn't identify the cause of the feeling, but as she sat, sipping coffee from an unending cup, the feeling passed and dulled. And soon, she forgot it had ever been there. She waved her fingers at the cold fireplace to her left. It roared to life with flame and heat. She wasn't cold, but there was something soothing about the crack and pop of a fire in a room. Listening to the hiss of flames, she sat watching the names on her list slowly go from gold to black as the Reapers collected them. In a world where time did not pass, the names changing was the only way to know time had ticked by on the other plane.

CHAPTER FOUR
LEAVE THE GHOSTS

May blinked at the hospital ceiling; the incessant sound of the beeping next to her threatened to drive her into insanity. She was alive, so she really shouldn't complain too much, and the new heart seemed to be doing well. But that damned beeping. She rolled her head on her pillows to stare at the offensive machine displaying all her vitals that confirmed she was, in fact, alive. It was still annoying as hell. She huffed a sigh and slowly, painfully, incrementally shifted herself up on her pillow and pressed the button to lift her into a more seated position. The TV was playing some reality TV show, with the volume lower enough she could barely hear it.

The flowers that had poured in, in the two weeks after her surgery had been squeezed onto a small rolling table and shoved against the window on the far wall. The blooms were wilted and drooping.

The door to her hospital room clicked open, and her favorite nurse—because when you're at the hospital as often and as long as May had been, you do get favorites—walked in. Kathy smiled a giant smile, full of teeth and crinkling eyes.

"Well, hello, sweetie. How was your nap?"

May didn't have the heart to tell her she'd lain there staring at the blank ceiling. Kathy was just too happy. She didn't want to disappoint her.

"It was nice," she said instead.

"Oh, good," Kathy said as she turned her attention to the damned beeping machines and her IV pole. "How's your pain level?"

May shrugged, then winced as it pulled on the stitches in her chest. "Fine."

"Mm-hm." She hummed at her, planting her hands on her hips. "You're improving at miraculous milestones, dear. Be happy."

She'd be happy when she was sure she wasn't dying anymore. It was far too soon for that naive behavior.

"Well," Kathy said when May continued to sit in silence, "Dr. Sato will be in later this afternoon to go over your latest test results with you."

She nodded and glanced at the clock on the wall across from her bed. Almost two in the afternoon. Her mom would be here any minute.

"Anything I can get you before I head onto my other rounds?"

May shook her head and forced a smile. She'd been warned before the surgery that depression could be a side effect afterward. That she might struggle mentally with the surgery more than she expected. Perhaps that was what she was feeling... or not feeling. After years of nearly dying, maybe she was just too jaded to believe she wasn't now. Though, as she looked around the room as Kathy was leaving, the mysterious Lady Death hadn't appeared again. She barely remembered that day. It was several weeks ago, right before she'd been approved for this heart. Everything was a bit of a haze, but then she was staring down at her body, and everything had come into sharp focus. It was too clear for her to think she'd been dreaming or hallucinating from the pain medications.

No. She wasn't clever enough to come up with the eternal being that had stood next to her.

Her door clicked open again, and her mom came busting into the room, a large canvas bag slung over one shoulder. "Mayflower!"

She rolled her eyes. For two decades, May had been too old for the nickname, but that hadn't stopped her mother.

"I come bearing gifts!" she said as she dropped her bag on the bed next to May. She riffled through it and pulled out this week's books.

"Oh, Fabio," May said, looking through the collection of old romance paperbacks her mom had brought. "What would I do without you?"

Her mom chortled, turning to the drooping flowers under the window, then touched a finger to each bloom, and they sprang back to life. Each full of color and straightening like it had been freshly cut. May eyed her mother's flawless and seemingly easy use of her Green Witch magic.

"You keep doing that, and even Joan will notice something is weird with the eternal flowers."

Her mom grunted and pulled the stiff chair over. "Joan couldn't find her way out of a paper bag without the bag needing an IV."

May laughed, a dry, dusty sound, but it was a real laugh, at least. Her mom gathered up last week's books and put those into her now-empty bag.

"Has Dr. Sato come yet?"

May shook her head and glanced at the clock again. Soon. Couple more minutes.

"So how are you feeling?" her mom asked.

"Alive," she said dryly, and looked to the door.

Right... now!

On cue, the ghost—a pale barely distinguishable shape—floated through the door. It walked the same path it had every other day, stopping at the foot of her bed. It was bent over, maybe reading something, then it turned and walked back through the closed door. When she'd first seen it, she'd yelped loud enough Kathy came running. She'd convinced herself then it was probably the morphine. That shit was strong and always gave her weird dreams. She had been awake... but surely, that's what it was.

Then, right on time the next day, the ghost had appeared again. It followed its same little path and disappeared. As the days crept on, May had accepted it wasn't the meds making her see the ghost. She just... could, so she'd started to create a little backstory for the ghost. So far, she had decided he was a resident from some far-back time. He'd died while doing his rounds, but he'd been so focused, so driven to finish his residency that even in death, he was still here. Doing his rounds.

It was a little depressing, she admitted. Maybe this week she'd come up with a new story for him.

"May?"

"Hm?" she asked, and blinked at her mom.

Her mom huffed and shook her head.

"Never mind."

May shrugged and was saved from an explanation by Dr. Mark Sato walking into her room. He was a no-nonsense, straight-to-the-point man in his fifties and a fantastic surgeon, one of the best in the area, but you'd know it, talking to him. He didn't act arrogant or like he was the smartest person in the room even though he undoubtedly was most of the time.

"Hey, Dr. Sato," May said, a soft smile on her lips.

Dr. Sato glanced at the two of them through his thin wire-framed glasses. "Hello, Miss Haines."

He stood at the end of her bed in a strange mirror to what her ghost had just done. He met her gaze, his almond eyes crinkling at the edges. "Your most recent tests look very good, Miss Haines."

"Oh, good," her mom breathed, and May glanced at her before returning her gaze to the doctor.

"How would you feel"—May's heart started to race—"about going home in the next day or two?"

Well, shit, maybe she could start believing she would survive this. Hopefully, she'd leave the ghost at the hospital.

CHAPTER FIVE
DEATH AND COFFEE

The house was quiet and dark, somber. Empty. Harper scanned the elderly woman's home before turning again to her body. She lay in her bed, tucked beneath her bedding as she'd been since going to bed the night before. Mirta's spirit glowered at Harper next to the bed, her arms folded tight across her chest, and her chin tucked as she stared at Harper. Her eyebrows pinched with disapproval.

"I won't go," she said for the fifth time.

Harper blinked at her, hand still held out. "You will bind yourself to this place for eternity if you do not."

"This is my home," she said, her Spanish accent thick. "I didn't leave when the neighbors threatened immigration. I wouldn't leave when my hijo said I should for my *health*." She spit the word like it was an insult. "I won't leave it now."

"You will haunt this home," Harper said again, hand slowly falling. "It will be a long, lonely, withering existence."

Mirta lifted her chin in defiance. "It is my home."

Harper pulled out her slim pocket watch and checked the time. Mirta's time clicked by, and she saw as the spirit's Tether bound itself to the floor beneath Mirta. She was tethered here, for all time now. To haunt. To wander the halls of her old home as time moved on while she remained trapped in her past.

"As you wish," Harper murmured, and turned away.

She stepped outside, the Arizona sun blazing around her as she studied the quiet suburban street. It was too hot for the mortals to venture outside, and it was empty, save for the few cars driving past the rows of simple adobe-style homes. It was a community, small and old, but she could see the history and stories in the homes. She turned away at the emptiness that caused.

A tug, a pulling sensation gave her pause, and she frowned. There it was again. She stretched her magic out, searching for... She didn't know what she was seeking. Whatever was causing *this* feeling. Her magic settled on the familiar soul of the witch with her broken heart not far from here. She could find any soul that had touched death, but why had her magic reached out to *that* soul?

Harper set off to see what had become of May Haines. Drawing more of her magic around her, she settled in with the living, no longer between planes. She slipped a simple pair of sunglasses over her eyes and followed the slight pull on her being, the tug all souls gave when they'd been touched by Death, and found the woman in a coffee shop tucked away from the main roads. A locals coffee shop, small and unassuming. Harper grinned at the name painted clumsily on the window and pulled open the door.

A bell dinged above her as she walked in, and several curious people glanced her way before returning to their conversations and drinks. The barista smiled up at her as the previous customer stepped away, but the smile faltered when her eyes settled on Harper. As it usually did. Even with sunglasses hiding her inhuman eyes, humans felt something *off* about her. Some deep ingrained survival instinct from the days Fae openly roamed and creatures that bled magic lingered in the lands. In the generations since the magical world retreated to the shadows, mortals had forgotten about them, but instincts remained.

"What can I get you?" the woman asked faintly, her voice a nervous whisper.

Harper smiled. "I'll just take a coffee, please."

The woman nodded and accepted the money Harper conjured into her hand with a simple creation spell, simple memory altering and acceptance.

Coffee in hand, Harper moved to the corner of the shop and settled in the hardback chair to watch May as she sipped her own cup. A scar was visible at the tip of her shirt in the center of her chest, still bright pink and healing. She'd gotten her new heart, then.

Harper smiled and sipped her bitter drink. The woman was thin, her cheeks still sunken and pale, but she was bursting with life and energy that wasn't there before.

Settling back in the chair, she looked away, letting her eyes rove around the room. It had been some time since Harper had just sat and let her senses explore. The coffee shop was filled with soft, whispered hums of conversations. Cars driving on the road outside added a layer of vibrations. Hisses and pops came from the espresso machine to her right. The bitter smell of coffee. Faint music played, low and quiet, from the speaker behind the counter.

Harper closed her eyes as she listened to the sounds—the sounds of life. It was an indulgence she rarely let herself have. Death shouldn't want to listen to life, but she did, and occasionally, she let herself have this little treat. It helped to remind her of the weight the souls left behind. It had been so long since she'd treated herself to this indulgence. She tried to remember when, but time was hard for an immortal being so she found she could not.

"So, you really do like coffee."

Harper's eyes snapped open to May standing next to her small table, with her own coffee in hand. May stared down at her, a soft smile on her lips, before pulling out the second chair and sitting without invitation.

Harper stared at her and felt, for the first time in an immeasurable time, surprise. "Excuse me?"

"You said you liked coffee." May sipped her drink, more foam and caramel sauce than coffee. "But I thought maybe you were just saying that because I was dead."

"You weren't dead." Harper answered without thinking and frowned at her. "So, you do remember."

May tilted her head, hair now dyed a bright blue and cut short and floppy around her thin face. Some short strands slipped over her eyes. "Shouldn't I?"

"Not usually. No." Harper sipped her drink and reached out with her magic to sense May's. Faint magic of a witch met her inquiring magic. Nothing special. Nothing that explained why May's magic had reached for her.

May hummed and sipped her coffee. "Maybe I'm special."

Harper hummed and sipped her coffee.

"So, what does Death drink?"

Harper looked down at her forgotten drink. "Coffee, with some milk."

"Hm. I thought you'd drink..." She tilted her head again. "I don't know. Something darker maybe."

"I enjoy a simple coffee." She looked at the sweet mess that May was drinking. "I see you do not."

May smiled, a giggle in her throat. "Who has time for simple? Live a little."

Harper chuckled low at the irony of a woman who'd nearly died half a dozen times telling Death to live.

"So, you got your new heart." She pointed a long finger toward May's scar and took a large gulp of her coffee. "Congratulations."

May fiddled with her neckline. "Yes. This one definitely works better than the other one. It's been…" She tapped out her fingers as she counted. "Eight months, and still no sign of rejection." She sipped her drink.

Harper blinked. "I didn't realize it'd been that long."

May smiled and nodded. "Time must move differently for you."

"Time has different meanings to an immortal. How much do you remember of your near death?" Harper asked.

May looked at Harper with narrowed eyes, mouth twisted in a grin, like she had a secret. "I remember a tall pale woman telling me I wasn't dead… yet. And being very mysterious behind all that long black hair. So…" She shrugged. "I guess all of it? Is it really that weird? I thought near-death experiences happened all the time."

She looked the woman over. A Green Witch but not a powerful one. She'd met stronger witches who had remembered nothing of their near-death experiences. Dreams. Flashes of lights or sounds. But never this clear. Harper touched the woman's aura with a gentle, questioning prod of magic. Her aura flared softly, and May's shoulders twitched at the sensation. Something in Harper's chest flared in response, and she frowned at the sensation.

"So, you're Lady Death. Are the stories about Grim Reapers about you?" May blinked at her, waiting.

Harper tilted her head at the surprising human. What was it about her that confused her magic so?

"Who could say?" She found herself saying. "Perhaps it was me. Perhaps it was a Grim Reaper."

May huffed out a breath of annoyance, a smirk on her lips. "What's a Grim Reaper, then?"

Harper leaned back.

"Is it a secret?" May asked conspiratorially, leaning forward.

"No," Harper answered, and couldn't stop her own smile.

It had been so long since she'd smiled, it almost hurt her cheeks to do so. Even longer since *someone* had made her smile.

May matched her grin and leaned further, and Harper found she didn't want the conversation to end.

"Grim Reapers," Harper said, and May's eyes widened with excitement, "are the Nephilim that assist in ferrying the dead. They are the forbidden offspring of angels and demons."

May blinked at her, mouth hung loose. "Angels and demons are real?"

Harper grunted a soft laugh. "You're having coffee with me."

"Excellent point," she murmured as she checked the watch on her wrist. She stared at her from under her lashes and floppy bangs. "What's with the sunglasses?"

"Eyes are the windows to the soul. I can glamour everything else to appear human but my eyes."

"Oooh," she breathed. "Mysterious." She looked again at her watch and huffed. "I have to go. My lunch is almost over." May stood and stared down at Harper with a tilt of the corner of her lips. "We should do this again."

"We should?" Harper asked with a raised eyebrow. "Like a monthly coffee date?"

Like a mortal? Like a friend? She hesitated, remembering the last time she'd trusted herself to another.

"Why not?" May folded her hands loosely over her chest.

"Maybe it'll give you something to look forward to so nearly a year doesn't go by in a boring blink of an eye, and I have more questions."

The last time she'd trusted a smile and kind eyes like that her heart had been broken and nearly carved from her chest. But she found herself drawn to this mortal, and she was... still... so very lonely.

Harper opened her mouth to counter, only to find herself nodding. "Maybe."

May nodded decisively. "See you in a month."

Harper watched as the interesting, and surprising, human left the coffee shop, her large bag swinging onto her shoulder. What was it about the witch that seemed to pull her? She let herself fade from the humans' plane before splitting the air. She cut deeper, deeper than her Underworld, and pulled the layers open. They fought her. These layers were too old and too stubborn to easily give way to even Death.

Eventually, they did, however, and Harper stepped through to a dark, silent world. The layers of the world slammed shut behind her, loud and violent in the silence that greeted her. The space felt large, giving the impression of vastness, but Harper couldn't see farther than several feet around her. A light emanated from nowhere, a glow with no source, just bright enough to show nothing. If there was a sky, it was as dark and void as the ground she stood on. Around her, floated silver strands so fine and thin they looked like spider webs. They floated and moved with an invisible breeze, an unfeeling wind.

"Fates?"

"Who disturbs?" a harsh voice echoed through the space.

"She does," a soft one, gentle and young.

"She always does," the third sister said.

Three beings stood in front of Harper. One with thin, wispy

hair, white with age. Her skin was wrinkled and sagging, her robes old and tattered. The second sister was a young-looking woman, her skin was smooth and unblemished. Her robes were sheer and flowing as she lifted an edge and tossed it over her shoulder. The third brushed her long dark hair back, skin touched with crow's feet at the corners of her lips and eyes.

All three stared at Harper with white unseeing eyes.

The Old One, known as the Crone or Atropos or Morta, and many more forgotten to time, snipped her shears at Harper. "Why do you disturb us?"

Harper flinched back from the large shiny shears. She didn't want to know what the shears that ended lives would do to her. The Fates had a power, a rank in the universe that was both higher and separate from hers, and she did not want to test who would come out against a direct confrontation.

Clotho, or Maiden, with her translucent flowing robes pooling around her waist, raised her thin, pale hand and wove her fingers around the threads. "She has questions."

Harper licked her suddenly dry lips. "I do."

The second sister appeared next to Harper, her measuring rod held loose in her hand. Harper's heart stuttered at the Fate's sudden appearance. The Mother held the rod aloft before pointing it to Harper's chest. "Many questions."

"We are not her bastard children to be ordered about," the Crone wheezed, and again snapped her shears.

"I've never ordered you anywhere, Crone," Harper snapped at the Fate.

"Hush," the Mother said, and stepped between the two to hold her rod to a newly spun thread held aloft by the Maiden. She tsked and shook her head, the thread shortening to nothing more than a few hand spans.

"I have questions about the human May Haines."

The Maiden turned her white eyes to Harper with a long

blink before reaching up for a thread. She pulled a long glowing thread down from the swirling mass. It was frayed in places, half a dozen that Harper could see, but she could not see the ends.

The Mother hummed and ran her fingers along May's fate thread. "Ah, this one."

The Crone nodded and tucked her shears into a pocket hidden among her ratty robes. "Her fate is ever changing, it is."

"Why?"

The Crone pulled more threads, fists full of them. "So many paths. So many endings."

She opened her hands, and the threads wove around each other, some separating and others weaving into braids. The Mother pointed to a long, pale, shimmering silver one. It was so silver it was nearly blue.

Something twinged in Harper's soul when the Fate's fingers brushed it. She swallowed, but her mouth was too dry as her thread wove and danced around May's.

"What does that mean?"

The Fates laughed, and it was a screeching, cacophonous sound that made Harper's hair stand on end.

"It means," the Maiden said gravely, "that you two are tied."

Harper frowned, her body stilling.

"It means," the Mother murmured, "that what happens to one, will effect the other."

Harper reared back, eyes wide, trying to form another question, any question, but the Fates were finished with this conversation. With a flick of their fingers, the Fates threw Harper from their domain, laughing and screeching, and the world shuddered at their voices.

CHAPTER SIX
WE'RE WITCHES, DEAR

May needed to be typing her report for the latest death she'd gone out on, but instead, she was sipping her coffee and staring at the computer screen. The cursor was taunting her with its blinking. May wrinkled her nose at the lukewarm coffee and set it down. She glanced around—which was pointless, as she sat in a pretty private cubicle—making sure no one was watching before dipping her finger into her coffee. A warmth filled her, and a quick thought to direct that warmth to her coffee, it magicked it back to being piping hot again.

Being a witch had a few perks. Not many, since she sucked at being a witch, but always-hot coffee was one. Her mother had lectured her growing up about her powers. She seemed to think May's lack of ability was from lack of trying and practice. As a college professor, her mother thought everything was solved with study and practice. Her dad was more forgiving and encouraging, but even he'd silently wondered why May had such poor aptitude.

May was halfway decent at making potions, but that

hardly took any skill. As long as you could bake, you could make a potion. She could handle a few spells with moderate effectiveness, but nothing with the ease or proficiency she should have.

She was, as she often joked, the dud of the family.

It was almost as if her magic was a stubborn ball deep in her chest. She could get it to work sometimes, but mostly, it just sat there. Ignoring her. Fighting her.

Her fingers crept to the collar of her shirt to tap against her collarbone just above her scar. She'd only been back to work for a few weeks, but it had been a blissful few weeks. The normalcy. The pattern of life. Her mother had wanted her to stay home longer, put off returning to life, but the second her doctors said she could, May went back to work.

Her medical leave was nearing the end of what it would cover, and she was out of paid time off. Her mom had hoped, believed, that May would use this as a reason to quit her job at the Medical Examiner's Office. She'd been disappointed, again, when May had insisted she stay. In the years since taking the job, she'd found she loved the forensic sciences. The puzzles. Her mom couldn't, or wouldn't, understand that.

May had needed to return to normal life. She needed to move past—forget—dying. Nearly dying. Whichever it was. She'd felt different ever since leaving the hospital after that last time, when she'd seen Death. All the books and *Reddit* threads said it probably was just PTSD. Maybe it was, but the appearance of Death sort of blew that idea out of the water.

May dropped her fingers and sipped her coffee, ignoring her computer screen that had gone dark from lack of movement. Her mind went instead to her surprising coffee date with the God of Death.

Was she a god? She certainly hadn't seemed like one today, joking and... flirting? May snorted at the thought, but then she remembered the golden eyes rimmed in orange, and her pale skin. She had been tall standing next to her as she lay dying in the hospital, but something about her being made her seem *more* than just tall. She had seemed like a god then.

A flicker in the corner of her eye caught her attention, and May turned. The office was quiet; most had already gone home for the night.

"Hello?"

She blinked and leaned back in her chair, peering around her cubicle wall. Another flicker of movement, then May squinted.

A shimmer.

Then a faint shape moved down the hall. It *floated* down the hall.

"Shit," May muttered, and turned back to her blank computer screen. "It's not there. It's not there."

Her heart hammered in her chest—her new, fragile heart—so she took deep, drawn-out breaths to try to slow the damned thing down. Peeking back around her cubical wall, she peered into the empty hallway.

That was the other thing that made her think it was *not* PTSD she was suffering from since her last near-death experience. The ghosts hadn't stopped at the hospital. Green Witches dealt with the living. They shouldn't deal with ghosts.

Ignoring them seemed to help. Eventually, they'd flutter off to wherever they came from, but they always came back. And she had the morgue at her back.

"Fuck," she sighed.

She tucked her collar tighter around her neck, and her phone chirped.

> Mother Dearest: come to dinner

May breathed heavily through her nose. Her mother had been bad *before* the heart transplant. Now she hovered in a way other helicopter moms would be jealous of.

> Me: Fine.
>
> But only because I'm starving and lazy.

It only took a few minutes for her to pack up her things and head out. It was a short drive through Oasis Point to her parents' place, even with evening traffic. They had a nice property on the edge of the city with a small chunk of land surrounding the house. Large desert trees like the mesquite and Texas Sage formed an impressive property line and wall around the house.

May parked her Volkswagen Beetle on the curb and walked through the short wrought-iron gate into the front yard. Several large ravens sat in the desert trees, staring down at her with black eyes. Past the trees and agave plants, May walked up the stone path to the front door. The yard was covered in desert flowers. Bright oranges and reds and pinks.

"Hey, pumpkin," her dad called to her from behind a bird of paradise plant under the front window.

"Hey, Dad." She tucked the strap of her bag higher up on her shoulder. "A little late for gardening, isn't it?"

Her dad, a short but muscular man in his fifties, straightened. His hair, chopped short in a high and tight as a leftover from his military days, was peppered more gray than the lush black it used to be.

"Pfft," he grunted, and walked over to her, hands covered in dirt, and knees of his jeans stained. "Now's the best time. It's not so damned hot. Anyway, I didn't mean to. I saw some weeds and got distracted, and here I am."

May chuckled and let him tuck her under his arm as they walked inside.

"So, your mom guilted you into dinner again, hm?"

She chuckled and let herself be led through to the kitchen in the back of the house. The large bay window overlooked the backyard, full of yucca and palm trees lining the fence line. The trees made for a fine privacy fence. May didn't have a memory where the yard and house weren't covered and protected by trees and bushes and plants.

"*We're witches, dear,*" her mom had said when she'd asked once as a kid, "*the last thing we want is people looking in.*"

That they were the largest, and fullest, and healthiest plants on the street during the hottest summers never seemed to enter her mother's mind as a thing that might make people "look in." Maybe people just thought their water bill was exorbitant.

Her mom was bent over the sink—her tall, lanky six-foot frame seeming too large for the kitchen—viciously scrubbing a pot of potatoes.

"Hey, Ma."

"Mayflower!" her mom shouted as she straightened from the sink and rushed over to her.

May groaned as her mom engulfed her in the hug, wet hands held awkwardly away from them.

"Mom," she whined, and patted her mother's back, "I hate that."

"I don't care," she quipped, and straightened. Her mother might be six feet, but May took after her dad and was only a whopping five, two.

May met her dad's crinkling eyes in a silent plea.

"Janet."

"Steve…" She smiled at the pair and returned to her potatoes.

May obediently sidled up to the sink and grabbed the peeler. Her dad patted her shoulder sympathetically as he passed her on his way upstairs.

"How are you feeling?"

"Fine," May said without looking up. "Just like yesterday."

"You're taking your meds?"

"Yup," she answered as she scrubbed potatoes.

"And you're not overworking yourself?"

"No, Mom."

"I worry."

I know, she thought but didn't bother saying. It was a repetitive conversation.

"I have a question," May asked as she wiped potatoes. "A... witchy question."

"Okay..." Janet hummed, watching her with a side-eye.

If there was such a thing as a witch search engine, it was her mother.

"Have you ever heard of any true accounts of the Grim Reaper or... Death?"

Janet put her potato down. "Are you asking if there is a God of Death?"

She shrugged. "Maybe?"

Janet was silent, and May refused to look away from her peeling. Eventually, the potatoes were peeled, and without a word, Janet picked them up and placed them into the boiling pot.

"Well," she finally said once the distractions were gone, "there are many, many accounts of Death. Each vary by culture and oral history. The only thing that's really consistent across the tales is that Death has many forms and that Death comes for us all."

Janet planted a thin hand on her hip and stared down at May. "But I suspect that's not the answer you were wanting."

May shrugged again and slid onto the bench at the table.

"Only Necromancers truly know the answer to that."

Necromancers. The word alone was enough to make May cringe. They were one of the dark arts, the forbidden arts. Necromancers raised the dead and touched things that weren't theirs to touch. No one should be able to alter death, and raising corpses for their own needs was as close to that as it got.

May shuddered and crossed her arms over her chest. "But we have so many stories. Surely, not only Necromancers can see Death. What about near-death experiences?"

"Oh..." Janet slid onto the bench next to May. "Those are different. Those are visions or fragments of memories from what we see on the other side. What they tell others..." Her mom shrugged. "Well, that's why we have stories."

May chewed her lip. "What about ghosts?"

Janet hummed, eyes locked on May. "Many people see them for many different reasons. Why?"

May waved her mom away. "No reason."

Her mom nodded as she looked away and took a deep breath. May braced herself for the question she knew her mother was prepping. "You've never talked about that day in the hospital."

May shook her head. Nope. She did *not* want to now either. Talking about it meant remembering how close to death she'd been... literally. She didn't want to talk about the past anymore. Every conversation shouldn't be about her nearly dying. She'd nearly died. A lot. Now she had a working heart. Couldn't we all move on now?

"You know, there are people that specialize in that sort of thing."

For some reason, that made anger rise in May's chest, and she angrily turned to her mom. "What *sort of thing*?"

Janet's mouth gaped before she gulped down a breath. "The... When someone..."

"Dies," May snapped. "The word you're looking for is dies."

"I know, May," Janet snapped back, and rubbed her hand over her face. "I'm just trying to help. And if you won't talk to me, then maybe—"

"Never mind, Mom," May said, and stood.

Okay, she admitted to herself. Maybe she had a *little* PTSD.

She stared out the back window and watched the orange setting sun as it gleamed off the yucca leaves, then slipped out the back door and into the warm yard. Even with the setting sun, it was hot enough for sweat to start at her hairline. May followed the flagstone path through the flowers. Her dad kept them thick and full, nearly wild, and they lined the flagstones winding through the yard. The path widened into a small circle clearing with a wooden bench where May sat with a huff and let her shoulders slump.

Soon, she heard the uneven gait of her dad walking down the flagstones. He rounded the bench and sat next to her with his own heavy sigh. Kicking his right leg out, he rubbed his knee. The orange evening light glinted off the titanium of his artificial leg as it stuck out from his basketball shorts.

"Your mom doesn't understand, but she tries."

May glanced up at him.

"Dying, even for a few seconds... well, it changes you. She doesn't understand that, but she tries."

A cold shiver went down May's spine, and she looked away. "Did things... change for you... after your IED?"

Steve slouched and placed his arm behind her, then tapped his fingers on her shoulder. "Lots of things did." He lifted his artificial leg and wiggled it. "This, for one."

She smiled but couldn't find the humor.

"And I got angry," he murmured into the silence. "And

mean. Mean to people I cared about. And I slept like shit. Well..." He shrugged. "More shitty than I had before."

She ignored all those things she was also doing. "Did your magic?"

Steve tilted his head at her. "My magic? No, not that I noticed."

May chewed her lip. *Had mine?*

"Do you want to talk about what happened?"

May shook her head. It had been over a year, but Death reappearing seemed to have reopened the wound she was determined to not acknowledge. While she was intrigued and excited to be talking to *Death*, she was irritated it reminded her of her actual death. She paused, realizing Lady Death hadn't talked about *her* death. She hadn't dwelled on the surgery or even seemed that excited about it. She was, May was realizing, perhaps the one person she could talk to who wouldn't care that she'd nearly died.

"Maybe one day," she finally said instead.

Steve nodded and patted her shoulder once more. He pulled his arms back and leaned forward. With a flick of his fingers and a muttered word too soft for May to decipher, she felt the warmth of magic flowing from his fingers. The wilting tulip straightened and brightened, its bloom replenishing. Steve looked at May with a smile.

"You try," he said. "Connecting with your magic can help ground you. It might help with your moods."

He was always trying to encourage her in a gentle, easy way her mom could never manage. May grumbled to herself but leaned forward. She stretched her hand out toward another wilting flower, drooping and tired from the day's heat, and her magic came slowly, sluggishly, as she tried to push it into the flower.

"Put your intention into the magic," her dad said as she concentrated. "Feel the life force in the earth."

May did as he said, planting her feet firmly on the ground, and pushed her intent into her resisting stream of magic. *Grow. Brighten.*

Instead, the flower withered and dropped more. Trying to connect with her magic was *not* going to help her mood.

She dropped her hand in a huff, and her dad sighed.

"Come on, your mom's going to be pissed if dinner gets cold."

She stood, offering her dad a hand, but he laughed and pushed it away as he stood.

"I'm not that old, come on."

Together, they returned to the house to eat.

CHAPTER SEVEN
A PALE HORSE AND A MISSING SOUL

Harper let her magic expand outside of her and radiate around her as she searched for the souls wandering the Forgotten Forest. Her magic touched them, little brushes of consciousness, as she moved through the silent trees. It was time, as it occasionally was, to remove those souls too malignant, too lost to remain on this side of the Maw. It didn't happen often. It took a great deal of anger or torment, and time, for a soul to fall into the bitterness and become a wraith, but when it did, it needed to be removed.

A soul slipped past her, its eyes downcast and unaware of her as she watched it go. She felt sadness, despondency, but nothing more, so she let it continue its wandering.

There.

She whipped her head toward the burning anger she felt against her magic. Extending her clawed hand, she *reached* for it and curled her fingers in. An inhuman screech rent through the silence around her as she held the wraith still. Snow silent beneath her steps, Harper finally made her way to the wraith as it writhed in her grasp.

It turned empty, hollow eyes to her, mouth gaping as it howled.

"Silence."

The wraith obeyed, but she could feel its anger and resentment. It had long ago lost any resemblance to the human it had once been. Now, it was nothing more than a vague shape, hollow black eyes, and a sorrowful mouth. Harper buried her claws into its chest and gripped it.

"You have lingered too long here," she told it, though she knew it couldn't understand her words anymore. She turned and started the long walk toward the Maw, her wraith in tow. "You cannot remain."

If she allowed it to, it would fester and contaminate the other souls, like an infection, and soon they would all be lost. And there were yet some who might find their way to move on.

As she walked, some souls, those with enough thought left or not so lost to their own grief, looked up as she passed them. Some with shock and fear. Others with sad resignation, as if they knew they would soon face the same fate.

"What happened to it?" came a soft, nearly unheard whisper.

The woman wore a gown several centuries out of style, hair piled up on her head in complicated curls. This soul—Harper searched her memory—Emilia, still held onto much of her old life.

"It lost itself to its anger."

Emilia turned sad eyes to the wraith, hands tucked demurely at her middle. "Are we all destined for that?"

Harper tilted her head with a soft smile. "Not all. I would be very surprised to find you had succumbed to such a fate, for example."

Emilia lifted her chin, a spark of pride flaring even this long in death. "A lady must endure."

Harper nodded and continued her trek, leaving Emilia to order nonexistent staff to set long-gone tables. Her ghost was an interesting one. She hadn't fought to remain but after all these years, still believed herself to be alive. Only with rare glimpses, like now, did she seem to realize. Usually, souls with such a grip on their life settled into haunt and refused to be ferried. Harper doubted Emilia would ever move on, but she had no worries about her becoming a wraith.

At the edge of the Forest, she moved quickly over the flat plain to the Maw. Once she cleared the tree line, the full view of the castle lay before her. It loomed to her right, large and menacing. The massive ebony structure took up much of the horizon in the distance. The spires, all six, thin and needle-like extended into the gray sky. Reapers—hooded, silent beings—moved through the plain. Some with souls in tow toward the Forest, others to the castle to be given their next name to collect.

Beyond the castle, stretched the Maw.

As Harper neared it, she could hear the whispers, moans, and cursing of the damned. The wraith, seeming to realize where they were, struggled anew in her grasp, but Harper simply flexed her claws in its chest, and it stopped.

"You are not bound for the Maw, wraith," she told it as she stepped a booted foot over the edge of the cliff.

The boundary flexed against her foot and held. It flared green with each of her steps, and like fish to food, the souls rushed upward, only to be rebuffed by the magical ward that kept them contained. They moaned, growled, and wailed as she walked, trailing her in a mournful parade.

Barking and howling sounded from behind her, and she knew her hellhounds were pacing the cliff's edge hoping for a soul to snack on.

Nearly halfway across, the howls of her hellhounds could

no longer be heard, and when Harper glanced over her shoulder, even her castle was a small black dot in the landscape. The souls moaned anew below her, and she hissed. With an angry flick of her fingers, she pushed them away with a wave of her magic.

"Away with you."

Screeching, they returned to the depths of the Maw, then she was met with blessed silence. She frowned down at the depths, wondering why the damned had swarmed to the surface. They usually hid when she was near. She paused in her trek, wraith still clenched in her grasp, and searched the Maw. Flexing her power, she sensed the barrier and tested it for weaknesses. It flared a soft green as her magic touched it and brushed along it.

It hummed in her mind, connected to her as it was, intact and stable.

"What has them stirred up, I wonder?" she asked the wraith softly, knowing it wouldn't respond.

She looked at the magic containing the damned once more before slowly resuming her trek, though she tucked the weird behavior into her mind.

After an eternity and no time at the same time, Harper stepped off the magical ward and onto hard, icy land: the Wasteland. Here, the wails and moans of the wraiths echoed hauntingly as if carried away by a wind that didn't exist. She released her claws from the wraith and withdrew her hand, letting it wail and screech as it fled from her. Here it was free to rage and scream with the other wraiths, and their taint would not reach the souls.

Hoofbeats echoed across the plain, and when Harper turned, the glowing eyes of her pale horse came into view as she trotted over. The large beast, as pallid as corpse's skin, huffed large breaths and nickered at her. She nuzzled Harper's shoulder, and she ran her hand along the long, broad neck.

"Hello, Silence."

She nickered again and huffed, tossing her massive head. Silence eyed Harper, her ethereal eyes wiser than any beast.

"Not yet," Harper said, and ran her hand along her muzzle.

Silence blinked and turned away to return to running the Wasteland. Harper watched her until she was gone from sight, a sad longing in her chest. She had rode her pale horse only twice before as War raged and Famine and Pestilence wreaked havoc behind him. And then, Death had followed.

When the angels warred with the Nephilim, her siblings had joined the fray. How could they not? Such destruction and anger. The Horsemen had to answer such a call. And again when the Nephilim rose up in rebellion of their new station, her siblings had rode then too, much to her dismay.

It was the first time she felt a conflict between her two roles. She was Death. She was to follow her siblings, but the souls she was taking, the ones War was cutting down with his broadsword, were those she'd sworn to protect. The angels had gotten involved then too, for the Agreement had been broken.

Harper suppressed a shiver and turned away. Those had been dark times.

The walk back to her castle was again instant and forever, her hounds yipping at her return. Armeal stood waiting for her, wings tucked tight to his back.

"Yes?"

"A Reaper has returned empty handed."

Harper shook out her long black coat as if she could shake the souls of the damned, and buttoned it. "And?"

"He insists the soul was missing."

"The Fates are fickle," she said, though she followed

Armeal as he turned to walk toward the castle. "The window for souls varies with each soul."

As they neared the large glistening doors atop the flight of stairs, a Reaper passed. His face, hidden by its large black hood and flowing robes, turned in Harper's direction and bowed as it passed. Her magic reached out and touched the Reaper briefly, an acknowledgment, before she entered the large entry hall.

"I know this," Armeal said curtly. "As does the Reaper. However, he refuses to move onto the next soul."

Her eyes fell on the Reaper in question standing still in the empty hall.

"What has happened?" she asked, though her voice was carried through the hall. "Explain," she demanded of the Reaper.

The shadowed hood turned in Harper's direction. "The body was there. The soul was not."

Harper's nails drummed on her hip as she planted her hands. "Could you have been late and the soul already broke free?"

The Reaper shook his head, and his pale hand clenched around the bonewood staff of his scythe. Harper sighed and folded her arms. Armeal blinked, his angelic face neutral. It was easy to see why humans thought the Nephilim were fallen angels, with the beauty and voices they had.

"Sometimes, souls *do* go missing if a Reaper is late," Harper said. "It is hardly cause for concern."

She glanced meaningfully at Armeal, a silent question, asking, "Why have you remained" and "Don't you have things to do," but the Nephilim stayed. He blinked, the briefest acknowledgment of her glance and command—one he chose not to respond to. She raised an eyebrow at him but turned her attention back to the Reaper. The Reaper flexed his hand on the scythe again. No Reaper liked the implication that they'd failed in their duty.

She drummed her fingers against her hip, confused why this Reaper was so determined. Souls refused the ferry often, especially if the death was traumatic. The window for collection was not often set, or they wandered sooner or later than they should've. But still, this Reaper fretted.

"Show me," she finally said.

The Reaper nodded and cut the air with his scythe. The air split as before, and the Reaper stepped through. Harper glanced once more at Armeal before stepping through after the Reaper.

Her boots landed in dirt and weeds. The sun was just rising here, and the early morning birds were loud in their declaration of the day. The trees stretched tall into the orange and pink sky, leaves dry and rustling on the slight breeze.

The Reaper appeared next to her, and with a gesture from his scythe, they walked a narrow path in the dirt. The Reaper was an Old One, his age and power radiating from him. Many of the older Nephilim gave themselves so fully to this life, this role, that they forgot anything else. Life in the Underworld changed them. Many of the Old Ones were Nephilim only in name now.

She glanced at him as they walked. "Do you remember your name?"

"No." He continued walking off the path and down the embankment of a small dry ravine. "I remember very little of my life before you. Fighting. Fear. Pain. This life is not that. It is a fulfilling purpose. I have no need for a name here."

She nodded, unsure what she'd been expecting. Reapers were not humans who liked to chatter.

Harper followed as they moved along the bed of the ravine. Not all Nephilim had settled into life as Reapers as well as this one had. Some had felt like they'd been trapped and rebelled. They had believed the words of a traitor, Yrien, and believed they could take the power of the dead for themselves. The lone few that surrendered following the fighting had been cast out of yet another home, only to be slaughtered by wrathful angels spurred on by War. The Nephilim Rebellion had been so long ago, even Harper struggled to find the memory.

The Reaper led her to a ravine, and at the bottom, nestled between small sagebrush growing out of the dry earth, was a worn and tattered tent. Peering inside, she found a skinny male wearing rags for clothes and a needle still in his arm.

"You searched the area?" she asked as she straightened. Around them, no ghost hovered. No aether lay on the scattered leaves and deadfall. No sign of a soul having wandered off.

The hooded figure turned to her with a hiss of robes and breath. "Of course."

She ignored the angry Reaper and knelt next to the body. It was cold and stiff, pale in a way only the dead can achieve. Holding her hand over the chest of the man, she *pulled*, searching for the thread of life that bound the soul to body. The silvery thing, now a pale yellow, fluttered into the air. The Tether was frayed and old, already breaking down from the loss of the soul after death. It didn't look cut, so it hadn't been stolen from the body.

She weaved the remnants of the thread around her fingers, feeling for the last memory. It was hazy and disjointed, as deaths filled with drugs usually were, but she squinted past the feeling. There was no fear. No pain.

Harper sighed again and dropped her hand, letting the Tether fall back into the man's chest. Standing outside the tent, she glanced again around the woods. The Fates *were* fickle with their time. Perhaps the Reaper was simply late.

The Reaper planted the end of his scythe in the dirt as if he could sense her thoughts.

"Why are you concerned?"

He paused, as if to gather his thoughts, boney fingers clenching his staff. "It should be here."

Harper raised an eyebrow at him.

"No," he snapped, and she gaped at the Reaper. "It should be here. I never misjudge the window. There is no anger or fury in the dirt around the body. It should not be haunting. It has not wandered."

Harper raised her eyebrows at the Reaper again, this time in surprised admiration. Those were details few Reapers bothered with.

"I am not Death," he rasped beneath his hood with a hint of his old Nephilim pride, "but I know my task. It is my reason for being. I do it with honor and this soul"—he stamped his staff into the dirt again—"is missing."

She looked around the area again and sent her magic out and around them, sensing, testing. She felt no soul. No ghost. No wraith. Harper pulled her magic back in.

"Do you remember," she asked carefully, "the last time souls went missing?"

Her blood cooled at the memory. The rebellion had started with missing souls. Power lay in the soul. Power, if you were foolish enough, to think you could conquer Death.

The Reaper next to her grew still, and it seemed he'd held his breath. "Yes," he finally breathed, soft and quiet, like a whisper from death.

"Do you believe this is that again?"

The Reaper was quiet and still. The insects buzzed and chirped around them, and off in the distance, a mourning dove cooed.

"No." The word was a rustle of paper on the wind. "None would be foolish enough to challenge you again."

"But you still think someone took it?"

Again, he was still, as if afraid to speak the words into being. "I do not know. I only know it is missing."

Harper stared into the dark hood, trying to see the face beneath. Eventually, she nodded, and the Reaper turned away. He split the world with his scythe again, and a pop filled the woods as the walls to the worlds snapped back in place. Harper watched the woods again, birds chirping and bugs trilling.

One soul missing. Not the start of another Reaper rebellion. Not another war.

"I certainly hope not."

Harper stood in the Forgotten Forest after her search with the Reaper. The tall, spindly trees surrounded her as souls and Reapers moved around her. Some had souls with them heading for the Forest, some without. One soul meant nothing. It's what she told herself as she stood there, watching. Thinking.

She caught sight of Armeal's white suit through the trees, his head held close to another Reaper's hood—a secret conference—before the Reaper turned away, leaving Armeal to glower after.

She clucked her tongue and turned toward her castle. She cleared the trees just in time to see the Reaper she sought walking down the massive steps of the castle.

"Nerwen," she said, nearing the Old One.

Her hooded head turned to Harper, her shimmering black

wings held tight to her body. The very tips of her feathers glimmered white, battling the black taking over completely.

"Death." Nerwen's voice was soft, like a whisper in the wind.

"A Reaper has returned saying a soul was missing."

Nerwen pushed her hood back, her pale-golden hair pooling around her shoulders, and purple eyes staring back at Harper. Her face had sharp angles and raised cheekbones, a beautiful angelic face. "Souls wander."

"Yes," Harper agreed. "But he was insistent. Have any others mentioned such a thing to you?"

Nerwen cocked her head. "To me? No, Death."

"Have you been on any ferries that were..." She shrugged. "Odd?"

Nerwen blinked her purple eyes. "No, Death."

Harper let out a breath. Nerwen was one of the stronger Nephilim, nearly as powerful as Armeal, and in the time before the Agreement, had been sly and cunning, noticing more than others. If she hadn't noticed souls disappearing...

"Though..." Her dainty whisper pulled Harper's eyes back to her. "I have noticed whisperings."

Harper frowned. "Whisperings?"

She thought instantly back to Armeal, head bent with the Reaper.

"Yes, Death. Whisperings." Nerwen gazed at the tree line behind Harper. "I do not know what they say, but there is the sense of... something beginning."

Harper's blood chilled. "Let me know if you hear anything else."

"Yes, Death." Nerwen replaced her hood.

Harper watched the Old One go. Something beginning... Nerwen was cunning and observant, but she was also skeptical of everyone and distrusting of everything. It was what made her such a successful spy in the warring times before the Agreement. Her faction had been brutally effective at eliminating other Nephilim. Were souls missing? Or had one wandered? Were the Nephilim whispering and plotting? Or were they simply speaking with each other as they had always done?

She sighed, hands planted on her hips.

"Lady Death," Armeal's voice called her, and she looked over her at him as he approached.

"What did you discover?"

She raised an eyebrow at him as he came to stand with her. "Why do you ask?"

"I wish to be helpful to you. I cannot do that without information."

She turned away from him to watch the comings and goings before her. "There was nothing. No explanation of where it had gone."

Armeal was still next to her, not even a rustle of his feathers.

"Souls wander," she said.

"They do." He nodded.

"It is nothing. It is one soul."

One soul did not mean history was repeating. It did not mean the Reapers had turned on her again. Feathers ruffled next to her, and she glanced at him with another raised eyebrow.

"You disagree?"

"I said nothing."

She snorted. "Your wings speak more than your voice."

He huffed a small breath, and she smiled at his annoyance. "Perhaps it is something."

"Have others reported souls they think are missing?"

He paused, and she turned, his face as neutral as always. "No," he finally said.

"So, it is the one soul."

If it wasn't, she would discover it.

CHAPTER EIGHT
THE GHOST

The month moved by slowly, unremarkably. It wasn't always this boring. Before May'd gotten sick, *really* sick, her time was chaotic and filled with dinners and nights out—friends. Then her heart got worse and she was in hospitals more than she was out of them. A few friends dropped off when that happened. She hadn't been surprised. Hurt but not surprised. Others had rallied around her. They visited her in the hospital and brought her flowers.

Then she had her transplant.

That was a long time in the hospital. And because of the immune suppressants she had to take to help prevent rejection, visitations were hard. More and more friends tampered off as the isolation dragged on. When May was finally released, she was still in no condition to go out. The friends she'd hoped would come back, didn't. Maybe they'd been shit friends all along and this just highlighted that. Maybe, and May thought this more likely, they couldn't handle a friend who always seemed to be dying. That's a lot of stress. A lot of mess.

She didn't blame them. Not really. There were one or two

she'd text around holidays or birthdays. A group chat of memes but no real substance. Really, it was fine. They reminded her of her time *before*, and somehow, all conversation seemed to go back to before she was sick; before she was in the hospital. She just wanted to be May now.

And somehow, that meant a coffee date with Death. She glanced at the time and smiled as she locked her computer and gathered her bag.

"Back after lunch," May said to her boss when she passed her office.

The drive was short to the coffee shop, and she parked around the corner on the street. It was far too hot to walk to coffee. The August sun was absolutely sizzling today. The AC hitting her flushed skin as she entered caused goosebumps to rise along her arms. Death was already seated in the corner with a small latte in her hand.

Even though Death was using magic to look more human, May remembered how she looked in the hospital. Her long black hair still fell down her back, hitting skin too pale to be a native Arizonan. A fine manicure with black polish tipped her hands, but she remembered the claws those pretty nails were hiding. Long and sharp, deadly at the end of dainty fingers.

May's lips curved in a smile as she moved to the counter to order. Once she had her drink, she slid into the chair opposite Death.

"You are late," she murmured.

May smirked. "You remembered."

Death smiled softly and eyed May's foamy drink, glancing over her sunglasses, her orange eyes peeking over the frame before she pushed them back up on her nose. "And your concoction this time?"

"This," May said with a grin, "is a caramel Macchiato Frappuccino."

"Uh-huh." Death sniffed, and sipped her own drink.

May ignored Death's judgment on her froo froo drinks and took a large gulp of the sweet thing. "Where'd you discover your love of coffee? Or do they have coffee in the afterlife?"

Death stilled for half a second before leaning back in the stiff wooden chair. "Well—" She sighed, her lips curving in a smile. "An Imam in Mecca, in the"—she tilted her head and frowned— "I believe you'd call in the fifteenth century, offered me some while I waited for a soul."

May leaned forward. "Really?" She breathed the word. "He could see you too?"

"Oh..." Death waved her dainty hand. "Those deep in their religion can sometimes see me. This man handled last rites for the dying, for those that made the pilgrimage, and so I was often visiting him for souls."

"And eventually he offered you coffee?"

Death smiled. "It was a religious drink then. Meant to aid in concentration in prayer and study. But I had long ago learned the joy of hot drinks. So, this strange new *coffee* was just another step in that journey."

"I guess that explains why you like a simple coffee," May said, stabbing her straw into the whipped cream to stir her drink. "I used to get coffee with my girlfriends. They always made fun of me for my crazy sugary drinks too."

Her smile faded, and she wished she had said nothing. She wasn't even sure why she had.

"Used to?" Death's question was soft.

May cleared her throat, shook her shoulders, and forced a happier tone into her voice. "Dying scares away even the closest of friends, it seems."

Death stayed quiet, but May felt her eyes on her as she stared into her drink.

"It's like they spend all their time preparing for you to die, mourning you before you're even in the ground, that when you survive, they're just... tired." The words spilled from May. She'd never talked about this with her parents. They'd asked where her friends went, and she'd just shrugged them off. Her mom wouldn't understand. Her dad could, probably, but she didn't want to talk about it with them. She didn't want to see the pity in their eyes. But Death... she'd understand. How could she not? She knew what it was like to be surrounded by the dying. "The couple who stuck around after my transplant kept looking at me like they expected me to break. Kept waiting for me to croak in front of them. I was a ghost to them."

May shrugged and pushed her drink away.

"The living," Death finally spoke into the heavy silence, "rarely know what to do with the dying."

"Yeah." May sighed and brushed her hair back. "What do your friends think of your coffee habit?"

Lady Death looked away. "Death walks alone. In this, we are alike."

Sad as it was, the words made May smile. "Death doesn't have any friends?"

Death frowned and stared into her cup, and she suddenly felt bad for asking. She had assumed she was alone by choice, but now, she wasn't sure.

"Sorry," she said as Death brought her shaded eyes back up. "You don't have to answer that."

"Friends," Death said as she leaned back, "are a strange thing to an immortal."

May nodded. "Maybe we can be friends." She tipped her cup against Death's in a subdued cheer. "Over coffee."

May steadfastly ignored the ghost hovering out of the corner of her eye as she typed her report not long after she'd returned from lunch. It had appeared nearly an hour ago and had seemed to take up residence in her cubicle.

She hit the keys on her keyboard harder than necessary and sighed, then rubbed her eyes and glanced over at the ghost again.

Still there.

"Dammit," she muttered, and turned to face it fully.

It stared back. It... he... hovered just off the ground, body too faint to make out many details.

"What do you want?" May whispered at him.

The ghost turned, and May barely smothered a gasp at the gaping hole at the back of his head. The ghost floated around the edge of her cubicle and into the hallway.

She sat, hand clasped over her mouth and heart pounding in her ears. *Okay*, she thought, *maybe it'll go away now*.

The ghost reappeared at her cubicle wall, glowering down at her.

"Shit." She angrily turned back to her computer screen. "Go away."

It moved closer and closer until it floated in front of her and she was glowering at her computer screen through the ghost's torso.

"Fuck off," she whispered.

It stayed right where it was.

"Fine." She pushed away from her desk. "What? You want me to follow you?"

The ghost glided through her desk and back out of her cubicle.

"I guess that's a yes," she muttered, and, feeling stupid and more than a little crazy, locked her computer screen and followed the ghost down the hall. The hole in the back of the man's head seemed to be the only thing that stood out with any clarity. It looked caved in, bludgeoned with something.

It was a quick walk through the small office area filled with desks and cubicles for the techs. The hallway was lined with small offices for the doctors, ending in swinging doors leading to the chilly exam room.

May rounded the corner, the small wall lined with gloves, booties, gowns, and hair nets, and the autopsy room opened up before her. Lined on the right were the stations, five in total. Two bodies were on tables. One was missing the back part of his head. The ghost, however, didn't lead her to his body but instead to the other table. May's slip-resistant, super comfy but horribly ugly shoes squeaked on her way to the table. Glancing down at the desk set up at the head of the autopsy table and at the exam logs laying there, she saw the autopsy for the male with the head trauma was nearly finished.

She ignored the autopsy technician. The two other assistants and the doctor were looking through the stomach. The ghost locked eyes with May before looking pointedly at the body, then fading from view.

What in the world...?

"What do we have?" May asked as she pulled the case sheet over to her.

Sarah, one of the autopsy technicians, pulled the sheet out of May's hands. "Kinda crazy, actually. These two were rock climbing over in Queen Creek Canyon. That one"—she pointed to the man her ghost came from—"fell, right. Bashed his head in on the landing. That one was found as an overdose at the base of the cliff they were climbing. Cops found drug paraphernalia all over the place and with their gear. Looks like these idiots were bouldering while high."

"Bladder, forty-one grams, empty," Seth, the assisting tech, shouted from the feet end of the autopsy table as he picked the bladder out of the hanging scale.

"Bladder, forty-one grams," Sarah echoed, and quickly scribbled down the weight on the chart.

Why had the ghost led her here? She tried to ignore the nagging fear from *why* she was even seeing ghosts to begin with. That was a bigger problem she didn't want to deal with just yet.

"Did you need something?" Sarah asked.

"No." May shrugged and folded her arms. "Just taking a break from paperwork. Thought I'd see if there was anything interesting happening back here."

Sarah nodded and went back to doing her paperwork, noting organ weights and measurements as they were shouted to her. May stood well back from anything messy, trying to figure out why the ghost had bothered her and led her back here. If the ghosts thought she was some sort of ghost detective, she needed to figure out how to put a stop to that.

She crossed her arms with a sigh. She was *not* getting involved in that shit.

Dr. Mikals moved to the next body and observed as the tech was removing the ribs and sternum, exposing the internal organs. May leaned her hip against the desk even though Sarah swatted at her. She looked around the room, but the ghost didn't return. May was starting to think she really was going crazy, but then she caught a shimmer out of the corner of her eye, so she blinked, focusing on the autopsy.

A little glimmer came from the chest cavity. Dr. Mikals did a preliminary check, and he didn't seem to notice it. May pushed off the table, taking a couple steps closer to the head of the autopsy. Straining to look without getting closer, May saw a silver thread, thin and fluttering as if moved by a breeze. May swallowed and glanced at Joanna, who methodically was going about her tasks oblivious to May's dilemma. Its end was frayed and torn, like an old rope, as it flapped in the wind she couldn't feel.

Dying, it seemed, had changed her magic. Had changed her. There was no denying it now. How much it had changed her was still to be seen. Maybe, May thought, she could pester her new friend about it over coffee.

"Weird," she muttered under her breath.

"What's weird?" Dr. Mikals asked, much closer to her than she'd thought.

"Oh, uh." She glanced down at the body for a reasonable answer. "He just looks so... healthy. No blemishes on his organs."

Mikals hummed as he nodded. "Yes, poor lad. Young and healthy, from the looks."

May nodded and peered back at the first autopsy as the tech was finishing sewing up the body. No strange thread there. Turning back to the young man, May watched the strange silver strands as they seemed to swirl and weave around his heart.

That's new. May forced herself to step away before her ogling drew attention.

She slipped out of the exam room before any more weird ghostly things happened. As she sat at her desk with her chin resting in her hand and twirling her bright-purple fidget spinner, her mind kept drifting back to the strange thread. The screen saver had long ago settled on her computer, its bright rainbow lines bouncing haphazardly around the screen.

"Hey."

May jerked at Sarah's soft voice and turned in her chair to see the quiet intern leaning against the cubical wall.

"What's up?"

"Nothing." Sarah shook her head and adjusted the strap on her bag. "Just saying bye. You leaving soon?"

May twirled her fidget spinner faster. "I have some reports to finish."

Sarah smiled, and her dark eyes glanced over May's shoulder. "It seems to be going well."

May grunted and tossed her spinner at the computer mouse, effectively waking up the screen. "I can't focus to save my life."

"You never can," Sarah said with a laugh.

May waved her off with a chuckle. "Have a good night."

She spun back around in her chair to face the dreaded screen and report, and Sarah's soft footsteps faded down the hall. Sighing, May slumped in her chair. Instead of focusing on the reports she needed to write, her mind went again to the odd thread. Why did one body have it and the other didn't? Why now? And why had the ghost been so determined for her to see it?

"Fuck it," she muttered, and pushed away from her desk, going toward the autopsy room. A quick look at the stored bodies would satisfy her curiosity, and then she could finally get the damned reports finished. Hopefully.

She moved quickly through the empty building, her footfalls louder than normal in the quiet as she turned into the autopsy room and down the back hall to the cold storage morgue. Swiping her key card, she entered the large room. The cold, dry air hit her face, and she wrinkled her nose at the sterile smell. Too cold to smell any decomposition or rot, but it didn't quite get rid of it either. Something about the mixture of sterile air and old death in the cold room made the smell worse.

The morgue wasn't as full as it had been. It'd been a slower month than normal, so only eight bodies were being stored here. A couple were waiting to be picked up by the mortuary, and one was still pending the toxicology. The three from today were at the back, waiting for their turn to be released.

May paused at the door as it swished shut behind her, and wondered just how crazy this was before shrugging and stepping farther into the room. She meandered past the rows of shelving. Two had been brought in today and were still in the transport bags, zippers sealed with the OME case seal. She wouldn't be able to look at those, so she kept going until she came to the three from last week.

With a shallow breath, she pulled the first drawer out. An old man, she couldn't remember what he'd died from. With one last breath, she pulled back the plastic sheet. Feeling more than a little creepy, she peered at the man's chest. No silver thread wiggled through the Y incision. Pushing the drawer back in, May moved on to the remaining two bodies. Neither of which had any signs of the strange thread.

Frowning, May retreated from the morgue and went back to her desk. There was no way she'd imagined that thing. Not after all the ghosts. But what was it? And why had the ghost wanted her to see it?

CHAPTER NINE
THE DETECTIVES

May huffed a sigh and rested her hip against the table. Last night, she was called out to a suspicious death during her on-call, and she was still feeling the lack of sleep. Her eyes felt like they'd had sand rubbed into them, and her head hurt. She stifled a yawn and rubbed her eyes. It's not like murders were few or far between in Oasis Point; being a smaller suburb of Phoenix, murders were definitely *not* unheard of, but that did nothing to make her feel better the next morning. And she wasn't even sure this was a murder.

If I lost all that sleep for nothing, I will be hella pissed at the detective.

"What's the matter with you?" Sarah asked with her own quiet huff as she settled her papers at the desk.

"I'm tired," she muttered.

"Why are you back here, anyway?" Sarah asked.

Great question.

May shrugged. "I was called out on this last night. The detective on scene thought it was suspicious, and I'm curious what the doc will find."

Was it outside of her purview to attend autopsies? Yeah. Would anyone really care as long as her paperwork was finished? Nope. She *was* actually curious what the doc would find. It had seemed like a heart attack to her. There wasn't any trauma on the body, and it wasn't like the guy was in peak shape, but the detective had been adamant that it was more than it seemed. She wanted to see if she could see what he saw. She disguised a look around the room with a neck stretch and shoulder roll. *No ghosts... yet.*

Behind her, two detectives fussed with their gowns and booties.

"Why are they here?" Sarah asked with a gesture over her shoulder.

"The cops?" May asked, glancing back at the pair. "Like I said, one thinks it's a suspicious death, so they want to observe."

"Oh..." Sarah's eyes bounced back and forth between May and the cops.

May chuckled. "You're not scared of them, are you? Trust me, they're more worried about stepping in something squishy than they are about anything living in this room."

Sarah side-eyed May but turned her attention to her papers. At the autopsy table, the technician started cutting, the external photos finally finished.

"Let us know if you find anything interesting, doc," the older detective said as he sat in one of the stiff plastic chairs against the back wall.

Dr. Kesler threw two thumbs-up from her spot by the sink, then turned back to watch the tech work.

"You're not going to watch?" the younger detective asked.

May tried not to obviously eavesdrop on the pair behind her but still tilted her head enough to listen. The younger detective looked familiar to her, she just couldn't place why or his name.

"Been to enough of these. I know what the insides look like when they're outside."

The younger detective murmured something to his partner and came to stand next to May. He was a youthful, thinner version of the potbellied senior behind them. His green eyes were wide and eager, watching the autopsy with rapt attention.

"Your first autopsy?" May asked.

"Yes, ma'am." His bright eyes flashed to her before bouncing back to the table.

"You're not going to barf, are you? Or pass out? It's fine if you do, just warn us first so we can get you a bucket or catch you."

"Yes, please don't crack your noggin on my floor, Detective," Dr. Kesler called without looking up from her work.

The detective chuckled, his tanned cheeks dimpling. "No, ma'am. I think I'll be okay."

"Dimples!" May blurted, recognition finally hitting. "You were at that really bad decomp a while ago, weren't you?"

He looked at her, a slight frown on his face, before his eyes widened with recognition, and he nodded. "Oh, yeah. The one with all the flies and maggots." He shivered. "Yeah. That was like... two years ago almost."

May held her smile, even as she felt the awkwardness of the situation creep up her spine. *Shit, shit, shit.*

It was still weird for her to be back at work after her long absence. Her life stopped for that year she was recovering from her surgery, but it hadn't for everyone else.

"Oh," she managed past the nerves suddenly clogging her throat, "that's right. I took some time off."

"Harding"— the man held out his hand— "Ethan Harding."

"May," she said as she clasped his hand with a nod. She was shit with names and knew that no matter how hard she tried... she would not remember Detective Dimples's name once he left.

"I'm okay to stand here?"

"Sure," May said, and glanced at the body of the middle-aged man as the rib cage was lifted away.

Her eyes widened when the bright-silver strand swayed into the air. *There that thing is again.*

"Have you found anything else to explain what happened to poor Steven Harrison?" May asked, her eyes glued to the thread.

"Yeah," the older detective called to them, "have you?"

Ethan growled a sigh, his eyes closing. "Nothing since you were at the scene last night, really. Just the overturned stuff in his yard. I think it looks like a fight. We did talk to some neighbors that said they heard shouting and arguing."

"Huh," she muttered. "Not what was said?"

"I still think it was a heart attack." Ethan's partner spoke from behind them.

They both turned to look at the senior detective.

"No reports of another person on scene." He held up his fingers as he ticked off his points. "No injuries that suggest a fight. No vehicles or persons on the neighbors' doorbell cameras were caught going to or from the scene."

"So what, in that, Doug, says heart attack?" Ethan asked a little acridly.

"My eighteen years of experience as a homicide detective says this *wasn't* a homicide, New Jack."

"Yeah, but a heart attack?" Ethan folded his arms.

"Those goddamned things hurt!" Doug scoffed. "I was screaming when I had my first one too!"

"First?" May gasped. "How many have you had?"

Doug smiled with a shrug. "Just two."

May's mouth dropped as Ethan snorted.

Just! Her hand went to her neckline, to the thick scar that sat just beneath her collar.

"If you don't stop with the doughnuts, you'll have a third."

"Nah." Doug waved off Ethan's concern. "The caffeine will get me first."

May felt her mouth go slack before she shook herself and turned back to the autopsy. *Good Lord.* She tapped her fingers on the tip of her scar.

"Doug's a different breed," Ethan whispered to her.

"Of human or detective?" May countered.

Ethan laughed, open-mouthed and loud. "B-both," he sputtered out through his laughter. "He's gruff, but he's good people."

May nodded and hummed. "He's something," she muttered under her breath, and forced her hand away from her scar. She'd lost track of how many heart attacks, minor or otherwise, she'd had waiting on the list.

"Hey, it's just a joke," Ethan uttered to her, seeming to catch her shift in mood.

"Dumbass," Sarah mumbled as she turned in her chair to glare at them. "She had a heart transplant last year."

Ethan jerked, his eyes wide and apologetic as he stared at her, then at the collar of her shirt where a bit of her scar poked out. Hastily, May shifted her shirt to hide it again.

"Okay, Sarah." She chided the young woman, even if she was silently happy at Sarah for coming to her defense. Clearing her throat, May shoved her hands into her pockets and stepped away from them to focus on the autopsy and the strand that was emerging from the chest.

It swayed in the air, as if searching for something in a ghostly wind. The tech had stepped back so the photographer could step in and take more photos. May grabbed a face mask from the table and cautiously stepped forward, careful to keep her hands in her pockets and away from touching anything.

She glanced at the camera, its flash popping every few seconds as their photographer snapped photo after photo in quick succession, and checked she wouldn't get in the way. Their photographer, Chen, her hot-pink hair pulled high into a ponytail, gave her a quick nod that she was in the clear and moved to photograph the victim's hands. May stretched her neck as she leaned, as close as she dared without stepping out of line, and peered at the strand floating above the heart.

She wanted to touch it, brush her fingers along it, but studiously kept her hands shoved in her pockets. It seemed to shimmer more than the last one had and reminded May of those old Edison-style light bulbs with the visible filament. Something about the floating, beautiful thing seemed to call to her.

"Notice anything?" Dr. Kesler asked, glancing up from the ruler she held along a scratch on the victim's right arm.

May swallowed and stepped back. "Nothing obvious."

Dr. Kesler nodded and glanced at the man's chest as the tech started to remove one organ at a time. "Yeah, nothing yet."

The impulse to touch the strand only grew as she watched it sway and stretch. Like it was reaching for *her*. It swayed mere inches from her. May looked over the body again and noticed a small blemish on the lungs. She knew it wasn't important. Smoker's lungs. But it gave her an excuse.

"What about this?" she asked, slowly extending her hand over the exposed chest organs to point at the lung.

She purposefully brushed the floating thread with her hand. Like a bad idea you can't ignore but should, she leaned into the impulse. The thing grazed her thumb, and she yelped as a numbing sting shot through her hand, hot and cold at once. Snatching her hand back, she cradled it against her chest, rubbing her fingers over the burning cold spot on her thumb.

Dr. Kesler's piercing-blue eyes shot to May, watching her like a hawk. "What the hell?"

"Sorry..." May's mind raced for an excuse, all while her heart pounded away in her throat. "I, uh, pinched my neck while sleeping. Must've tweaked a nerve... or something."

Kesler's eyes bounced between May and the body several long, silent moments before she blinked, with a frown between her brows.

May ignored the pounding in her chest.

Dr. Kesler watched her face still. "You're sure you're okay?"

"Yup," May muttered, and forced a smile, ignoring the searing pain in her arm. "Really. Just a pinched nerve."

May shoved her tingling hand back into her pants pocket, where it should've stayed, and walked as quickly away from the table as she could without looking like she was running.

"You all right?" the cute detective with the dimples whose name she'd already forgotten asked as she passed him.

"Yup," she said, and continued back to her desk. All right, so she ran away, but as long as it didn't *look* like she ran away, May didn't really care.

She dropped herself into her chair with a shaky breath and finally pulled her hand out of her pocket. It looked normal. Even as she rotated it this way and that and held it under her desk lamp, it was a normal hand. The numbness was slowly receding, but when she poked the spot the thread had touched, it was ice cold still.

"What the fuck," she breathed, and shook her hand out. "What the fuckity fuck."

All right, so May was willing to admit that was probably a really bad idea, but there had been a pull, a desire to touch that stupid glowing string.

"Not doing that again," she muttered, and took a long swig from her water bottle and focused on her breathing, on slowing her panicked heart rate. "Stupid," she mumbled, and turned toward her computer screen.

I am not getting involved in ghost detective shit.

She focused on her paperwork, avoiding any desire to return to the autopsy. It wasn't her job, anyway. Normal or otherwise. She'd lost track of time, engrossed in her mundane work, when a soft throat-clearing behind her pulled her attention.

Dimples stood there, looking sheepish.

"What's up?" she asked.

"Hey—" He cleared his throat again. "I didn't know about... I didn't know you'd been sick."

Shit, shit, shit.

She did not want to have this conversation. She just wanted to be normal and not nearly dying. "It's fine." She smiled at him and meant it. "You couldn't have known."

He nodded and looked relieved. "Okay. I just didn't want you to think I was some heartless prick."

She laughed, and it surprised her. "No, no, I don't." She turned around in her chair. "So, what was the verdict?"

"Oh." He huffed and shrugged. "Doc's not sure. But the track marks on his arm leads her to think an overdose. We're gonna have to wait for toxicology."

"Isn't that better than a murder?"

"Yeah." He frowned. "As long as that's what it is."

"And you're still not convinced?"

He chewed his lip and leaned his shoulder against the cubicle wall. "I don't know. Just... something in my gut, you know, says it's not just that." He pushed off the wall. "Who knows, maybe someone gave him a hotshot."

May chuckled. "A what?"

"Hotshot. An injection of drugs, usually a lethal dose or something. Anyway, thanks for your help last night."

"Sure," she said as he left.

Sitting at her desk, she flexed her hand. The numbing pain had long since faded, but still, May wondered what had actually happened. She looked over at the large desktop calendar that covered half of her desk. Tomorrow was the first: the standing coffee date with Death. She'll know. May just hoped, shaking out her hand again, that she hadn't actually done something stupid.

CHAPTER TEN
A MISSING REAPER

Harper stood at the Maw, her boots hanging just over the edge of the cliff. The souls beneath swarmed and howled. Arms folded, Harper tilted her head at them. They were angrier than normal. More active. Her hounds ran the edge of the cliff, their low barks and growls vibrating through her bones. One came and sat at her side—sleek, black, and almost to her elbow. They were thin creatures, nearly skin and bone. Despite that, there was no doubting their strength. It was in their long legs, too long for their bodies, and large muzzle filled with glistening teeth. Their eyes held intelligence and purpose.

Harper dropped her hand to its head and ran her sharp claws through the hound's downy fur. It leaned into her, closing its amber eyes as she moved to scratch behind the pointed ear. It curled its ninetail around its paws.

"What do you sense, hm?" she asked it softly, and turned her attention back to the Maw.

A yip sounded in the distance, and the hound at her feet sprang and charged off to meet its packmate. Harper reached for her magic buried in her and flung it out from her fingertips at the damned swarming near her feet. Strands of glowing green wove into the barrier and swatted at the damned crowding the surface. With screeches, they sank again to the depths.

They're testing it.

But why? Why would the damned think the magic keeping them contained was weakening? So far, it was only weak souls, mostly human souls, that were rearing up to test the magic. The older, stronger beings were staying well within the endless pit. It was causing her hounds to run themselves into a fury as they growled and snapped at the air wafting from the cage.

"Lady Death?"

She glanced at Armeal, hands tucked tight against his chest and wings held high. Her lips twisted in a grin before she could stop herself.

"They won't attack without cause."

"I do not trust them."

She rolled her eyes. As if sensing his fear and liking it, several hounds bounded over, tails whipping frantically.

"Away!" she barked, and they retreated with whines. "They like your fear."

"I fear," he said stiffly, "because I do not trust them."

She grunted. "What is a Reaper to do..."

He ignored her with a deep breath.

"Do you need something?"

"There is a wraith," he said, "in the Forest."

Harper frowned and looked toward the woods, the tall leafless trees stretching into the pale sky. "Again?"

He nodded, golden eyes moving to the Maw. "It was brought to my attention by a returning Reaper."

The lost do not turn so often. She was sure she'd removed the last wraith before it had contaminated any other lost souls. "I will handle it. Thank you, Armeal."

Armeal nodded, still watching the Maw before slowly retreating from the edge. Harper set off for the Forest, mind and magic stretching to feel for the wraith.

After depositing the wraith into the Wasteland, Harper returned to the Forest. She would not allow the wraiths' touch to fester the souls here. Moving silently through the trees, snow settling on her shoulders, she sensed for any contamination. Lost souls floated around her, most unaware of her presence. She lost track of the time she spent among the trees, searching, sniffing out any other festering anger and rage before she was satisfied there was no lingering effects.

Still, she could not shake the feeling that something was wrong, like the stillness before disaster or the breath held before a fight. She was on edge. An aching longing filled her chest. A searching feeling she couldn't explain. She felt that something had...*happened*. Snow landed on her cheeks as she stood there. Thinking. Sensing.

Shaking the snow from her, she stormed back to her castle. In her office, the rows upon rows of the Books of the Dead did little to calm her nerves. She pulled the most current book from the shelf and set it heavily on her desk. Quickly flipping through the thick pages, she noted how many names glowed golden, souls not collected, and how many were black. There were some, as there always were, but there were more than there should've been. Too many were... missing.

She bared her teeth at the book, a growl working its way up

her throat. The damned. The wraiths. The feeling that clung to her shoulders like a bad omen.

Coincidences were a fallacy humans believed in to explain magic and the supernatural.

"Reapers!" She sent the command through her magic, touching each and everyone. *"Gather."*

She felt their responses through the magic, a soft nod against her mind.

It didn't take long for the Reapers to assemble, silent and unmoving, in the Great Hall. The black stone shimmered around them, the marble pillars stretching to the ceiling. Armeal stood off to the right, his white suit and glorious wings on full display among the sea of black, a display of his strength. The few Reapers sporting wings in the crowd and those that did kept them tucked tight to their bodies.

Turning her attention back to the sea of Reapers and scythes, Harper breathed long and slow.

"I feel a sense of apprehension in the Forest."

There was a subtle shift in the air, like the wind changing directions, and she knew she had all their attention. A few of the younger ones pushed their hoods back, their eyes shining at her.

"I have sensed it as well," an Old One rasped from the crowd.

"I believe…" she said slowly, reluctantly, "souls may be missing."

A hiss from one of the Old Ones in the back broke the soft mutterings at her declaration. She found him, recognized his magic, and gave him a subtle nod.

"Stolen?" a younger Reaper asked near the front of the crowd.

"Perhaps. Perhaps a different magic is at play." She did not want to believe they were being stolen. Lost, perhaps, or waylaid by some Necromancer's magic. But the knowledge to capture a soul...

She held up her hand at the increase of murmurings and the ruffling of feathers and wings. "There are more missing than there should be. That does not mean they are being stolen. That also doesn't mean they are not. It means that more are not where they should be." She huffed a breath. "But something is changing. The damned are restless. The lost are angry."

"What do you ask of us, Death?" the Old One asked, the one who first noticed.

She stared into his hood, searching for the orange eyes she knew lay beneath it. "Be vigilant. Report any odd thing you sense. Trust your senses."

He nodded, a small dip of his hood.

"The Old Ones among you remember what happened the last time souls truly went missing." More hisses and the scrapes of staffs sounded against the marble. "We cannot allow that to come about again."

"There are no traitors here!" a Reaper shouted from the crowd.

"We do our duty," another rasped.

She raised her chin. "I know."

Armeal shifted with an angry shake of his wings. His wings always spoke more than his voice... She watched him with a narrowed gaze before turning back to the crowd.

"I am not saying anyone here is disloyal." She spoke clearly so there was no mistaking her words. "I only warn of what has once happened and the risks if something like that happens again. The souls are my domain. I will find what is happening, but I will rely on your assistance. Now, back to your souls."

They muttered and nodded before dispersing. Harper watched them leave, and soon, the giant hall was empty except for a younger Reaper, hood back from her face. Armeal's steps were soft as he appeared at Harper's side.

"What business do you have?" he asked.

The Reaper's eyes were a dull gold, nearly bronze, and the skin of her face had tightened around the bones of her skull. Her hair, which had once been a lush and bright blond, now hung straight and thin and white as bone. Harper blinked at Armeal, dismissing him with her gaze as she turned to the Reaper.

Her voice was raspy but delicate. "You spoke of trusting our senses."

She nodded and waited.

The Reaper blinked again, glancing over at Armeal before speaking. "I think a Reaper is missing."

Armeal angrily snapped his wings again, but the Reaper did not take her eyes from Harper.

Harper stepped closer and waved Armeal off when he moved to step with her. "How do you know this?" she asked the Reaper.

She lifted her bony chin, the spark of Nephilim arrogance returning. "He is my friend."

"That doesn't explain why you think he is missing."

She tucked her chin, her stance softening from arrogance. "I cannot find him. I have looked. I have waited. I cannot find him."

Missing? Or taken?

Fear settled like a rock in Harper's stomach. "How long has he been missing?"

The Reaper blinked and a sharp frown appeared between her thin brows. Time was difficult with Reapers. It was difficult for Harper, as May had demonstrated. Time passed so differently, and often times, seemed to not move at all.

"I do not know how to answer that, Death."

Armeal snorted, as if he'd have some other answer to give, and Harper turned on him with a snarl on her lips. "Be silent or be gone!"

His clear eyelids closed over his eyes, and he stepped back.

"How many souls have you ferried since you last saw your friend?"

The Reaper's brow smoothed, and she blinked again. "Seven."

"And his name?"

"He is an Old One. He calls himself Talsk. I do not know if it is his name."

"It is if he says it is." Harper's stomach fell, and for the first time in her easy memory, she tasted the sharp, bitter taste of fear on her tongue.

She had to swallow before she could speak. "Do you have a name?"

"Esiel."

"Thank you, Esiel."

She watched Esiel leave, hood pulled back into place, before slowly turning to Armeal.

"Seven ferries is not such a long time," he reminded her.

"No," she agreed, "but that he is missing at all..."

The last time Reapers went missing... the last time their loyalty was questioned... Harper narrowed her eyes at Armeal. His second eyelid blinked closed, and he stepped back.

"Perhaps it is a Hunter," Armeal murmured.

She snorted and waved the idea away. "No. The Fae had retreated to their hidden forests. A Fae Hunter hasn't stepped outside their lands in centuries."

"What about the witch?"

Harper glared at him. "What about her?"

Armeal shrugged. "She seems to have inserted herself into your confidences. She's had more than usual near deaths, and the Fates are overly ambiguous about her fate. All at the same time as souls go missing and now a Reaper."

She raised an eyebrow. "Into my confidences?"

A position he wishes he held, no doubt.

He huffed, feathers rustling. "It is quite a coincidence, is all I'm saying."

She lifted her lip in a snarl and turned away, dismissing him as she did. He nodded in silence and slipped away.

Coincidences did not exist...

CHAPTER ELEVEN
THE DESERT LAND OF PHOENIX

Harper looked over the list of names in her Book of Souls, many of the glowing, golden names turning black—successful ferries. She flipped through the pages, clawed finger sliding down the list of names. A few flickered and shimmered, and she paused over those. One name being, Katherine Lang. That soul should've been collected by now. Frowning, Harper sent a query of magic out to the Reapers, finding the one that had taken that ferry and called it to her.

The Reaper stepped into her office not long later. He was a younger Nephilim, his magic weak and feeble as she tested hers against it.

"You went for this soul?" She pointed to the name in the ledger.

The Reaper pushed his hood back and glanced down at the page. He blinked his pale-yellow eyes and nodded once. "Yes. It was not there."

Harper frowned and looked again at the name. "Had it wandered?"

The Reaper shrugged his thin shoulders. "It was not there."

She sighed through her nose and looked at the Reaper from under her lashes, reminding herself that not every Nephilim was as attuned or thorough as the Old Ones.

"All right," she said. "Thank you."

He nodded, pulled his hood back up, and left.

Slicing her claws through the layers of the world, Harper stepped into the dimly lit hallway of the nursing home. She wrinkled her nose at the smell of disease and poorly kept hygiene that permeated the halls, then turned toward Katherine's old room. The nameplate was still on the wall beneath the room number, but as she stepped into the room, she saw it had been stripped of any belongings and bedding. The empty room was dark, the blinds pulled against the harsh Arizona sun.

Harper sniffed, sensing the magics in the air as she walked slowly around the small room. Touching her fingers to the mattress, she detected stillness. Peace. An acceptance of the end. She straightened from the bed and looked around again and found nothing that would cause the soul to tether itself here. Pulling the stale air over her tongue to taste it, she found the slightest tingle of familiar magic. Ancient. Powerful. But then it was gone again.

She turned to the hallway, unseen by the living, and searched out the dead. Places like these, homes for the dying, always gathered souls. The lost, the forgotten. Their souls gathered here, where families had left them.

Harper caught the glimpse of a soul, more solid than the other waifs floating by, and stepped in front of him. His hunched frame stuttered to a stop, and he dragged his eyes up to her. The man wore a three-piece suit, tattered and patched, with a pocket watch draped at his waist. He gaped at her, toothless mouth snapping as he glowered at her from under bushy eyebrows.

"Out of my way."

"Eugene," Harper said, holding her hand out to stall him.

"No," he barked, and tried to scoot around her on stiff legs with a cane. "I didn't go then, I won't go now!"

She put her hand on his boney shoulder, knobbed from the arthritis that had tormented him in the end, and curled her claws into him to hold his attention. "I am not here for you. You have long ago bound yourself here, not even I can change that now."

He glared at her, smacking his lips. "Then what do you want?" He waved his cane at the hallway ahead of them. "I have people to see."

People who had been dead for decades. She glanced down the hallway, knowing all the souls of the people he knew had left. Eugene had strange moments of lucidness. He knew he was dead. He knew he was wandering halls in a repeating pattern, but he also stopped by the rooms of his friends and spoke to no one, repeating conversations that had once happened. It was a strange hell he'd created for himself: trapped in the repeating history of his life while knowing he was dead.

"The woman here"—she pointed over her shoulder at Katherine's room—"do you know what happened to her?"

Eugene huffed but followed her finger to the room, smacking his lips again. "She was going to stay. She said so."

Harper's eyes widened. "Did she?"

"No!" he yelled at her. "The dame must've changed her mind." He huffed. "Not proper for a lady to be so wishy-washy like that."

But the soul hadn't been collected. Katherine's name still glowed golden.

"Who took her?"

Eugene shook himself free of her grip with strength he never had in life. "Agh!"

He shuffled away from her then and returned to his endless walk. Harper watched him go before looking once more into Katherine's empty room.

Returning to her office, Katherine Lang's name still flickered. It didn't mean her soul was missing. It could've wandered before the Reaper arrived. It could've tethered itself somewhere else. The elderly, especially those removed from their homes, had a tendency of finding themselves back there in death. But still...

Harper found another flickering name on a page. No Reaper had gone for this name yet. Taking the name, she stepped into the mortal world for it and found herself in a crowded home, people gathered around the body of John Wilkes on the floor. Paramedics stood nearby, gathering their things.

John's soul flicked the ash from a ghostly cigarette and crossed his arms. "Well," he said, voice rough and crackly from a lifetime of smoking, "they all did say smoking would get me in the end."

Harper walked over next to him, and they watched his family cry as the finality of the situation settled in.

"I just didn't think it'd be a stroke."

Harper looked over at him as he continued to smoke his endless cigarette. "What did you think?"

"Oh—" He puffed a cloud of smoke. "You know. Lung cancer probably. Oh well." He flicked it again. "This was quicker."

Harper held her hand out to him, which he took with no hesitation, and she brought him to the Underworld as quickly as his stroke had taken his life. He left through the trees, smoke puffing up from him as he went, then she turned to seek out

Armeal. She searched for him through the trees of the Forgotten Forest but didn't see him.

"Fineli," she called to the Old One as he passed her. Fineli wasn't originally his name, but it was the one he'd chosen after the Agreement. She didn't know if it was an effort to distance himself from who he'd once been, or if he couldn't remember the old name. Fineli was another Old One nearly as rebellious as Armeal. He wore his Reaper cloak like an afterthought. Hood thrown back and front open, he kept to his more traditional garb from before the Agreement, loose-fitting pants with a tunic-style vest, but at least he had the respect to keep them black. The sleeves were shorn off the cloak, exposing the pale-gray skin of his arms.

He glanced at her, the frown that always seemed to mar his delicate face creasing his forehead. "Death."

"I was looking for Armeal, but he is away," she said. "Have you seen him?"

As annoying as Armeal was, as grating as his rebellious nature was, he was an observant Nephilim.

"I haven't, Death." He frowned harder. "He has been gone for some time."

Gone? Harper filed that away for later.

"Well," she said instead, "have you noticed any missing souls?"

He wrinkled his nose. "No, Death. You asked we report such things if we see them. I have not."

"Yes, yes." She waved away his snappy words. "I was just... never mind." Shaking her shoulders, she turned away from the Reaper.

Again, she stood over her desk, studying the names in her ledger, and a Reaper stepped in, slow and hesitant. Harper looked up at the hooded figure.

"Yes?"

"Death," the Reaper said, her voice nearly a whisper.

Harper raised her eyebrow at the Reaper, and she slowly stepped into the large room.

"I have a soul that was not where it should be."

"Missing? Or gone?"

The timid Reaper stopped in front of Harper and her desk. She reached a boney finger out and pointed to the glowing name on the page: Jeff Holden.

"Missing," she whispered, "I think."

"Why do you think it is missing?" Harper asked as she noted the name.

The Reaper shrank back at Harper's question, her shoulders rising around her.

"I only ask," Harper said, "so I understand. Not to criticize."

The Reaper relaxed her body but stayed hidden beneath her hood. "No reason for it to be gone, but it was."

Harper looked at the other names she had collected of potentially missing souls. "Could you have been late?"

The Reaper shook her head. "No, Death."

Harper raised an eyebrow at the Reaper again. "You're so sure?"

"The dead," she muttered, "are kinder than... I arrive early and wait. I am never late."

Kinder than her siblings, no doubt. "And where was this soul?"

"In the hot lands of Arizona."

Harper narrowed her gaze at her. "Where in Arizona?"

The Reaper tilted her hooded head. "I think the mortals call it Phoenix."

Harper looked at her list of names. Too many souls were missing from those hot desert lands. Katherine Lang. Jeff Holden. The man in the woods. Too many to be a coincidence. Not that those existed, anyway.

Harper looked up at the timid Reaper. "Thank you."

She nodded and turned to leave when Harper stalled her. "Do you have a name?"

She stilled, hand hidden in the long sleeve of her robe clenched around the staff. "No one has given me one."

"You should give yourself one."

Her glowing eyes appeared from deep within the hood. "Perhaps."

"Last question," Harper asked. "Have you seen Armeal?"

"I do not know the name."

"The one in the white suit."

The Reaper shrank away. "No. I have not seen him."

She scurried away, allowing Harper no more questions. Harper glanced again at her list of names. Why Phoenix? What was happening there? And where was Armeal?

CHAPTER TWELVE
THE TETHER

Harper's orange eyes stared back at her from the large mirror. The edges were rusted, the patina slowly spreading more and more inward as the years crept on. She remembered when the mirror was crisp and clear, not a blemish on it. That had been some time ago. She could simply magic away the patina, make it new again with little effort, but she liked the look. She liked the reminder that time here does, in fact, move. Even if it was hard to track it.

Everything about the castle was clean and orderly, pristine. The little bit of chaos in her quarters helped to ground her. As did the crackling of the candles that wavered in the corner of her vision, the flames casting wistful patterns on the walls.

Sounds. Change. Chaos. Reminders that there was life outside her silent throne.

She puffed a breath before turning away and waving her hand through the air. A small gust of wind flew from her fingertips, extinguishing her candles. Smoke rose in swirls throughout the room. She needed to talk to the witch, to May. She would never admit such things to Armeal, but he was right. May had appeared far too coincidently. The souls were missing from the area she was in. Nearly circling her like she was the epicenter of a storm. But why? That, she couldn't figure out.

Out of the corner of her eyes, she caught Armeal in an alcove as she passed, and he dipped his head in a nod.

It was clear to her now that someone was taking souls. A witch perhaps. Someone had learned how to capture them before her Reapers were getting to them. A Necromancer? She pursed her lips. Possibly. They were the most likely to be able to see the souls and even the Reapers, thanks to their Grave Magic.

Outside, the clouds swirled overhead and lightning crackled over the Maw. Her eyes lingered there, searching. The hounds paced the edge, low growls filling the otherwise quiet courtyard. It all was making Harper anxious. She looked away with a huff and flicked her clawed finger through the air. Focusing her energy into separating the layers of the world, and the air in front of her split. She held the edge open, the world straining against her grip to close.

"I'll be in the human world," she spoke, knowing Armeal would hear.

"Back soon?" Armeal muttered from behind her.

She glanced over her shoulder and saw him standing on the obsidian steps.

"Soon enough," she said. *Where had he been?* She narrowed her eyes at him. His brother's betrayal had started like this too. She let the split in the worlds slam behind her.

She could find any soul that had touched death, but she could find May's faster, easier than any other. Was that why the Fates said she was tied to this? She didn't know and didn't understand their riddles, so she shook their foolish words away and found May sitting at a small, shaded table. It looked like the backside of a building, probably the office she worked at. The small picnic area was shaded by large trees, though she suspected the heat was near intolerable even in the shade. She approached the witch and eased her magic around her, settling herself in the mortal world, and May looked up with shocked eyes.

"Oh, hi, um…" She glanced around and sat up from the book and salad she was hunched over. "What're you doing here?"

Harper flexed her magic around them. "I thought we could talk."

May smiled widely without hesitation, and Harper felt the smallest pang of guilt.

"Okay." She seemed to look Harper up and down. "Don't you get hot?"

"No," she breathed, and brushed her long braid back over her shoulder. "I do not feel things like that. Why do you ask?"

"Because it's the surface of the sun." May smiled and plucked at Harper's sleeve at her wrist. "And you're always wearing this long black coat and boots and freaking pants. You look like a goth girl."

"I like them," Harper said, sitting at the wooden picnic table. "I see you don't seem to mind the heat."

She groaned. "Oh, it's hot, but the office is freezing from the AC, so I'm warming up like the lizard I am. Are you sure it's not just because you're used to it?"

"I do not reside in Hell," she snipped with a sniff of her nose. "I feel it is hot, but it doesn't effect me. I don't burn from the sun. Nor do I freeze in the snow."

"So, Hell *is* a place, not a myth?"

She hesitated. This wasn't what she wanted to talk about. This wasn't the purpose of her visit, but as reluctant as she was to admit it to herself, Harper enjoyed the mortal's company.

"That is a very complicated question with no easy answer. I would say, perhaps, the Greeks came the closest, but even I do not know what dwells past the Underworld."

May's eyes grew unfocused, and Harper watched her fight with the question as her eyes bounced from her and away again.

"Ask," she said.

"I don't want to imp—"

"Ask."

May had died, but Harper never took her across the plane. She'd never seen the Underworld, her home. She found she wanted to share it. Share it with someone who might enjoy it.

"What's it like?" May breathed, her elbows resting on the table.

Harper thought of the crowds walking along the street. Their laughter. Their noise. Their life. Harper could feel May's eyes on her.

"The Underworld?" She pulled her eyes back to May. "No hellfire and brimstone, but it's bleak. There is no life. No sound. The trees of the Forest are barren, the soil dead. Souls of the lost and tormented wander the plain. A constant cloudy haze blocks the sun. The snow... I've come to enjoy the snow."

"Sounds lonely."

"Yes," she breathed, and it sounded sad. "It is."

That loneliness was part of the reason she'd offered her home to the rejected and hunted Nephilim. She had hoped they could bring friendship, companionship, sounds to her world.

It had not gone the way she had hoped.

May hummed, a soft sound, and sipped from her water bottle. Harper stretched her magic out, and May's magic, soft and quiet and buried, flared in response, and May's shoulders twitched. Pushing her magic out farther, Harper touched souls of the living in her search. She felt nothing out of the ordinary. No strange magic flared.

"Well... since you're here." May started, and Harper focused on her. "A weird thing's been happening at work."

Harper straightened, and that strange *otherness* in her chest returned. "Weird how?"

"Ummm..." She dragged out the word in a high-pitched sound. "So, I don't know if you know this or not..." She glanced around them. "But I'm... a... witch."

"Yes."

May blinked at her, mouth slack. "Oh. Oh, so you knew?"

Harper chuckled and twisted her lips in a grin and leaned in close. "I am a being of magic and history and gods. You think I can't see magic on others?"

May's cheeks flushed and she nodded. "Well, sure, okay. When you say it like that."

Harper waited while May settled, rubbing her forehead before grasping her water bottle.

"Well. Before, my magic was"—she shrugged— "it wasn't anything exciting. But now, I can see the dead. I can hear them sometimes. I—"

Harper frowned. "It happens sometimes when you are so close to the border of life and death. Especially given how often you were."

"I, hey." May frowned. "Okay, my obvious mortality aside, a couple of dead guys came in and there was this... thing." She gestured with her fingers near her chest, a deep frown between her eyes. "This silver-looking thread thing and—"

"What?" Harper breathed. "You could see it?"

May nodded. "Shouldn't I? You just said it happens sometimes."

Not that. Harper didn't know how May was connected to

what was happening with her souls, but she was now convinced she was. "What was this person's name?"

"I... I don't remember. I can check. Why?"

Because more had gone missing... This one might be one of my missing. Harper pressed her lips tight.

"Well—" May let out a breath. "Anyway, the second one was brighter, different somehow, and when I touched it—"

"You touched it!" she shouted, shock getting the better of her for the first time in centuries.

"Sorry," May muttered, shrinking back into her chair.

"You should not touch it," Harper bit out. How this witch was still alive was a question she would try to weasel out of the Fates later. The power contained in a Tether could send even the strongest of Nephilim to their knees.

"Obviously, I got that now." May's voice was petulant. "It was like it was calling to me. It wanted me to."

Harper stilled and turned all her attention to May. No one should be able to hear the call of the Tether. Not even the Reapers could hear it. Mortals cannot see it. Cannot hear it. Cannot survive touching them. Yet, this witch could.

"How many?" she asked, mind still racing.

"I've seen two. What is it?" May asked, her voice shaking and low.

She took a deep breath. "It is the Tether to the soul."

May's eyes widened and her face paled.

Harper watched her with unblinking eyes. "Souls are missing, and I think someone is stealing them."

"Well, it's not me!" May shouted, hands flying into the air. "Wait!" She pointed an accusing finger at Harper with narrowed, angry eyes. "Did you come here because you thought I was responsible?"

Harper blinked and leaned back.

"You did!" May pushed back from the table with a loud, angry chortle. "What the hell?"

"Coincidences do not exist," Harper said slowly, letting her magic flare and ride along May's. She sensed, felt, waited for a sign the witch was more than she seemed. "Mortals cannot see the Tether. Yet, you do. You survived touching it. It *called* to you." Harper narrowed her eyes. "Only I can hear the Tether's call."

May threw her hands up again and stood, pacing the small, shaded area, hands rubbing on her pants. "I don't know what any of that means or why I can do it."

Harper slowly withdrew her magic. "I can see that now."

May turned angry eyes to her. "I thought we were friends."

The accusation hit Harper so hard in the chest she had to swallow before she found the words. "Friends are a complicated thing for an immortal."

May sniffed. "Yeah, so you've said."

Harper took a deep breath. "I don't know what role you have in what is unfolding, but the Fates have decided you do have some role to play."

"Do I want to know what the Fates are?" May grumbled, and folded her arms across her chest.

Harper shrugged. "They have many names. Maiden, Mother, Crone. Hecate. Past, Present, Future."

"I don't want a role in any of this."

The Fates had said their threads were tied together. Harper sighed. "The Fates have decided."

Harper barely kept her lip from turning into a snarl. She didn't like this feeling that the Fates were maneuvering around her. Maneuvering *her*. The Fates dealt in mortal. Others. Not *her*. She should be above their machinations. May's lips were too thin, too pale, as she stared into her forgotten coffee.

"I did *not* want to get wrapped up in this shit," May muttered under her breath.

Harper tilted her head and leaned forward. "Wrapped up in what?"

May huffed an annoyed breath and dropped her arms, meeting Harper's eyes. "Supernatural shit. One of the ghosts I saw... he—It was like he needed me to see something. He bugged the fuck out of me at my desk until I followed him back to the autopsy room. He basically led me to the body of his friend, and that was the first time I saw the Tether... thing."

Harper narrowed her eyes on May. Was she *just* a Green Witch? The dead, the spirit realm, rarely bothered with others. Not unless they felt some connection. A Green Witch, rooted in the earth and living and growth, would be the last thing Harper expected spirits to connect to.

"What happened when you touched the Tether?"

"I..." She shrugged and swallowed. "It shocked me. My arm went numb."

Harper's breath left her in a rumble. "I need to see the body."

May's mouth gaped before she was able to form words. "I can't—You can't just—"

"They will not see me."

"Right," May said, her voice soft. "Right."

She stood, and May stared at her. "Now?"

"Now, May."

CHAPTER THIRTEEN
THE BODY

May huffed a breath, frowning at Harper. "Fine." Folding the corner of the page on her book, May started packing up her small lunch.

"It's not often people steal souls, I'd bet."

"No," Harper said solemnly.

Only one had managed to capture souls. Yrien. She was one of the first Nephilim, and it showed in her strength. She'd been nearly as powerful as her mother— and as beautiful. The Archangel of War would've been proud had she not been fooled by a demon. Looking back, it shouldn't have surprised her that Yrien never settled into her life in the shadows. Yrien had been a strong-willed, proud creature. As set in her self-believed righteousness as her mother. Harper had trusted her, confided in her, considered her more than, perhaps, just a friend, but she should've seen the betrayal coming.

May slung her bag over her shoulder and turned toward the building. It was a large gray building. Utilitarian in design. A few windows sat along the side—offices, she assumed—near the front door they'd driven past. The rest was nondescript brick. May pulled out her white key card and glanced at Harper with a question in her eyes. Harper dropped her glamour, letting it fall from her in a wave, then let herself fade from the human world and into the gray space between. The in-between, where ghosts and spirits roamed.

Harper nodded to her, and she keyed in. There was a soft beep as the door unlocked, and then they were inside. She followed, her foot-falls silent. May waved at a few coworkers as she passed them and nodded to others. They moved through a near labyrinth of halls before she finally found her desk and dumped her bag unceremoniously on the chair.

A woman with freckles and red hair stopped at May's desk. "Have a good lunch?"

May took a deep breath and nodded as she stepped past the woman. "I did, Sarah, thanks."

Sarah smiled and turned to follow May down the hall of offices and desks.

"So, who is he?"

May looked over her shoulder at Sarah with a frown. "Huh?"

"Or she?" Sarah amended with a shrug. "No judgment."

"What?" May's eyes danced over Sarah's shoulder to Harper before she hastily turned away and resumed the walk.

"Whoever you meet on your monthly lunch date. Are you meeting your boyfriend? Girlfriend?"

"I didn't meet anyone."

"No," Sarah agreed with a sly smile, "not today. But you do... Who is it?"

"If I was meeting anyone I was dating, I hope I'd do it more than once a month," May said dryly. She glanced over at Sarah again, who'd stopped at one of the last desks. "Just a friend I know from when I was in the hospital."

"Oh," Sarah whispered, as if talking about sickness and death would bring it upon her. "I see."

May rolled her eyes and continued into the exam room and around into the freezer storage. Once inside, the cold making May's breath fog in front of her, Harper asked, "Who's Sarah?"

May watched Harper from the corner of her eye, then started scanning the labels on the drawers. "An autopsy tech," she stated.

May grunted when she found the correct drawer and pulled it out, then unzipped the bag and laid it open, putting the hastily stitched-up Y incision on display.

"I don't know how much you'll be able to see with him closed—"

Harper extended her clawed hand over the dead man's chest and *pulled* for the Tether. The frayed end slithered into the air through the cuts in the skin.

"Oh..."

She peered closer at the Tether and clenched her teeth as anger and fear settled in her blood. The color had dulled, now a soft-pale yellow. She lowered her hand, and the strand fluttered before laying down across her fingers. A small jolt shot up her arm, and with it, memories. Pain, fear, the sense of running. Disjointed, incomplete memories.

"This man died in fear. Terror clings to him. Pain."

"What does that mean?"

She dropped the Tether, and it returned to the body, curling up in the chest. "It is his last memories. His last thoughts. Emotions last the longest."

Fury built in her chest, hot and violent. Whoever was doing this was murdering them before their time. Stealing what was hers. Trespassing in her domain. Pain seared in her palms as her nails bit into her flesh. May's lips were pressed into a thin line, her hands clenched tightly around her chest as she hugged herself.

"This does not concern you."

She would find another way to deal with this soul thief. Ready to cut the layers of the world open, she turned away, but May's hand gripped her arm tight. Her hand shook, squeezing Harper's wrist, but her hold was firm and uncompromising.

May scoffed, loud and angrily. "Fuck you, dude."

Harper snapped surprised eyes to May.

"You come here and *accuse me* of being the one stealing people's souls, and then have the nerve to say it doesn't concern me?"

Harper blinked, surprised and shocked. She wasn't used to such anger being directed at her. To her. The Nephilim were not so brazen to her face, and the dead... the dead were different.

May shrugged, her folded arms jerking against her chest. "So I can see the fancy Tether thing. And can see ghosts. And all that other *shit*, and you're just going to what?" She shrugged again, jutting her chin out like she was demanding an answer. "You're going to deal with this yourself? People are dying. Being murdered."

"I am Death, Keeper of the Underworld and Rider of the Pale Horse," Harper thundered. "Who do you think *should* fix this? The souls are *mine* to guard and keep."

"And you expect me to ignore murders even as they pass across my desk?" May's eyes were angry. "You want me to ignore that? After the *audacity* you came in here with?"

"Yes."

May pulled back, her cheeks flushed with anger. "I can't. I can't pretend people aren't being murdered, that they're souls aren't being stolen. I work at the Medical Examiner's Office, for hell's sake! My job is investigating deaths."

"This isn't a human problem," Harper insisted.

"You just said my fate is stuck in this." May persisted.

Harper hesitated. She didn't know what their twined fates meant, but she was Death. If she couldn't solve this problem without the help of a mortal, what did that mean for her?

No. She shook her head and turned away.

"I'm in this already." May continued when Harper was unable to speak. "I'm already involved. Let me help you. The dead are going to continue to come by my desk. I'll see them even if I don't help you. I'm in this already."

"So it would seem," Harper whispered. "But that doesn't mean the Fates control me."

May scoffed, but Harper angrily sliced the layers of the world and stepped through.

"You can't just run off!" May shouted at her as the world slammed shut.

CHAPTER FOURTEEN
YOU SHOULDN'T ARGUE WITH THE FATES

Harper ripped the world open, anger harshening as her claws dug through the layers.

"Fates!" she shouted, her voice thick with growling anger.

The nothingness of their domain echoed her shout, and the threads of lives around her trembled. The Crone appeared and snapped her shears at Harper.

"You disturb, Death."

Harper snarled at the Crone. "You meddle in my affairs, old woman."

The Mother, measuring rod held out like a stick to hit something with, stepped next to her sister. "You overstep yourself, Death."

Whispering, like spiderwebs on the back of her neck, brushed past Harper as the Maiden, her sheer robes flowing around her, stepped around Harper. "She is angry."

Harper cut a hard glare at the Maiden but remembered herself enough to hold her tongue.

"I spin the webs," the Maiden said, her voice ethereal despite the anger thick in the air, "for my sisters to shape." She gestured to the Mother. "She measures the lots. Sets the thread." She spun around the group to place gentle hands on the Crone's shoulders. "And she cuts the threads and sets the destiny."

Three sets of white glowing eyes turned to her, and Harper withered beneath the fury that seemed to burn her skin.

"*Your affairs are ours to meddle. Your fate is created, destined, and set by us.*" Their voices overlapping, booming, nearly deafened Harper.

She fell beneath their power to one knee, head bowed and breath straining, before the Fates lifted their power from her. Harper was left gasping, staring at the floor of the swirling void.

"Perhaps," the Mother spoke softer, her feet padding around Harper, "Death wants to try again."

Harper gritted her teeth, holding back the snarl and words she wanted to say, and stood stiffly.

"You are no god here, Death," the Crone wheezed, her scissors snipping open and closed.

"I have been thus," Harper huffed, "reminded."

"What does Death want, then?" Crone snarled.

"My name is Harper," she snapped.

The Crone laughed, a loud cackling sound that grated on Harper's nerves. The Crone reached into the swirling mass of threads and pulled down her shimmering blue thread, tied even tighter with May's tattered one. "You think you're a being worth a name? Like your servants?" The Crone scoffed. "You are a being beyond mortal names."

The Mother held her measuring rod between her hands as if she still debated smacking someone with it.

"Explain the witch May Haines."

The Mother tsked. "Again, you ask this."

"Explain," Harper demanded, managing to keep the venom out of her voice, lest she be forced to both knees.

The Maiden danced over, her fingers twirling along the twisting, turning threads, making Harper's spine tighten. "They weave together. They are bound now. No undoing that."

"But why?"

The three cackled and laughed.

"Wrong question," the Maiden sang as she moved around them again.

I hate these things, Harper thought, and unclenched her jaw.

"Is May involved in the theft of souls?"

"She's not, not involved. Not yet."

"That doesn't even make sense," Harper muttered. "How is she able to touch the Tether and survive?"

They hummed and shrugged. Harper bared her teeth but kept her words to herself.

"Why do the ghosts seek her out?"

"Wrong questions," the Maiden sang again from somewhere behind her.

"Enough," the Crone snapped.

"No," the Mother said with a soft look at the Crone, "let her have one more question. Maybe she'll get this one right."

Harper's breath stilled in her chest. They were likely to throw her out, and after her entrance, who knew when they would speak to her civilly again.

"Will... I need the witch's help to find my souls?"

The Mother, face aged with gentle crow's-feet at her eyes and laugh lines in her cheeks, stalked forward until she was nearly nose to nose with Harper.

"Yes," she whispered, then snapped her fingers, throwing Harper from their realm.

She landed hard on her ass, momentum snapping her head back against the marble floor of her office. Her teeth slammed together, sending numbing pain through her jaw and the metallic tang of blood across her tongue. Raising a trembling hand to her face, she lay there, seething and head pounding.

That was a little unnecessary, she thought with a groaning sigh.

Footsteps had her opening her eyes as Armeal leaned over her, staring down with a birdlike tilt of his head.

"Lady Death?"

"Why are you in my office?" she asked. "And where have you been?"

Armeal glanced over at her desk. "Ferrying souls. Where else would I be?"

She sighed and let her hand flop to the floor. *Excellent question.*

He turned golden eyes back to her, face impassive. "May I ask why you're on the floor?"

"No." She rolled to her feet, and he shuffled out of her way.

"More souls are unaccounted for."

She paused, jaw clenching, and turned away. It was time, she decided, to look upon the past.

Harper's steps were quiet in the silent halls. It didn't matter that she wore black boots or walked on cold black marble. Death was silent. She moved through the dark halls, turning corners and taking narrow stairs down into the depths of her castle. No Reaper wandered here. She twisted her fingers, and a soft glow rose above her. Just enough to light her way and cast a flicker of yellow light on the walls around her as she continued her trek down. At the end of the long corridor stood a door covered with intricate engravings of Nephilim, angels, and demons.

She flexed her fingers, and the magical light brightened as she stared at the iron door as tall and wide as the corridor. Angels, wings flared and swords drawn, glare down from the top of the carving while demons, with their horned heads and tails, reach up from the floor. Nephilim cover the center, shrouded in Reaper cloaks and reaching for scythes.

She blinked in the flickering magic light before slowly reaching for the large latch. The door swung open on silent, willing hinges to reveal a pitch-black room. Stepping inside, Harper flared her fingers wide, and the magic brightened the whole room. The obsidian marble continued into the room, a giant cavern of black.

Pedestals of black rock rose from the floor in neat and orderly rows. A notch in the top of the rock, the perfect size to hold the staff, was cut into each one. Reaper scythes rested in the pedestals, the shimmering silver blades cresting the rock. Harper passed each one solemnly. These were the fallen—the Nephilim defending their duty, upholding their oath. The loyal. Names of those that had them were etched into the stone.

Many lives were claimed on each side by the Nephilim Rebellion.

Some pedestals she passed were empty of the Nephilim's scythe. Not everything had been reclaimed after that final battle. The angels made off with their share of spoils, and more than a few Fae managed to swipe a blade or two. Those, she'd recovered. The Fae should've known better than to think they could keep such things. But the angels...

Harper raised her lip in a silent snarl as she stared at the empty markers. Those weren't theirs to have, and the theft grated on her. She would have torn down the pearl gates to take back what was hers—if that side of death hadn't been barred to her.

She moved farther into the cavern and came to the back where another set of stone markers stood. These, however, were not monuments to the loyal, or memories to their deeds.

No. These were markers for the traitors. Their scythes were thrown on the floor at the foot of their marker. The names etched into the stones had been gouged out. Harper slowly raised her hand to a marker, the one that started it all, and gently ran her fingers along the matching claw marks across Yrien's name. She was the first. The first Nephilim and her first Reaper. She'd brought many with her into the Underworld, into the new life that had been promised.

Her first, perhaps, companion. The first, and last, being she'd trusted her heart too.

And Yrien had thrown it all back in Harper's face. She flexed her claws into the stone and scratched out more of Yrien's name. That pain was still fresh, even after all these centuries. The pain and embarrassment and shame. The heartbreak.

Her scythe hadn't been found in a battlefield that stretched for miles. Another theft of the angels. Harper let out a sharp breath and dropped her hand. Probably Yrien's mother. It would be fitting for the Angel of War, so foolishly betrayed by a cunning demon, to claim her fallen daughter's weapon.

She left Yrien's marker, a bitter taste in her mouth as she did, and turned to the one next to it.

Artheal.

Yrien's second-in-command.

Armeal's brother.

Theirs was a story she'd never understood. Some angels had been tricked by their demon counterparts into thinking they were other than what they were. Like Yrien's mother. As one of the archangels, one would think she was smarter than that.

She didn't think Artheal and Armeal's mother had been tricked, however. If she believed Artheal, they had been raised by his mother for some time before their true parentage had been discovered and they were cast out. Artheal, with his infant brother. The two couldn't be more dissimilar. While Armeal was arrogant and prideful, Artheal had been quiet and gentle. Almost too gentle for a Nephilim. Perhaps his time with his mother had crafted that personality. Armeal had an air of bitterness to him, as if he blamed his brother for not having the same.

She stared at the empty marker for Artheal. His scythe was among those not recovered.

The betrayal burned in Harper's chest like it was new, fresh. She had offered her domain for the Nephilim to live. To survive. She swore to protect them against those that had hunted them. And still they had betrayed her.

Yrien had betrayed her.

She ground her teeth and turned away with a huff of breath.

It wasn't happening again. It couldn't be.

The thought of another betrayal burned her chest. The Fates' words, that she would need May, a mortal, carried heavy shame in her chest. Who was she, if not even Death could protect her realm? What did that make her? She had felt sympathy for the rejected Nephilim. Felt sorrow for a kin so rejected by every side that she had opened her home to them. Offered them a life. A kinship she hadn't realized she'd wanted for herself until they were here.

Maybe it was the nature of the Nephilim, she mused as she stared at Artheal's scratched-out name. They were sired by demons, after all. Their nature is dark and untrusting. Looking over the podiums of those that had betrayed that companionship, her mouth turned down in bitter pain. If they betrayed her again... she wasn't sure she had any room in her heart for them in her home. If they turned against her again, perhaps this time she'd cast them all out.

The soft flutter of feathers pulled her attention to Armeal standing still and silent behind her. His eyes, wide and shocked, moved in quick succession from one pedestal to the next. Anger burned in her chest at the intrusion.

"I did not know this existed," he murmured, mouth slack. His eyes finally fell on his brother's pedestal, and his lips firmed into a tight line.

Harper shifted her shoulders, rolling them, and stretched. "I did not think your kind sentimental."

"We aren't," he said, eyes never leaving his brother's gouged name. "Usually."

He took a cautious step closer. "Why is this here?"

Harper hissed out a breath. "You may not care about your fallen siblings, but I mourn the loss of those who fought beside me."

He stepped even with her, wings held tight to his back. "Then why keep these?" He jutted his chin toward his brother's name.

She looked back at it, her angry claw marks like a wound. "Even in their betrayal, they deserve something marking their existence." She glanced at him from the corner of her eye before turning again to the disgraced monuments. "No one deserves to be forgotten."

Armeal turned to her in a jerky movement before glancing back at his brother's name. He took a deep breath, his wings shaking like an angry raven, before turning sharply on his heel. "Some do."

CHAPTER FIFTEEN
GHOSTS AND HEARTS

May's hands were sweaty on the steering wheel, and it had nothing to do with the temperature outside. The red stone of the large hospital looked right at home in the desert, the cacti and desert shrubs the landscapers chose, adding to the appearance. It was an unassuming building, even if it was huge. It shouldn't be giving May sweats and a dry mouth, but it did.

She'd spent far too much time at the Mayo Clinic of Phoenix already. She was tired of this hospital. As thankful as she was that they'd saved her and given her this new heart, she was ready to never walk into this building again.

Too many ghosts lingered in these halls—metaphorical and literal.

She took a deep breath and one more long gulp from her water bottle before shutting off her car. She'd taken the day off work, even though this checkup wouldn't be long. She was always too unsettled afterward to focus on work. Far too many emotions were stirred up at these appointments: fear, sadness, relief, grief.

"Fuck it," she muttered, and finally left her car for the short walk across the parking lot. Even in the early morning, the sun was already hot, though the breeze ghosting across her skin still had the coolness of night to it. That wouldn't last long. Inside the lobby, the AC was already going hard, and the sudden temperature shift made her skin pucker in goosebumps. May turned quickly to the elevators and pushed the button for the Transplant Division.

The door to the small waiting room had frosted glass, obscuring the area inside. She assumed it was for privacy but hated that she couldn't see how empty or full the room was until she was already inside. She preferred an empty room. Then there weren't worried families making quiet small talk, or patients pointedly avoiding each other's gaze. She pulled the door open and breathed a soft sigh of relief when she saw the room was empty.

Thank God for early appointments, she thought as she crossed the room to the receptionist.

She'd long stopped telling her parents of these appointments. She couldn't handle their fretting, hovering. The careful questions and nervous glances were enough to send her over the edge of insanity. Now she just called her mom with the outcome of the appointments. Rather her mother's wrath than her worry.

The perfectly, neutrally polite receptionist checked her in, and May turned to sit in the overstuffed and stiff chairs. Only to jerk to a stop with a sudden breath.

Shit.

A ghost, thin and barely there, floated near the door. She'd missed it when she'd walked in, and now they locked eyes. Gathering herself, she quickly settled in a chair and waited. The ghost seemed to ignore her as she floated on the other side of the room. The body was hardly there, just a filmy outline that implied a person. May made out the face, a blurry approximation of a teenager, from the corner of her eye as she tried to ignore it. Hospitals were full of the dead. And their ghosts.

May took a deep breath and looked away, staring instead toward the door leading to the exam rooms.

The ghost glided over and *sat* in the chair next to May.

Shit.

She shifted, continuing to ignore it.

"I know you can see me," the ghost girl said, her voice a whisper through time. It seemed to echo across a distance, faint and far.

May shifted again and prayed the nurse came for her soon. Maybe the ghost would stay here.

The door clicked open, and a nurse stepped out with a clipboard. "May Haines?"

She stood with a jump, eager to be away from the ghost. "Yup."

The nurse smiled at her and led May down the hallway of doors and into her room. To her utter dismay, the ghost followed. In the room, the nurse took her vitals and asked the same routine questions they always asked, then said the doctor would be in shortly. Like a reheated play.

"I don't know why they bother," the ghost said, voice ethereal in the room. "The doc comes in and asks the exact same. Like—" She huffed an echoing sigh. "Why even bother writing anything down if you're not going to read it?"

"Go away," May whispered harshly.

The misty form of the ghost wavered, like she'd been blown by a wind, and out of the corner of her eye, May noticed another shimmer. A shimmer like what she'd seen last night at the death scene. It only lasted for a second, but it was enough to make her spine straighten and her hands sweat.

The ghost humphed and flickered again.

"Why are you here?" May whispered at the ghost girl.

"I died here," she said matter-of-factly.

"Right..." May huffed and pushed a shaky hand across her face. "But why are you *here*, bothering me?"

Right then, the door clicked open and her stern-but-kind cardiologist walked in. "Hello, Miss Haines," Dr. Sato said with a small bow from his neck.

May smiled while ignoring the ghost. "Dr. Sato, I've said you can call me May."

He blinked at her the way he always did—not rude, but never indulgent. "Miss Haines, I looked over your echocardiogram from last month. Everything looks very good. I don't see any enlarged vessels, and the valves look good."

She nodded and wrung her hands together on her knees.

Dr. Sato clicked through the computer against the wall in the small room, nodding slightly as he did, before facing her. "Any shortness of breath? Light headedness?"

"No." She shook her head.

"See," the ghost said with a sigh, and May had the distinct impression she was folding her arms in annoyance. "Why even have the nurse come in first?"

May took a deep breath. Over Dr. Sato's shoulder, she saw a faint haze in the air like a halo of wings, but when she blinked, it was gone. She frowned and shook her head, focusing on Dr. Sato's questions.

"Your bloodwork," he said as he clicked something else on the computer, and May leaned around to try to see, "also looks good. Your immunosuppressants are at good therapeutic levels. No elevated white blood cells, good red count..."

He scrolled through the rest of the results.

"How's your stomach?"

"Good. That new drug you had me try has been much

better." The last immunosuppressant she had been on made her so nauseous she couldn't keep down most of what she ate.

"And how is work going? You've been back for several months now, yes?"

"Yes." She nodded. Dr. Sato had been one of the few people on her side about going back to work. He agreed that getting her out of the house, going back to a regular routine, would go further in helping her recover than sitting at home. "I still take it easy, but for the most part, it's all back to normal."

"Very good." He clicked something on the computer and turned back to her. He slid his small, framed glasses up onto his bald head and gave her a rare, uncharacteristic smile, though small. "You're progressing very well. I think we can push your follow-ups out to once a quarter."

May smiled, tears of relief prickling at her eyes. She nodded, unable to speak just yet. One more step toward normalcy. One step closer to normalcy.

"As much as I enjoy seeing which color your hair will be each month," Dr. Sato said, "I will enjoy knowing you are healthy enough to not need me as much anymore."

She laughed and wiped her nose. "Thanks, Doc."

"I'll let scheduling know." He nodded, a small bow from his shoulders again, and left.

May sat for a moment, enjoying the relief, the weight lifting from her, before standing and gathering her purse. The ghost stared at her, not any more corporeal than before. "Why did you follow me?"

The ghost shrugged her transparent shoulders. "You felt... familiar. There was a... pull."

May frowned. "A...pull?"

The ghost wavered and floated closer, arm hovering around May before gliding back. Ghostly shoulders shrugged again. "Why is he following you?"

May froze and glanced over her shoulder at the spot the shimmer had appeared. "Who?"

But the ghost only shrugged and drifted away, disappearing through the wall of the exam room. She looked again at the spot she'd seen the shimmering... something. Was it another ghost? If it was... why?

She shook herself, eyes going around the room once more, before leaving the exam room.

CHAPTER SIXTEEN
MERELY A GENERAL

Harper watched the Nephilim from her balcony moving to and from the Forgotten Forest, either leaving for a soul or returning with one. Armeal had been markedly absent again, no Reaper knowing where he'd slunk off to. It felt too similar to what his brother had done. The repeat of such a betrayal made her bones hurt. Was he the one stealing souls? She didn't know. She couldn't decide. He'd been nothing but loyal, but now... now he was disappearing and absent. She sighed heavily through her nose. Then there was May. Mortals can't see the Tether. They can't survive touching it. The raw magical power held within the Tether is too much for the human mind to contain, for their body to channel... and yet May touched it and survived. Not even her Reapers were capable of such feats.

So, what was she? And what was her involvement? Harper believed May when she'd said she wasn't the thief, but she'd believed Yrien too. And Artheal.

A flash of white in the sea of black caught her eyes.

"*Armeal*,"—she sent her magic to him—"*come.*"

She saw when he felt her call, heard her command, in the twitch of his shoulders. He glanced up, and their eyes locked. For a heartbeat, she saw his brother's face in his. She set her jaw and waited.

"Lady Death?" Armeal's voice was hesitant from behind her sometime later.

She turned, and a thick layer of snow had gathered on her shoulders. She shook the snow from her long overcoat as almost as an afterthought. What to tell him? Should she tell him anything? Harper blinked as she searched his face, as if she could find something in his high cheekbones or hawk nose that said whether he was planning to betray her. Everything she'd known to be true was now in doubt.

She either doubted everything or trusted something. Her soul hurt too much at the thought of doubting everything. "The Fates," she finally said, "have implied the witch is directly connected to the souls' disappearance."

He scoffed, his wings fluttering behind him. "How? She is mortal."

"They surprisingly wouldn't say," she drawled.

"Fickle creatures," he muttered.

"We are faced," she said, turning around again to face her domain and resting her hands on the balcony banister, "with several options."

Armeal came to stand next to her, though he kept his hands clasped in front of him.

"Either a human has learned how to cut a soul from the Tether and is behind the theft of the souls, or..."

"Or," he said after she failed to continue, "another traitor is among us."

"Seeing as there are very few things in the world that can do such a thing."

He blinked. "The Reaper scythe."

She couldn't stop herself from turning to stare at the side of his face. With his silky chestnut hair curling around his ears, he really did look like an angel. He stood still under her stare, eyes forward as if ignoring her gaze stopped it. With a huff of breath, she turned away.

"You are one of the eldest among your siblings. What is your thought?"

His lip curled into a snarl. "They are not my siblings."

She raised an eyebrow at him. "Such hatred for your own kind. Why?"

He met her eyes with an angry glare, jaw clenched. "You have no kin," he spat. "You do not understand. They are my kind. But they are not my kin. I had a kin."

"I have kin," she growled back, though she didn't understand why she had this desire to meet him in this argument. What did she care if Armeal thought she had family?

Armeal scoffed, loud and full of arrogance. "Those three do not count."

Harper curled her lip at him and forced herself to turn away. "You're right. Your kin betrayed both of us. Mine have done no such crime."

He jerked at her words, and a small part of her, the part not angry and seething that he was right, felt guilt at her words. "You know the other Reapers well," she said, ignoring the stiff stance of his shoulders. "Do any strike you as ones able to do this?"

His shoulders rose and fell with his giant breath. "No. Though not all have buried their pride as well as others, none would do this."

She glanced at him from the corner of her eye. *No*, she thought as she stared at him. Perhaps not all had. He was quiet as his gaze grew introspective. He wasn't stupid. He shifted his yellow eyes back to her.

"You think I have betrayed you."

"Have you?" She kept her voice soft while watching his every move. Was she too trusting of her Reapers, too confident in the oath they'd sworn so long ago? They had betrayed her once. Was she so naive to think they would never again? "Where have you been?"

Armeal blinked his clear eyelid closed over his golden, shimmering eyes. He held himself with a careful grace and stillness as he bore her glare, and she remembered he'd been a warrior before the Agreement. Strong, lethal. She could see that lethality in his stance.

"If I had betrayed you and were now caught, the obvious answer would be to say 'no' to try to save myself. You would, however, expect that, so it's safe to assume anything I say will be subject to scrutiny."

Harper nodded once, a dip of her chin. Snow fell around them and settled again on her shoulders.

He tilted his head and tucked his wings in tight. "However," he continued, "we are having this conversation in private, away from your hounds and the Maw. If I were to accuse someone I had already come to the conclusion had betrayed me, I would do it where I could set my hounds on them or toss them into the depths of Hell. So, I would guess that you haven't yet decided."

Harper raised an eyebrow. "Perhaps I am less showy than you and want to exact my revenge away from prying eyes."

Armeal's lips tilted in a small smile; his old arrogance peeking through his eyes. "You didn't know my life before the Agreement."

She fanned her fingers out to him. "Enlighten me."

He looked away. "That story is mine to keep." He watched her with ancient eyes, tilting his head slightly. "You think I am my brother."

She met the challenge in his gaze, the accusation, and did not deny it. "Where," she asked again, "have you been?"

She saw the indecision in his eyes and extended her claws.

"Watching your witch," he finally said.

She jerked in surprise. "What?"

"And talking to the others."

She narrowed her eyes at him. It was a convenient answer. Was he stealing souls or searching out the one who had? "How do I believe you?"

Without a word, he lifted his finger to his mouth and bit, his sharp short canine piercing his flesh. He held it out, a bead of blood welling on the tip. "I offer the only truth that matters to my kind. I am sworn only to you and have not betrayed you to anyone. I have not uttered a lie to you."

A blood oath. The strongest and unbreakable of oaths. Offered freely and without condition, it was, in the Nephilim world, the most sacred offer. She held her own finger out, and he turned his hand over, his singular drop of blood falling to her finger. She swiped it across her tongue, and the truth of his oath rang through her blood. That weight was now lifted from her shoulders. There was at least one Nephilim she could trust.

She nodded. "Thank you, Armeal."

He bowed and flicked open his clear eyelid. "Whatever you believe of my brother and I… it is wrong. I am not him."

She blinked. "No," she murmured, "for you are alive."

He dipped his chiseled chin. "I am alive."

She watched him a moment longer before nodding and shifting the snow from her shoulders again. "So, tell me what it is you've been doing, then."

"Like I said. Watching your witch."

Harper's back stiffened.

"I did not trust her, nor did I trust your blindness around her."

"Blindness?" Harper snarled the word.

Armeal merely raised an eyebrow. "I think the humans have a phrase... something about seeing through rose-colored glasses? It is not the first time."

"Careful," she growled, and flexed her claws.

His clear eyelid flicked back over his eyes, and he took a small step back. "The souls are missing from the area she lives in. The souls began going missing not long after she survived her last near-death moment. You yourself say coincidences do not exist. The human has clouded your judgment. I needed to be sure if you wouldn't."

Harper spun on him with a hiss, her teeth bared. He stepped back with a flutter of wings and feathers as he tucked them tight to his back and took a deep breath.

"I did not trust her. But, having watched her for some time, she is, it seems, a simple mortal."

Harper turned away, seething at his words. Had she been clouded?

"What else," she bit out, "have you learned?"

He shuffled his feathers. "I tried to speak with the Nephilim, but—" He sighed. "They do not speak freely around me." Harper tilted her head, and he answered her unvoiced question. "They see my proximity to you as a betrayal of them. A station above them. But they speak with Luras."

She knew Luras. An Old One older than even Armeal. He'd been a general in their wars, cunning and brutal. Since his life in the Underworld, he'd kept to himself and had done his duty without complaint.

"And what did Luras have to say?"

Armeal looked uneasy, and that was enough for Harper to forget about the slight and fury he'd done her. "He said he'd heard whisperings. Rumors. That *she* is back again."

Impossible. Harper's breath stilled in her chest.

"But Luras dismissed the rumors. Yrien is dead. But there are whisperings and rumors that someone... pretending to be her, perhaps, is gathering power."

"A Nephilim?" she asked.

He shook his head. "I do not know. But who else would have the knowledge and power to pretend such a thing?"

So, she thought as she turned back to stare at the snow-covered valley. *Someone has still betrayed me.* Again.

"Why?" she asked the snow around her.

"Why... what, Lady Death?"

She glanced at him and sighed. "Why do they always betray me?"

He stayed behind her, silent.

"I offered them my home. Brought you in like family. And still, I am betrayed." She finally turned to him. "Why?"

He blinked at her and spoke in a soft voice, softer than she'd ever heard from him before. "Because we are not your family."

She jerked like she'd been slapped.

"Our family chased us away and hunted us down. Siblings fought siblings for power and station and alliances. Family," he said gently as he stepped closer, "as you think of it, is not something we understand."

"Is that why they will never accept me?" she asked, her voice small.

He tilted his head at her. "We can respect you. We can swear loyalty to you. Those are the things that matter to a Nephilim. We are not children to be minded. We are warriors without a war or leader."

Harper blinked, realization settling around her. They needed tasks. Purposes. More than simply fetching souls.

"If..." she spoke slowly as the idea was forming in her mind. "I had you find the ones you trusted the most and appointed them as leaders. Assign each with a group of the younger ones..."

Armeal smiled, and it was, perhaps, the first time she'd seen the stoic Nephilim do such a thing. "I can organize them, Death."

"Then," she said, "I trust you to organize the Reapers in a way you see best. Continue your monitoring of May. We still do not know her involvement. Search for Talsk as well. He has yet to return, and I believe him to be truly missing now."

Armeal nodded and turned to leave.

"Be the leader they need."

"No, Death," he said over his shoulder as he stepped away, "you are our leader. I am merely a general."

CHAPTER SEVENTEEN
THE SCENE

May drummed her fingers on her desk, her chin propped in her other hand with her elbow resting heavily on the edge of her desk. She was staring at the preliminary report for Steven Harrison's file as the cursor blinked at her from the screen. The thirty-two-year-old died of a drug overdose. Or murder, if you had a God of Death as your source. Behind her, a small ghost fluttered around the opening to her cubicle. May refused to turn around and engage with the thing. It had become a battle of wills, hers to refuse to turn and the ghost's determination to get her to.

She checked the case file and found the detective's contact information easily. The line rang three, then four times before it clicked and a male voice spoke.

"Detective Harding."

"Um..." May stammered and tried again. "Hi, this is May Haines from the Medical Examiner's Office."

"Oh, hi." His voice changed from casually neutral to the voice of someone talking to a friend. "How are ya?"

"Good." She grabbed a pen and furiously clicked it. "I just

wanted to let you know we have the toxicology back on Harrison's case. The doc is still finalizing the report, but I wanted to give you a heads-up since I knew you had—"

"A crazy theory?"

She laughed. "I was going to say a vested interest."

He chuckled over the phone. "What'd it say?"

"Stupid high levels of heroine. Doc's going to call it an overdose."

The line was quiet for a beat. "Any metabolite?"

May blinked. She hadn't looked to see if the metabolized chemical was listed in the report. "Um, hang on, let me look." She quickly pulled up the toxicology report and scanned the results. "Nothing listed. So he didn't have time to break down the heroin before he died."

"And how much heroin was in his system?"

May scrolled up in the report. "Oof," she said. "He's high. One hundred twenty milligrams per milliliter."

Ethan whistled on the other end. "That's a lot of heroin."

"Yeah…" She paused. "You still think this is a …What did you call it? A hotshot?"

"I just think," he said slowly, "that it's a little suspicious that a long-term drug user overdoses so fast that he can't even metabolize some of the heroin he's used. And that there's that much in his system. Is it possible to think someone gave him an injection after he'd been knocked out or rendered incapacitated?"

She paused again, thinking over the autopsy report.

"Just because we didn't see any traumatic injury to his head doesn't mean he wasn't knocked out, right?" He continued.

"Well… no." She agreed. "Especially if he died before the bruise had time to set."

"I'm just saying. There were signs of a struggle. Or… at least signs we can't rule out as *not* being a struggle. And the shouting the neighbors heard."

She frantically clicked her pen, thinking. "Okay. I'll talk to the doc and express your concerns."

"Thank you, ma'am."

She snorted. "Ma'am is my mom. I'll let you know what the doc says."

Dr. Kesler was in the middle of another autopsy when May went to talk to her. It always struck her as slightly humorous that people could have normal office conversations with organs laid out on a table between them. Because that's exactly what happened most times.

"The police don't have anything more about this maybe fight?" Dr. Kesler asked as she sliced through the cross section of heart and stuck small pieces into a jar for later testing.

"No, but it is still open."

"Hm..." Dr. Kesler moved onto the lungs, making quick, sure slices and looking through. "Oh, a small hamartoma," she muttered, and continued cutting.

"Do you think that's what did him in, doc?" the tech asked from the table.

"Yeah, never mind the bullet to the head, this little noncancerous thing certainly did it." She chuckled and focused back on May as she moved to the next lung. "Well, there isn't enough evidence in the body to say one way or another. I'll list the overdose as the cause but leave the manner pending for now."

May nodded. "I'll let him know, thanks, doc."

She threw her mask into the trash as she left and slipped out her phone.

> Me: Docs going to leave the manner pending until your investigation is finished

She typed the text out to Det. Dimples as she walked back to her desk. Just as she was sitting down, the phone rang.

"Medical Examiner's Office."

"Hey," the voice on the other end said. "Detective Barton. I'm on an overdose."

She sighed and pulled out her notebook. It was her turn to take the next case, anyway. "Alright, give me the details."

"Pretty simple," he said, and she could hear chatter in the background. "Neighbors called in a welfare check after not seeing him for a few days. PD arrives and finds him deceased. Needle on the ground next to him."

Tingling on the back of her neck made May turn around, phone cord wrapping around her as she searched her cubicle. There was a shimmer at the corner of her eye, and when she turned toward it, she swore she'd seen the outline of wings before she blinked and it was gone.

"Okay," she said, turning back but feeling like someone was watching her. "Text me the address, and I'll be right there."

It took her longer than she'd thought to drive across town to the dead man's house. When she pulled up, her beat-up yellow bug fit right in with the older used cars and car parts. The address was an older trailer park, the streets cracked and uneven. No sidewalks lined the roads, and most yards were thin in the way of grass. The homes, while old, appeared well-kept. The skirts on the manufactured homes weren't riddled with holes or falling off like so many others she'd seen.

As she stepped out of her car, and the blessed air conditioning, the sun instantly started to bake her skin. May had been blessed with a nice olive skin tone. The kind that never burned, only tanned. Even so, May was quick to move out of the sun and into the shade of the single wide. She clutched the strap of her bag over her shoulder and felt the lanyard around her neck. The thick yellow lanyard with the black "MEDICAL EXAMINER" words were hard to miss. She patted her ID card where it hung, reassured it was there.

She moved quickly toward the patrol officer standing in the doorway of the single wide. He smiled and handed her the crime scene log without a word. She scribbled her name on it and ducked inside, where it was, at least, cool.

"Sorry it took me so long," she said as she walked over to Det. Barton, who she now recognized as Det. Dimples's partner. "Traffic was a mess."

"Hey, I'm paid by the hour." He walked over to the sofa in the living room right off the front door. "Here's"—he checked his notepad—"Aaron White. Born August six of 1976. We have a large history with him involving drugs: overdoses, dealing, selling, public intox."

May nodded, and after writing that down in her own notepad, started taking photos, documenting the scene. Poor Aaron looked like he'd lain down to sleep, stretching out on the couch. One foot hung off and was resting on the ground. It could've been a normal nap if it wasn't for the vomit dripping from his mouth and the half-lidded eyes nearly all dead seemed to have.

Again, came a tingle on the back of her neck, but she brushed it off, telling herself it was the detective's eyes.

"We think a friend might've been here when he used," Det. Barton mentioned.

"Why's that?" she asked as she snapped more photos of his arm, the track lines clearly visible.

"There's the needle"—he pointed to the floor beneath Aaron's hand—"but there's no foil, no burnt spoon, no unburned heroin. Someone cleaned up."

She looked around the room herself, noticing there wasn't any other signs of drug use near the body. While weird, it wasn't unheard of. People would often clean up the scene and flee, afraid of being arrested for the drug use, instead of calling for help. May turned back to the couch only to jerk.

What the hell? She stared at the shimmering, almost glowing liquid pooled beneath Aaron, just the edge of it visible from under him. Glancing at the detective—who either hadn't seen it or couldn't—May took a deep breath to steady her suddenly racing nerves.

Snapping her gloves on, she moved some of the loose clothing around, trying to see the liquid more. She wanted to touch it, felt like she needed to. May shook her head, recognizing the same call the Tether seemed to have. Death had been *very* mad that she'd touched that; May couldn't imagine she'd be any less mad if she touched this stuff.

Besides, she scolded herself as she continued to stare at the glowing viscus-looking liquid, there was a rule among fire fighters, cops, the OME: if it's wet and sticky and not yours, *don't touch it*. And here she was... wanting to ignore that rule.

The impulsive urge to touch it grew until, with a huff and glance at the detective at the front of the house, she dipped the tip of her gloved finger into the pool. She jerked away with a barely held back shout when the same burning cold pain as when she'd touched the Tether shot up her arm.

Okay. Okay... She breathed through her nose and stood. Glancing again around the room, she saw no ghosts or... well, Death.

As she finished her part of the investigation and scene documentation, she watched for more supernatural things to appear but only saw the large pool of glowing... stuff on the couch under Aaron once the body snatchers moved him.

If Lady Death is ever finished throwing a tantrum, she thought to herself as she and Det. Barton followed the gurney laden with Aaron outside, *I'll have to ask her.*

"Well, thanks," Det. Barton said as the body was loaded into the transport van.

Just those few minutes outside in the summer sun was enough for Det. Barton to start wiping his forehead with a rag and for May to be uncomfortably hot.

"Anytime," she said as she started toward her car. She waved over her shoulder at him and hurriedly slipped into her car. The second the door closed, she let out a breath in a huff at the suffocating heat inside. She jammed her keys into the ignition, desperate for some air. As she pulled away from the curb, her eyes caught a shimmer in the air, like a heat illusion but more solid. She stopped and turned in her seat to watch the spot. Squinting, focusing, she swore there was a shape in the shimmer. A shape... like a tall person leaning against the trunk of the sad tree, too thin and too starved of water.

She reached out with her magic, and her blood warmed with its use. She directed her magic, like a hand reaching, to the tree and whatever stood next to it. As it got closer, as it reached for the trunk of the tree, something hard and unyielding swatted back at her magic.

"Ow!" She gasped, dropping her magic.

May wheezed a hacking, barking coughing fit before she could get a breath. Clearing her throat, she glanced back, but whatever had been there was gone. With a shiver, she put her car back in drive before something else could happen.

CHAPTER EIGHTEEN
HELP OF A WITCH

Harper stood at the edge of the Maw, her hounds racing around her ankles. The spirits were restless... again. Damned spirits rose to the surface and crowded against the barrier. Hand outstretched toward it, she pulled her magic, her very being, and sent it toward the barrier. The draw of magic twinged her insides as she layered more magic over the weakening threads of the barrier. The emerald-green threads flew from her fingers, hand stretched out toward the abyss, and wove into the shimmering shield. These threads, this shield, yanked on her life force, and it stung like a bitch.

This constant, persistent testing of the barrier by the damned was weakening it. The damned would only test it this often if they thought they had a chance at freedom. Did they also realize, did they sense what the Fates alluded to, that she could not command her realm? Did they sense the theft of the souls?

Dropping her hand, she glared at the souls as they screeched away and returned to the depths. Did they think she was weak?

The urge to rend the world apart burned in her chest. Hands clenched enough to draw blood from her palm, she forced herself still. Acting rashly would accomplish nothing. The hounds at her side whined and yipped, long rough tongues swiping at the blood dripping from her clenched fists.

"Away!" she shouted with a swat to one's nose.

"Death!" Armeal raised his voice over the barking of the beasts.

She glared at him, mood still foul. To his credit, he did not flinch away.

"I have seen no signs of Talsk yet. Your witch was sent to a death. She could see the aether."

Harper sucked in a breath. "Another cut soul?"

He nodded solemnly. "So it appears. And—" He took a breath, and Harper braced herself. "I believe she was able to see me."

Of course she could, Harper thought with near-angry irony. *She can see everything else.* She turned with a growl back to the Maw.

"Death."

She ignored him.

He spoke to her back, anyway. "What else was said by the Fates about the witch?"

"Why do you think anything more was said?"

"Because." He spoke to her back, far enough away that her claws could not reach him. "You have been... angrier than usual. Snappish, one could say."

She turned with a wry smile. "Snappish?"

"It was the least likely to get me in trouble, but I have other options."

"Of course you do," she muttered, and turned back to the Maw. She could speak her fears to the void. Maybe then they would be swallowed up by it. "They said I would need her help to find my souls."

She heard the soft flutter of feathers. "And you have not sought it out yet because?"

She whirled on him in fury. "Must I admit to every being in these lands that I am incapable of keeping my own house in order?" Her shout echoed across the frozen lands, and she took a large step toward him. "Do you enjoy hearing how weak I must be to need the aid of a *mortal*?"

His throat flexed as he swallowed, but he did not step back, though her claws were well within reach now. "Did they say you were weak?"

"What?" she snapped.

"Did they," he repeated slowly, "say you were weak?"

No. She blinked.

"I hated my brother," he said without warning, and the change shook Harper. "Hated him for what he'd had of our mother that I did not. Hated him for uncountable other reasons I shall never share, but I still mourn his loss because he knew me. There must be something to this witch of yours, that you continue to seek out her company."

She settled back on her heels, at a loss for words.

"You have no kin." His painful words rang back to her from where they'd buried themselves in her heart.

"Are you saying..." Harper frowned at him, words coming dangerously slow. "That I need the witch's help, not because she is better suited for the task, but because I need a *friend*?"

His wings fluttered, feathers shifting and smoothing. "I am saying, you should speak to your witch."

He stood well within reach of her claws, which were curled in anticipation, but he did not flinch away. Lesser Nephilim would not have stood so tall. They wouldn't have bore her anger and temper as easily as he did. She relaxed her claws slowly, one finger at a time.

"Fine," she muttered, and his eyes widened in shock.

Harper sliced her claws through the air. She had no need to wander the human streets, no desire to appear human, so she focused her attention on May's soul and its location. Its pull, faint as it was, guided her to split the world near it. When she stepped through, she was in a hallway of an apartment building with four doors and a set of stairs at the end of the hall. She turned to the door with the "3" and knocked. She didn't bother with glamour for this visit and kept a careful watch on the quiet hall.

There were sounds of a lock moving, and soon, the door was open and May's wide eyes were staring at her.

"Hello," she said in surprise, and stood with her shoulder leaning against the door frame.

Harper raised an eyebrow at her. "Are you going to let me in?"

May folded her arms against her chest. "Are you going to stop acting like a child?"

"Child?" She gaped.

May cocked her head and waited, her purple hair slipping over her shoulder.

"And how have I done so?"

"By storming off in a fit and not finishing a conversation like an adult," May said, all but raising her nose in the air. "I suspect you are... like... millions of years old. I think that qualifies as an adult."

Harper's mouth hung, then she huffed and settled herself. "I am..." The words were foreign in her mouth, and she wondered briefly if she'd ever spoken them before. "Sorry for how I last spoke to you."

May watched her for a moment before nodding. "Thanks," she said, and stepped aside for her to enter.

She slipped into the small apartment and into the living room off the kitchen. A worn but tidy sofa and loveseat were set in the corner of the room with a simple rectangular coffee table. Harper looked around the living room. It was kempt, but lived in. The shelves were dotted with tokens from trips and gifts.

"Want some tea?" May called, already in the kitchen.

"Yes"—she settled on the couch—"actually."

Her long legs bumped into the table as she sat. May busied herself with pouring the tea, and she raised another eyebrow as May handed her a large mug of strong black tea, and with plenty of cream and sugar.

May shrugged at her look. "You strike me as a secretly indulgent tea drinker."

"I drink plain coffee," she said as she sipped the liquid. Warm and sweet and perfect.

"That's coffee." May sat on the other couch, her own mug of tea clasped between her hands. "Tea is different."

Yes. She grinned as she sipped more tea, the steam curling around her face. *It is.* She ignored the fact May guessed that fact so easily. One problem at a time.

"Tea warms the soul," Harper muttered, remembering the small ancient woman who had said such words to her once.

May glanced at her from over her cup. "Where'd you discover tea?"

Harper smiled. "A long time ago, though it feels like a moment ago. In ancient China, though it was not called that then. A small woman, old and broken by sickness and a life of hard work, had uttered those words to me."

"Really?" May leaned forward.

Harper smiled, a small laugh working its way up her throat. "Her name had appeared in my Book of Souls many times, but I believe she would die like she had lived: on her own terms at her own time. In the end, she had been unable to walk, her joints twisted and knobbed. Her hands were curled in on themselves, but she still insisted on finishing her cup of tea before I took her. 'Tea warms the soul,' she had said to me, 'for the journey to come.'"

"That," May murmured into the silence, "is adorable."

Harper chuckled. "It was the only adorable thing that woman ever said. She was full of spitfire."

May chuckled as well. "But she didn't offer you a cup."

"No." Harper smiled and sipped her tea. "But I had to see what this magical liquid was that this woman was so adamant she finish it before I took her."

Silence grew as the conversation ended. May hummed softly and set her cup aside. "So, before... You were kind of an asshole." She blinked her bright eyes at Harper. "I thought we were friends."

She took a deep breath, only to hesitate once more. Frowning, she tried to shift her thoughts into something that would make sense. May waited patiently across from her but never lowered her gaze.

"Friends..." she finally said slowly. "Friends are a foreign idea to me. Forgive me if I make missteps. Companions, friends, kin." She sniffed. "They are things I do not have."

May took in her words silently.

"The Fates say your path is tied with mine. I don't know what that means. I will admit," she said, softly like a secret, "I feared it meant you were replacing me."

May's mouth dropped, and she straightened but waited for Harper to finish.

"It took the advise of another to see that perhaps you are not replacing me but are here to help me."

May took a deep breath, and slowly, a smile spread. "Sounds like advise from a good friend."

Harper jerked at the words. Armeal? A friend?

No, he was loyal. He was fulfilling his duty. But friend?

"Or companion," May said with a shrug, and picked her tea back up.

He had been with her from the beginning. Arrogant, angry, stubborn, and with enough pride for all his siblings. But he had never faltered in his duty. Even when she'd accused him of such. He had become her general. Was that friendship?

"So," May said into the silence as they sipped their tea, "how can I help?"

She let out a long breath and settled the mug in her lap. Her long fingers looked strange and pale holding it. Harper didn't need to eat or drink, but she enjoyed it. It made her feel alive in ways she never had.

"I will admit," she said with a sigh, "that I do not know. You can see things no human should, things only I can."

May chewed her lip. Next to her on the couch, her phone screen lit up, and Harper could hear the soft buzzing coming from it. May glanced down and silenced it.

"So, what does that mean?"

"I don't know," she said again, beginning to hate the words. "This has never happened before."

"Oh!" May jerked. "That reminds me. I saw some glowing... stuff at a dead body I went to earlier."

"Aether." Harper glanced again at the phone as it lit up. "A byproduct of the soul being severed from its Tether prematurely."

"Oh," May said, distracted as she looked down at her phone. "I guess that explains why it shocked me."

"You touched it!" Harper exclaimed, hand going to her eyes. "You must stop touching things."

"Well, I didn't know," she said, and picked her phone up. "I'm sorry she isn't going stop unless I answer, one sec."

Harper waved her fingers and sipped her drink as May held the phone to her ear.

"Mom."

"Why are you ignoring my calls?" a woman's voice said through the speaker.

"Mom, I'm busy. That's all."

"You are always busy."

May pinched the bridge of her nose. "Sorry."

A sigh, crackly and garbled, came from the phone. "Don't be sorry, just talk to me."

"Okay, Mom, I would, but I actually do have someone over."

"May, are you just saying that to get off the phone with me?"

"Hello!" Harper shouted from behind her mug. May shot wide eyes to her.

"Oh, shit. I'm sorry. Look, call me later, okay?"

"I will, Mom."

"Okay, don't forget your meds, and practice your magic!"

May punched her screen and tossed the phone down. "You could hear her?"

Harper sipped her tea and smiled. "She does that often?"

May sighed. "Yeah, she's a bit of a helicopter parent."

Harper wondered about May's attitude. "Is it not pleasant having someone check on you?"

May stilled. "Uh, it is, but it can get a bit much when it's *all the time*. Anyway..." May huffed and combed her hair back with her hands. "Souls being stolen. People being murdered."

"Quite."

"Why would someone want... to steal life?" May asked, her tea forgotten in her hands. "That's what you're talking about, right? Someone is doing this to steal the power of life."

"The soul," Harper corrected. "Life is gone when the body dies. They are stealing the power in a soul."

"Why?"

Harper felt the anger building again. The fury from someone thinking they could, that they had the *right* to take what was hers.

"Why does anyone want power?" she growled out.

"Okay." May met her eyes. "Okay. So, how do we figure out who it is?"

"That," Harper said, her voice dipping dangerously low, "is the question. Very few things can sever a soul. A Reaper scythe is one."

"What else?"

Harper flexed her hand, claws on display.

"Oh, right. Just those things?"

Harper shrugged and put her mug aside. "There have been a few witches over time that have been capable of enchanting items, but that magic is long gone."

"Are you sure?"

Harper set her jaw. She wasn't sure of much anymore, but she refused to utter the words *I don't know* again. "It is rare, I should say."

It was possible the knowledge had been passed down in a family line, a coven, or mage circle. Her mind went again to Yrien. She'd known the power of the soul. Could she have told someone before her death? Would she? There was also the matter of several scythes unaccounted for at the end of the war.

And there was still the missing Old One, Talsk.

"Has this happened before?"

"Once."

May waited expectantly for an answer. Harper blinked and looked away, not wanting to talk about the Nephilim Rebellion, or the one that started it. She shook her head. Yrien was long dead. Harper thought the damage had also been done and finished, but it seemed more and more things were repeating.

"What was the name of the man that died whose ghost gathered you for his friend?"

May held up a finger and stood, talking as she returned to the kitchen. "I remember you asked about that before you stormed off in a *mood*, so I looked it up."

Harper clucked her tongue but waited patiently as May returned with a scrap of paper.

"Edward Orthander. What are you going to do with it?"

"I'm going to ask him what he saw and why he sought you out."

May nodded. "Why do you think ghosts are seeking me out?"

Harper stilled at May's words. "More than one has done this?"

May rocked her head from side to side. "Well, sorta. I was at a doctor's appointment and a ghost followed me around. She said I felt familiar. What does that mean?"

Harper sniffed the air around her, but again found no magic that would explain. "I do not know. If they are going to continue, see what they will tell you. I'm going to ask Edward what he remembers of his death. Maybe he can explain why he sought you out."

May watched with wide eyes as Harper stepped into the cut in the world.

CHAPTER NINETEEN
HAUNTINGS

From May's lived-in apartment, Harper stepped through the slice in the world and onto the sun-baked desert sand. Even in the height of summer with the heat drying every bit of water from the ground, the low-lying shrubs still flourished. The desert plants, spindly and thorny, thrived in the heat and aired land. The rocks around her rose to massive heights, towering as cliffs and mountains in the canyon.

She'd followed the pull of Edward Orthander's soul to the desert canyon, and ahead of her, towering over her, stood a tall rockface. It's flat, sheer face dominated the space. The wind blew against her face, hot and dry, and with it, came a tang of magic. A scent that tickled the back of her mind. She whirled on it, chasing the memory in the wind, but it disappeared just as quickly as it had arrived. Frustrated, she clenched her jaw.

"It was fun to climb," Edward whispered near her shoulder.

Harper spotted clips wedged into the rock, rising in a steady line up the face. Edward joined her, staring upward, his expression wistful and his eyes full of longing. He pointed to a path of clips and bolts that wound up a different section of rock—a particularly difficult-looking side.

"I placed those anchors myself. Jim and I came here all the time."

From Harper's angle, she could see the edge of the gaping wound in his skull. Not every ghost kept the injury of the body, but those traumatic deaths tended to. That pain and fear and trauma etched itself in the soul. She faced him.

"What happened here?"

Edward stepped around her to an obstructed view of the cliffside. "We were like brothers."

Harper sighed. She was hoping he would be more lucid, but the ghost seemed trapped in the sorrow of death. The longing of a life gone. She stepped in front of him again and *pulled* him with a touch of her magic, sending it into his chest while she snapped her fingers at the end of his nose.

He jerked, and a sense of awareness returned to his eyes.

"What happened?"

His eyes widened in horror as the memory of his death—and the truth of what had happened to him—came rushing back.

"I fell. I fell. He wasn't there. Jim wasn't on belay. Why wasn't he on belay?" He reached for her, translucent hands grabbing her shoulders. "Why wasn't he there! He knew better!"

Harper grunted under his onslaught and reached her claws into his chest.

"*Be still*," she commanded, and he slowed his panicked ranting until finally, he was silent. She resisted the land's pull, the trauma pinning him to this place—this memory—with claws buried in his chest. "Think to after the fall. You were here. Where was Jim?"

His face went slack, pale eyes racing back and forth as he

struggled to think past the haze of death, the shroud of trauma. "Gone," he said faintly. "I was here. Waited. I watched my blood..."

"Was anyone else here?"

His eyes fell to the spot he'd fallen, the rock still covered in a dark-brown stain dried by the sun. "What?"

She flecked her claws. "Was anyone else here?"

He brought his eyes back to her, but they were already growing distant again. "Yes..." he breathed the word on a sigh. "Yes..."

"Who?"

He frowned.

Harper sighed. Hauntings were so difficult to deal with. They so rarely remembered anything not related to the death.

"Why did you go to the witch for help?"

That seemed to bring him back to himself, and he blinked with awareness again. "I followed Jim. I kept waiting for him. So I followed him... us. But then there was this pull. This *feeling*... like... like I knew it."

Harper frowned, hanging on his words.

"I went to her. I don't know why. I just... knew she would help." He wavered, his form flickering in and out of shape. Her time with him was dwindling. "I asked for help. I asked her where Jim was. But I never found him."

With one last flicker, like a flame in the wind, he was gone, and her hand was left clutching at nothing. Lips back from her teeth in a silent, seething snarl, she dropped her hand. Why were spirits pulled to May?

She spun on her heel with a huff and turned instead back to the breeze. It was faint, a soft, gentle thing that caressed her cheeks. She walked upwind, sucking large breaths of air into her lungs as she did. Somewhere, that scent lingered. It had to. She circled the area, sniffing and tasting the air. All she could smell was the sharp tang of sagebrush and the piney smell of the Cyprus pines that dotted the canyon mouth. Distantly, Harper heard the laughing chatter of people hiking. Frustration gnawing at her, she returned to the blood-stained rocks.

There!

The faintest hint of magic.

She fell to her knees in the dirt, face lowered like a scent hound as she pulled the smell from the earth. That familiar, painfully familiar scent. It reminded her of something. A time she was happy. Happier, anyway. But the memory was coated with anger and sadness.

Realization hit her like a slap to the face, and she jerked upright with a gasp.

Yrien.

The Nephilim was dead. She'd delivered the fatal blow herself. So why was her scent lingering? She fisted the dirt and sand, claws biting into her palms. Why had she been catching whiffs of it for decades?

Why, Harper thought as she slammed her hands into the earth, *was Yrien still haunting her?*

Her claws were still buried in the sand, hours, days, minutes later, when she finally came back to herself. What was it that grabbed her attention? Harper leaned back on her knees, frowning. Something had—

There it was!

Distress.

She stood in a flurry, sand and dirt falling from her hands as she searched for the Reaper sending such feelings. Slicing her claws through the world, she tore through the portal. Her Reaper stood in the shadows of skyscrapers as she hunched away. The same Reaper she'd spoken to earlier, the timid, too gentle one without a name, backed away from a tall, imposing being with their sword drawn.

Harper's lips peeled back in a snarl as she stepped in front of her Reaper. The sword, a long, slim, delicate-looking thing, thrust forward toward the cowering Reaper.

"Fae do not hunt what is mine!" she shouted, and grabbed the Fae's blade.

The steel cut through her hand, but she couldn't feel the pain over her rage. She yanked the blade from the Fae Hunter, who stumbled after it, and her claws sank into his throat.

"They are sworn to me and under my protection," she hissed into his face as she flexed her claws.

The Fae's black eyes widened, and his golden, honey-brown skin paled. He gripped her wrist but didn't struggle in her grasp. Harper knew he was old, as his power hummed under her skin, and judging by the amount of hooped rings lining his long-pointed ear, he was a successful Hunter.

"The Agreement was voided." He gasped around her claws.

She raised an eyebrow at him and threw him back. He caught himself before falling and stood tall, staring at her. The Fae's arrogance nearly rivaled that of the Nephilim. She turned and looked at the Reaper who huddled in her shadow.

"What were you doing on the mortal plane?"

The Reaper flinched. "Waiting for the soul." Her boney hand extended from her too-long sleeve and pointed at the blanket draped over several boxes against the side of the building. A foot stuck out of the makeshift tent.

Harper turned back to the Fae with a growl in her throat. "Does that sound like the Agreement is voided?"

He took a step back as his eyes bounced between the body and them. Blood ran dark and thick down his neck, but he paid it no mind. Finally, he said, "No, it does not."

"Make sure it is known among your kind," Harper said, taking a slow step after him. "I am forbidden from taking a life myself, but my hounds are under no such obligation. They have missed the taste of Fae flesh."

He blanched, grabbed his fallen sword, and retreated into the shadows. Harper watched until she was satisfied he'd left before turning back to her Reaper. The Reaper slowly straightened and picked up her fallen scythe.

"Thank you," she whispered. "I did not think you would come."

Harper frowned and tilted her head. "Why wouldn't I? I gave all of you my oath of protection in exchange for your service. I stand by my oaths."

The Reaper turned away and slowly headed back toward the body. "Perhaps, as Nephilim so often broke our own, we did not believe yours."

Harper sighed. "You did not defend yourself against him?"

"No," she said as she resumed her vigilance. "I have had enough of war."

Harper sighed, unsure of what to say to the Reaper.

"I have picked a name," she said just as Harper opened the portal.

"Oh?" she asked over her shoulder. "And what is it?"

"Serenity."

Harper smiled. "It suits you."

CHAPTER TWENTY
FAILED GREEN WITCH

May stared at the small potted plant on her kitchen table. A simple little ZZ plant, or a *Zamioculcas zamiifolia* for the specific folks, but who wanted to bother with that mouthful? Its dark-green leaves, shiny and waxy, stretched upward on the thick stems. Hard to kill, it was the perfect plant for her. It didn't need special light. Hardly any water. It thrived on neglect.

Perfect for her to practice on.

She reached for her magic, that resistant ball that always seemed *just* out of her grasp. It wiggled and resisted her, but she managed a small thread. She directed it toward the ZZ plant, trying to tie her small thread of magic to the stem.

Sprout, grow. She tried filling the little string of magic with her intention.

May searched for the magic of the earth; even far away in her apartment, she should be able to feel the earth's magic. She couldn't, but any Green Witch should.

She pushed her magic to the plant and watched in dismay as the stem shriveled.

"This is bullshit," she grumbled, and pushed the plant away.

She dropped her head back with a sigh, then turned to the other problem facing her. So much for not getting involved in ghostly problems. She liked puzzles, solving things, and uncovering mysteries. It was what drew her to the Medical Examiner's Office in the beginning. She liked being part of a team that solved how someone had died. The research into a person's life to discover their death seemed... oddly poetic for a girl who seemed to always be dying.

She snorted a laugh. *Used to always be dying.*

And now she was Death's investigator. Or... so it seemed. Even after Lady Death had apologized, her disappearance had been abrupt. She shook her head, abandoning the kitchen table and embarrassing plant to curl up on the couch. She should figure out dinner but instead clicked on the TV. Her phone chimed next to her on the couch, and she frowned as she picked it up to read.

> Det. Dimples: Heard you were the on call.

Smiling, she typed out a quick reply to Det. Harding, though Det. Dimples would always be his contact name.

> Me: Yup!
>
> Unless it's smelly then I'm taking a pass lol

The three little dots popped up, then his response chimed through several moments later.

> Det. Dimples: Ha!
>
> Not smelly. Just a little weird. You good for a 21?

May frowned. "A what?"

She clicked the call icon on her phone. It rang twice, then his voice popped over the speaker. "Hey."

"A what?" she asked.

He laughed. "Sorry. 10-21 means a phone call. Sorry, old habits. But hey! You figured it out anyway."

She grunted and leaned over to her laptop sitting closed on her coffee table. "Lucky me. So, what's up?"

"Well, I'm actually glad you're the on-call, because this one's... It's not suspicious, but it's a little weird."

Her heart jumped in her throat. Weird how? Why was he asking her? Was she overthinking this?

Probably.

She made herself take two deep breaths and open her laptop, pulling up her case file program. "Ooookay. Weird how?"

He chuckled, and the background nose quieted as she heard a door shut.

"Remember the case with Harrison? The overdose I thought was a murder?"

"Yes." The room suddenly felt too small. Was this another murder she could tell no one about?

"Kinda like that. Scene looks like a struggle, shit's everywhere. He's obese as hell, alcohol everywhere, and his estranged wife says he drinks booze like it's water. But it just... it just doesn't look right. It's weird."

"Uh-huh." May nodded, standing to pace in her small living room. "Okay. Text me the address, and I'll get my things."

"Copy that."

The phone clicked as he hung up.

"Okay," she said to herself, and took another deep breath. "Okay."

May pulled her sputtering bug up to the curb behind several police vehicles. Two still had their red and blues on. A small crowd had gathered outside on the front lawn despite the oppressive evening heat. A patrol officer stood in the doorway to the small single-story home, clipboard in hand, and she spotted Ethan's beat-up Impala parked farther up the street.

Turning the car off, she wiped her sweaty palms on her jeans before grabbing her camera and bag from the passenger seat as she stood. She slipped the thick camera strap over her head and slung the bag over her shoulder. Glancing around the yard, she noticed nothing suspicious. May snapped a few quick photos of the front of the house, then approached the patrol officer guarding the crime scene.

"ME, right?" he asked.

She nodded. "Yup."

He nodded and thrust the clipboard at her. "Sign in, please."

"Yup."

She scribbled her name into the log and ducked under the bright-yellow tape. After snapping on her gloves, she reached for the boot covers next.

"Hey, May," Det. Harding called before his head popped out of a small bedroom to the side. "I'll come talk to you over there."

She glanced around the small living room, with a kitchen to her right. A coffee table was on its side, couch pillows on the floor, and a recliner that had seen better days was tipped over. Like Ethan had said over the phone, beer bottles and cans scattered the floor and there was an empty twenty-four pack on the kitchen table.

May studied the floor to find a clean-ish space to drop her bag. "Looks like there was a fight."

"Right," Ethan said, and planted his hands on his hips. "Weird, like I said."

"Where's the body?" May asked while rooting around the giant medical examiner's bag for the case marker and her own clipboard of information.

"Through the bedroom to the left. Bathroom through there too. Kitchen to the right. Laundry and another bath off the kitchen to the back door."

"Okay. Let me snap some pictures here, and then you can tell me all about it."

She quickly took photos of the space, Ethan doing his best to stay behind her and out of them as she went. When she got to the bedroom, with a pair of feet sticking out of the doorway, May paused and examined the bedroom.

The shimmering glow of the aether covered the bedroom floor. It was splattered on the walls like an arterial bleed. She had to remind herself to keep her mouth closed, to breathe evenly through her nose. Her fingers tightened on her camera.

What the hell?

"Right, meet Mr. Lars Benion." He held out an Arizona driver license to her, and she took it with shaky fingers. "Neighbors called in a welfare check on Lars when they noticed his car hadn't moved in a while and no one answered the door. Officers arrived, knocked, looked in some windows, then went around back to this bedroom window"—he pointed to the window at the back of the room—"and was able to see the body on the floor. They kicked the front door in, and voilà."

"Everything was locked when PD got here?" she asked.

"Yeah," Harding said, then pointed to an open window in

the back. "But after we took photos, we opened a couple windows for some air."

She nodded and snapped a picture of the driver's license, then started taking photos of the deceased Lars.

He had that been-dead-a-minute funk to him that smelled somewhere between bad fruit and rotten meat. She slung the camera back around her neck and pulled out the clipboard. After filling out all the biographical information, doctor information, and what Ethan had told her, she stuffed it back in the bag and snapped on some gloves.

"I'd guess he's been down for at least twenty-four hours, but not more than a day or so."

May picked up Lars's hand and bent his joints. "Rigor has already broken and..." She lifted the edge of Lars's discolored white T-shirt and pushed her finger into the purple discoloration on the edge of his back. When she pulled her finger away, there was no white outline where her finger had been. "And lividity is set with no blanching. Yeah, I'd say maybe two. And the mess in the living room?"

"Neighbors haven't heard anything weird in the past few days. Ex-wife, who's outside, said he drinks booze more than water."

"I thought you said estranged."

He grunted and waved his hand in the air. "Estranged, ex. She can't make up her mind which she is."

May chuckled and snapped a few more photos of the lividity.

"If he's piss drunk, all that out there could be him tripping over himself. Knocks over the table and trips over the chair on the way to the bedroom. Falls one last time and dies where he lands."

May hummed as she felt around Lars's skull. "Possibly." His skull felt intact, but his neck was looser than it should've been. She poked around his thick neck but couldn't tell if it was broken. The autopsy would reveal it.

Standing, May finally turned back to the bedroom covered in spectral ooze and started snapping pictures. Not that anything would show in them other than the unmade bed, the piles of laundry on the floor, dated and old furniture, and a dead man in the corner.

Why was this one so different? Why did it feel so violent?

"Hey, Harding."

May glanced over her shoulder at the patrol officer who had poked his head into the room.

"Harding, the wife wants to talk to you again."

"Son of a..." Ethan muttered under his breath. "Yeah, okay. I'm coming." He looked back at May.

"I'm good. Ask if he had any drug use."

He nodded and retreated from the house, the young patrolman following.

Letting out a shuddering sigh, May glanced around the room in the silence that followed their departure. She slowly meandered around, opening the odd dresser drawer, looking for anything out of the ordinary, or any drugs. Finding none, she packed up her few items and hauled the ME bag back onto her shoulder. She retreated from the room and looked around the trashed living room again.

Was it a fight?

Had he tried to fight off whoever came for his soul? Or had he been drunk and trashed the place himself, and the attacker came for his soul after? Glancing back at the dead man in the corner, she was guessing the first option.

So why have the fight at all? None of the others had. All the others appeared to be overdoses, but this one looked violent. What changed? Why?

Chewing her lip, she turned away, intent on waiting for the

transport team in her car, when a shimmer caught her attention from the corner of her eye. With a glance at the front door, and the thoroughly bored patrolman staring off into space, May picked her way over beer cans to the overturned coffee table. Squatting down, she sifted through the papers, TV remote, and more beer bottles to find the shimmering thing she'd seen. It looked like a scrap of black fabric, but the more she studied it, the less sure she was that it was black. The color seemed to move and blend as the light hit it.

She reached out and plucked the material gently between her forefinger and thumb. It was silken smooth, nearly weightless. It did not belong in this world, whatever it was. She stuffed it into her pocket.

"Find something?"

May jerked at Ethan's voice and hastily stood. "No. It was nothing. Just trash."

"Oh. Well, the wife, ex—whoever, said he overdosed once a few years ago. Said he died for a few minutes before paramedics Narcaned him and brought him back. Heroin was his drug of choice back then."

May nodded. *A near-death experience...* Did that mean he could see who attacked him? Was he like her?

"So, did you find anything?"

May shook her head and walked out of the house, Ethan following her. "No. Neck seems weird, but we'll have to wait for the x-rays. If the house was locked up like you said and he's as drunk as it looks, then this really could be just him drinking himself to death."

"It is weird, though. Right?" Ethan asked as he leaned his hip against her bug.

She tossed her bag and camera onto her passenger seat and leaned her hip against her car, mirroring him. "I'd say it's weird."

"Sometimes, I think I overthink these things."

May shrugged and wiped sweat from her temples. "I don't think that's a bad thing. I am, however, going to wait in my car with the air conditioning for transport to get here."

Ethan smiled his dimpled smile at her. "Smart."

She slid into her car and started it. Eventually, blessedly cold air blasted from her vents, and she pulled out the scrap of fabric. It was softer than even the most expensive silk she'd ever touched. Like a whisper of air on her skin. Draping it across her fingers, it seemed to almost camouflage them.

"I guess invisibility cloaks really are a thing," she muttered to herself, grabbing her phone.

She shot off a text to the transport team with the address information and dumped her phone into the passenger seat. She scanned the street, noting the way people glanced in their direction as they passed. Some were cautious and others curious. While she waited, her gaze drifted—and landed on a figure standing several houses down. The evening light shimmered in the haze, and she narrowed her eyes, trying to make out his features, but the distance and the glow swallowed the details.

Like he was a heat shimmer. Again.

Her pulse jumped in her throat.

He shimmered and seemed to disappear in the evening.

"Shit," she muttered, and pulled for her magic, the little spark deep in her chest.

"Away with you, doer of wrong." Her skin felt flushed as the magic flared gently. "It stands as a shield, united and strong. Against dark forces that threaten my peace."

The magic wove around her simple warding spell and settled along her skin. A cough rose in her throat, and she gulped down warm water from her water bottle. That should last until she could get to her parents'. It might be time for a stronger warding spell.

"Oh!" May's mother gasped dramatically as she opened the door. "She graces us with her presence."

"Never mind." May turned around with a huff, only for Janet to pull her into a hug.

"Don't be dramatic."

"I'm the dramatic one?" May huffed with a smile and let Janet guide her into the house. "Where's Dad?"

"Bowling with friends."

Janet led her into the kitchen, where she seemed to thrive if she wasn't in front of a room full of students. May snagged a banana off the counter and slipped onto the stool on the other side. The cough had lingered on the drive over, and again, she huffed a cough as she broke into the banana.

"Why are you coughing?"

May rolled her eyes at her mom. "It's just the dry air. I'm fine."

Janet leaned over and placed her hand on May's forehead, anyway, frowning at her while she did. May jerked away when she lingered too long. "Mom. I'm not dying. I have a dry throat."

"Well, forgive me for caring."

"I just—" She huffed. "I just want to not be dying all the time. Can we talk about literally anything else?"

"Yes." Janet smiled gently at her. "Tell me about the girl you had over."

Fuck. May dropped her head onto the counter. She'd walked right into that one.

"Is she..." Janet hedged. "A friend from work?"

"Kinda," she said, and sat up. "She does... similar work."

"Oh!" Janet perked up and leaned on the counter. "What kind?"

"She handles next step... sort of things."

"Like a mortuary."

May chuckled. "Sorta."

Janet hummed. "And you're..."

"Friends, Mom."

"Okay, okay." She held her hands up in surrender and went to the fridge for a drink. "You know, some daughters share these things with their mothers."

"Yeah—" May chuckled. "Some."

Janet chuckled back and handed her a soda. "So, what brings you over?" May cracked open her soda and glanced up at her mom, who shook her head with a smile. "You never come over just for fun."

Oof, May thought, instantly feeling shitty. She cleared her throat awkwardly. "Well, I had some more questions about ghosts. And if you had a strong warding spell... that was also easy."

Janet narrowed her eyes. "Why do you need a warding spell?"

"Ummm..." She dragged the word out. "Because I think a ghost is following me around?"

Janet leaned back from the counter, eyes wide and mouth slack as she stared down at May. She blinked at her, mouth gaping, before walking around the counter and sliding onto the stool next to May. "Excuse me?"

"Well—" May forced a chuckle. "I see dead people. Surprise!"

The joke landed flat with her mother, but in fairness, she couldn't force herself to laugh at it either. *Shit.* She sobered with a sigh. "I can see ghosts now. Since the hospital. Since... well, since I died."

"Why haven't you said anything?"

May jerked. *Because I thought I was going nuts? Because I thought I was evil? Because I didn't want to?* "Look, I just... It's a lot to come to terms with. Okay? Normally, they just sorta hover like annoying exes, but lately, there's one that seems to be following me. It's creeping me out."

"Okay," Janet said soothingly, and patted May's arm. "Does it seem malevolent?"

May shrugged. "It just sort of... lingers in the shadows. I don't really want it to get close enough to figure out if it's malevolent or not."

"Okay," Janet said again, this time offhandedly as her eyes grew unfocused. "Well"—she focused again on May—"there are plenty of warding spells that should work."

"Yeah, but easy ones," May said with a whine.

"May," Janet huffed. "You need to practice. It's the only way you'll get better."

She dropped her head back in a huff before looking at her mom again. "I cast a simple rhyming spell earlier. But those don't last long."

"May," Janet snapped, to May's surprise. "I've told you. The rhyming spells you do are not *real* Green Magic."

She slouched on her stool. "It worked, didn't it..."

"No," Janet snapped again. "When you cast those, you're not pulling from the earth. You're not pulling from the magic in living things."

So what am I pulling from, then? May wondered. And why did it feel so natural? She didn't bother asking, however. She'd done that dance with her mom before. Many times. She never got a straight answer out of Janet. Nor a satisfying one. It basically boiled down to "Don't do it" and "Because I said so."

"Here," Janet said. "This one is simple."

She held her hands between them and took a deep breath, so May trepidatiously did the same.

"Now," Janet said, closing her eyes, "focus on the earth. The magic that runs along and through it. All that magic is buried deep in Ley Lines. Focus on it and pull from the earthen magic."

May huffed but closed her eyes. She tried to feel for the magic her mom described. Faintly, she could sense *something*, but it felt odd and different. The magic of the earth didn't respond to her, didn't want her reaching for it.

"Now," Janet continued, "take that magic and weave it around you. Picture the grand canopies of the Amazon jungle. Or the thick Redwood Forests in California. Weave it around you while imbuing the magic with your intent: absorb, protect, hide."

May grunted and opened her eyes. She couldn't weave any magic into a fancy leaf shield when she hadn't been able to pull any magic to start with. Janet sighed and slowly blinked at May. Disappointment was in the slant of her eyes, the slump of her shoulders, and the tilt of her head. And she wondered why May didn't want to come by often...

May clucked her tongue. "A totem, maybe?"

"Don't you even want to try again?"

No... She thought petulantly. "Fine," she said instead.

She closed her eyes, trying again to reach for the magic in the Ley Lines, but like before, it slipped from her. Like water through her fingers. Grinding her teeth, she grabbed for any magic, only to open her eyes in a huff. Her eyes watered, and she angrily blinked the frustrated tears away.

"Are you even trying?"

"Yes!" she shouted at her mom. "I am! It never works. I can't feel the earth."

"You have to open your heart to it," Janet stated, as if May hadn't spoken.

"You think I'm not?" she yelled.

After an uncomfortable staring contest, Janet sighed. All of her mother's disappointment and belief that May was in fact *not* open to it was in that long, mournful sound. It was a sound May was overly familiar with. The same sigh she heard every time she'd failed another Green Witch skill.

"Fine." Janet stood and disappeared into the back of the house.

May pushed her soda away like a petulant child. Her mom always made her feel that way when it came to magic. *"Just practice,"* she'd say over and over and over. And May had. All the way to college before she decided that maybe the witch part of her life was just not going to happen the way her mother expected. It made sense. Her career path hadn't gone the way Janet wanted either.

She straightened as her mom came back into the kitchen and held her hand out. In her palm was a small obsidian rock carved in the shape of a lion's head. The mane flared out to the edge of the stone, deeply carved lines making it look like wind was blowing in the lion's face.

"This should ward off anything that wants to do you harm. As long as they themselves aren't exerting a stronger magic. Keep it with you."

"Thanks, Mom," she said as she plucked the totem from her mom's hand and stood, heading toward the door.

"You don't want to stay for some late dinner?"

"No," she said without looking back, "not tonight."

She couldn't bear the look of disappointment over the entire length of a dinner.

CHAPTER TWENTY-ONE
I WAS SENT BY DEATH

Sitting at her desk the next day, May ran the strange, otherworldly material through her fingers. She still didn't know what it was. The totem was wedged in her pocket, constantly reminding her of her mother's disapproving eyes.

"May?"

She turned to the opening of her cubicle.

"They're about to start the Benion case."

"Oh, thanks," she said to Sarah, and pushed away.

She headed down the long hallway to the exam room, slipping on a gown as she went. Yesterday's deceased was set up at the end station with Dr. Kesler during a cursory lookover already.

"Hey, doc," May said as she approached.

"So…" Dr. Kesler planted her hands on her hips as she studied Lars. "You have concerns about this one?"

She nodded. "Scene presented with signs of a struggle, which could be explained by his drinking, however, when I examined him on scene, I had concerns about his neck."

"Think it's broken?"

May shrugged. "Maybe."

"Well," Dr. Kesler said as she walked over to the computer against the wall, "let's see what the x-rays say."

She clicked through the computer files and pulled up Lars Benion's x-rays. "Survey says..." She opened another file. "Yup. Broken neck. Good call, May."

May's heart jumped into her throat.

"Now, let's see if it was a fall or something a tad more violent."

"You'll be able to tell?"

Dr. Kesler shrugged. "Hopefully. Was the detective observing this?"

May shook her head. "He said to update him, but he's working leads."

"Okee dokee." Dr. Kesler pulled on her gloves and turned back to Lars.

May watched as they began the autopsy, pulled out her phone with shaky fingers, and typed out a quick message to Ethan.

> Me: Cause of death is a Broken neck. Autopsy starting. Will advise.

The dots appeared nearly instantly.

> Det. Dimples: Holy shit. Found a neighbor who saw a strange car sitting down the street the days leading up to this. Might be the baddie.

May swallowed, but her mouth was dry, then she locked her phone and slid it back into her pocket. She returned to her desk to finish paperwork while the exam went on. Eventually, Dr. Kesler informed her she would most likely be putting undetermined as the manner of death, pending the police investigation. She couldn't say how the neck was broken, and with no other information implying foul play, it would likely stay as undetermined.

Now, at home, May didn't know what to do. She paced her small living room, feeling the need to do something. She just didn't know what, and Death hadn't exactly given her a set of instructions to work with. Her orange tabby, Loki, stared at her from his spot on the couch. He'd nervously followed her when she'd started pacing, but after tripping over him the fourth time, he'd angrily meowed at her and retreated to the safety of the couch.

Suddenly, Loki's ears went flat against his orange head, and he stared at the door. May paused, slowly turning to the door, and someone knocked.

Loki hissed.

Shit, shit, shit.

"Guard secrets and whispers untold. A fragrant fortress, a haven to hold," May whispered, putting power into her words as she set the spell on her door. She pulled that magic in her chest, the one her mother didn't seem to understand or acknowledge, and her chest warmed as her rhyming spell settled into place.

They knocked again, louder, and May gasped, choking on the air and coughing.

Guess surprise is out. May crept to the door to peer through the peephole and frowned at the man that stood staring at her door. She didn't recognize him, and given how striking he was, she'd remember seeing him. Even through the distorted fisheye lense of the peephole, she could tell he was tall. He wore a pale suit, which was a clean sharp cut that belonged nowhere near her neighborhood. She reached for her phone in her pocket, then she felt the tingle of magic along her skin. Her deadbolt clicked and the doorknob turned.

"Shit."

The man pushed the door open, and their eyes locked. Her heart stuttered, and her breath came fast and ragged through her open mouth. Behind her, Loki hissed and growled. The man took a step, only to frown and pause on her doorstep. He looked around the doorframe, then back at May.

"This simple spell won't keep me out."

May took shaking steps back. "What do you want?"

"To talk."

"Bullshit." Isn't that what all bad guys said before they killed you? May felt a hysterical laugh creeping up her throat but continued to slink backward. The man frowned, then muttered something in a language she'd never heard, and with a fizzingly pop, her spell collapsed.

No. Her hands trembled, and he stepped into her living room.

"Leave," she ordered, trying to sound firm instead of terrified.

"I do not wish to harm you."

"I don't believe you." May's voice shook as she brought her clenched hand to her mouth. "Last time I ask."

The man scoffed and stepped closer.

"*Burn*," May whispered, and blew on her now-open hand; her one good spell. She reached for the magic she didn't understand. The magic her mother said was *wrong*. The magic that seemed to be *hers* and listened to her intention. It came without a fight and when she asked it to. Flames eagerly leapt from her palm in a hot, scorching heat. He shouted and jumped back, falling to his back in the apartment hallway.

She dropped her hand and lunged for the door, but halfway to slamming it closed, he shoved his fancy leather loafer in the way. He glared up at her, holding the door open with a force she didn't understand. She strained against him, putting all her strength into closing the door. Half his face was burned, the skin red and charred, but as she watched, it healed. Burned skin and blisters smoothed, new skin overtaking the black.

"What the f—"

"I was sent by Death."

"—uck." May stared at him, mouth hanging open. A cough climbed up her throat, either from the struggle or the smoke, so she hastily cleared her throat.

"Now, may we speak?"

Down the hall, a door clicked open, and her neighbor poked her head into the hallway, gray hair a curly cloud around her. "¿Qué es esto? Even I can hear this racket."

"S-s-sorry, Maria!" May stuttered without taking her eyes from the man on the floor. "My... friend... fell."

Maria humphed and said something too fast in Spanish for May to catch, then slammed the door shut again. It hadn't sounded polite.

"I swear on my honor as a warrior I will not harm you."

The words felt like they had a weight she didn't fully understand. They meant a promise in a way words used to, in the old days, with old magic.

"Fine," she finally said, and let the door fall open.

The man stood slowly, eyeing her with narrowed eyes, and entered her apartment. He stayed near the door as he surveyed the room. His blond hair, long and flowing in a way only Fabio had mastered, stood out against the harsh glare he had on his face. He was almost angelic, save for the seething anger in his eyes.

"So—" She cleared her throat, hand gripped painfully around the obsidian in her pocket. "You know Death?"

He looked down at her, because *damn*, he was tall, and glared. Suddenly, his eyes went wide, and he frantically looked around her apartment before turning narrowed eyes back to her.

"Wha—"

He gripped her arm in a painful, iron-tight grip, and yanked her hand from her pocket.

"What the fuck, Fabio!" she screeched at him as she uselessly tried to wrench her arm from his grip.

Ignoring her shouting, he shoved his hand into her pocket and plucked out the scrap of mystery fabric. He released her and sniffed the shimmering material.

"Where," he asked with a growl in his voice, "did you get this?"

Heart beating frantically in her chest, she stepped back and reached for her power again. Her chest warmed, skin flushed and hot. Her breathing wheezed in her throat. "How do I know you're not going to just kill me?"

I am not about to end up on a true-crime podcast.

He curled his lip, like the idea was so disgustingly beneath him it insulted his very being. "If I were to, I would have already."

"That doesn't make me feel any better." She took a deep breath and huffed past a cough. "What are you? Why did you heal like that?"

She felt a shimmer in the air, like a magic wind brushing against her skin, and suddenly, Fabio was shimmering, changing. His hair brightened. His brown eyes shifted to a bright-golden glow. The most striking change, however, was the massive white wings that now hovered over his shoulders. May gasped as her eyes ran along the feathers dropping nearly to the floor, where the tips were tinged black and golden veins seemed to spread through them.

Oh my God. May gaped at him. "Are you an angel?"

His lip curled in a snarl, and she saw he sported a set of pointed canines. "Do not insult me."

Death sent him. He's got wings. May's mind struggled to come up with an answer until suddenly it clicked. "You're a Reaper."

The snarl remained on his face as he slowly held up the scrap of fabric. "Where. Did you. Find this?"

"At a scene," she said in a rush. "At a crime scene. I think the guy was murdered, but the only evidence is the aether splattered everywhere."

He blinked, and she noticed he had a second, clear, eyelid at the corner of his eyes.

"Why?"

"This," he said as he slowly slipped the fabric into a pocket of his suit, "is from a Reaper's cloak. It also... has the smell of someone who should be gone."

She waited, but he failed to enlighten her further. "Okay, so what do you want? Why did Death send you?"

Fabio shifted his shoulders, his feathered wings ruffling, and then the magic breezed across her skin again. His image shifted, like a heat mirage, then his wings were gone and his golden eyes were a boring brown. She shivered at the magic ghosting over her skin.

He smoothed a hand along his white suit jacket and stiffly sat on the couch. May slowly settled herself across from him. His frame dwarfed the couch, more than even Death's had.

"You shouldn't be able to see the Reaper cloak. You were able to see me, which makes my job of following you unobserved rather pointless."

"That was you!" she shouted with an angry finger point. "I thought an evil ghost thing was going to try to kill me!"

He simply raised a perfectly carved eyebrow at her.

"Also!" May jabbed her finger at him again. "Why are you following me?"

"Because Death commanded it."

She opened her mouth to snap more obscene things at him, but he held up his hand. She snapped her jaw closed with a loud clack of teeth and settled her hands on her lap.

"I was sent by Death to watch you. You have, it seems, an ability to be involved in things you aught not to be."

May resisted the urge to interrupt, to speed him along.

"So I was sent to observe you. When it became clear you could also see me, despite my Reaper cloak, I thought to try a"—he tilted his head in a decidedly bird way—"different approach."

"Okay..."

Fabio, or whatever his name actually was, blinked his human eyes, though there was nothing human in his gaze. "I was also sent to locate a missing Reaper. I believe you can help me in this task."

She drummed her fingers on her knees, heart in her throat, as her brain tried to process his words.

"I need a drink," she declared, and went to the kitchen.

CHAPTER TWENTY-TWO
SUPERNATURAL DETECTIVE SHIT

The electric kettle bubbled on the counter in front of her as May drummed her fingers against the cold surface. She tried not to think of the Reaper sitting in her living room or acknowledge the glare from her cat as he sulked in the corner of the kitchen.

Why did Fabio think she could help find a Reaper? Why was one even missing in the first place?

The switch on the kettle popped as it reached the boiling point, and mechanically, May poured the boiling water into the pot. The smell of the earthy black tea reached her, and she let out a soft breath. Tea always helped. She placed two mismatched mugs on the small tray with the pot and carried it back into the living room. Fabio was where she'd left him, sitting on the couch and taking up most of it with his bulk. Even though his glamour hid his wings, she knew they were there, so she stared into the space they should be.

With a shake of her head, May turned away from the invisible, magical wings and set the tea service down on the coffee table between them. Fabio raised an acrid eyebrow at it.

"I do not understand your obsession with hot drinks. Nor do I understand why Lady Death shares it."

May blinked mid-pour and set the pot down. "Okay. No tea for you, then." She wrapped her hands around her mug and left the second empty on the tray. After a deep breath and a gentle sip of the still-boiling liquid, she set her eyes on the Reaper again. "Alright, Fabio, you want to start from the beginning?"

"Armeal," he said with a *tone*. "Death sent me to watch you, as I've said. It seemed easier to reveal my presence to you, as you seemed aware of it already. I also was sent to attempt to locate a missing Reaper. I believe you can be of use to me."

"Okay, see," May said, "that's where you lose me."

Again, he raised his eyebrow in a way that made her feel stupid and annoyed.

"Why—" She sighed and shook her head. There were so many questions that started with "Why," and she was having problems picking just one.

"Why has a Reaper gone missing?" Armeal, though he would forever be Fabio in her mind, said. "That is the question I also do not know. Things are shifting in the Underworld, and we do not know why. Ghosts are being troublesome. Souls are missing. Reapers are unaccounted for." He tilted his head like a bird again. "Why was I sent to watch you? You seem to be involved in the missing souls and the troublesome ghosts. And the Fates have deemed you to be involved. That has even Death's curiosity piqued. Why do I think you can help me find Talsk?" He straightened his head. "Because the Fates have deemed you involved. I think if we find Talsk, the other threads will connect as well."

May blinked at him, tea forgotten in her hands.

The corner of his lips twisted in the smallest hint of a grin. "Human minds are simple. The questions were easy to assume."

"Did you just call me stupid?"

Now the bastard grinned.

"So, why do you think I can help you find a missing Reaper?" May asked, tea forgotten on the table between them.

Armeal was quiet across from her, his eyes dark and brooding. The muscles in his jaw flexed and clenched, like he fought with the words he wanted to say.

Finally, he leaned back and let out a soft breath. "Because the last time Reapers went missing, I had assistance looking for them. And this time, that person is gone."

May blinked, fingers absentmindedly rubbing the top of her scar on her chest. She leaned back, mirroring him with her own sigh. "If you want me to be your sidekick in this supernatural detective shit, I'm going to need full disclosure. I'm not getting involved if you don't trust me to *be* involved."

Armeal sucked his teeth but nodded with a curt dip of his chiseled chin. "Fine."

She folded her hands in her lap.

Armeal cleared his throat with a huff of breath. "There was a rebellion between the Nephilim. A small group thought they were above their station, their calling, and refused the call of Death. They thought they deserved more." The words were ground out, like stones crashing against each other. "A Nephilim," he spat the word, "a traitor, swayed the weak-minded of us to her side and challenged Death."

Armeal held up the mysterious cloth. "This smells like her. She is dead. Has been dead for centuries, but this appears... Souls are being stolen. A Nephilim is missing, and now this." He shook his head, eyes downcast. "I fear another rebellion is upon us. I hope it is not that, but I fear it is."

"What does it mean, if it is another rebellion?" May muttered.

Armeal tucked the cloth away with a shake of his head. "A

war with the angels. Perhaps the Fae, if they dirty themselves with the idea of leaving their safe havens."

"That sounds bad," May whispered.

"We need to learn where this cloak came from. How whoever has it came upon it."

"When you say 'we,' you mean me, don't you?"

Armeal tipped a tight-lipped grin at her. "I must search for Talsk."

May nodded slowly, mind spinning and heart racing. The cloth was found at a crime scene. Det. Dimples was already assigned the case, so it would be easy enough to dig deeper with him.

"What would having the Reaper cloak do?" May asked.

"The wearer would be invisible to human eyes. They would be..." He paused as if searching for the right word. "Not entirely in this realm."

"Like the in-between Death is in when she's here but not... here, here."

He nodded.

"So," she said, thinking out loud, "it would allow them to sneak up on people. Which would explain no witnesses at the scenes Dimples thinks are murders." She dropped her head back. *Which means they really are murders.*

"Okay," she finally said to the ceiling. "And if I find anything...how am I supposed to find you?"

She lifted her head to watch him, eyebrow raised.

Armeal blinked at her, then looked around the room before plucking her small compact mirror off the side table. Clicking it open, he swiped the pad of his finger across his tooth, then pressed the bloody tip to the mirror. A zing of magic flared in her blood in response to whatever magic he cast. It was hot, spicy, and familiar before it disappeared in a rush. Armeal snapped the mirror shut and handed it to her.

"Speak into it, I will hear."

May looked at the closed mirror in her palm. "Just a smear of blood, huh?"

"There is power in blood magic."

May grunted ironically. "Blood magic is dark magic. We're taught we shouldn't use it. That it leads to corruption."

Armeal frowned and tilted his head.

"Sacrificing your own body, or more specifically, the body of others is wrong."

He frowned harder. "Is it? Why?"

May blinked, about to respond with her mother's words "*Because it is*," but she paused. She didn't understand why. She asked her mother that constantly and was never satisfied with the answer.

"Humans have sacrificed and bled for power throughout your existence," he said when she remained silent.

"Murder is wrong." Her protest was soft even to her own ears.

"I never said murder," Armeal replied with a hard stare. "I said bled."

She didn't have a response, or even a reason to give him, so she looked away. It was wrong because she was told it was wrong, but she didn't understand. Didn't accept the answers given to her by her mother. There must be something, though, she thought. Or else, why was it so strongly enforced?

Armeal snorted and stood. "Humans and their ridiculous sensibilities. I never understand them." He gave a pointed look at the mirror she still clasped in her hand.

"I'll call if I find something."

He nodded, and, without another word, disappeared before her eyes.

CHAPTER TWENTY-THREE
NOT ALL HAVE BURIED THEIR PRIDE

Harper stood over the body as police milled around her, oblivious of her presence. Uniformed patrol stood at the doors, both front and back, as suited detectives stood with hands on hips and glowering faces. Upstairs, there was a similar scene with more detectives. At the front door, Harper caught a glimpse of the medical examiner investigator being signed in, but the woman in nondescript black scrubs and an OME T-shirt wasn't May, so Harper paid her no mind.

No, what held her attention were the two bodies without souls.

The body in front of her, the husband, lay in a pool of his own blood. His chest was cleaved open from collarbone to breastbone. Like an ethereal shadow, silver aether mingled with the dark-red blood on the ground. It poured from the man and spread farther than even his life blood had.

Harper snarled at the scene and moved up the stairs to the second victim. She lay in the hallway, sprawled on her stomach as if she'd been running for her life before being cut down. A large stab wound—stained a dark, almost black—in her back, was the source of the blood here. The wound was large and gaping, bigger than any simple knife could cause, but again, that wasn't her concern. The narrow hallway was covered in spattered aether. The walls practically glowed with it.

She didn't need to feel the Tether to know these people died in pain and terror. What she didn't understand, however, was why the change. These people had been murdered, brutally, and their souls taken. Why? Why now?

The hole in the woman's back had Harper's blood boiling and her hands clenched, claws digging into her palms and drawing blood. These wounds were inflicted by a scythe. A Reaper scythe. She recognized the wounds easily enough. The urge to shatter the world around her grew in her veins, but she slashed her bleeding hand through the air and rent the layers open. To kill humans with the scythe... to *interfere* in such a way, was forbidden. It was the way of the Reapers. It was not their duty. The world split without resistance, like it felt her fury and did not wish to delay her.

Her boots landed on the hard black marble of her castle. The large entry hall loomed around her, and fury pulsed within her.

"*Reapers!*" she bellowed, and forced her life's magic into the command.

Every Reaper heard her command, felt it in their blood. And they answered.

Those already in the Underworld came quickest, and soon, every Reaper gathered in the hall around her. She glowered at them, fury and seething anger still boiling her insides. A Reaper had given their scythe to another. Or worse, a Reaper was responsible for the thefts, the murders. It was an inescapable fact. Before, Harper could pretend it was a human with strong magic. Or a Fae that had left their courts. Or even a rouge angel. But those scythe wounds, so distinctive, ruined any hope of pretending she hadn't been betrayed. After a war with her own Reapers, the damage a scythe could inflict on flesh was forever etched in her mind.

The air was thick with tension and confusion as she met each and every one of their eyes.

"Present your scythes," she said, voice loud and clear through the hall.

Murmurs echoed through the hall, soft whispers and mutters. Like old papers falling.

The Reapers held their scythes in front of themselves for her inspection. Some muttering under their breaths, others nervously shifting under her gaze. Harper went from one to the next, checking each Reaper had their scythe, checking for the smell of human blood on the long, hooked blade.

"Are you calling us traitors?" one Reaper asked, voice cold and bitter, seething with his own fury.

Harper snapped her eyes to the Nephilim that had spoken deep in the crowd. The Reapers silently separated, leaving a direct path from her to him.

"You accuse us without words of betraying our duty," he spoke again, throwing his hood back, and planted his scythe at his feet, bony, pale hand clenching the staff.

Harper met his hollowed eyes, the eyes of an Old One, and lifted her chin. "How else do you explain a scythe cutting down humans?"

Her voice echoed in the silent hall.

The Nephilim lifted his chin, thin lips peeling back to reveal long fangs. "There are many missing scythes from the fallen."

Murmurs and more than a few muttered affirmatives filled the air.

"And I cannot account for that which is already missing,"

Harper said, stepping closer. "But I can quickly eliminate any question here."

"By calling us traitors," another Nephilim spoke, her voice soft and unsure.

Harper paused, eyes moving around the hall again.

"Have we not earned your loyalty?" a third spoke from the crowd. "Or are we just your slaves?"

"Slaves," the Old One mocked, eyes bright with the challenge.

Recoiling, a hiss slid through her clenched teeth. She never had imposed her will on them, only protected them and offered them a home when all others had cast them out. She had only ever asked one thing of them: ferry souls. And for this, they hated her? Harper ground her teeth and took a deep breath. Her anger from earlier made her reckless, and she wanted to slash the throat of the Old One in front of her, remove any hint of challenge in his eyes, but these beings were hers to protect. It was her oath to them. And she always upheld her oaths. Even when she was constantly reminded they did not.

"You think," a new voice shouted into the tense stillness, and Armeal stepped next to her, "this is the life of a slave?"

He looked around the group. Soon, the Old One she knew as Luras stepped free of the crowd. "Slaves would not be allowed to *whine* so incessantly over so *little* work."

Luras flared his black wings, and those around him scurried to avoid them. Another set of wings, feathers white at the root, flared, and Harper recognized Nerwen standing to her right.

"Your leader has given you an order," Armeal barked. "And your generals echo it. Present"—his eyes narrowed at the crowd—"your scythes."

Slowly, the crowd assembled themselves into something

akin to rows. She watched as a group gathered in front of Luras, and then Nerwen, with Armeal standing behind his two chosen generals. His stance was wide legged, arms folded and wings flexing behind him. He radiated authority, power, anger.

She stepped slowly to Armeal and raised an eyebrow at him.

"You found your generals, then."

He glanced over at her before nodding his chin at Luras. "He hates my very existence, and I hate his. If given the chance, we both would go for each other's neck, but he is a cunning leader with the respect of many of the younger Nephilim, and I've never known him to break a vow. Nerwen"—he jutted his chin at her—"well... I'd rather her spy for me than against me."

"You think she would?"

"No," he said without hesitation. "She is loyal to her word once she gives it."

She nodded.

"And both," he whispered, so low she was sure even the other Nephilim wouldn't be able to hear, "both tire of war and long for an easy existence."

She smiled, glad that at least three chose this life and did not simply settle for it. Chose the life *she* offered them.

She turned to the gathered Reapers and stepped between the two waiting Nephilim. "You are not my slaves. However, I cannot ignore the fact that a scythe was used to cut down humans. Souls are being stolen, and Reapers are missing."

She had their attention; it weighed on her like a beam across her shoulders. "While it might hurt your *pride*..." The word was laced with the anger she couldn't ignore. "I must check among you first. I do not want to find traitors among you. I hope I do not, but the past has taught me well. I would think you have learned your own lessons from your siblings' betrayal."

Murmurs again, soft and embarrassed.

She met the angry eyes of the Old One who had challenged her. "Present your scythes. Then we may move on."

"Now, Kian," Luras snapped at the Old One who still hesitated.

Reluctantly, with slow movements that spoke of insubordination and resentment, he presented his scythe for her inspection.

"Not all have buried their pride as well as others." Armeal's words echoed back to her as she inspected Kian's scythe. She would need to keep an eye on this one. His anger seemed to go deeper than others'.

The rest of the inspection passed in silence, without a word spoken or a whisper breathed. She let out a breath of relief after inspecting the last scythe. None were missing. None smelled of human blood. A weight lifted from her soul. None here had betrayed her. Her relief was short-lived, however.

If none here, then who?

Harper looked over the crowd of Reapers. They waited, for judgment perhaps.

She returned to Armeal and stood close, her words only for him and those he trusted.

"A Fae Hunter attacked a young one."

He hissed, his fangs glistening as he pulled his lips back.

"I... *deterred* him," she growled. "But if one Fae believes the Agreement is breached enough to risk my hounds, then others may."

"I understand," he said, and with a nod, moved to Luras and Nerwen. They spoke, heads bowed together before the three straightened. Armeal glanced back at her, but Harper nodded and told herself to trust him with the decision they had made. "Going forward, until this thief is dealt with, we will now ferry souls in pairs."

A few hands clenched their staffs, but no one spoke.

"An Old One with the younger." He gestured to Luras and Nerwen. "They will make the assignments. Someone, something is stealing souls that are our duty to collect, and the Fae are getting bold enough to attack. We will not be an embarrassment to the one who shelters us. We will not be struck down by some *mortal* thing that thinks itself eternal."

A few Old Ones in the crowd murmured. The hatred between the Nephilim and the Fae went back to the Nephilim's very creation. Two prideful, powerful, immortal creatures perfect at killing and hard at being killed: they were the perfect challenge for the other.

"And," Armeal continued, "we will not let what is ours to collect be stolen."

He snapped his wings shut in a gesture of dismissal, and Luras and Nerwen went about pairing the Reapers together. Armeal watched on. As they dispersed, she did not miss Kian's glare, his eyes full of too much anger.

CHAPTER TWENTY-FOUR
THE TOUCH OF DEATH

May sat in her car in front of her parents' house, fingers tapping nervously on her steering wheel. She hadn't been able to sleep in the days since Fabio had descended upon her apartment. In the silence that filled her living room after his abrupt departure, she was left with more questions than ever. Armeal was just as obtuse as Lady Death about what they wanted May to do. Find a Reaper cloak? How was she supposed to do that? These immortal beings needed a lesson in conversation skills.

Another massive question that had been burning in her mind was *What is blood magic?*

Her parents made it sound as if she was selling her soul to the devil to use it, but Armeal, who was definitely not the devil—probably—acted like it was just another magic. So who was wrong? Or were they both right? She shook her head. Those questions were why she was parked outside her parents' house. The judgment of her mother kept her from walking inside with her questions.

May jumped in her seat, heart in her throat, at the overly loud *ding* from her purse.

"Why is it even that loud?" she muttered to herself as she dug her phone.

> Pops: You gonna sit out there forever?

She exhaled a loud breath and looked over at the large bay window just visible from the street. Her dad stood in it, waving at her. Feeling embarrassed at being caught, May gathered her purse and trudged up to the house. High above her, a raven cawed. She met the bird's large eyes, and it moved its head this way and that as she watched it. Ravens were signs of many things, depending on what you believed, but one was consistent through all types of magic: a great change was in your future.

May's heart stuttered as she watched the bird, its large black eyes locking on hers before it cawed and took off. They also represented the link between the living and dead.

"Great," she muttered, and shook herself.

Her dad met her at the door.

"You seem pensive," he said as a greeting, and wrapped her in a side hug.

May weakly returned the hug. "I got myself wrapped up in some..." She did *not* want to wrap her parents up in the same mess she was in. "Just some cases at work are bothering me."

She felt only a little bad about the lie.

"The murders?"

May's eyes snapped to her dad as he walked into the living room and sat back on the couch, reaching for the TV remote. "The what?"

"The murders." He pointed at the TV with the remote, news muted on the screen. "They've been all over the news.

Some guy was killed in his home, and over in Chandler, a husband and wife were killed in what looks like a burglary gone wrong. The news is connecting them to some sort of crazy serial killer."

May's eyes were glued to the broadcast. In the b-roll footage, she saw the house she was at several days ago and even spotted Detective Harding's car on the curb. Then it moved to another house, the footage shot from a helicopter, based on the angle. Crime scene tape surrounded the house and the yard, police cars filling the street.

"The news keeps throwing around crazy names for the crimes, as if we're still in the 1990s and serial killers still exist," her dad was saying.

"Technically, anything involving three or more murders in a similar sequence is considered a serial killer," May muttered, still watching the news footage.

"You know what I mean." Her dad scoffed and switched the channel to a rerun of *Jeopardy*. "A real serial killer, like the Golden State Killer or the Boston Strangler. Not just people going around robbing and killing people."

"Wha— " May shook her head and turned to her dad. "What? Never mind." He chuckled at her. "Where's Mom? I have a question for her."

He thumbed over his shoulder. "Her study, grading papers, I think."

She tossed her bag onto the old recliner in the corner and headed down the hall.

"You staying for dinner?" her dad shouted at her.

"No," she shouted back.

Her mom's door was open at the end of the hall, and she was bent over her desk, papers stacked next to her, reading glasses perched on her nose.

"Yes, you are," she said without looking up. "You're already here."

She sighed but didn't argue and instead slumped into the small chair facing her mom. "What're these on?"

Janet scribbled a note at the end of the paper she was reading and set it aside. "*The War of the Roses* as told by Shakespeare."

"For a history class?"

"Shakespeare wrote historical plays."

May narrowed her eyes. "I don't think that's the same thing."

Janet blinked at her and took a deep breath.

"Anyway..." May grinned at her. "How can I help you? I heard something about a question?"

May slouched farther in the chair. "So..." May started, only for her words to fail her.

Her mom raised a thin eyebrow at her. "So?"

May cleared her throat. "What makes a magic evil?"

Janet frowned and leaned back in her chair. "Haven't we been over this before?"

She shifted in her seat under her mother's pinched gaze. "I just... I don't understand. Why is blood magic evil? Why is Necromancy evil? Is it *evil* or just..." She shrugged. "A different type of magic?"

Fabio's words had settled in her stomach like a rock, or too much pasta, ever since he'd appeared in her apartment. *Why was it wrong?*

Janet frowned and leaned back again. "Because Necromancy, blood magic, and curses are forbidden magics."

"Because they're..."

"Wrong." Janet snipped when May hesitated. "Those magics deal in sacrifice and control. Controlling another's will is wrong, May. And interfering with the natural order, life and death, isn't meant for us."

May frowned and stared at the desk. Were they wrong because they were Green Witches? Their magic dealt entirely with finding balance within nature and honoring life. But would their magic look wrong to a Blood Witch?

"I see your brain working. What are you thinking?"

May shrugged and took a breath. "But why is it forbidden? Necromancy," she said quickly at the look of horror that had spread across her mother's face, "I get. Raising the dead. Bad. No good. Curses, I also get. But is the magic evil, or the person using it?"

"Both," Janet said emphatically. "Sacrificing life forces for power, like with blood magic, corrupts the person doing it. Cursing another person is really no different than harming them with a knife or your fists. In many cases, it's *worse*, for the effects are so long-lasting. Necromancy is unnatural. We aren't meant to interfere with the natural course of life and death," she repeated her earlier words.

May chewed her lip. But was that because they were Green Witches and their magic worked by having a deep connection to life?

"A person with good intentions doesn't choose magic that causes pain or harm or choose to *inflict* harm for good."

But May had seen the world of death and murder. She could think of plenty of reasons someone would want to hurt others for very good reasons. Righteous reasons, even. There was a reason vigilante justice existed. Looking at her mother's frown, she didn't think that was an argument she would win, however.

"Honestly, May." Janet scoffed. "What has gotten into you?"

"Nothing," she muttered with a shrug. "Just... picking apart a question."

She retreated from her mom's office before it could turn into a real lecture and trudged back into the living room. Her dad was still lounging on the battered couch, remote in hand, watching *Jeopardy*. She collapsed onto the couch next to him in a huff, bouncing Steve on the cushions.

"Hey, pumpkin."

"Hey," she grumbled.

"Mom kick you out?"

She looked over at him and sighed, then turned to the TV.

"Mom told me about the ghosts."

May looked at him from the corner of her eye. "Yeah?"

"Yeah. Is that what's behind all the questions about good and evil?"

She shrugged and sank farther into the couch. "Maybe."

Her dad sighed and threw his arm over her shoulders, tucking her in close. "Look, kiddo. I can't help if you don't talk."

She grumbled but let her dad tug her close. "I just don't understand magic."

"Sure you do," Steve protested.

"No, Dad." She sat up and looked at him. "I pretend I do. But I don't feel the Ley Lines like you and Mom. I don't feel the earth's energy. I don't think magic is evil or good. I think it's the person using it that determines that, but Mom says all Necromancy is evil. All blood magic is evil. I just don't get that."

Her dad watched her solemnly.

She shrugged, and now that her words had started, they didn't seem able to stop. "Like, is my magic evil? I'm not doing evil things with it. But I don't know where it comes from. It's not the earth."

"Maybe you just don't recognize it as the earth," her dad said, but May frowned. "Sometimes, it takes years and years of practice and honing your skill to understand it."

Practice. May groaned to herself. She doubted her problem had to do with practice.

"Maybe it doesn't feel the same to you as it does to me or your mom. That doesn't mean it's not Green Magic."

Doesn't mean it is, either. Her dad was nicer, gentler than her mother was, but he still believed it was a matter of skill. Neither seemed to want to consider the idea that May's magic was not theirs.

"Yeah," she said noncommittally. "Maybe."

She settled back in her dad's arm and pushed away the feeling of disappointment.

"So, ghosts, huh?" he asked after a moment of silence, the TV softly playing in the background.

"Yeah," she said, and accepted the change of topic. "It started when I saw Death in the hospital."

He tensed against her. "You what now?"

"I saw..." She looked at him again and felt like a little girl. "I saw the God of Death. Not one of her Grim Reapers." She shook her head. "No, I saw *her*. Death. She has blazing orange eyes and pale, pale skin."

Her dad was silent next to her, face a little pale in the flickering TV light. He nodded like he was working something through his mind, a deep frown between his eyes. May twisted her fingers together.

"Death, huh?"

May laughed, and it sounded a little crazed. "Yeah," she finally said. "And she likes coffee."

"What the fu—" Steve pressed his fingers to the bridge of his nose.

May let out a giggling breath.

"You have coffee with Death?"

"Sometimes," she said with a smile and a shrug. "I think she's lonely."

Steve laughed and covered his face. She wanted to tell her dad the rest: the murders, the missing souls, the Reapers. But she didn't want to involve them. She needed to protect them from this.

"Okay," he said, and smoothed his pants, as if he could smooth away the complexity of what he'd heard. "Okay. Well, one step at a time, I suppose."

Her stomach rumbled, loud and hard. "Can the first step be food?"

He grunted and chortled. "Sure, yeah. Let's eat."

"And then," May said as she followed her dad, "I'm going to need some warding spells."

"Why do you need more warding spells?" her mom demanded after an awkward dinner explaining that she not only saw ghosts but talked to Death.

"Why does anyone need warding spells, Mom?"

Janet clucked her tongue and folded her arms. "Sass will not help."

May barely resisted rolling her eyes. That most certainly wouldn't help. "I need something to protect my apartment."

Janet narrowed her eyes at May. "What have you gotten yourself into?"

May sighed and rubbed the headache forming between her eyes. "I just... Can you help me, Mom?"

Janet didn't lessen her glower, but she stood and walked

down the hall to her office. Once she returned, she set the family's thick leather-bound grimoire on the table between them. "I'll always help. But that doesn't mean I'll do so without question."

"As long as you're all right with me not always answering them," May said, and reached for the book.

Janet held it tight, and May released her grip on the cover with a huff. "Your father keeps reminding me you're an adult," she said as she flipped through the pages. "That doesn't mean I have to like that either."

May smiled.

"Now," she said as she settled on a page, "let's look at shields first."

"Aren't those going to be mostly defensive?" May asked, and craned her neck to try to see the page.

Janet glowered up at May from under her lashes. "Warding spells *are* defensive. Do you want offensive spells too?"

I mean... wouldn't be a bad idea. "Maybe something with a little..." She shrugged. "Encouragement to stay the hell away?"

"May Elinor Haines," Janet said in a low voice.

May flinched back.

"What is going on?"

"Better answer that one, kiddo," Steve hollered from the living room. "That's her I'm-not-playing voice."

Yeah, I got that. May rubbed her face, not wanting to tell them everything she'd actually gotten herself involved in. She didn't want to bring that trouble and worry to them. Not after they'd spent so many years waiting for her heart to give out. Not when her mom had just finally started to relax.

"I can't tell you. I don't want to involve you."

Janet's face went red, but before she could say anything, May stopped her. "It's dangerous. It... *could* be dangerous. I don't want to bring that to you."

"Well, uninvolve yourself, then!"

"It's not that simple." She sighed. "I'm helping Death. I—There are things I can help with, and if I can, then a lot of bad things can be stopped."

Janet drummed her fingers on the table, her lips pressed into a thin, disapproving line. The recliner creaked as Steve leaned forward to peer around the corner of the wall to watch.

"Matters of the grave and death should not be your concern," her mother finally said.

May sighed. "Mom. I'm an investigator at the Medical Examiner's Office. I'm literally paid for it to be my concern."

"You know what I mean," she snapped, and looked away with a huff.

"I'm involved in it whether I help or not," May murmured. "I'd rather help."

"This is about the murders," Steve said, and came to stand in the kitchen behind Janet. "Isn't it?"

May met his worried eyes. "It's not... *not* about the murders."

Silence and worried eyes stared at her.

"May," Janet said softly, her eyes sad and worried, "we just got your heart fixed. Your body is still weak—"

"Mom," she snapped, "I'm not some broken child."

"But you are *my* child."

May dropped her head and sighed. "Sorry." She took a deep breath and met her mother's worried eyes. "But people are dying. Green Witches are supposed to care about life, aren't they?"

Janet held May's eyes for a long, silent time before nodding with a breath.

"Well," Janet finally said and closed the book, "I think we need the—"

"Yup," Steve said, and pulled the grimoire from her hands before taking it back to her office.

"My back is hurting," Janet said, and stood. "Let's move this into the living room."

They solemnly moved into the living room, TV on mute, and waited for her dad to return. Janet's hands were clasped tightly, and May felt a pang of guilt that she'd brought this worry to them... again. Steve returned not long after, a slim book in his hand. He handed it to Janet, who took it with a reverence May hadn't seen from her before.

"Now," Janet said as she placed the small pamphlet in her lap. "I have a few spells we can try that might have the... *bite* you're looking for. I created these a long time ago, but I always had a feeling they were going to be needed."

"What?" May frowned at her mother and peered at the little book. "What kind?"

"Ones with *bite*." Janet flipped through the pages. "I have quite a skill for offensive spells, which... as a pacifist, I had conflicts about. Now..." Janet settled her brown eyes on May. "What sort of thing are we keeping out?"

"Uh," May breathed. "Well, the human kind. And... maybe the dead kind? And—" She took a deep breath. "It might be a good idea to also keep out the Nephilim kind."

Janet's hands shook where she'd gripped the corner of the page. "Nephilim? As in from the Bible?"

"Ummmm," May whined as she drew out the word. "That's kind of complicated, but yes. Kind of."

Janet took a long, shaky breath and turned to the book in her lap. Steve stood on uneasy legs and walked to the kitchen. May followed him with her eyes as he slowly came back, two glasses of whiskey in his hands. He handed one to Janet who threw a large gulp of it back, and she winced as it burned her throat.

"All right," she said, voice a little raspy from the whiskey. "Let's see what I have."

They went late into the evening going over the spells Janet had in her little grimoire. In the end, they found one that, once set, May only needed to activate or deactivate. None were quite as offensive as May was hoping, but she settled on what they'd decided on. Her dad followed her home to set the ward, a complex spell that hid her apartment from thought from any seeking it. As he was leaving, her dad had turned to her with a serious face. "You will owe us a full explanation eventually."

She'd nodded, again feeling guilty she couldn't tell them everything even after they'd so willingly helped her. She supposed that was part of being a parent.

Now, alone in her apartment, she inspected the ward set around her door. She could barely make out the complex strands of magic that made up the spell. With trembling fingers, she reached out and gently touched the spell. Magic buzzed up her arm, and she faintly tasted dirt and moss in the back of her throat. May reached for that bundle of magic in her chest, and it flared softly as she pushed the tiniest bit of her own magic into the woven strands.

Burn.

Her magic wove around her father's spell, and they settled among the strands, along with the taste of ash in the back of her throat.

CHAPTER TWENTY-FIVE
THE LAST MEMORY

Lars Benion's home called to May as she sat in her bug, parked on the side of the road. She swallowed her beating heart and gripped the keys in the ignition, not yet bringing herself to turn her car off. She'd had the stupid idea as she was leaving work for the day that since the fabric—the Reaper cloak scrap—was found here, maybe there was... other stuff... here.

The idea of breaking into the empty house had gnawed at her as she drove. It was a terrible idea, an illegal idea. But...

But she was supposed to be helping. She kept telling her parents she needed to help. Lady Death and Armeal both came to her asking for help. Even if they didn't exactly know what that meant, she needed to start doing something. So, she would do just that. She couldn't just sit there and wait for more murders to come across her desk, watch as they continued to be closed out as something else, and wonder at what to do. She needed to act.

She remembered from her investigation the day of that no

one else lived at the residence and, sure enough, as she sat here watching, the house was still dark and quiet.

"I can't believe I'm considering breaking and entering," she muttered to herself. As if she hadn't already made up her mind.

Taking a deep breath and slipping on some exam gloves, May exited her car and walked around the house to the side yard. She also remembered that PD had opened the back window because of the smell, and she hoped...

"Sweet," she whispered as she walked up to the still-open window.

She looked around the yard and found a small storage box up against the house, then dragged it over to the window before climbing onto it and removing the screen. Sliding the window open farther, she glanced around once before taking a deep breath and hoisting herself through it. May landed in a heap and a thud beneath the window.

That looks so much more graceful on TV, she thought with a grumble as she pushed herself to her feet and ignored the twinge in her ankle.

The house was just as they'd left it when everyone had finally left the scene. Beer cans were still scattered throughout the living room, the recliner still tipped onto its side. The smell of death was still in the air, though was faint and stale.

"Okay," May breathed, and looked around. "Lars had a near-death experience."

Walking slowly through the living room, careful not to disturb anything, she came to the front door. Turning to face the living room, she tried to put herself in Lars's point of view.

"Maybe he can see something, see past the Reaper cloak."

Except Fabio said humans can't do that... She sighed and folded her arms, chewed her lip.

"He must've," she said again, and walked into the living room. "His neck was broken. The chair is tipped over. *Some-*

thing happened. Drunk or not... So—" She huffed and walked the path of overturned things into the bedroom. "Let's pretend he can see something." She entered the bedroom and stood at the doorway where Lars had fallen.

"He sees something, runs. It chases him and then—" May huffed again. "Catches up to him and breaks his neck? Maybe if he's pushed, lands without bracing himself, which would make sense since he's drunk..." May continued to mutter to herself as she tried to picture it. "Breaks the fall with his face and then his body lands next. That could be enough force to break his neck if he's not expecting it."

May shrugged and looked around the room. "Probably, anyway..."

The aether was still softly glowing on the walls where it had splattered before. It had dulled with time to a soft, barely-there glow and faded completely in some areas. As she stared at the glowing marks, the urge to touch it grew. Like it had with the Tether. She wanted to touch it. She knew it would burn and zing through her blood, but still... Maybe now that it was old?

She chewed her lip again and bent down to a spot on the floor with a large pool. It flickered and flared.

It reminded May of bioluminescent pools that exist around the world.

With her heart in her throat and trembling fingers, May peeled off a glove and reached for the glowing carpet. Her fingers shook, and she paused right before touching her fingertips to it.

"This is one of my worst ideas," she muttered before taking a deep breath and setting her fingers into the aether.

Immediately, *something* zipped through her arm. It burned like fire but froze like ice at the same time, and her heart stopped long enough for her breath to freeze in her chest before she was gasping and panting. The... power... burned through her, and suddenly, memories flashed through her vision.

Lars's memories.

She felt fear and panic. A blurring, stumbling feeling that made her nauseous and dizzy. A haze stood at the door, shimmering in the sunlight, and Lars blinked his drunk eyes to try to clear them. He saw the swoop of a hood and the arch of a scythe. She felt his panic escalate to terror as he saw the thing move toward him. He ran and stumbled, then the memory started to fade.

May squinted her eyes shut and forced herself to hold her hand to the aether. *Focus!*

Pain flared across her knees and hips as Lars crashed into the recliner and fell before pushing himself upright and running for the bedroom. Something crashed into his shoulder and pushed, then he was falling and then—

She gasped as she felt the nothing of death and then a burning, searing cut in her chest. Ripping her hand back, she cradled it to her chest as she fought down the urge to vomit. Taking deep breaths barely helped as she quivered and shook from the power fading, the man's terror still lingering in her own body, and that horrible *stillness* she recognized as dying.

She pawed at her chest, searching for an injury. That tearing, cutting *agony* convinced her she'd been cut open, but her palms came away free of blood. The pain, the iron grip on her chest and the press of it against her heart, and the feeling of *dying* again made a cold sweat break out over her skin. She shuddered, her breath coming back and irregular as she knelt, shivering like she had a fever.

"I'm alive," she wheezed. "I'm alive."

She had to keep reminding herself she was alive. That she wasn't the one who had died. That she wasn't dying now.

It took longer than she wanted to admit for the shaking to stop, for her breathing to return to normal, for feeling to return to her arm. The nausea didn't settle as she slowly pushed herself to her feet, swaying but staying upright.

She had no memories of actually dying, just suddenly waking up staring down at her sick body and Lady Death, silent and tall, next to her. But feeling Lars's death felt familiar. It felt like what she'd felt but hadn't remembered until now. Nausea grew until she was gagging, mouth thick with spit, and she had to breathe heavily through her nose before the feeling settled.

"That—" She huffed. "Was a terrible idea."

She stumbled through the house back to her window, and just as clumsily as she'd entered, crawled back out. It was made more difficult by trying to keep her ungloved hand from touching anything it would leave a print on. Eventually, she got outside, then slid the window shut and put the screen back in place before heading back to her car.

It was nearly dark, the sun just barely peaking over the horizon.

Shit, she swore to herself and started her car. She'd been inside much longer than she wanted to be.

And for what? She shook her head as she pulled away from the curb; she was no closer to figuring out who the hooded person was. All she'd gained was a searing migraine, rolling nausea, a bad taste in her mouth, and a memory she didn't want.

Her headache didn't lessen as the night went on, unfortunately. May hadn't really learned anything for her trouble, which made her mood worse as she lay on her couch scrolling through various social media apps. She'd learned how he died, sure, but nothing that would help Fabio or Lady Death.

On an impulse, May switched to *Facebook* and searched for Lars's profile. She found it easily enough, though he didn't seem to really post anything to it. A few memes and random profile photo updates, but nothing else. She clicked through his friends list, which was short: his estranged wife, an aunt named Martha Jameson, a sister named Victoria Thormunt, and a few random friends.

May spent a few minutes clicking through the family's pages only to be equally disappointed when she saw that Victoria never posted and his aunt, Martha, only shared stupid recipe videos.

"That would literally never make a cake," May muttered as she tossed her phone away. "Why do people watch those stupid 'hack' videos?"

She reached over her head to the side table and felt around for the compact before finally finding it. Clicking it open, she looked at the shiny, reflective surface.

"Um, hello?" Silence. "Fabio?"

More silence.

"Fine," she muttered, and clicked it shut.

She must've dozed after that because when knocking jerked her awake, the apartment was dark and her back was cramped from lying on her old sofa.

"Wha..." she muttered, and looked around. Her headache was gone, but she had cottonmouth from her nap on the couch.

Knocking again, louder.

Loki hissed from the hallway.

May clambered from the couch and hurriedly opened the door to an angry-looking Armeal.

"Oh," she said as she stepped aside so he could enter. "Why didn't you just pop in like how you left?"

Armeal glared at her. "Because you've now warded your apartment."

Right...

May flipped on a light switch and cleared her throat.

"Have you found something?" he asked dryly.

May shrugged and folded her arms. "I went back to the scene with the Reaper cloak. I didn't really find much, but I did see how he died."

Armeal's eyes widened. "How?"

"I..." May hedged. "I touched some of the aether."

Armeal's already wide eyes threatened to fall out of his pretty face as he eyed her up and down. "And you still live."

May spread her arms. "Clearly. Look." She snapped to get his attention as he continued to stare at her. "The guy didn't know what he saw, but he saw something wearing a Reaper cloak and holding the blade of a scythe."

Armeal frowned at her.

"Well... he saw a thing wearing a hood, and it sorta"—May wiggled her fingers—"shimmered. I made the logical leap. He'd had a near-death experience, maybe he could see ghosts and stuff too."

Armeal didn't seem convinced. "Perhaps," he drawled as he continued to look her up and down and... Did he just sniff her?

"What!" she snapped at him.

"Humans cannot survive touching the aether. Yet you touched it *and* saw the last memory. Something only Death can do."

May blinked at his words as they stole any response she had.

"Not even the eldest of the Nephilim can do such a feat."

The silence was loud as those words settled into her. Armeal watched her carefully, his inhuman gaze searching.

"What are you?"

It was asked with curiosity, and as she stared back at the Nephilim, she saw he wanted an actual response.

"I'm a witch," she muttered.

He tilted his head at her, waiting for more.

"Just a witch," she said, firmer than she felt.

He hummed and finally looked away. "If you insist."

His answer angered her more than she expected it to, so she reached for her apartment door in a huff.

"Get out."

He watched her again as he passed, softly saying, "If you insist."

CHAPTER TWENTY-SIX
AN ANGEL'S AUDACITY

Harper waited in the dark hospital room. The only light was the blue glow from the screens and monitors. The soft beeping, growing slower and slower, the only sound. The young man appeared asleep in the bed. He was pale and thin, skin sagging around his skeleton. The knitted beanie had come off his head at some point, and it laid crumpled on the edge of the pillow. One last beep, then the flat line. This time there was no rush of doctors, just a single nurse who checked his pulse and checked the machine again before noting the time in his chart. The man's soul slipped from his body and appeared next to Harper.

It was a repetitive thing. A dying person in a hospital bed. Before humans had created this thing they called modern medicine, deaths were in homes. They were surrounded by family, by loved ones. It wasn't so cold. It wasn't so... clinical. The deaths were so drawn out and painful. In their attempt to lengthen life, humans had also lengthened suffering.

He glared at her with tears brimming his eyes. Lips pressed tight against the anger and regret and sorrow she could see in his eyes. She held her hand out, but he refused to take it. Harper blinked softly and moved to grasp his wrist. He was stiff and resistant in her hand, but he had no choice now. He'd fought until he couldn't and still had that spirit to him. For a split second, she had the thought to argue with him. She hadn't given him cancer. This wasn't her choice. She was simply here to help him to the next point in his journey. After splitting the layers of the world, she pulled the soul into the Underworld with her.

Her grip on the soul loosened as her feet touched the snowy ground. It slipped from her fingers silently and floated off into the trees. Harper suspected that one would wander for some time before finding peace. If it ever did. She watched the soul disappear through the trees before taking a deep breath and heading toward her castle. As she cleared the Forgotten Forest, the Maw opened ahead of her, and she paused.

The hair stood on the back of her neck as Harper looked around the snowy plane. Magic ghosted across her skin on the wind, and it stung. She hissed at the recognizable burning pain of Celestial magic.

"Interloper!" She stormed across the plane, hounds howling at her scream.

Her boots thundered on the obsidian stairs, her angry steps cracking the stone beneath her. Nerwen strode away from the wall, and Harper slid to a stop.

"Which one?" she asked, eyes narrowing over the Reaper's shoulder into the Great Hall.

"Raphael."

Harper's breath hissed between her teeth. "An Archangel." She slid her eyes to Nerwen. "Hide the young ones."

"Do you think this is the first wave?" Nerwen asked, her wings quivering.

"That's what I intend to find out." Harper moved into the Great Hall.

In the center of her hall, stood the Archangel Raphael. As if this was *his* hall. His wings, glorious white things, were fanned out behind him. His Celestial magic radiated from him in a glow—the halo that humans who'd had the misfortune of seeing a Celestial believed was a sign of righteousness. Harper slowly stepped closer to the angel, flexing her clawed fingers one by one.

"You are trespassing, angel." Her voice echoed in the hall.

Raphael turned his too-wide eyes, too far apart in his skull to ever be mistaken as human, to her. "Death." He blinked and clicked his teeth.

"You do not belong here."

His pale eyes looked around the hall, and Harper could sense Old Ones moving around the edge of the great black room. He dropped his folded arms, his hands slipping free of the long cream sleeves.

"Reach for your magic or that sword, and I will rip your wings from your spine."

His eyes cut to her, but his hands stilled. Harper stepped closer, ignoring the burning pain of his magic against hers. "What is your purpose here?"

"I do not understand you, Death." Raphael ignored her question, his pale eyes looking past her again to the Reapers lining the walls. "You do not need the help of these vermin. You have suffered much since bringing them in." He finally turned back to her. "Why do you bother? They are not your kin."

She heard feathers ruffle and shift behind her in the still air. Out of the corner of her eye, she saw Luras shift the grip on his scythe.

"My reasons are mine and not for you to wonder at."

Raphael sighed and looked askance at her. "Everyone wonders why you took in the strays. Death walks alone, after your siblings waged devastation, war, and suffering." He gestured at the gathering Nephilim with fingers too long, like a spider's legs. "What do they do? Where is their purpose?"

Her jaw clenched. He may be an angel, but he was in *her* domain. The Underworld was forbidden to their kind, like she was forbidden from theirs. That he stood here, in her home, insulting her, was a slight she would not bear. She would not be lectured like a lesser thing. Her magic answered, unfurling in a brilliant green flare around her. She reached into the depths of the Maw, to the countless imprisoned souls—the demons, the monsters—and drank in the power of the dead. It flooded her veins.

Her hounds howled and barked in the distance. Their cries rose into a cacophony of sound that even the damned feared. Raphael's eyes shifted again. Even the angels feared her hounds.

She pushed her magic on him, and the thin green strands wrapped around him as it tore from her fingertips. They circled his neck, settled on his shoulders, and tightened around his wings. His skin burned black like ash where her magic touched. His glow dimmed. The luster of his skin paled. His eyes widened as his feathers dulled. As *her* magic conquered *his*. She *pushed* her magic on him, the power of the dead, until his knees buckled under the strain and he fell with a grunt.

She flexed her hand, tightening her magic around him, and smiled at the sight, much like a trussed-up bird.

"Do not lecture me on my own *existence*, bird." She tipped his chin with her claw, the point held daintily to his stony flesh. "I was a being before you were even a consideration."

Raphael strained, the veins in his neck bulging as he withstood her magic crashing against his. It burned her, the two magics crashing together, but she withstood it. Her skin started to burn, patches of red spreading up her arms, but not half as bad as his. She pushed her claw into his chin and forced his neck to bend even more as she stared down into his eyes.

"The arrogance you have"—she bent low—"to come here to *my* domain and lecture *me*."

She stepped back, releasing her magic, and Raphael stood with a growl and falling feathers. He shook his wings angrily as his face flushed red. Already, the blackened marks were fading.

"Why," she asked again, stalling whatever rampage he was preparing for, "are you here?"

Raphael snarled, his lips curling away from blunt teeth. "We know the Agreement is in jeopardy. Get your house in order, or we will rescind our side of it."

Harper stilled, as did the Reapers along the walls.

"This is your only warning." He stepped back, shaking his robes straight, and flexed his wings, knees bent, and, in a blinding flash of magic, disappeared.

A low growl vibrated in her throat as she turned to face the Old Ones. Her burns faded, and soon, her skin was smooth and pale once more. Nerwen pushed through the Reapers, eyes wide and nervous. Luras peeled away from the far wall and slowly approached.

"We cannot risk a war with the angels," Luras said. "The Fae perhaps, but not the angels. Not both."

Harper turned to him with a jerk. "You will risk war with my siblings if we don't do as he says. Once they get involved, I am bound to follow them."

"I remember," Luras said gravely.

Nerwen shifted. "I've been watching. All the pairs are accounted for. None are missing. No reports of Nephilim not doing their duty."

"Which means," Harper said, and rolled her shoulders

against the tightness in her back, "that either they are hiding better than we think, or there are more traitors than we expect."

The two shifted, their eyes meeting in a nervous glance.

"Lady Death," Armeal's voice boomed through the hall as he strode toward them.

Harper quickly dismissed Luras and Nerwen with a look. They both shuffled away as she turned to Armeal. He carried a small canvas bag in one hand, and it was weighed down by whatever round-shaped thing it carried. His golden eyes raked over her, a deep frown marring his forehead.

"I heard an angel was here."

She snorted and shook out her hands. "The audacity of those things." She sighed and grew grave. "Things are worse than we thought if the angels are interfering."

He nodded. "Indeed, Death." He held up the bag he carried and dropped it into her waiting hand. She felt the weight of the item and the roundness of it. She loosened the drawstring and let the bag fall open. A skull, bleached white by the sun, stared up at her. Pointy canine teeth in the upper jaw. The lower mandible was missing, but she knew a Nephilim skull when she saw one.

"I believe I found Talsk."

"Where?"

Armeal sighed, and the sound was enough to extinguish her anger and exhaust her. He sounded tired and defeated. "In a canyon outside the city the mortals call Phoenix."

"Of course it was," she muttered, shoulders dropping. She stared at the skull, but not even her anger could rouse her from the exhaustion she now felt. "Just his skull?"

Armeal nodded. "Whoever did this was smart enough to scatter his remains. The scent was so faint I struggled to find even this."

"His scythe?"

Armeal shook his head, and Harper's stomach sunk.

"There's more," he said, and slipped his hand into his suit pocket to pull out a scrap of Reaper cloak. He held it out to her. She took it stiffly.

"This was Yrien's." She could smell the scent easily; it haunted her still. It had been following her. "Where did you find this?"

He sighed again. "Your witch had it. She said she found it at the scene of a stolen soul."

They were both silent as the uncomfortable truth started to settle around them.

"How sure," Armeal asked, his voice soft, "are we that she is dead?"

I killed her myself, Harper thought as she stared at the cloth, but everything pointed to her. Everything pointed to someone who was dead.

"I don't know," she finally said, her voice a whisper in the hall.

CHAPTER TWENTY-SEVEN
PAD THAI AND NAMES

May hesitated, staring at her phone screen with Det. Harding's contact before clicking the little call icon. It rang through to voicemail, which is where May's courage gave out, so she hurriedly ended the call before the recording finished. She let a breath out and dropped her phone to her desk.

"Stupid," she muttered, and turned to her computer screen.

She had Lars Benion's case file pulled up on her screen. It was still pending. Like she told Dimples it would be. She wanted to ask about the investigation and pester him for information. Something more useful than what she'd been able to learn. But pestering a homicide detective for information about their case was risky. They were a territorial bunch and even more suspicious. She wanted information, but not at the risk of alienating him.

As if her thoughts summoned him, her phone rang with Det. Dimples's name lighting up the screen.

"Hello."

"Hey," Det. Harding's voice came through, "I saw you called. What's up?"

"Hey, hi." May glanced at the autopsy report. "So, what's up?"

Muffled voices in the background overlapped Harding's. "Uh, nothing really. You called?"

Shit, that's right. "Oh," May hedged, pen twirling frantically in her fingers. "I was just checking in on the Benion case. Have you guys gotten any further on it? The doc was asking."

Always blame someone higher up.

A pause. "Uh, a bit."

"Yeah?"

Harding paused again, and May worried she'd pressed too hard too soon. Then she heard him take a deep breath. "Well, I'm pretty sure I've identified the guy in that suspicious car. Luckily, one of the houses around the corner had a doorbell camera that *just barely* caught his plate."

May's heart sped up. "Oh, that's great!"

"Yeah, so now I'm just tracking that down."

May nodded again, even though Det. Harding couldn't see, and chewed her nail. "And you think he's your suspect?"

"Maybe," he said noncommittally.

May rubbed her forehead. She wanted the name but felt dirty asking for it. It wasn't information she would normally have access to, even though he'd probably tell her if she asked. He was nice that way. Sharing.

There was more laughter and talking in the background. "Hey, I'm on the phone!" Harding shouted, and then more muffled voices. "No, that's the shittiest restaurant in the city," he said to someone in the background.

May chuckled.

"Sorry, my squad wants to go get Chinese at that skeevy place on Main and Ninth."

"Oh." May laughed. "No, not that place. There are so many better options!"

"Ya, but they give half off to cops so..."

"I'm still not sure that's worth the tummy troubles." May laughed.

Det. Harding echoed her laugh. "It's not. Hey..." He paused, and May held her breath. "Wanna grab some lunch?"

She checked the time, a little early for her lunch break, but she could make it work. "Sure. Where at?"

"You pick. Anywhere that's not going to give me a code brown."

May laughed, gasping into the phone. "That's not a real thing!"

"It is!" Det. Harding laughed. "I swear!"

May tried to control her giggling, her breaths coming in rapid gasps. "How about the Thai place by the theater?"

"Yeah, I can do that. On fifth, right?"

"Yup." May was already grabbing her oversized purse. "See you in fifteen."

It wasn't until she was standing in the restaurant lobby, hands clenched around the strap of her purse, that she thought accepting a lunch date in order to pry information from the cute detective might be a little shitty. But she was already here, so she'd have to deal.

"Hey," Ethan Harding said as he walked up next to her, sliding sunglasses on top of his head, his smile dimpling his cheeks.

The waiter nodded at them and directed them to a quiet

corner table in the back of the crowded restaurant. May took a seat, dropping her bag over the back of the chair.

"This place looks great," Ethan said as he scanned the QR code for the menu.

May nodded but didn't bother to look. This was a regular haunt for her, and she knew exactly what she wanted.

"Back again!" Lek said enthusiastically as he approached their table. He was a short man, thin and wiry, with a mop of dark hair falling into his eyes.

May smiled at Lek. "Of course!"

Lek turned his dark eyes to Ethan. "Ooh, and you brought a friend." He smiled meaningfully at May. "This is new."

May felt her cheeks burning, and Ethan watched the interaction with a soft smile and wide eyes.

"So, what do you want?" Lek asked Ethan in his thick, clipped Thai accent.

"Oh, I don't know yet." He gestured to May. "Start with the lady."

Lek scoffed. "Oh, she's going to get her regular." May smiled and nodded. "See. I know."

Ethan chuckled and hurriedly glanced through the menu on his phone. "Um, I'll do a chicken pad Thai."

"Good, good. How spicy? Level goes one to five."

"I'll do a four, thanks."

"Ah..." May stopped Lek from walking away. "Is Mom cooking?"

Lek grinned and nodded.

"Yeah, he's gonna do a three."

Ethan looked back and forth at them before saying, "Sounds like a three."

May turned to a bewildered-looking Ethan.

"Come here a lot?" he asked with a laugh.

She matched his laugh. "It's really good and close to the office."

They were quiet for a moment as the laughter settled with the awkward silence that comes between new acquaintances.

"So," Ethan finally said, leaning forward, "you think it was a murder, right?"

May blinked, the abrupt change in conversation jolting her from her thoughts. She reminded herself to stay cautious. She *knew* it was murder; the certainty sat heavy in her chest, but how could she possibly explain that? A premonition whispered from a soul didn't belong in any case file. It barely belonged in the real world, and yet here she was, carrying it like a secret too strange to share. "I don't think it was a simple fall that broke Mr. Benion's neck, no."

Ethan nodded and clasped his hands on the table. "Okay. See. I don't think so either, but the rest of my squad thinks I'm trying to find a murder where there isn't one."

"Why do you think that? Is your squad just"—she shrugged—"missing something or...?"

Ethan huffed and shrugged, shaking his head while staring down at the table. "Just a gut feeling. I don't know. The whole thing just feels weird. I can't really explain why. And that weird car just sitting down the street?" He shrugged again. "I just want to run everything down so I can know for sure."

Lek returned and placed a water glass in front of Ethan and a tall bright-orange Thai ice tea in front of her. She couldn't help the gleeful squeal she let out as she stabbed a straw into the drink.

"So, what are you going to do?" she asked after sucking down a mouthful of the sweet drink.

"Well, I'm going to track down this James person and see what's up with him. I'm having forensics process the bottles that were on scene for prints, maybe I'll get lucky. Although, they're pissed."

May grimaced. She remembered the dozens of beer cans and bottles littering the floor.

"So, this James guy..." May eased in. "He the guy in the car?"

She fluttered her fingers, pulling the littlest bit of magic and pushing it across the table.

Ease the lips and loosen the mind, let slip the words of secrets bind.

As soon as the magic settled in Ethan's chest, the guilt settled in hers. It was a slippery slope, using magic to influence others but she needed to know. She needed this information. Her mother's words came back to her, that some magic was evil no matter how it was used. Was this wrong? She cringed to herself. She knew it was. Influencing people was dirty. But was doing so with magic really any different than charismatic people doing it with words? Or was this what it looked like when someone tried to justify their wrongdoings?

She shook herself. More than just his case rested on the information he had. In this instance, she decided it was worth it. Just this once.

"Yeah." He nodded and leaned back as a steaming plate of pad Thai was placed in front of him. May smiled at her giant bowl of Tom Ka. "James Thormunt. He's got a history of a lot of suspicious activities. Neighbors seem to be creeped out by him. A few thefts from gas stations. Nothing crazy violent, though."

"Hm." May frowned. Why was that name familiar? "But he was outside Benion's house?"

"Yeah. He drives this old green Honda," Ethan said, and took a quick gulp of water. "Holy shit, this is hot."

May giggled. "And you wanted the four."

"Normally, I can do spicy," Ethan protested, and sipped more water.

"Not when Mom's cooking." She giggled. "She cooks like she's still in Thailand. White-people spicy isn't a thing she can do."

"Clearly." He cleared his throat and continued. "Yeah, anyway. This James guy was seen by neighbors a couple of times sitting down the street, and a few even caught him in their cameras. As far as I can tell, dude doesn't live in the area. It's residential, so it's not like he's going to work through there. It's suspicious."

May nodded and spooned sour coconut soup into her mouth. It was definitely weird. She pushed aside the guilt of sneaking the information from him with a spell. It was necessary. Wasn't it?

They ate their lunch quickly, Ethan going through three more glasses of water in the process. He was called back to his office as they were finishing, sparing her an awkward goodbye as they returned to their jobs.

She hadn't learned much, but she had a name. And nowadays, everyone was online.

May sipped her wine, laptop open and balanced on her thighs, as she scrolled through different open-source people searches. James Thormunt was a unique enough name that luckily, there weren't a ton of results to sift through. After a quick *Google* search and then again to *Facebook*, May finally figured out why the name had felt familiar. James Thormunt was married to Victoria, Lars's sister.

She chewed her lip and eyed her phone. She should tell Harding. It was the nice thing to do after he'd given her the name. Even if it was helped along by her spell...

She huffed and picked up her phone.

> Me: Sorry for the late message, but I was looking through Lars's file and saw his next of kin is listed as his sister.
>
> Victoria Thormunt

She picked at her lip.

> Det. Dimples: Yeah, we caught that when we ran history on Benion

May huffed. Obviously, the cops would've figured that out without her.

> Det. Dimples: We're tracking James down tomorrow to see if he'll explain why he was in the area when Lars died. But now it looks a bit less suspicious that he was in the area of his brother-in-law's place.

"Oh." She sighed as she read his message.

That was disappointing. She tossed her phone away and looked back to her laptop. Loki jumped up, purring, and curled into her hip, staring at her.

"Don't judge me."

He blinked and tucked his head onto his paws.

She clicked submit on the screen to pay the extra twenty-five dollars to get expanded results. Maybe there was still something with James Thormunt worth checking out.

"I feel like a stalker," she muttered, and sipped more wine. "But damn, the stuff you can find online."

The results loaded on the page, and soon, she was looking

at two addresses, both within the city, a date of birth, and even a telephone number.

"This really should be illegal."

Loki chirped and twisted against her, throwing his paws in the air as he rolled upside down. She scratched his chin and was rewarded with air biscuits and more purrs. May checked the time on her computer—10:42.

She chewed her lip and finished her wine. Before she could change her mind, she snapped photos of the addresses with her phone and pushed off the couch. Loki chirped at being disturbed and leapt from the couch, meowing the whole way to the bedroom.

Nodding, and not letting herself think too hard on what she was going to do, she shoved her feet into her sneakers and grabbed her keys.

The drive to the first address was quick, especially this late at night, even though it was on the other side of town from her apartment. As she approached the house, a small bungalow in an older neighborhood, she turned her headlights off. She crept by, squinting at the house and looking for a green Honda. She didn't know what model of car, but any green thing at this point would do.

The driveway had a motorcycle parked next to the house, and no green car. With a sigh, she turned the corner in the neighborhood and flicked her lights back on.

"Let's see what the second one has," she muttered, and punched the address into her GPS, then frowned at the map.

"Well, this already feels more correct," she whispered as she traced the path to the far edges of the city.

She took a deep breath and started driving. As she got farther out on the winding side roads and the lights of the city faded behind her, her palms grew sweaty. Her heart was in her throat, and more than once, she checked that she still had cell service.

You're so stupid, she thought as she pulled down a long lane off the main road.

There were farmhouses on the lane spaced far apart with land separating them. The road was dark, no streetlights dotted the soft shoulder. A few houses had lights on, a window here or there, a porch light, but many were dark. Her GPS alerted the house was coming up on her right, so she slowed down. She didn't bother turning her lights off this time. The houses were set back from the road far enough she doubted many would notice a lone car driving by. As she passed the correct house, the hair on the back of her neck stood up.

In the dirt driveway leading to the house, sat a little green passenger car. The light over the side door to the house was on, haloing the car. A light was on in the upper window of the two-story house.

She wanted to leave, to drive away and forget she'd ever come looking for this house and its green car. She sped past the drive to do just that and grabbed the black lion head totem she kept in her pocket. The soft zing of magic fell from her, and she shook her head as the totem dispelled the magic.

That was a powerful aversion spell.

She kept her grip on the totem and drove farther down the lane until she was away from the house. Well past the house, she pulled onto the shoulder and shut off the car. She wanted to know more about the magic on the house and that aversion spell.

Shaking out her hands and taking a deep breath, May quietly closed her car door and walked along the dark shoulder back toward the house. The yard was enclosed with a chainlink fence from the roadway with a gate closed across the gravel driveway. She held her hand out, fingers soft and questioning as she felt for the spell that had turned her away.

Again, she was hit with the terrifying feeling, the urge to run away, to leave and forget. But she was expecting it this time and gritted her teeth against the sensation, even as it made her hands shake and heart race.

The magic woven around the property felt... wrong, slimy against her fingers, tainted. She shook her hand out and pulled it back, fingers curling into her palm.

"What the hell," she muttered under her breath, and crept along the fence line.

She moved slowly, carefully, watching the porch and windows as she did. The magic seemed to follow along the fence.

Another light flicked on in the house, and May fell into a crouch in the darkness. She held her breath, heart hammering in her chest and ears as she waited for a door to open, a shout to break the silent night. But nothing came, and after what felt like hours, the light went off again and the house was dark.

Hands sweaty and shaking, May slowly, terribly slowly, retreated from the fence and away from the house. She stayed in her crouch, legs burning and knees cracking, until she reached her battered Beetle. She crawled inside with a huff and stuttering breath, sweat slipping down her temples.

"Well," she said, panting as she started her car, "I think I found him."

It was disgustingly late when May finally slunk into bed. When her alarm went off what felt like seconds after her head hit the pillow, she groaned and flung her hand out to silence the offensive sound.

"Shit," she groaned, and pushed herself upright. If she didn't sit up now, she wouldn't make it to work.

She dragged herself into the shower and got dressed, barely leaving her apartment in time to make it to work without being late. An hour later, she fell into her chair with a heavy sigh and a full cup of coffee, still wishing she was asleep.

"Late night?" Sarah asked as she walked by.

"Yeah," May said, nursing her coffee.

"You're not on call, are you?"

"No," May said, hoping Sarah would leave her alone soon. "Just a late night."

"Ooooh," Sarah breathed, and waited for more details, but when May just blinked sleepily at her, she huffed a sigh and left.

Her phone dinged with a text from Det. Harding, but she ignored it and called her mom instead.

"Morning. Are you okay?"

"Yeah, why wouldn't I be?"

"Because you never call while you're at work," her mom chided.

Oh. "My bad," she said, and cleared her throat. "I had a question."

"About?"

She checked over her shoulder and lowered her voice to a soft whisper. "Do you know what kind of magic leaves a slimy residue on the spell?"

Silence was followed by another cluck of her tongue. "Only one thing I know of that leaves a slimy residue: Necromancy."

Shit. "Thanks."

"Why?"

"You don't want to know. Thanks, Mom." She ended the call and dropped her head against the back of her chair.

Shit, she thought again, and looked at the text from Ethan.

> Det. Dimples: You won't believe what I found.

That made May straighten up.

> Me: What'd you find?!

She waited, staring at the screen as the "read" message finally popped up under her text. Then the three dots. And then...

> Det. Dimples: Thormunt's car was in the area of the Chandler homicides.

May's hands stilled. Whatever doubt she might've had that Thormunt was connected to the homicides, disappeared. The fact he was neck deep in Necromancer magic didn't make her feel any better either. At best, it meant he was versed in more magic than she was. At its worst, it meant he was exponentially more powerful than she was.

CHAPTER TWENTY-EIGHT
LEY LINES

Standing on the balcony, Harper watched the Reapers moving through the courtyard below. They moved in pairs, as they'd been instructed to. A sharp bark ringing through the cold silence pulled her attention away from the conspiring Nephilim and to her hounds. A group had gathered near the edge of the Maw, and their barks and growls grew in intensity. She pushed away from the balcony and leaped over it. Wind rushed at her, pulling her black coat up and streaming her hair behind her. Then her boots thudded to the ground, her knees bending to absorb the energy of the fall before she strode toward the Maw.

She stormed toward her hounds as they growled and yipped at the precipice of the Maw. With a snap of her fingers, the writhing mass of bodies moved, and Harper stepped to the edge. Her hands clenched, claws digging into her palms, as she took in the hoard of damned pushing against the boundary. It flared and bowed against the souls' efforts. Stretching out her hand, she extended her magic along the boundary. Like an extension of her, her magic moved along the woven magic. She felt for gaps, for weakening threads, for holes. Her magic found none... yet.

Taking a deep breath, Harper *pulled* her magic to her and flung her arms wide. Her magic rushed from her—her life force, her will—and she wove it into the barrier. The shimmering magic flared a bright green as she reinforced the shield against the damned.

The souls moaned and screeched, many turning and fleeing as she entwined her own soul into the barrier. Harper's arms fell to her sides as the damned disappeared back to the depths of the Maw.

Her hounds soon dispersed and resumed their patrols along the Maw's long shore. A few Reapers nodded their hooded heads as she passed. As much as she would never admit it to him, Armeal had been correct. The Reapers didn't want a family, but they needed direction. Order. Since Armeal had tasked Nerwen and Luras with organizing them, she had noticed an ease that hadn't been there before. An acceptance, almost, in the air. Even if they were still angry at being paired together. Many took it as an insult to their strength, but that was what she got for dealing with Nephilim pride. Luras and Nerwen dealt with the moods and rebukes.

Even with the Reapers settling, she was still tense. The missing souls were causing imbalance in the Underworld, and the dead seemed to sense it. As Reapers passed her, she couldn't stop herself from studying each and every one. Was this one betraying her? Was that one the thief? Was this the one that killed Talsk?

The murder of a Nephilim was a hard task. They were not killed easily. Was it the Fae? One had already attacked. Had they started attacking earlier? There were too many questions.

Back in her office and surrounded by the smell of parchment and old leather, the tightness in her shoulders eased some. She leaned over her desk, hands braced on either side of the Book of Souls, and glanced through the names. Many that had glowed a soft light were now inked in black—souls collected. Only a few remained.

A soft tremor of thought, an inquiring thread, touched the edge of her mind, so Harper glanced up at the closed door.

"Come," she called, and settled herself in the chair.

Dark hair fell across her cheeks, and she brushed it behind her ear.

The door creaked open, and a Reaper glided into the room. It came to stand in front of her desk and tapped the butt of its scythe on the marbled floor as it stopped. She blinked at it, waiting.

"Death." The voice was low, not yet the papery wispy sound of the older Reapers. "The Old One paired to me has not returned."

She straightened in her high-backed chair. "What?"

Its pale hand tightened on the staff of the scythe. "We were sent for a soul. Once in the mortal lands, the Old One disappeared. I waited, but then the soul needed collecting, and I could wait no longer."

Her claws dug into the carved armrest. "How did the other Reaper simply *disappear*?"

Again, the pale hand clenched its staff. "We were late to the soul. It had already wandered. We had to search the area for it. We separated in order to find the soul."

The muscle in her jaw twitched, and she had to unclench her teeth.

"It is our duty to fetch the souls." The Reaper's voice was angry now, defiant.

"Of course," Harper said. "I do not fault you for finding the soul. Your duty is always first to the soul."

The Reaper's hand relaxed on the staff, and the hood dipped with a small nod.

"Do you know the Old One's name?"

"He called himself Enil."

"Which soul did you collect?"

The Reaper frowned and then leaned forward to peer at the open Book of Souls on Harper's desk. She pointed a bone-thin finger to a name.

Harper nodded and forced her claws to retract from the chair. "Thank you."

The Reaper retreated from the room, swishing robes the only sound. Harper drummed her fingers on the arms of her chair. That soul was collected from Phoenix. She clenched her jaw. Everything centered on that desert land. Why?

May.

That was the only thing she could think of. May was at the center of this all. She just didn't understand why.

Even in the moonlit sky, it was hot in this desert. Heat radiated up from the baked earth through her boots, in the air as it brushed against her cheeks. This late in the year, even the low shrubs had dried and shriveled, their leaves brown and dry. Harper snorted in irritation and turned to face the breeze. She'd started in the center of Phoenix and slowly, methodically, worked her way around and out until she was finally walking the desert that surrounded the southern side of the city. She'd searched, sensed, *tasted* the air as she'd gone, looking for that haunting magic.

The desert seemed nearly endless until—

There!

Her head snapped toward the scent, faint but there.

Yrien.

She followed the smell deeper into the desert toward a lone mountain in the flat lands. As she neared the mountain, she noticed motes of magic in the air, swirling and glittering. The magic grew thicker as she came to the outcropping of rock surrounded by tall cacti and twiggy bushes.

Here, the magic swirled and settled.

Why here?

Harper searched the area. She pulled the air into her mouth, tasted it, scented it, and frowned. It stopped. As if the being had simply disappeared. As if…

Harper bent and touched the earth beneath her, *feeling* for the magic that coursed through the earth. She found it buried and nearly forgotten in the day and age. A Ley Line.

The path all magic takes from point to point. A gathering of magics. The earth was covered in Ley Lines, like a spider's web draped across the earth. The points could be formed by a gathering of magical beings, like the Fae's courts, or if a particularly strong magical calamity happened. Or in a natural place magic gathers. And Phoenix happened to have one of those points.

She growled, slicing through the air with a swift swipe of her claws, then stepped through the portal to where the Ley Line ended. Her feet landed in a splash of shallow water. Ahead of her, loomed tall canyon walls, rock a deep red that permeated the area. The small river ran between them, spindly grass filling the low banks. She'd been here before. The rock climber had died in this canyon. Her lips peeled back with another snarl.

This time the scent was easy to catch. It flowed with the winds from the narrow canyon. Hands clenched tight, Harper walked downstream into the canyon. She followed it to a bend, a little pool nestled into a cutout in the canyon wall. She trudged to the bank, soaked to her waist. Her coat was a heavy weight on her shoulders, and with an angry shrug of her shoulders, she magicked the water away.

The magic in the air pooled and gathered against the canyon wall, but the trail seemed to end there. It simply... disappeared.

"They're hiding in the Ley Lines," Harper spoke to the air.

That's how the Old One, whoever carried Yrien's scent, had stayed hidden for so many centuries. By remaining in the Ley Lines, emerging only when necessary. Only an immortal being could exist in the pure magical realm of a Ley Line. It would be painful. The magic would threaten to pull it apart, but an immortal being, a *Nephilim*, could manage it.

Teeth grinding together, Harper felt blood drip from her palms as her claws cut into them. With an inhuman shout, a growl of a sound, she slammed her fist into the canyon wall, leaving a crack in its wake. The sound reverberated like a whip, and birds nestled in the bush took flight in a startled burst.

She was beginning to wonder if Yrien was truly dead, and if she wasn't, how in the heaven and hells had she survived having her heart ripped out.

Back in her office, Book of Souls open before her, she huffed a sigh and looked to the stoic Nephilim waiting before her. He wisely did not comment on her brooding mood, though his second eyelid flicked shut.

"Another is missing."

His shoulders shifted with his breath.

"Enil," she said.

He nodded.

She stared down at her Book of Souls, at the names that glowed and flickered. Many were inked in black, but more, simply flickered. Souls waiting, wandering. Not being collected.

Reapers were not collecting souls.

He seemed to notice her gaze as he shifted his stance. "Nerwen reports pairs are finding that the soul they were sent for is missing." He took a deep breath. "And now another Reaper is missing."

Has he been killed like Talsk? Or is he helping steal the souls?

"I will search for him."

Harper sighed again. "They are using the Ley Lines to hide."

His feathers ruffled, soft and raspy. "Could even a Nephilim survive for long in a Ley Line?"

Harper rolled her shoulders. "Not without great pain and torture. It would test even the strongest of you."

"It will be," Armeal said, his words stiff and halting, "nearly impossible to find a Nephilim in a Ley Line."

"I know," she whispered, and the words felt like a defeat, an admission.

The words hung heavy in the air around them, and they both were silent as it settled across their shoulders. The feeling was broken, however, when a sharp, crisp knock on her office door startled them. Luras stood, looking grim as he pushed his hood back.

"Death," he murmured, his eyes moving between her and Armeal, "I searched for you."

"I am here," Armeal stated, eyes narrowed.

"Clearly." Luras sniffed and turned his eyes back to her. "I have heard whisperings among some of the young ones."

"Go on," she said with dread in her belly.

He hesitated for a fraction of a second, but it was enough to make Harper's blood run cold. "They are whispering of choosing a side."

"What... side?"

"They will not say, not to me, and those that may know are keeping the secret." He took a deep breath and planted the staff of his scythe firmly on the stone floor. "But, if I were to guess, the side is either yours or whoever is taking up Yrien's cause."

The words rung around her.

This. Again.

Dread like she hadn't felt before settled in her chest, heavy. It hurt to breathe. Her mouth was too dry to swallow.

Armeal licked his lips. "Do you think"—his voice was stilted—"we are facing another rebellion."

"No," Harper said solemnly. "It has already started. What we risk now, is war with the angels."

Even in death, Yrien was waging her war.

CHAPTER TWENTY-NINE
WE HAVE A MURDER

May scrolled through more of James Thormunt's *Facebook* page, chin propped in her hand. He didn't have much of a social media presence. Anything she could find was years old. He was a normal-looking guy, with dark short-trimmed hair. A scruffy beard. Tan skin. He might have Native American ancestry or Hispanic. Or he might just be tan. The few photos he'd posted showed a smiling, happy-looking man with a pretty lady by his side.

Then about five years ago, the posts stopped. Family post yearly on his birthday, but he never seemed to respond.

"So, what happened to you, Mr. James?" she muttered, and closed the app, tossing her phone aside. "And what do I do now?"

She'd driven past his house once more, but the car hadn't been there. There had been no more murders, that she was aware of, anyway.

So, what was he doing?

The office phone rang, and after a sigh, she answered.

"Medical Examiner's Office, this is May."

"Hey, it's Detective Williams from Oasis Point Police," said a rough voice.

May glanced at the time—

4:40.

On-call hours started at five, and she could easily forward this to the on-call investigators for after-hours work.

Let's see what it is first. If it was smelly, it was definitely going to the after-hours person.

"Hey, detective. What do you have?"

"Hey, we're out on a homicide near the reservation border. I'm giving you a heads-up, we're probably about an hour from being ready for you."

Shit, never mind. May sat up and clicked to pull up her case entry program. "Okay. Do you want to give me the details now, or when you're ready for me?"

"Now's good if you are."

May tucked the phone against her shoulder. "Yup, hit me."

"Got a currently unidentified male. Possibly Native American. We're about half a mile south of State Route two-oh-two, off Princeton Road. I'll text you a pin, it'll be easier. Body was found in the middle of a field."

"Alright." May typed as quickly as she could, keeping up with the detective's words. "How was he found?"

"Some kids looking for a spot to hook up noticed some shoes sticking out of the weeds. Looks like blunt force to his head so far."

"Alright," May said again. "I'll let the doc know. Shoot me a text with the address and when you're ready for us to head down."

"Yes, ma'am."

She drove out with Dr. Kesler nearly an hour and a half later to a nondescript field off the freeway. Businesses lined the roads to the east with a few trailer parks nearby. Mostly, it was farmland or empty field. They followed the GPS directions down a small dirt access road with the glow of red and blue lights in the distance. The ME truck bounced and jerked over the rough road as Dr. Kesler parked behind the Oasis Point major crime trailer. With her heart in her throat, May grabbed her bag and slung it across her shoulders and hopped out of the truck.

Dr. Kesler followed with her own backpack. They picked their way through the tall grass, mostly stomped down by the many boots of the detectives and forensics team.

"Hey, doc," someone hollered in the distance, and May caught a raised hand against the glare of lights.

They met the detective at the edge of the bright-yellow crime scene tape hung limp along the tops of bushes and grass.

"Detective Williams." The older detective held out his hand, first to Dr. Kesler and then to May. "I'm the lead on this one."

"Alright, give me the rundown. May"—Dr. Kesler turned to her—"do you want to start with photos?"

May nodded and pulled her camera from her bag, then started with photos of the edge of the scene while the detective started with his briefing.

"So, dispatch was notified by a 911 call from some kids about 1500 this afternoon. They noticed the man's boots first, and after getting closer, found the body. Forensics have gone through the area, and we can't find any bullet casings. Looks like blunt force to his head, anyway."

"Alrighty." Dr. Kesler paused, and when May glanced over, she saw Dr. Kesler scribbling notes in her little pad. "And have you identified him?"

"We have a tentative ID, but we haven't been able to confirm it yet. I think there's a wallet in his back pocket, though."

"Alright, well you're about to find out, then." She tucked her notebook back into her backpack. "Are we good to go in?"

Det. Williams lifted the crime scene tape and gestured them inside. May followed, careful of where she stepped. The area around the body was flattened, the grass having been trampled by all the officials. He was lying on his side, with his chest flat against the ground. The man's legs were tangled, as were his arms. May's stomach fell as her eyes settled on the body. There was a large bloody wound on the side of his head, and the closer she got, the more it looked like a chunk had been cut away. The blood was crusted and dried, but she could tell it was thick. The man's black hair was stuck to his skin, trapped in the blood, and there was a definitive deviation in the side of the skull. But that wasn't what made her stomach sink. No. It was the silvery, glowing liquid that pooled under the man's chest.

Another soul stolen.

It wasn't a large pool, but it was just visible from her vantage point. She looked around the grass but saw no more of the magical blood. There should've been more.

"He wasn't killed here," she muttered before she could stop herself.

Two sets of curious eyes turned to her.

"Why do you say that?" Dr. Kesler asked.

Det. Williams watched her with a curious intensity.

"Uh..." She swallowed and pointed to the wound on his head. "There should be more blood around him, but it appears mostly contained to him. And the body's positioning implies a body dump."

Dr. Kesler nodded and turned to Det. Williams.

"We also think a body dump." He nodded and pointed north of the body where there was a longer strip of crime scene tape. "Before we smashed all the grass down, there was a distinct track from a vehicle leaving that direction and meeting up with another access road."

"And I concur about the blood," Dr. Kesler said. "Good eye, May."

May nodded and began photographing the body. As she worked, detectives came and went around them. Det. Williams lingered at the edge of the scene until Dr. Kesler reached for the bulge in the man's back pocket and pulled out a thick wallet.

"Detective?" She called him over, looking through it for an ID. She pulled out an old ID, dirty and warn. "Arizona ID for a..." She rubbed the dirt to better see the name. "Aaron Loudhorse Jones."

"Yup, that's who we thought it might be. He's a local transient one of our patrol guys knew."

Dr. Kesler nodded and held the ID out for May to photograph before putting it back in the wallet. Going through the wallet quickly, she found mostly random pieces of paper with scribbling, or cards for local homeless shelters and resources. "Okay, let's roll him, May, and we can grab the last of our photos."

May nodded and stepped around the body as Dr. Kesler gripped Aaron's shoulder and hip, bunching the dirty clothing in her hands.

"One, two, three." She pulled the thin man and rolled him onto his back.

Now, May could fully see his chest and the limp, cut Tether.

Well, she thought as she snapped her photos, *I know what Thormunt was doing when he wasn't at home.*

She completed her photos, and Dr. Kesler finished with the body as the transport team arrived in their body van. May leaned against the hood of the ME truck while they went about the grizzly business of bagging up the body. She checked the time on her phone and groaned. It was past eight, and her growling stomach let her know how upset it was at missing dinner.

"Hey."

May looked up at Det. Dimples as he ambled over. "Hi."

He leaned against the grill next to her and crossed his arms, his sleeves rolled to the elbows in the harsh heat.

The air smelled of blood, warm and rancid. Birds circled high in the sky, and a few brave ones landed in the outskirts, hidden by the tall grass. Ravens cawed around them.

"Got any good leads?"

He shrugged. "Yeah, some. We just got back from canvassing the businesses along the road. A bunch have cameras, but we'll need to hit them again in the morning when they're open."

She nodded. "Do you think our guy, James, is involved?"

He stilled next to her before glancing down at her. "Do you?"

She shrugged, unable to make herself say "yes" when she knew she wouldn't be able to explain.

"It's not really in line with the others," Ethan said, mostly to himself, it seemed. "But his car was at the other scenes in Chandler, and those looked like break-ins. Then the broken next guy. None really have a pattern. So"—he rubbed his chin—"I can't really say this doesn't match when none of them do."

He looked down at her again. "Why do you think he's involved?"

"I didn't say he was."

He watched her, his hazel eyes narrowing the slightest. "I don't know you well, but I've figured out that you're very specific with your questions."

She met his stare but couldn't find any words to give him. Eventually, he nodded and looked away. "I guess we'll see."

It was nearly midnight when May finally dragged herself into her apartment. She was painfully tired, but before she could sleep, she needed to do one more thing.

Tossing her bag onto the floor near her door, she pulled her small compact from her pocket and clicked it open.

"Fabio?" She grimaced. "I mean… Armeal?"

Feeling more than a little silly, she took a deep breath. "I think I figured out who the killer is."

Nothing.

With a sigh, she clicked the compact closed and fell onto her couch in a huff.

"I should get in bed," she muttered to herself, eyes falling shut under the weight of exhaustion. "Or I'ma end up sleeping here."

A tingle across her skin had her sitting up and looking around. Then a shimmering split the air, and soon, Armeal was stepping out of the hole in the world.

May jumped up, heart in her throat. Armeal stared down at her with unreadable eyes.

"You should reactivate your ward," he said. "You found something?"

"Uh," May stuttered, and shook herself. "Yeah."

He blinked at her, white suit impeccable like before.

"I'd offer you tea, but I remember your aversion to decent beverages."

He simply blinked at her again, and she collapsed back onto the couch, too tired to be annoyed.

"I'm pretty sure the person who's responsible for the thefts and murders is this guy named James Thormunt."

Armeal sat stiffly on the other couch, Loki hissing and growling from the corner of the room before running into the bedroom.

"My cat seems to hate you." She folded her arms. "He's a pretty good judge of character."

Armeal was quiet still, and May sighed.

"So," she said, "I sort of thought Lady Death would come since this is like... kind of important information."

He frowned at her. "Lady Death is dealing with her own problems at the moment. It would be wise to not distract her."

"Oh..." She huffed and dropped her head back onto the couch. "Well," she spoke to the ceiling, "I'm pretty sure he's our guy. He's also a Necromancer, which really sucks."

"That is an unfortunate development. Necromancers are..." May lifted her head at his pause. "Troublesome."

She grunted a laugh. "So, now what?"

"He must be stopped. And any cohorts he has must be revealed."

The way he said *stopped*, the coldness in his voice, the finality in his eyes, made May's stomach twist.

"When you say 'stopped,' you mean killed. Don't you?"

Armeal blinked, long and slow, but he never broke eye

contact. "Yes. For his transgressions against Death, his punishment must be death and imprisonment in the Maw."

I do not want to know what that is, May thought, a chill settling over her.

Not because they were talking about murdering someone, but because she had no qualms about it. If James Thormunt was the man behind the murders and stealing souls of countless others she wasn't aware of, he needed to be stopped. Permanently.

A chill settled on her shoulders because she agreed.

"Another Reaper has gone missing," Armeal said, pulling May out of her thoughts. "I may not be able to assist as much as you wish until I locate him."

"Another? Is that... a lot?"

"Yes," Armeal said as he stood with a jerk to his suit. "There are problems brewing in the Underworld. The first Reaper was killed. I must find this one before he suffers the same fate."

"So"—May stood on shaky legs—"killing Thormunt might be up to me?"

She hated the way her voice squeezed at the end.

He met her eyes. "It may."

CHAPTER THIRTY
A LINE OF BLOOD

"How'd you know?"

May jumped, sloshing coffee all over her hands from her too-full mug. "Jesus Chri— " she muttered and held her dripping coffee away from her lap. "What?"

"How'd you know?" The question was harsh and accusatory from Det. Harding, who stood glaring at her from the edge of her cubicle.

"Who let you back here?" May set her coffee down and wiped her hands. "Also, hi, how's your Monday going?"

Her weekend had been filled with crises of morality and consciousness. It should bother her that killing a man may rest on her shoulders, but all she could think about was how not to get arrested for murder. The fact she, a supposed Green Witch, couldn't find one iota of hesitation in her being about killing him, had her spiraling in all sorts of ways. Did that make her evil like her mother lectured? Was she coldhearted for not caring? For only worrying about how to cover up the murder?

It had left her with poor, fitful nights and depressing days before she finally decided she'd worry about that later. When? She didn't know, but later.

Ethan folded his arms and glared down at her. "Well, my Monday is going like this: I come into the office and learn that a vehicle that looks suspiciously like James Thormunt's vehicle was seen on the access road the day the body was discovered. And while the rest of my unit thinks I'm Captain Ahab with this guy, you're the only one that asked if I thought James was involved with our homeless body dump. Which leads me back to, how'd you know?"

Shit. She stood and gripped his arm. "Let's go for a walk."

May led him to the small outdoor break section at the back of their building. There was a picnic table on dry and dying grass under the shade of a tree. Mostly, people came out here to smoke.

"Okay," May said, and let go of him. "I didn't know. I was just... guessing. Hoping?" She shrugged. "I was making small talk. I don't know anything about the murder."

He watched her with narrow eyes. Slowly, the corners of his eyes relaxed and the pull of his mouth loosened. He looked away with a self-conscious laugh.

"I was starting to think you were in on it."

May forced herself to giggle with him. "I'm not nearly that clever!"

Ethan ran a hand through his hair and planted his hands on his hips. "Sorry. I just..." He shook his head. "I know Thormunt is involved. Somehow. I just can't... prove it."

May chewed her lip and felt all sorts of scummy. He was on the right track, and she couldn't tell him that. Though, she could nudge him perhaps. "But..." She drew his attention away from the spot on the ground he was staring at. "You said his car was at the dump site."

"Maybe his car," he corrected with a huff. "The others

don't think so, like I said. But it's his car. The camera was too far away and too grainy to get a plate or much detail, but I know it's his car."

"What was his involvement with the Chandler homicides?"

Ethan shrugged again. "The same as these. His car was in the area. On the same street as one of them. But nothing puts him at the actual homicides."

"Isn't that enough to interview him?"

"Oh—" He huffed. "It's enough. But he won't come in. He'll talk to me over the phone, denies any involvement, and says it's only a coincidence but won't come in for a formal statement."

"What about him being at the Benion scene?"

Ethan sighed a grumbling breath. "Said he was there trying to talk sense into his brother-in-law and get him to go to rehab. They had a verbal argument, and he left."

Oh, May thought.

"And I don't have enough to force him to come in for a formal interview otherwise."

"Really?" May asked.

"Being weird and creepy and suspicious doesn't always equal illegal," he said with a half smile.

She smiled at him, feeling all sorts of shitty again, and thumped him on his shoulder. "I believe in you."

"Thanks."

"So, what are you going to do?"

The heat was baking her, even in the shade of the tree and building. It was too hot to be having this conversation outside, but she wasn't going to leave when he might tell her more.

He gave her his dimpled smile. "Cop stuff. Now, I should leave before I do anything else stupid. Sorry again for barging in like that."

"It's okay," she said as he started to walk off. "Don't you want to go through the building?"

"Nah." He waved her off. "I'll walk it off."

May watched him go, worried about what "cop stuff" meant. Ethan had no defense against a Necromancer. Not as though she did either, but at least she had an idea of what she'd be facing. She chewed her lip, thoughts racing, before succumbing to the heat and returning to the air conditioning inside.

That night, when the sun had well and truly set, May drove out to Thormunt's house. She pulled down the lane, headlights off, and parked on the shoulder again before turning off her car. She could just make out Thormunt's house two houses down. The lights were off as far as she could tell. Her heart hammered in her chest, and her breathing came just a little too fast.

But she was committed to the plan.

Even if it was a little risky.

She slipped her compact out of her purse.

"Armeal?"

"Not now" came the faint reply from the mirror, like a radio from underwater.

"But I need a spell. I need to cast a spell that'll notify me when someone crosses it."

There was that familiar shimmer across her skin, then Armeal was standing next to her car, looking pissed. May hurriedly exited.

"You're a witch, you do it."

"I need your help," May whispered.

"Because you refuse to use the magic in your blood?" he asked dryly.

Folding her arms, she refused to answer that question. She didn't really have an answer, anyway. Was she refusing to use the magic she had? Was she afraid of it? Or was she afraid of what her mother would say about it?

He sighed, his feathers fluttering softly behind him. "Simply place your intent in a line of blood," he said, as if speaking to a child.

"B-but"—she backed into her car door—"I'm not... That's..."

He sighed again and actually had the audacity to roll his eyes. "It is a simple spell."

"But it's *blood magic*," she whispered back harshly.

"Yes." He mimicked her harsh whisper. "What do you think your fire spell is?"

May jerked and gulped. Was that what she'd been doing? Was that why she was so afraid to acknowledge it? He blinked at her before sighing again, then, without another word, sliced his wrist with a blade he pulled out so fast she never saw it. He held his bleeding wrist above the road and walked, dropping a small line of blood across the asphalt before coming back to her.

"Thank—"

He gripped her hand and sliced the knife across her palm before she could say anything and pulled her down, pressing her bleeding palm to the blood on the ground.

"Ow! Asshole!"

Sizzling burned her hand, and the blood drops on the ground glowed a bright red before falling dark again. The power burned through her, stalling any further words she might've had for the Nephilim, as it seemed to burn up her chest.

And then it stopped.

"This way the spell is tied to you. All I did was activate it." Armeal released her and stood as she leaned on her hands and knees, breathing heavily. A cough rose up her throat. "It will not last long, a few days, before it fades. I will not waste more blood to do this again." He glared down at her.

May tried to speak but only coughed.

"You're welcome," he said dryly, and disappeared without a sound.

"Fucker," she wheezed to the asphalt, and shakily rose to her feet. May noticed a slight... awareness... at the back of her mind that seemed to be the spell Armeal had cast.

Eyeing the spot the blood had once been, May hesitantly walked across it. In the back of her mind, she saw herself walking across the road. It was a flash, quick through her mind, but it was enough. Now, at least, she'd know if Harding showed up at Thormunt's. Or... if Thormunt came and went.

Unfortunately, she'd also know if any other random person drove down the road... but she'd take what she could get.

CHAPTER THIRTY-ONE
I'M A WITCH, DIMPLES

May rubbed her head, pressing her fingers into her temple. The road was just busy enough that several times a day, she got flashes of cars or bicycles, and it was driving her insane. It had only been two days, but it was enough to test her sanity. Loki jumped onto the coffee table and pawed at the compact. May dropped her head back onto the couch and sighed, but then there was a flash, an image in the darkness.

Harding's car drove over the line.

She sat upright and looked at the clock. Nearly 8:00 p.m.

What was he doing out there so late?

No other cars followed his. He was alone. Why?

"Surveillance," she said as the idea came to her.

Thormunt hadn't passed over the line since she set it. He was probably home. And Harding was heading right to him.

May chewed her lip, threw caution to the wind, and grabbed her keys. But she paused at the door to her apartment, house key held between her fingers. What the hell was she going to do? She wasn't a cop, and despite everyone else thinking so, she wasn't a supernatural cop either. How was she going to help?

"Shit," she breathed, staring at her key.

She'd never fought a Necromancer. She'd never fought *anyone*. The one sparring match at a boxing gym in college did *not* count.

"Dammit," she muttered, and shoved her keys back into her pocket, pulling out the magical compact instead. "Armeal?"

Her reflection stared at her, silent.

"Armeal. I need your help."

Her eye blinked back at her in the reflective glass. With a nervous huff, she snapped it shut. Maybe nothing would happen, and she'd sit there in the dark for nothing, but... what if something *did* happen? What if Thormunt attacked Harding? He had no warning of what he was facing. What if this was her chance to end Thormunt and not get framed for murder while doing it?

Shit. She reached for her cell and quickly dialed his number. It rang and rang before finally going to voicemail.

"Dammit," she muttered, and dialed again, only to get the same outcome.

Shoving her phone into her pocket, she reached for her keys.

The pounding in her chest increased the closer she got to Thormunt's. She took the turn off the freeway, hand shaking on her steering wheel. Checking her GPS again, she pulled down the long road that lead to Thormunt's. May turned off her lights and crept down the road, keeping an eye on her GPS, and the road for a blacked-out Impala. It was nearly impossible to see in the distance. The road was too dark. She drove as close as she dared before pulling onto the side and killing the engine. The house was just ahead of her, and she could make out the glow of the window lights.

She sat in silence, her breathing too loud, and waited.

And then, suddenly, a dome light clicked on in the distance, and she could just make out a car door opening. She jerked upright and tried to track his movement in the darkness, but she could barely see him. A blur of shape approached the fence line. Her mouth dry, May stepped out of her car and strained her ears in the silent night. Crouching, she half ran toward Thormunt's property and knelt in the high grass at the edge of the fence. She listened, trying to calm her heart, and saw several windows with lights, and there, tucked against the side of the house in the driveway, was the green Honda.

Where... She squinted in the darkness, searching for Harding.

A shout broke the silence, and the hair on the back of her neck stood on end. May straightened, then heard another strained shout.

"Stop!"

Harding.

May stood and ran past the front of the property to where she last saw Harding.

"Stop! Police!"

Shit-, shit, shit, shit.

The panic in his voice made her teeth clench, her own heart beating in her throat. More shouting came from Harding, and May took the sharp turn up the fence line toward the house. Her palms were sweaty, and she could taste the bitter adrenaline in the back of her mouth. She ran, the chainlink fence to her right, on shaky legs and nearly tripped twice in the darkness.

A sharp crack of a gun firing had May dropping to the ground, her ragged breaths puffing the dirt in her face. After another loud crack of the gun and shouting, May pushed herself onto her hands and knees, shakily, against every instinct, and started forward again. Then she heard it.

The growling. Low and inhuman.

The sound made her pause, her heart seeming to stop in her chest.

"Stop!" Harding's voice was a fever pitch, high with panic.

May pushed to her feet and ran toward Harding's panicked voice.

She pulled on her magic, that resisting knot in her chest, and yanked it, her blood warming as it reached her palm.

Burn. She focused that burning into her palm. A flame erupted from her skin, illuminating the area. The knot of magic in her chest loosened and flexed as she grew her flame.

She found Harding on the ground, scooting back from where he'd clearly fallen, staring at the thing ambling toward him. He still had his handgun pointed at the growling creature.

"Holy shit!" she shouted as her eyes registered the walking corpse growling in front of them.

It was an old dead, with skin a pallid gray and sunken eye sockets. The jaw hung at an odd angle, like half of it wasn't fully connected. Thin hair hung limp and greasy from its skull, where parts of the underlying bone shone through. Three holes, bullet holes she guessed, peppered his chest, but no blood ran from them.

May reached down blindly for Harding. "Up, up, up!"

She grabbed a handful of shirt and tugged. Thankfully, he listened and climbed hastily to his feet.

"What the hell?" he shouted when he saw the flame in her hand.

She backed away as the corpse ambled closer. Ethan brought his gun up and fired two more quick shots, one striking the corpse in the chin and the other its shoulder. It shook from the impact but continued on.

"I don't think that's gonna work!" May shouted, and stumbled backward. Her foot caught on a lump of dirt, and she landed hard on her ass, her fire going out as she fell. Her vision went black with the sudden lack of light, the growls from the corpse feeling even louder in her ears.

She felt a hard hand clamp around her ankle and screamed, the sound cracking in her throat. Ethan kicked the corpse hard in the face, throwing the thing backward with the force. He pulled her up much like she'd done him, and his hands shook where they gripped her shirt.

"How do we kill it?" His voice was panicked, unsteady. Eyes too wide.

Everything burns... eventually.

She pulled on her magic again, the heat of it warming her already too-hot body, and sweat broke out on her temples. The corpse lurched toward them again—hands outstretched, mouth agape. May caught its rotting arms mid-lunge, the stench of decay coating the back of her throat. She screamed as its cold, rubbery skin met hers and, with a desperate cry, shoved fire through her hands and into the dead flesh.

Burn. Burn, burn, burn.

Her blood burned as if it was on fire as well, and she coughed from the smoke, her chest aching.

It screeched an inhuman, guttural sound as the flames raced up its arms, and jerked away. She made a fist, the flames in her hand curling around her fingers, and threw the fire at the thing. A ball of flames hit the corpse in the chest, and like it was made of tinder, it erupted into a fireball.

"We've got to go!" May turned and started pushing Ethan. "Go, go."

He needed no further urging, and together they ran

through the tall weedy grass, their backs hot from the burning corpse behind them. It screeched into the night before suddenly stopping. The smell of burned flesh filled the air, making May gag as they ran. As they reached the road, Ethan grabbed her arm hard. She could feel the shaking. He still held his gun limp at his side.

"What the f—"

"Put that away," she interrupted, out of breath. "And follow me. I'll explain, but we need to leave right now."

"But I—"

"Right now!" she screamed, and ran to her own car.

She climbed in, limbs shaking, throat clogged with dirt and the smell of burning flesh, and stomped on the gas once she saw Harding behind her. She drove home, ignoring all stop signals and speed limits while gripping the steering wheel hard enough her knuckles hurt. As she pulled into the parking stall, she had a half-delirious thought that the jig was up. Unsteadily, she got out and waited as Ethan's Impala parked in the spot next to her.

"Come on," she said as he got out and locked eyes with her.

She imagined she looked as bad as he did, eyes wide and face too pale. Ethan followed her silently up to her apartment and into the living room. He stood in the room, staring at nothing. At least he'd holstered his gun.

"Sit."

She moved to walk past him, but his hand jerked out and seized her wrist in a painfully tight grip.

"What are you?"

She paused and met his wide, terrified eyes. "I'm a witch, Dimples."

CHAPTER THIRTY-TWO
YOUR FIRST ZOMBIE

"You're a what?"

"Witch," she said as she pulled free from his grip and went into the kitchen. "And that was a zombie. I need a drink."

She moved into the kitchen, and out of habit, reached for the kettle.

"I don't want tea," Ethan said from behind her. "I want some damned answers."

She turned to him, feeling disconnected from herself as he stared back. "Right," she finally said, and instead grabbed the whiskey she kept tucked away in her cabinets for really bad days.

Ethan shrugged when he saw the bottle. "Yeah, okay. I'll do some whiskey."

She poured two large glasses and handed him one. They stood there and stared at each other.

Ethan rubbed his face with a trembling hand, smearing dirt across his forehead. "Holy shit," he muttered, and paced in her small living room. "I can't be here. I-I discharged my firearm. There's a protocol. I have to—"

She stared into the brown liquid.

"I fired my weapon."

"At a dead person. I don't think that counts," she muttered.

He froze. "Tell me what the hell is going on."

May gulped down a large mouthful of the whiskey and moved into the living room. Ethan sat across from her; he still hadn't touched his whiskey, as if it sat forgotten in his hand.

"So," she started, then clamped her mouth shut with a clack of teeth. "So," she tried again. "Witches are real. Magic is a thing."

He stared at her, mouth slack.

"Your cases have some overlap in a... a magical case I'm dealing with."

"You're not joking, are you?"

"Well"—she shrugged—"I can show you some more magic, but I think I'll just remind you we fought a reanimated corpse about an hour ago."

He shook his head and finally gulped down nearly half the whiskey.

The bounce of his knee made her anxious.

"Okay," he eventually said. "You're a witch and can do fire stuff."

She nodded.

"And that thing was a zombie."

She nodded.

Ethan made the sign of the cross and drew in a long, steadying breath. "So, explain this magical case you said you have and how it overlaps with mine."

May hesitated. How did she explain without explaining *everything*?

"Well," she started, "someone is killing people and stealing... well, stealing their souls. Your suspect is also *my* suspect."

"You did know!" He pointed angrily at her with his shout. "You knew Thormunt was involved. Here I am working my ass off and doing surveillance that nearly gets me eaten by a fucking corpse, and *you knew the whole time*?"

"How was I supposed tell you?" she shouted back, whiskey sloshing over the lip of her glass. "Not like you'd believe me if I said 'oh, hey, a fucking ghost told me it was Thormunt!'"

Ethan glowered at her, eyebrows nearly pressed together in his fury, but as he pointed at her, whiskey sloshing, he slowly lowered his hand. "Fuck," he breathed, and drank the last of the whiskey.

"Fuck," she agreed, and finished her drink.

The whiskey was already burning in her stomach, and the tingle of alcohol was buzzing through her blood.

"Look," she said, lips feeling the alcohol, "I tried to help as much as I could. That's why I put the spell on the road, so I'd know if you went there."

He stared at her, hands hanging limp between his knees. "That's why you showed up."

"Yeah, you're fucking welcome." She stood and retrieved the whiskey from the kitchen and brought it to the living room. Without asking, she topped off his glass and refilled her own.

Ethan sat silently as he drank his drink, May doing the same. The anger seemed to have been burned out of them, the immediate adrenaline disappearing and leaving exhaustion in its wake.

"You said he's stealing souls? Do you mean that literally?"

She nodded. "You don't need to worry about why. You don't want to be involved in that."

He guffawed and rubbed his hand over his face, only to flinch and look down at himself. Lifting his collar to his nose, he sniffed and grimaced. "This is crazy. If I couldn't still smell it, I would think I've lost my mind."

"It's very real, I promise."

He sighed, a heavy sound, and dropped his head. "Why did we come here?" he finally asked.

"My apartment is warded."

He watched her for a moment before dropping his head and muttering, "Of course it is."

"What were you doing out there?"

He sighed and leaned back against the chair. "Surveillance. Thought maybe I could catch him throwing something away I could use or"—he shrugged—"maybe catch a pattern. I thought I'd walk the fence and see if I could see anything. It was my last idea before I'd have to drop it. I was running out of options to work on Thormunt. That's when the"—he waved his hand—"whatever that thing was, found me."

"Added security," she muttered. "Kinda cliché for a Necromancer, but..."

He looked like he wanted to ask but instead just shook his head, closed his eyes, and dropped his head back. "So, now what?" he asked the ceiling.

May suddenly regretted drinking so much whiskey so fast, as the room started to sway around her. "I don't know." She set her half-full glass down and slouched on the couch. "At least, right now, I don't know."

He sighed. "Sounds like a tomorrow discussion."

She stood, only to pause. "You should probably stay here for the night."

"Why?" he asked with narrowed eyes, standing as well.

"He'll for sure know he's been caught now that his pet's been destroyed. We don't know if he saw you or me. And my apartment is warded."

"Apartment is warded," he said along with her. "Right."

She thumbed toward the bathroom. "I have some old sweats you'll probably fit in, but I'm claiming the shower first."

He sighed, raising his hands in defeat. "Fine, right."

She nodded, feeling awkward and unsure. He waved her off halfheartedly and sat with his whiskey in his hands. She nodded, mostly sure he wouldn't have a mental breakdown while she was in the shower, and clicked the bathroom door shut behind her.

She leaned against the door, the emotions of the night sneaking up on her, and took a shaky breath before pushing them aside, and turned the shower on.

Later, as she lay in bed unable to sleep, she couldn't get the zombie's screams out of her mind. Every time she closed her eyes, she heard it. Smelled it. Felt it grab her ankle. Seeing it, hearing it, she thought she might understand why her mother always said Necromancy was evil. It was hard, she admitted to herself in the dark, to see that thing and think it could ever be used for good. Or had any place in the world. It was wrong. Unnatural. It was, she decided, evil.

With a huff and tears in the corners of her eyes, May pushed her covers aside and crept to her door. Creaking it open, she peered into the living room toward Ethan but couldn't tell if he was awake or not. She tiptoed into the living room, eyeing the couch Ethan had stretched out on.

"Can't sleep?" his mumbled voice asked in the darkness.

She jumped, heart in her throat, and crept over to the couch, then sat on the floor, back against the couch and Ethan.

"No," she whispered.

He grunted, a tired, soft sound. "Yeah."

"Is this," she hesitated, "the first time you've…"

"Nearly died?" he asked for her when she couldn't.

"I guess."

He was silent for a heartbeat before he took a deep breath. "No. I was in a shooting when I was on patrol. I wasn't injured. But I shot the guy that nearly got me. Nearly got my partner."

"Did you kill him?" she asked so softly she wasn't sure he'd hear.

"Yeah," he said just as softly. "I'll never forget the bullets flying by me. It was like I could feel them as they passed. Feel the brush of them as they zipped through my clothes. I don't know if it was actually that close, but it sure as hell felt like it."

She was silent as she pulled her knees to her chest and hugged them.

"The smell of gunpowder always brings it back. Not the sound." He shifted, and when she glanced up, she saw he'd flung his arm over his eyes. "The smell. The gunpowder brings back the taste of adrenaline in my mouth. The fear that had me sick to my stomach. And the slow-motion bullet holes appearing in the guy's chest."

"I can't stop hearing it scream," she said, chin on her knees.

"Yeah." He dropped his arm and patted her shoulder. "Yeah, that'll suck for a long time."

She took a shaky breath and nodded, burying her chin in her knees again.

"It'll be the little things you don't see coming that'll bring it back. Shit you don't expect."

"Sounds fun," she muttered, and sniffed.

"A blast," he drawled, and let out a dry chuckle. "But you'll be all right."

"Yeah? How do you know that?"

"Cuz," he said sleepily, "you ran into the fight, not away. You're already made of sterner stuff than the regular person."

She smiled into her knees and listened to the soft sound of him snoring. Carefully, she slipped out from under his hand and went into her bedroom for a pillow and blanket. She returned and curled up on the opposite couch, and finally slept, listening to the soft human snores.

The next morning was stilted and awkward. Ethan sat in her living room wearing her borrowed Army sweats and undershirt, surrounded by too thin pillows and blankets. May was painfully aware of her bed head, her short purple hair sticking at every which angle. She stood awkwardly at her counter, watching the coffee drip into the pot.

"So," Ethan muttered, and flopped into a kitchen chair. "Morning."

May glanced at him. "Morning. Did you sleep?"

"No."

May nodded, chewed her lip, and went back to watching the coffee. "Right," she whispered, and pulled the coffee pot out.

She quietly brought the creamer, sugar, and mugs over and sat across from the pale-faced detective. Silently, they each poured and fixed their coffee.

Eventually, May cleared her throat. "Do you have to get to work or...?"

He shook his head. "I text my sergeant. Told him I was sick and taking a personal day."

She nodded and took a big gulp of her coffee. Ethan stared into his black coffee.

"Were you military?" he asked, and May jerked.

"What?" she asked, and he flicked the baggy leg of the green sweats. "Oh, no. My dad."

"Ah." He nodded and returned to staring at his mug.

God, May thought, her anxiety rising, *help me.*

"So..." Ethan took a long swig and thunked the mug onto the table. "Witches are real."

She nodded.

"And magic is... real."

"Yup."

"Vampires? Werewolves? Demons?" he asked in rapid fire succession. "What about fairies and dragons?"

"No one's seen a vampire for a century, and werewolves have been hunted to near extinction. Although, I think a pack lives in Europe somewhere, not sure. Demons..." She shrugged and was about to say no, but then she remembered Armeal. He was the son of a demon. That meant they had to be real. The thought sent a shiver down her spine. "Assume it's all real at this point."

He stared at her before slowly blinking. "Shit. Okay. Alright."

He dropped his head into his hand and took several deep breaths.

"Would this be easier if I lied?"

"No." He lifted his head and squared his shoulders. "No. I'd rather not be surprised in the future."

She smiled softly at him and lifted her cup. "I can almost guarantee you'll be surprised many times to come."

He glared at her, and she flinched.

"Sorry."

Ethan stared at the table like he was searching for answers, his brows knit tightly together in a frown, before nodding and squaring his gaze on her.

"So, what's next?"

"Well..." May pushed her coffee aside. "I think we need to break into Thormunt's house."

She'd been thinking all night of what to do next. It might

be up to her to kill him. A task she prayed would not fall to her, but after seeing the corpse ambling after her in her nightmares all night, she would do it if she had to. She reminded herself he was a murderer. A serial killer, really. No human jail would hold him, not if he really wanted out. She needed to figure out who, if anyone, Thormunt was working with, then she and Armeal would deal with him. Armeal dragged her into this disaster—dragging him right back through it was the least she could do.

Ethan blinked at her. "Excuse me?"

"Yeah." She nodded and leaned forward.

"I can't break into his house." He scoffed. "None of the evidence would be admissible, not to mention, I'd be fired and arrested. Besides—" He huffed and stood. "There is protocol."

May watched him tiredly as he paced her kitchen. "Protocol for zombies?"

"And that!" He turned on her with a pointed finger. "You really want to go back there with zombies running around? I sure don't."

May shook her head, rubbing her hand over her tired and dry eyes. "No, no I don't. But do you want him running around at all?"

"No!" Ethan shouted, throwing his hands up. "Protocol. This needs to go through proper channels."

"And what are the proper channels for a Necromancer that murders people, steals their souls, and raises the dead?" She challenged. "Look," she said when he remained silent under her glare, "I don't want to go back either. I don't want to be eaten by damned zombies! But—" She took a deep breath. "The *proper channels* for James Thormunt aren't your channels."

She watched him until he stilled and slumped under her gaze.

"He's not going to court... is he?"

She shook her head. "If he's the one stealing the souls, no. No, he will not be. This isn't an issue for human courts and justice."

"And if he's not your guy?"

He is. She sat back with a shrug. "Then he's all yours. But I'm telling you, he is."

He watched her with serious, hard eyes, his jaw clenched. "Fine," he finally said. "How do we get into his house without zombies eating us?"

May chewed her lip. "I don't know." He glowered at her, and she held her hand up. "Let met think."

Ethan sighed through his nose before nodding. "Fine. Text me when you want to meet. Until then, I need..." He rubbed his face. "I just need to go."

"Okay," she muttered, and walked with him to the door.

Silently, he gathered his dirt-stained clothing from yesterday and, with no more words, left.

CHAPTER THIRTY-THREE
MORE IS AT RISK THAN SOME MISSING SOULS

The apartment was painfully quiet after Ethan left, and the idea of going to work made May want to throw up. After shooting off a quick text claiming bad sushi, she sat at her kitchen table. Staring. Thinking. The screaming kept forcing its way into her thoughts, and she struggled to push it back into the little trauma box it belonged in it. She twisted her neck, trying to dispel the tension that had her shoulders tight and back stiff, but it did nothing for the building headache.

She groaned, knee bouncing frantically under the table.

How was she going to kill someone with that kind of magic? And why the hell was it her responsibility? She dropped her head into her hands, breathing fast and shallow.

"Shit, shit, shit."

She wanted to talk to her mom about her magic and why it had... done what it did. She had summoned fire before, but that felt... different. It felt *good*. It wasn't the Green Witch magic of her family, she knew that, but it had to come from somewhere. Right? Maybe it was a different kind of Green Magic. She snorted to herself. It wasn't Green Magic. She had a horrifying suspicion of what it was, but she wouldn't let herself speak those words, even to herself.

She wanted to talk to her dad. He knew what it was like to face something trying to kill you and knew what it was like to survive it. But she couldn't involve them in this.

She didn't want to be chased by zombies, or fight for her life, or know supernatural serial killers were wandering around town. How did a cup of coffee with Death lead to all this?

Death was who she needed to talk to. Maybe yell at her a little. Rubbing her knees, she shakily pulled out the compact.

"I need to talk to Death," she said into the mirrored surface.

"She is busy" came Armeal's distorted reply.

"I don't give a damn," she snapped.

The silence was damning. May remembered she was trying to command the God of Death and an immortal Nephilim... yet she still didn't give a damn. She snapped the compact shut and tossed it onto the coffee table.

Dropping her forehead back into her hand, she focused on taking deep breaths, on keeping the panic at bay. She was feeling like this was a pretty one-sided friendship when a glow broke through her closed eyes. Lifting her head, she saw a shimmering line in the air. The world split as Lady Death stepped into her apartment draped in her signature black coat—part trench, part something older, with sharp lines that reminded May of a war-era military overcoat. Her dark hair fell down her back, and she turned an orange gaze to May.

Lady Death tilted her head when she saw May, a frown between her eyes.

"What has happened?" she asked as she sat at the table with May. "You seem... quite upset."

May felt tears crawling up her throat, and she had to take a deep breath to keep them from spilling out. "I don't think I can do this."

Lady Death blinked, her strange eyes and cat-like pupils roving over May's face, assessing.

"This isn't fair," she said, taking a deep breath against the surprise rush of tears. "I never wanted to be chased by zombies. I never even wanted ghosts talking to me!"

Death continued studying her, head tilted. "I do not know why this is happening."

"Why don't you kill him?" May asked, pushing against the tears threatening. "Or Armeal? I don't think I can do this."

She took a deep breath and felt a betraying quiver in her chin. Feather soft, cold fingertips brushed her temple, pushing her hair away, and the soft tingle of magic grazed her mind, gentle and caressing. Her panic subsided, her tears retreated, and her racing heart slowed. Then she could breathe without the threat of suffocation.

May turned wide eyes to Death. "What did you do?"

"I cannot erase emotions, but I can age them. Dull their effect on you." Harper smiled tentatively. "Time has different meanings for death. I can alter how it happens to others, in small ways."

May could feel the fear in her chest, but it felt old, dull. It wasn't gone. Just... quieter. She took a deep breath and didn't feel the press of tears or anger. Slowly, Death removed her fingers from May's temple. Later, she might feel differently about the alteration to her emotions, but right now, she was just happy the panic was gone, that she had *some* control over her emotions again.

"What happened?" Death asked gently again.

May slumped against the couch, resisting the urge to bump shoulders against Death. "The detective went to Thormunt's," May muttered, as if she was afraid speaking too loudly would bring the panic back. "I went after him. I knew he wouldn't have any chance against a Necromancer. I don't know what I thought I'd be able to do."

She sighed and let her head fall back against the couch cushion, staring up at the ceiling.

"I don't want to be chased by corpses. Killing him sounded easy when it was just words, but now... I've nearly died enough times."

With a heavy breath, May turned her head toward Death, who watched her with still, unblinking eyes.

"Why can't you kill him?" she asked again.

Death blinked with a sad smile. "I am Death. Not War. I ferry the souls of the dead to their next journey. I do not strike them down. I must remain impartial. Death simply is. I cannot take sides. I cannot pass judgment on the living. I do not decide who lives, who dies, nor do I decide when. The Fates control that."

"What if you did?" May asked petulantly.

"I cannot," Death stated. "It is a rule so firm in the fabric of magic that I could not disobey it even if I wished. If I took action against the living, what would stop the living from making deals with me for who lives and who dies? Chaos would ensue."

"Oh." May lifted her head. "But what about Armeal?"

Death tilted her head. "He could. And if you wish to no longer be involved, then the task will fall to him. However, he is rather occupied with locating more missing Reapers."

May chewed her lip.

"There is..." Death said slowly, and if May didn't know any better, she'd say fear was in her words, "a concerning converging of events."

May shifted on the couch and propped her elbow on the back cushion as she faced Death.

"Souls are taken. People are murdered for them." Death continued. "The souls of the damned begin to resist their prison. Souls of the wandering are restless. The whole Underworld is restless and..." She shook her head at whatever she was going to say. "Reapers are resisting their duty. They are resisting *me*. All at the same time."

"What do you think it means?"

Death met her eyes, and May was shocked to see true fear in them. "I fear it means the Necromancer was directed to do this by someone who should be dead. I fear it means much more is at risk than the loss of some souls."

Whoever owned the Reaper cloak, May thought, remembering the same fear in Armeal's eyes when he found it, *whoever that is, they're afraid of them.*

"The Necromancer needs to be *ended*." Death growled the word, and May remembered that while she seemed a calm, passive person on her couch, she was still the God of Death, and her souls were being taken. "But more importantly, I must learn who his master is. Thormunt did not seem the kind to rise to this level of magic when I encountered him before. Something... some*one*... guided him."

"When did you meet Thormunt?"

Death shrugged. "Before." She shook her head. "Time is... difficult. His wife was dying. But it wasn't her time. Later, when it was, a Reaper went for her, but she had tethered herself to the earth and now haunts it. She refused to pass."

She didn't want to remain involved, but it sounded like if she backed out, more people would be murdered. Thormunt could continue whatever he was planning, and the police would be unlikely to catch him. Even if they got enough evidence to charge him, they wouldn't be able to *stop* him.

Could she sit back, knowing what was happening, and watch it?

Would she able to live with herself if she did?

Was that worse than the weight of what she would have to do if she didn't?

She rubbed her face with an angry huff. "Shit."

Death raised an eyebrow at her.

"I can't just... ignore everything." She dropped her head back again with a huff. "Shit."

Death raised her hand, long dainty fingers barely brushing May's forehead with the tips of her fingers again. "Be careful."

Heat flooded May's cheeks as she turned to look at Death.

"You are the most interesting human I've encountered in a long time."

"Just interesting?" May asked before she could think.

Death grinned. "Not just interesting."

May's lips tilted in a smile. "Lady Death thinks I'm more than interesting," she teased.

"Harper."

May lifted her head with a frown.

"My name is Harper."

Her lips formed an "oh" before she clamped her mouth shut. It never occurred to her Death would have a name; never occurred to her to ask.

"And you are," Harper said back with a smile.

CHAPTER THIRTY-FOUR
THREATENING BUSINESS

May needed to get out of the office. Harper's magic had dulled the panic and fear, but it was still there, and during the quiet hours at the office, it was the most noticeable. She didn't break down in a panic attack this time, but she was antsy. Fidgety. In the couple of days since the zombie, May started a habit of having lunch at the coffee shop. It was a nice distraction that didn't raise questions with her coworkers.

She ordered a simple ham and cheese sandwich to go along with her coffee, an iced Frappuccino this time, and sat with her easy lunch at one of the empty tables. Nibbling her sandwich, she scrolled through *Facebook* on her phone and was enjoying the sugar rush from her coffee when a shadow crossed over her table. Glancing up, she smothered a gasp as James Thormunt sat in the chair across from her. Her phone forgotten in her hand, she stared ahead, and her sandwich fell to the wrapper on the table.

James smiled at her, and if she didn't still smell the burning flesh of his zombie, she'd say he looked nice. Polite.

"Let's not make a scene," he said, and scratched at his beard.

It had the look of one that was once well trimmed and neat. Now, it was too long to be neat, but too short to be intentional. Sitting across from her, he looked older than his *Facebook* photos. His skin had a pallor to it that made her think he was sick or spending far too much time indoors, and his eyes were creased at the corners with wrinkles, and a twinge of yellow overtook the whites of his eyes, the early display of jaundice.

Or—she tried to swallow around her dry mouth—*that was what Necromancy did to a person.*

"What do you want?" she whispered.

James shrugged and slid her sandwich over to him. "Depends on what you want."

"I don't—"

"If you want into my business—" He took a bite of her sandwich. "Then I'll get into yours."

She swallowed. Well, tried. Her mouth was too dry, throat scratchy.

"It takes a lot of work," he said around a mouthful of ham and cheese, "to raise a corpse. A lot more work to make it sentient enough to follow orders. You destroyed my property. My work."

"A corpse isn't your property," she bit out at him.

James shrugged one shoulder. "Hm, well. We'll have to agree to disagree, then. Why were you at my house?"

"How did you find me?" she asked instead.

He chuckled like she'd asked a dumb question, and dropped what was left of her lunch onto the table. "Necromancer secret. I suggest you stay out of my business."

May hid her shaking hands under the table. "Or what?"

"Well." H sighed. "I'll have to involve the police, won't I? Report the trespassing. Harassment. Maybe the stress of a major surgery and returning to work so soon was too much." He shrugged again and let out a slow breath, and May grimaced as it brushed her face. "I don't know. Maybe you snapped. But a criminal investigation into an investigator from the Medical Examiner's Office wouldn't be good for you."

"You don't have any proof I was on your property," May said, even as her heart beat hard in her chest. How did he know so much about her? Where she worked, her surgery...

"Don't I?" James asked with a smile.

Was he bluffing? Or had they missed something?

He sucked his teeth. "Why were you at my home?"

May raised her chin. "Witch secrets."

James chuckled, a dry, raspy sound that sent shivers down her spine. He nodded while his eyes moved over her face, assessing. "Did she send you?"

May held still, keeping her face impassive. *Death?* she wondered. *Or who...*

"You have a—" He sniffed the air and reached across the table. "An aura."

James held his hand out to her, palm extended, and the slimy, oily feel of his magic brushed over hers. She resisted the urge to swat his probing magic away, to flare hers, to burn him.

He dropped his hand with a huff and frowned at her. "Are you a Necromancer?"

"No!" she shouted too loudly, and several people glanced their way.

"Huh," he said, and sighed.

"No one sent me," she said, answering his earlier question. "Who gave you the scythe?"

He twitched like he was surprised and leaned back. "Who said I have one?"

May smiled. "I know you have one. How else are you cutting away the souls?"

James sucked his teeth again and narrowed his jaundiced eyes at her.

She leaned forward and pulled on every detective show she'd ever watched. "Why do you need souls, anyway?"

He grunted and ate the last of her sandwich. "This is the only polite warning I'll give."

She leaned back, not surprised he didn't answer.

"Stay away from me, and I'll stay away from you," he said with another smile that didn't reach his eyes. "Deal?"

She nodded, her breath shaking in her ribs. "Fine."

He stood, wiping his mouth with the back of his hand, and stared down at her. His eyes were hard with anger, his face drawn and stripped of its earlier politeness. The person who killed others and stole their souls stared down at her. She tried not to wither under his gaze, and eventually, he turned away, leaving the shop as silently as he'd arrived.

"He did what!" Ethan shouted over the phone at her.

Once her hands had stopped shaking and her breathing had returned to a normal rhythm, she had called Ethan.

"Told me to stay the fuck out of his business," she said breathlessly in her car outside her office.

"Did he threaten you?" he asked, and she could still hear the seething anger in his barely controlled voice. "What exactly did he say?"

May rubbed her lips. "Threatened to report my trespassing

to the cops. But he knew about my heart transplant, where I work. Where I go to lunch."

"That's the thing that worries me the most," Ethan said.

"Can't you arrest him?"

"For what?" He nearly shouted again. "Nothing he said amounts to a threat, and technically, we did trespass on his property."

"Shit," she breathed, and dropped her forehead to her steering wheel.

"Besides," he said softer, "this feels like a test-me, I-dare-you sort of stunt, and I don't think we want to do that. He wouldn't be this bold if he didn't have something in his back pocket."

"You think he has proof we were there, you know, besides the zombie briquette."

"No…" There was silence for a beat. "He wouldn't want to reveal that. It has to be something else. Maybe the implied threat that he knows more about us than we do about him."

"That's not comforting."

"No, but your apartment is warded."

Hers was, but not his place. Not her parents'. Not her coworkers'. Who knew who else could be at risk from Thormunt.

"This puts a rush on us," he said. "We can't risk dilly dallying."

"No," she agreed, and lifted her head from the steering wheel. "And we need to be more careful."

He agreed, and the call ended quickly after that. She felt lightheaded from the stress and near hyperventilation.

"Fuck, fuck, fuck, fuck," she whispered, eyes closing as she took deep breaths.

Someone knocked on her window, and May jumped with a

shout. Sarah stared at her through the window, frowning. Taking a deep breath, May gathered her purse and got out.

"Wow, you're jumpy," Sarah said with a laugh, and walked toward the building with May.

"Yeah," she said breathlessly, with a false smile.

How was she supposed to go back to work like a Necromancer hadn't just threatened her during lunch?

CHAPTER THIRTY-FIVE
HE'S AN ASS

May lay buried under a pile of blankets, an empty wineglass abandoned on the coffee table. The TV flickered in front of her, but she wasn't really watching—just staring through it. She'd checked her ward three times before forcing herself to stay put on the couch, clinging to the illusion of calm and a second glass of wine. Earlier, she'd called her parents, told them to put up wards too. She passed it off as an overzealous relative of a case she was working—just a stalker, nothing serious. Which wasn't really that far from the truth. It happened occasionally when someone was convinced their loved one had been murdered when they hadn't been. They'd argue and yell and fight with the autopsy findings. It wasn't a hard stretch for her to tell her parents that had turned into a stalker. They weren't happy, her mom was furious, but they put up their wards and didn't ask if it was related to ghosts.

It was late, a glance at the clock said nearly ten, but sleep was hard still. Even after Harper's magic trick, the dreams were... hard, and after Thormunt's appearance yesterday at lunch, her nightmares had taken on a new threatening appearance. Loki was curled up on her feet, having given up on trying to get her to bed hours ago with his petulant meows.

On the couch arm above her, her phone dinged.

> Det. Dimples: You up?

She read the text from Ethan, and after a moment of hesitation, typed out a quick reply.

> Me: Ya. Why?

His reply was quick.

> Det. Dimples: So sleeping sucks. Want to order a pizza and not talk about zombies?

A laugh burst out of her without her expecting it, startling Loki, who chirped at her in irritation.

> Me: Sounds great.

It didn't take long for Ethan to arrive at her apartment, which made her think he was already in the area. He knocked on her door with three sharp, quick knocks that startled her.

"You knock like a cop," she said as she let him in.

"Ha," Ethan said as he walked inside with a six-pack of beer. He held it up like an offering. "I didn't come empty handed."

She smiled, even though she was never much of a beer fan, and returned to the couch. Ethan set the beer down on the coffee table and pulled his phone out as he collapsed against the opposite couch.

"Any preferences?"

"Nothing with pineapple," she said. She curled her legs under her, knees braced against the arm.

Ethan glanced up at her from under his eyelashes. "You're one of *those* people?"

She wrinkled her nose. "You mean correct people? Pineapple should never be on a pizza."

He grumbled a rough breath. "I'm sorry you have such poor taste in pizza."

"Who hurt you?" she asked with a laugh, which he softly echoed.

May was glad he laughed, joked with her even a little bit. She'd been so long without friends, without someone to joke with, it felt almost foreign.

He tapped away at his phone, leaving them in a heavy, awkward silence.

"Here"—he handed her the phone—"stick your address in."

She quickly typed her address and handed it back to him. "So," she muttered as he tucked his phone away.

"Oh, I figured a good supreme was the way to go since you're opposed to decent pizza."

She chuckled softly. "Thanks, but I was going to ask how you were doing."

He stared at the wall across from him, and the usually soft ticking of the clock seemed disproportionally loud.

"It's not every day your world is turned upside down," he uttered. He still stared at the wall. "But I see a lot of fucked-up shit every day at my job. People do horrible things to each other. All the time. For no reason."

Ethan finally turned and looked at her. "If I can come to terms with that, I can come to terms with this."

"Sorry you got dragged into it."

He shrugged. "Shit happens. How'd you get wrapped up in this? Are you some sort of paranormal investigator?"

She laughed. "Oh, no. Not at all." She let out a breath and thought back. "I started seeing ghosts. It kind of spiraled from there."

"So, what changed?"

She dropped her head back and hummed at the ceiling. "I died." She lifted her head at the silence. "Only for a minute. Or... I think, it was technically two and a half."

"Your heart?"

She shrugged. "Yeah." She tucked the collar of her shirt down enough for him to see the tip of her scar. "Got a new one, though!"

He smiled. "Congratulations."

"Thanks," she said.

Silence returned, broken only by the soft ticking of the clock.

"So, umm," she hedged, "Thormunt."

"Any ideas on how we'll get into his house and not die? Or get caught?"

She blew a raspberry. "Not really. I'm a witch but..." She shrugged. "I'm also sort of the dud in the family. I'm good with fire, but not much else."

"Well," Ethan said with a small chuckle, "fire seemed just fine last time."

"Yeah," she said noncommittally. But what if there were more? Lots more?

"Do you guys think he's still there?" she asked.

Ethan leaned against the couch, arms spread over the top. "Dunno. A couple neighbors called in some shots fired calls to dispatch after our... adventure... so there's been more patrol activity over there, but he hasn't been seen. I was able to get a warrant for his phone location information, but I'm still waiting for the results. That can take a while."

Shit. She didn't want to go in blind. She didn't really want to go in at all... but that was a separate issue.

"We've been able to connect him to most of the victims, though," Ethan said. "Which earned me a giant *I fucking told you so* to my whole unit."

"Oh?" May perked up. "How?"

"How else?" Ethan snorted. "Drugs. We were able to get into the phones from the Chandler murders and found his number in there. Looks like he's a small-time heroin dealer. And all those scenes that aren't murders but are, had connections to dealers, and when I looked back through the photos, I found heroin paraphernalia at all of them. And then, you know Lars was his brother-in-law. Maybe that fight he told me about wasn't just words."

"Huh," she said. "So he's killing his clients?"

Ethan shrugged. "Easy pool of victims if you think about it. They'd know him. Let him in. Agree to meet him."

May hummed that she agreed. *And,* she thought, *even easier if he was invisible.*

Knocking on the door startled them both.

"Damn, that was fast," Ethan said as he looked at the door, but Loki hissed and growled.

May jerked, heart in her throat as possibilities raced through her mind. Had Thormunt found her?

"Or..." Ethan stood too, glancing between the door and May. "Maybe that's not pizza."

The knock came again, louder, more persistent.

"Witch!" Armeal shouted through the door. "Lower this ward and let me in."

Ethan turned wide eyes to May as she huffed out a long breath, relief making her jittery.

"You're about to meet another magical thing," May warned. "And he's kind of an ass."

CHAPTER THIRTY-SIX
GHOSTS AND SECRETS

"I'm about to meet a what?" Ethan said, voice a little too high.

May gave him an apologetic smile and lowered the ward as she opened the door to a pissed-off Armeal. He pushed past her into the apartment, causing Loki to spit and hiss, and then he scampered off the couch and into her bedroom.

"My cat really hates you," May said dryly as she shut the door.

Armeal glowered at her, then turned angry eyes to Ethan.

"Armeal," she said as she gestured to Ethan, "this is Detective Ethan Harding. Detective, this is... Armeal."

Ethan, the well-behaved person he was, stuck his hand out almost on reflex. Armeal looked down his nose at the outstretched hand before turning cold eyes back to May.

"He needs to leave," Armeal said cooly. "We have a task."

"He is an ass," Ethan muttered as he took his hand back.

"He knows," she said to Armeal, and wiped her suddenly damp hands on her jeans. "He's in this with me."

Armeal lifted his human-looking lip in a decidedly not human snarl. "More humans…"

She lifted her hands. "He's Velma to my Fred since you insisted on involving me in the supernatural detective shit."

He glowered but made no more demands.

"What's the task you insist we do?"

Armeal shifted his eyes to Ethan again before settling his inhuman glare on her. "Things are escalating in the Underworld. We must end this quickly."

"Escalating, as in…"

"War." Armeal's declaration was met with stunned silence.

"I'm sorry," Ethan said into the building silence. "But who the fuck are you?"

Armeal's eyes snapped to Ethan, and the anger in them had May quickly stepping between them. "He," she said to Ethan, "is complicated. But… um, well, short story is, I'm friends with Lady Death, he's her assistant"—Armeal growled behind her, sending shivers down her spine, but she steadfastly ignored it—"and he's definitely not human."

Ethan's wide eyes looked over her shoulder before snapping back to her face. She smiled again in apology, then turned to face Armeal.

"Not that I'm complaining, but why the rush?" May asked, still standing between the two. "You haven't exactly had an active hand in this before."

Armeal glared down his nose at her. "More souls are missing. Reapers are choosing sides in a conflict that risks a war with the angels. We can wait no longer. We must know who he is working with."

May swallowed, but her throat was dry. The thing she'd been avoiding thinking about was here. She'd have to make a decision soon.

"Okay," May said, adrenaline making her winded. "Guess we're forgoing the pizza."

"Okay"—Ethan stepped around May to face them both—"if we're doing this, we're doing it my way. You might not be human"—he pointed at Armeal—"but *we* don't want to end up in prison for this."

May tried to breathe past her suddenly pounding heart. *Prison. For murder.* The thought made her palms sweat.

"I'll drive," he said. "We'll wear gloves and touch absolutely nothing unless we have to. Put everything back where it was. If he's there..." He paused, and May watched his jaw flex and clench. "Well. I'll deal with that when we come to it. If he's not, we're not getting arrested for burglary."

May nodded, hands shaking just enough she shoved them into her pockets, and Armeal stayed silent.

The inside of the Impala was as beat up as the outside was. The driver seat had a hole worn into the right side of the backrest. As he started the car, he lowered the volume of the police radio tucked away beneath the dash. May glanced at the rear-view mirror and met Armeal's irritated eyes. The visual of the giant Nephilim stuffed in the backseat of a shitty car nearly sent May into hysterical giggles.

She controlled herself.

Barely.

The drive was silent and long, broken only by the soft police chatter from the radio. Ethan took a longer, back-roads path rather than the quick direct route. Maybe he was afraid of being followed. Maybe he was worried about being seen.

Either way, she didn't ask. It didn't matter in the end. When they finally got to the long road that led to Thormunt's house, he turned his headlights off and crept along the dirt road. May's mouth was dry, her heart thumping in her chest. He stopped quite a ways from Thormunt's property.

"Why are you stopping here?" she whispered even though they were alone in the car.

"Because," he said back just as softly.

She waited for the rest of the answer, but Ethan just killed the engine and opened his door.

"Just because," she muttered to herself, and exited the car.

They closed their doors softly, quietly, and she met Ethan at the trunk. He opened his trunk and pulled several blue gloves, then handed her a pair that she yanked on with practiced ease.

"Flashlights?"

"Not while we walk up." Ethan pocketed a flashlight and closed his trunk with a soft thunk. "Follow me."

May rolled her shoulders to try to ease the tension that had them creeping to her ears and followed him along the gravely road. She had to focus on her steps so she wouldn't trip on the uneven ground. Suddenly, Ethan stopped, and she looked up in alarm as she crashed into him.

Armeal huffed and walked around them.

"No one is here," he said as he continued walking toward the house.

"What about zombies?" May whispered harshly.

Armeal growled and kept walking.

"Guess no zombies," she muttered to Ethan.

Silently, they followed.

The three cautiously approached the front door on the narrow porch. The wood banister was old, and even in the darkness, May could tell the paint was faded.

"Do you have a spell or something for the lock?" Ethan asked.

May glared at him. "I'm not Harry Potter."

"What the f—"

With a growl, Armeal stepped between and gripped the doorknob. He twisted, and the mechanisms snapped as they broke.

"Dammit," Ethan swore, and stepped into the house after the angry Nephilim. "Do *not* break anything else."

May followed, closing the door behind them.

"Can we turn the lights on?"

"No," Ethan said as he slowly walked through the living room. "The lights can be seen from the road."

She grumbled and looked around the room while digging out her cell phone. It was a simple living room, sparsely furnished. The furniture had a layer of dust on them as if they hadn't been used in some time. Picture frames hung on the wall. As her light passed over the glass, she could see the cobwebs that clung to the frames. The stench hit her first—stale, sour, and sharp enough to make her gag. It reeked of urine, and it clung to everything. Thin and worn carpet spanned the living room floor.

"Since he's not here"—Ethan's voice startled her from behind—"what are we looking for?"

Armeal spoke ahead of them in the room without turning around. "Signs of his master. Someone set him on this path. The scythe he's using. The Reaper cloak. Anything magical."

He stared down at her in the dark room. "A scythe. And a..." He paused. "A magical robe."

"Yup," she squeaked out, and turned back to the sparse contents of the room.

May wandered to a shelf covered in dust and cobwebs

tucked against the far wall. She shined her phone light on the small photo frame on the shelf.

"A wedding photo?" May asked, and peered closer at it.

Beneath the layer of dust, May could make out Thormunt and a woman dressed in wedding attire on some beach. "Oh," she gasped as she recognized the woman in the photo. "Harper said she had died," May muttered.

"Who's Harper?" Ethan asked as he continued looking around the room, behind the old sofa and its pillows.

"Um—" May cleared her throat. "Lady Death."

Ethan's response was a strangled grunt.

She stretched up on her toes. "Oh," she said softer, spotting the urn with the name "Victoria Thormunt" engraved on the small base. Reaching up, she rubbed her thumb across the date under the name. "She died last year."

May hesitated, licked her lips, then reached up and removed the lid from the ceramic urn. Tipping the jar toward her, she found it empty.

Weird, she thought, *why keep an empty urn?*

Necromancy couldn't bring people back to life. Everyone knew that. It could put movement into bodies, bring a basic level of survival to their minds, but nothing akin to a soul. Basic consciousness. Nothing more. Thormunt was stealing souls. Gathering power. Someone might've given him the ability to steal souls, but he still would've needed a reason to.

She didn't like the idea forming as for why.

May put the half-formed thought aside and moved into the kitchen. Here, it was a little more obvious someone lived in the house. Food cartons covered the counters, and dirty dishes were stacked high in the sink. Pizza boxes and takeout were piled in the corner. Through the kitchen, a small hallway led to a set of bedrooms and a bathroom. One room was smaller and empty. She glanced in the bathroom as she passed it, but the smell coming from it was enough to hurry her along. In the main bedroom at the back of the house, May found a cluttered room. A door to an ensuite was tucked in the corner.

May glanced over her shoulder at Ethan in the hallway and flipped the light on in the bedroom.

"Hey!" Ethan shouted in a hoarse whisper. "What did I say?"

"It's the back of the house," May said, and pocketed her phone. "Who am I going to alert? The deer?"

The room was orderly, a stark contrast to the state of the kitchen, though a layer of dust coated most of the surfaces. The dresser was covered in dust and cobwebs, the rings and bracelets scattered on the top forgotten in time. Photos were turned down on the nightstands and dresser. Clothes were piled on a chair in the corner, but the floor was clear. Old medical supplies were tossed onto the end table in a pile.

May wandered around the bed, looking at the items scattered around the room. Life seemed to be frozen in the past.

"It's like he stopped living when she died," May whispered.

"Grief," Ethan said behind her in a low voice, "does strange things to a person not prepared for it."

She gently poked through the items on the dresser, careful not to disturb them. A small bowl, one used to hold keys or rings, sat at the edge. She sifted through the items and saw loose change and a button. A man's watch laid in the bowl, the metal dull from grime and lack of wear. The band was a metal link that had once been a shiny silver. May glanced at Ethan puttering around the room behind her and picked up the watch. The face was a simple silver and gold Seiko. Turning it over in her hands, she saw a small inscription on the back: *With all my love, Victoria.*

"Hey," Ethan said, "I think this might be what you're looking for."

She came around the bed and found Ethan on his knees, bent low to look under the bed.

"Why? What is it?"

Ethan pushed himself up and gestured to the floor. May pulled her phone light out again and looked under the bed.

She gasped as the light hit a black scythe. The long, curved blade glimmered even in the dim cellphone light. "Holy shit."

She reached out with a shaking hand and slowly, with trembling fingers, touched the smooth black staff. A tingle went up her arm as she gripped it. With a deep breath, she pulled the scythe out from under the bed. She stood and held the thing in front of her. Ethan stared at it with wide eyes.

"Is that..." He took a deep shaking breath. "Is that a damn Grim Reaper scythe?"

"Yes," she breathed.

"The Grim Reaper is real?"

"Well." She shrugged and pulled her eyes away from the scythe. "That's a more complicated question than you'd think."

Ethan shook his head and held his hands up to stop her from continuing.

Armeal appeared in the doorway, his eyes narrowing on the scythe. He pushed past Ethan and held his hand out. After a moment of hesitation, she slowly placed the scythe into his outstretched hand. He ran his fingers over the smooth wood, bringing it close to his face as he peered at it. His hand moved along the staff, then suddenly stopped. Armeal's eyes narrowed, and he flipped the staff over to stare at the spot he'd touched.

"What?" Ethan asked.

Armeal ignored Ethan, his eyes widening.

May stepped closer and tried to peer at whatever caught the Reaper's attention.

"What is it?"

His eyes cut to her, and she stepped back at the glare in them. She was about to ask again when a shimmer over his shoulder caught her eye. She peered around him at the translucent haze. As she watched, it settled into a woman's shape.

"You're..." May whispered, and stepped around Armeal.

Thormunt's wife's ghost stared at her with sad, hollow eyes. Her hair, once vibrant and red, was limp around her.

"No one's there, May."

"I can see ghosts," she whispered to Ethan, not looking away from Victoria.

"Right..." he breathed behind her.

"She has tethered herself here," Armeal whispered. "She is haunting."

Victoria looked past her at the scythe, still firmly in Armeal's grip, and frowned. Then she turned and moved out of the bedroom. She paused in the hall and glanced over her shoulder at May. When she still didn't move, Victoria jerked her head down the hall. With a sigh, May followed the floating ghost down the hall.

"May," Ethan called after her. "Where are you going?"

"I don't know," she said as she followed Victoria back into the kitchen. "But I think she wants to show me something."

Victoria floated to a door at the back of the kitchen that she'd overlooked before.

"A closet?"

"No." Ethan stood next to her. "That's a basement door."

He reached for the doorknob, and a shimmer of magic brushed against May's arm.

"Stop!" She grabbed his wrist, inches from the door.

Ethan pulled his wrist back, and May slowly held her hand out toward the door, just above the surface. Magic flared and flicked up to her palm, stinging and burning, and she yanked it back to cradle against her chest.

"It's warded," she said, glancing at Ethan, "with something strong."

She turned to find Armeal leaning against the wall, arms folded across his chest as he tiredly watched them. He slowly raised an eyebrow at her.

"Are you even a witch if you can't disarm a ward?"

She pursed her lips at him and folded her arms. "I'm a Green Witch! Wards aren't in my skill set."

His eyes narrowed. "You're a witch that can cast fire spells, see the dead, and talk to gods. Whatever you are, you are not a Green Witch."

He pushed off the wall, however, and came to stand in front of the door. She muttered nonsense under her breath, having no comeback for him. His words were too close to home. Too accurate.

Armeal sniffed and tentatively held his fingers to the warded door. His lip curled as the magic flared against his skin.

"You were correct. It is a simple spell but strong. I cannot disarm it unless I trigger it, and I do not want to melt my skin off."

"Jesus Christ," Ethan muttered. "Let's not do that."

May chewed her lip. "What if I burned it away?"

Armeal looked down his long nose at her, eyebrow raised incredibly high. "Are you capable of such a spell?"

Maybe. "Yes," May said with more confidence than she felt.

The look on Armeal's face told her he didn't believe her. He sighed heavily through his nose before dipping his chin. "It should work. As long as you can deflect enough of the spell before it burns *through* you."

May took a deep breath and shakily faced the door. Ethan slinked back until he was blocked by the fridge. She raised her hand, palm out, toward the door. Focusing, pulling on the stubborn magic in her blood, she gathered it in her open palm.

Her body heated. A cough rose in her throat from the smell in the kitchen, and she pushed it aside. A giant wall of fire. That was all she needed.

She pictured a bonfire in her mind's eye, large and burning, the flames licking into the sky, and gathered that heat and fire into her open palms. Armeal stepped behind her, and she followed his movement from the corner of her eye.

Little bitch, she thought and took a deep breath.

"Ready?" she asked.

"Sure," Ethan whispered from behind her.

Victoria's ghost shimmered and weaved before blinking out.

After one more deep breath, May ignited her bonfire.

CHAPTER THIRTY-SEVEN
THE NECROMANCER'S SECRET

The ward exploded against her fire. The flames ate at the curse, burning it away, but still, the ward expanded out. It burned through her fire quickly, faster than she'd expected. She pushed more of her magic into her flames, her body dripping in sweat as she overheated. Her flames grew and roared as they ate at the expanding ward. Suddenly, she was ripped from her feet and thrown back as the last of the ward's magic burst past her flames and sizzled out.

Smoke and an acrid smell that clung to the back of her throat filled the room. She coughed violently and cleared her throat and blinked around her.

Armeal had a painfully hard grip on her upper arms as he placed her back on her feet. She frowned at him.

"I suspect Lady Death would personally hold me accountable for any damage you sustain."

The thought put a smile on her face even as she coughed again.

"Did it work?" Ethan asked from his position behind the fridge.

May turned to the now burned door and raised a trembling hand to check. "I don't feel any ward. I think it worked."

Armeal stepped in front of her and pushed the door open without hesitation. May rolled her eyes and stepped after the Nephilim down the stairs.

The smell hit her almost instantly, making her gag and retch.

"Decomp," Ethan said behind her, his voice thick from holding back his own gags.

I know, she wanted to say but was afraid of opening her mouth. It was some of the worst decomposition she'd smelled in a long time. Sour meat and bowels, shit and urine, and the distinctive smell that all dead has. Whatever was down here, was old and rotting. She came to the bottom of the stairs and stepped into a small living room space. Carefully, she felt along the wall for a light switch and flicked it on. A TV sat on a console in front of a worn couch. A coffee table with old magazines and remote controls. Shelves.

But what pulled her attention, what Armeal was also staring at, was the closed door at the back of the room. Soft growling sounds came from the room. Scratching. Shuffling.

"Oh my God," May whispered as Victoria's ghost again appeared and floated next to the closed door.

Victoria's weeping eyes pleaded with her, begged her.

"Open it," she uttered Armeal.

The Nephilim didn't argue this time and slowly pushed open the door. The smell instantly worsened as a shriveled corpse turned toward them. Rotting gray flesh hung from the mostly exposed skeleton. Limp hair hung in clumps from the patchy skin left on the skull. One of her eyes hung from its socket. She crawled toward them, only to be stopped by a chain on one bony ankle. She growled and rasped as her rotting arms reached for them.

Around the corpse were bodies of animals. At least, May gulped, parts of animals.

"He was feeding her," Armeal said from his spot closest to the corpse.

Behind her, Ethan vomited.

Tears soaked May's cheeks as she stared at what was left of Victoria's body.

"This isn't natural," Ethan said.

Armeal growled in agreement. "Necromancy never is."

Victoria's ghost pleaded silently with her, her own eyes weeping. May raised her hand, already engulfed in flame.

"No," May said to Ethan, "it's not."

She pushed forward, jaw tight, the flame spitting and twisting in her palm as she poured everything she felt into it—disgust, fury, and raw power. Her blood warmed and almost burned with the flame as it burned red, then orange, and then white. She threw her fire at the corpse. It erupted in flames and screeched an inhuman sound. The sound made May cover her ears and wince. She wanted to turn away, but she didn't. She forced herself to watch as the flames consumed it. Victoria, silent and tearful, held vigil over the flames with her.

Eventually, the flames were gone and there was only smoldering ash and sludge where the corpse once was. The smell of burned flesh clung to the roof of her mouth and back of her throat. It made her gag. Victoria's ghost floated in front of her, and she smiled.

She was going to make Thormunt pay for what he did.

"Do you know where he went?"

Victoria shook her head, and May sighed. *Damn.*

"You deserve to move on," May said to her.

Victoria shrugged sadly and floated away, fading from sight.

"She has tethered herself," Armeal said again, quietly. Sadly. "She cannot move on."

"We need to leave," Ethan said urgently. He walked up next to her and placed a gentle hand on her shoulder.

May nodded, tears gathering in her eyes, her throat tight. She turned, trudging back up the stairs, and felt the weight of the death behind her. The woman had died a year ago, but this was worse. Keeping her body alive and chained in the basement, feeding it animals, while her soul watched in horror... It was so much worse.

Suddenly, the thought of having to kill James Thormunt was less disturbing. It was less awful. Now, she felt it was what he deserved.

The others followed silently until they were back in the living room.

"Why would someone do that?" Ethan asked.

I'll ask him right before I kill him.

May watched Armeal as he strode to the corner, scythe still in hand. She shrugged as she looked at Ethan. "I don't know. Everyone knows, especially Necromancers, that you can't revive the dead. Only reanimate the body. The mind, that is gone. Maybe he thought... maybe he hoped he could bring her soul back. Maybe he couldn't let go of her body." She shrugged again and wiped at her damp cheek. "I wonder if that's what he was gathering the souls for. Maybe he thought that would give him the strength to bring her back."

Armeal grunted, lips pressed in a thin, determined line. "Someone gave him the idea that was possible."

"Who?" May asked. "What does that mark mean to you? That one you saw."

The silence hung in the air. She held his gaze, even when he narrowed his eyes in an indignant glare. Ethan shifted next to her.

Finally, he blinked. "It is," he said, each word tight, like he resented speaking them, "the mark of a very old Nephilim. A Nephilim... who should be dead."

"Why would his scythe be under a Necromancer's bed?"

"Why a human has her scythe isn't the important question," Armeal said. "How is she still alive, is."

"Who is... she?"

"Did she send you?" Thormunt's words echoed back to her. It hadn't been Death he was taking about.

Armeal's eyes grew distant before he whispered, "Yrien."

There was more to that story, May could feel it, but here and now wasn't the time to hear it. She turned to Ethan, throat still tight. "What are we going to do about the body?"

He shifted on his feet again, eyebrows furrowing. "Leave it. Tomorrow, I'll call in an anonymous tip pretending to be a neighbor that heard something. Once patrol gets to the door... they'll smell it."

She nodded and turned to the door. "Let's go home."

Armeal had disappeared into the night without a word as soon as they'd left the house, and May and Ethan walked back to their car. It seemed a much longer walk than it had before.

The drive was quiet. Tense. May fought back tears. Ethan's hands were white on the steering wheel. She could feel Ethan's eyes on her as they drove, but she stared out the window forlornly. She couldn't get Victoria's eyes out of her mind. The sorrow in them. The betrayal.

"We need to figure out where Thormunt is." She spoke to the window, the dark world a blur to her.

"I'll see what I can find tomorrow at the office. Hopefully, we have location information by then," Ethan said. "His plate must've been picked up by a camera somewhere."

She nodded, the weight of what she had decided to do heavy in her chest.

CHAPTER THIRTY-EIGHT
SO, YOU'RE ALIVE

Harper couldn't stop staring at Yrien's scythe. Armeal stood silent, still, wary as she stared at it, clutched in her hands.

"Surely, she's not alive."

Harper clenched the staff hard enough the bonewood cracked. She didn't believe that anymore. Not now. Not after being told that Necromancer had *her* scythe. She remembered, so long ago, so faint a memory, a simple thing James Thormunt had said:

"*But she told me,*" the man had said, "*she told me there was a way.*"

It had been there, in front of her, all this time.

He believed he could resurrect his wife's soul. Because Yrien had told him he could... with the power of souls.

Souls for a soul.

Harper growled, the sound vibrating through the black floor and in the silent air. Armeal stepped back. She screamed a harsh, animal scream and cut the air with her claws, rending the world apart. Her coat fluttered around her as she stepped into the desert sun, the red rocks and canyon high around her. The Ley Line thrummed beneath her feet.

The layers of the world crashed shut behind her as she slammed the butt of Yrien's staff into the dusty earth.

"Don't hide now!" she shouted, her voice carrying through the layers of the world. "Not now that the mystery is gone!"

Laughter, clear and delicate, an angel's song, danced around her.

"Took you long enough."

Harper felt her eyes on her back as she slowly turned. Her golden wings were held wide behind her, beautiful, shimmering things. Yrien's mother was said to have loved her daughter's wings. Yrien looked much like she had eons ago. Beautiful, angelic face and soft-blue eyes like the sky. Her long white hair was cut shorter, falling to her chin now. It had once fallen well past her shoulders. Harper remembered it being as soft as silk between her fingers.

"So," Harper murmured, "you're alive."

"Surprise," she sang.

Harper felt the same pang of sorrow the last time she'd seen Yrien. Sorrow and hatred. Betrayal and heartbreak.

"What?" Yrien smiled, though there was no warmth in her gaze. "No words of welcome? No joyful reunion? You loved me once. 'Together for eternity,' you once said."

"And then you betrayed me." Her words were cold and bitter. As heartbroken as she felt.

Yrien tsked. "I don't know. You were the one that ripped my heart out."

Harper stepped closer, lowering Yrien's scythe toward her. "How did you survive that?"

"Oh." Yrien smiled and skipped backward. "I'm not giving away all my secrets."

Anger built in her chest. Fury that still... *still*... after all this time, she treated this like a game. Fury that she was still here, still betraying her. Again.

"You tempt the angels' wrath, *again!*" Harper adjusted her grip on the staff. "You risk all their lives!"

Yrien sobered, her face growing cold and hard. "And you still think a life of servitude is a life worth living."

"*Enough!*" she bellowed, and swung the scythe.

Yrien ducked it easily, but Harper swung again. The long, curved blade hooked for her throat, but Yrien grabbed the top half of the staff, her hand gripping just below the blade. Her strength shocked Harper as they both pushed against each other.

"I'm not letting you cut me apart this time," Yrien growled, pulling Harper close.

She beat her massive wings, and the force of them blew Harper back, her grip slipping from the staff as she flew. She landed hard on the baked earth. Fury gave her strength she didn't know she had.

Her own wings burst from her. Large, massive things of jet black. They shimmered in the sunlight, purple and pearlescent colors shifting in the light. She beat them and was lifted from the ground. A quick flutter had her back on feet. Harper's wings arched high above her, blotting out the sun and cloaking her in shadow. The heavy tips of her vast feathers dragged across the ground like dark banners. Their sight made even Yrien pause, her eyes going wide.

"It was rumored you had some," she said as her eyes roved over them.

"Surprise," Harper growled, and snapped her left wing out with all her strength. The claw at the tip of her wing bone, as sharp as all her claws, caught Yrien across the face, and the force of the hit drove her head back at a painful angle. She cried out and crumpled, hand to her face.

Blood, bright red, dripped through her fingers as Yrien glared at her, but Harper didn't stop. Not now. Not this time. She brought her wing down again, pounding Yrien hard on her head, then she leaped forward, her claws out. Yrien jerked back, legs and wings working, but Harper was faster, and her claws sank into the meat of Yrien's wing.

She screamed for real as Harper dug her claws into those beautiful golden feathers and tore the flesh. But bone snapped and the joint popped as she pulled and tore. Yrien's shrill cry burned Harper's ears, cracked her heart open all over, but she did not release her. She used her grip on Yrien's pride and joy, and pulled her close.

"Where are my Reapers?" she shouted into her face.

"They aren't yours," Yrien bit back.

Her wing's claw had sliced Yrien's cheek open from the corner of her eye to her chin, and blood poured down her neck from the wound.

Pain!

Harper grunted as she felt metal slice across her belly, but still, she reached for Yrien's neck. Harper's claws cut across the beautiful white flesh of her neck, but Yrien jerked and fought, so Harper couldn't get her claws to sink. More pain seared Harper's chest as Yrien flailed and struck nearly blindly. Harper yanked her hand, and the last of the joints in Yrien's wing snapped.

A burst of power hit Harper in the chest and threw her back again. She righted herself with a few flaps of her wings as she hovered and watched Yrien with caution.

Her beautiful wing hung limp and useless at her back. Yrien's eyes flicked to it, her face twisting with pain, but her teeth bared in a snarl, breath ragged and blood streaking her cheek. She turned furious eyes to Harper, glaring at her from under her brows.

"That was uncalled for."

Harper felt the warmth of blood running down her, but she ignored it, pushed it aside, as she settled again on her feet. She picked up the scythe from the ground, staff cracked.

"Where are my souls?" she thundered.

Yrien scoffed, and the sound grated on Harper's nerves, fury boiling in her veins.

"Did you kill Talsk?"

"He saw me," she said. "I couldn't let my surprise out yet."

"Why the human?"

Yrien limped away, wincing as her wing jerked with the movement.

"He was gullible. Easy to persuade." Yrien limped farther back.

She lifted the scythe. "Why use a human at all?"

Yrien laughed, a brittle, angry sound. "Look how long it took you to figure it out. Why wouldn't I?"

"But... why?"

Why. There were so many questions in that one word. Questions Harper knew she wouldn't get answers to. She flexed her massive wings and flew toward Yrien, blade aimed to cut the Nephilim in half. Time slowed, sound silenced, as she saw the blade inch closer and closer.

She felt the rush of power, hot and cold at once, as she brought the scythe down.

And it sliced through empty air, the blade cutting deep into the earth.

Yrien's laughter as she sank into the Ley Line echoed softly off the canyon until it was silent again.

The gouges across Harper's stomach and chest slowly knit back together. The only sign she'd been injured were the cuts to her clothing and the thick dark blood.

The staff shattered in her grip as she squeezed it.

She didn't know how long she stood there staring at the shattered pieces of the scythe.

"Death?"

Armeal's voice startled her out of her reprieve.

"You have been gone for some time."

She turned and saw Armeal staring at the broken scythe. He lifted his eyes from the shattered staff and moved over her torn and bloody clothing.

He stared with wide eyes. "You have been injured."

Harper couldn't bring herself to care or be worried. "Yrien is alive," she said instead. "She is behind all of the missing souls. She recruited the Necromancer."

"How is she alive?" Armeal asked incredulously.

I will not leave her in enough pieces to heal next time, she thought, and gathered the pieces of the scythe.

"Gather the Nephilim," she said instead.

She let them see the blood crusted on her clothing. The tears. Her wings flexed large and wide behind her. The Nephilim gawked at her, many with their hoods pushed back. Their mouths hung slack and their eyes were wide. Her feathers ruffled as she flexed her wings, shimmering like oil or a moonless sky—like the cloaks worn by the Nephilim. She had sacrificed her many of her beautiful feathers for those cloaks.

"I will not mince words." Her voice echoed through the hall. "Yrien is alive. I'm sure many are already aware."

The crowd shifted and the rustling of their robes filled the hall. Luras and Nerwen shifted and glanced over at her.

"Leave," she commanded in a booming voice. "Follow her

foolish plan. Die beneath the Fae's blades and run from the angels."

They muttered now, and Armeal stepped closer behind her.

"Those that stay, will remain under my protection, but I will not protect traitors. I will not harbor those who think me a slave driver. I will not fight for you a second time."

Nephilim looked to each other. A few started stepping back.

"I will not have another war!" she bellowed, and they all stilled. "So *leave!*"

They were still as they waited to see if it was a trap. But then they started to turn. Some threw off their Reaper cloaks. She observed silently, heart closing as more and more turned away. Armeal stood next to her, his wing gently brushing hers as they watched Nephilim leave.

In the end, less than she feared had left. More than she'd hoped. Many hovered and clustered around Luras and Nerwen

"What now, Death?" Armeal asked under his breath.

"They will tend to the souls here. It is no longer safe for them to leave the Underworld."

"You will ferry the souls yourself?"

"Yes," she whispered, and turned away. "As I have before. Alone."

CHAPTER THIRTY-NINE
THIS CHANGES EVERYTHING

May sat at her desk, distracted and tired. Morning had come too quickly, but she'd already missed too much work. Her reports were piling up and her email box was uncomfortably full. Armeal had disappeared quickly after Thormunt's house. He hadn't said anything about what the next step was and ignored her calls on the mirror.

"Okay." She sighed and pushed herself upright. "You can do this."

Pep talk finished, she opened her inbox and started the long, arduous task of dealing with her emails. Fortunately, most were simple: releases to mortuaries, reports from the toxicology labs, and submitting completed reports to those that had requested them.

She was cradling her third cup of coffee, nearly finished with emails, when muttering and loud conversation pulled her attention from her computer screen. Poking her head out of her cubicle, she gawked into the hallway.

" ... don't believe..."

Sarah shook her head, mouth agape. "For real, though."

May frowned. "What's happening?"

Sarah and Darlene looked over at her, then headed her way.

"The body they brought in last night," Darlene said. She shoved her hands into her scrub pockets.

"What about it?"

"You haven't heard?" Sarah gasped, and May had to focus not to narrow her eyes.

Obviously, or I wouldn't have asked.

Darlene nudged Sarah.

"PD got a welfare check last night, and when they got there, they could smell decomp. I went out on the call."

May's heart stuttered, and her mouth went dry. "Not so weird." She forced herself to say.

"Normally, no." Darlene continued. "But when they went in, they found a burned body in the basement. What's even crazier—" She took a deep breath and paused for effect. "Turns out, the lady probably died like... a year prior."

May's mouth went slack. "What do you mean 'probably'?"

Angela came out from her cubical a few spots down the hallway. She was one of the senior investigators at the office and tended to keep to herself. That she was coming over to join this water-cooler moment surprised May.

"Because," Angela said, "we can't find any record of her death."

"Oh..." May breathed the word. That *was* weird.

Is that why he had an empty urn?

"The detective on scene was telling me they ran history for the lady, and her brother had called in a bunch of welfare checks on her. He was saying he thought his brother-in-law had killed her. But he was a huge drunk so most of his calls sounded like nonsense."

"Oh, shit," Angela said under her breath.

"Cops said they found an urn in the house, but we can't find any records of her death ever being reported to us. I pulled her medical history and found she was being treated for breast cancer about three years ago, then she just stopped showing up to her appointments."

"And no one called to be like 'hey do you still want your chemo?'" Sarah asked, drawing a self-conscious giggle from Darlene.

Angela shot the intern a withering glare but answered. "They did. But she said she was refusing treatment." She shrugged.

"And then she died at home." Sarah picked up the story. "And her husband just... kept her."

The group shook their heads, but May remembered Victoria's sad, beseeching eyes. Begging. Pleading for peace. The sight made her stomach roll.

"Hey," Angela said. "You okay?"

The other two had already wandered down the hall.

"Yeah," she muttered, and rolled back to her desk. "Just... Yeah. I'm fine."

Angela lingered in her cubicle. "You sure? You've been—" She took a breath. "I know we don't really talk, but you've been different lately."

"I'm fine."

"Okay," she said at last. "If you want to talk. We see a lot of shit, and we don't ever seem to talk about it until it's too late."

Great, she thought. *Now I feel like an ass.*

"Thanks," she said as Angela was turning away. "I've just got some personal stuff going on."

She nodded, her long hair flopping over her eyes.

Some personal stuff. May snorted and turned back to her computer. *If that's what I'm calling this mess...*

She propped her elbows on her desk and dropped her face

into her hands. Her phone buzzed, and she cracked an eye at it. Ignoring it, she closed her eyes again.

It buzzed again.

Shit.

She picked it up with a huff.

> Det. Dimples: We need to talk
>
> Now.

Ethan's texts sent her stomach into summersaults.

> Me: Meet me at the coffee shop on Main
>
> Det. Dimples: Copy

She grabbed her bag and threw it over her shoulder. As she passed Angela's desk, she stopped long enough to say she had to run a personal errand and would be back in a couple minutes. Angela frowned at her but nodded.

The coffee shop was just around the corner from work and a quick walk. Soft music was playing from the speaker behind the counter. The colorful, mismatched chairs were a welcome sight. She ordered quickly and chose a table in the far corner.

Her knee bounced, and she forced herself to breathe steadily and slowly.

Not long after, Ethan walked in looking as frazzled as she felt. He quickly found her and joined her at the small table.

She sipped her chai. "What's the matter? Why'd you text?"

"I got the results of the phone warrant for Thormunt's cell. There's no data for the last couple of days, so he turned it off."

May closed her eyes. "When we killed his zombie."

"I searched for hits on his license plate, and there's been a few. So he's still in town."

She nodded. "Where at?"

He shrugged. "He's been uptown a lot. In the older rich area near the Park Preserve."

May froze. Her parents lived in that area. She'd told them to put up their wards, but she needed to come clean about why now. She needed to warn her parents.

"My parents live in that area."

Ethan swore under his breath.

"Text me their address. I'll see what I can do about extra patrols."

She nodded, even as she knew it was pointless. If he still had the Reaper cloak, which he likely did, no one would see him. She took a deep breath and tried to calm her racing heart. Her parents were accomplished witches. They were strong. Their wards would hold. She just needed to warn them to make sure.

She grabbed her phone from her purse and quickly pulled up her mom's contact.

> Me: Everything ok at the house?

"So, he's still in town, which is good, I guess," Ethan said. "Since your friend still needs to... kill him, I guess."

May nodded and glanced down at her phone again. Armeal did... or she did. She didn't really know what Armeal was doing. Was he taking over that task now that there was some war brewing? Or was she still expected to handle this?

"His license plate hasn't hit anywhere near his house though, so there's a chance he doesn't know what happened last night."

Her phone dinged and she jumped.

> Mother Dearest: Yes, why?

May rapidly typed out her response.

> Me: Dad ok?

> Mother Dearest: Yes…

> Why May?

She let out a breath and slumped in her chair.

"What?" Ethan asked.

"My parents are okay," she said, hands shaking with relief. "But I need to go talk to them."

"Yeah, yeah." He nodded. "I get it. Let me know if you need anything, and if I learn anything, I'll call you."

She nodded, already grabbing her purse.

May raced to her parents' house. Pulling up to their curb, she threw her car into park, her car jerking to a stop. The front door opened as she got to it, her dad staring at her with wide eyes and a slack mouth.

"What the hell's the matter?"

She pushed passed him and slammed the door shut. "Where's Mom?"

"Teaching." Her dad stared down at her. "You know that. What is going on?"

She forced herself to take a deep breath, but it didn't help the fear rolling in her stomach. This was all her fault. They wouldn't be in danger if she hadn't gotten involved. Tears pooled in her eyes.

He watched her, eyes moving over her face, then he tugged

her in for a hug, large hands moving gently up and down her back. "You're okay."

"It's r-r-really b-b-bad..."

"Nothings that bad," he said into her hair.

She saw Victoria's body again, her weeping eyes, smelled the burned skin, and cried harder. She felt that same, burning hatred toward the man who would do that to another person, the man who had killed so many, and knew she would feel no remorse when she killed him. And that made her sob into her dad's chest. What sort of Green Witch feels no remorse for murder?

She let her dad hold her, let herself cry until she hiccuped, but then she remembered why she came. Pushing back, she looked blearily into her dad's eyes.

"You're in danger."

He paused, eyes growing serious. "Been in danger before."

She nodded. "This might be a bit different."

He took a deep breath. "Well, you'd better fill me in, then."

He led her, with his arm around her shoulder, into the kitchen, where he started a kettle of water and pulled mugs down from the cupboard. She sniffled, wiping tears from her soaked cheeks, and watched. He grabbed his own blend of herbs, ones he'd grown and dried and mixed, then he set two steaming mugs on the table and sat next to her. She wrapped her hands around the mug, ignoring the burn from the too-hot ceramic.

"This has to do with the ghosts," he finally said. "Doesn't it?"

She nodded and blew on her tea. Clearing her throat, she looked up at him. "A Necromancer has been murdering people and stealing their souls. I've been helping Death find out who that is. I found him, Dad."

His face was stern as he nodded.

She took a shuddering breath and pushed aside Victoria's haunted eyes. "A few days ago, a detective was watching his house. He got into some trouble with a zombie."

He nodded, eyebrows furrowing.

"I burned it. I had to," she hurriedly added. "It was coming at us, and Ethan was on the ground. I had to stop it, and I didn't have any time. I wasn't prepared for a *zombie*. It was coming and growling and—"

His hand on her arm stopped her rambling words. "You protected your partner. It's what you do."

Her breath stuttered, tears slipping down her cheeks, but she nodded. Partners... is that what they were now?

"Yeah, I did." She sniffled. "Anyway, I thought we got away without being seen, but..."

She shook her head and gulped down her hot tea. The soothing, settling spell her dad had set on it churned in her belly, but she was too upset, too afraid, for it to work.

"Last night," she continued, "we went to his house. He was gone already, but we found... It doesn't matter what we found. I destroyed it, but Ethan, he's been trying to find him. And his car has been in this area the last four days."

"You think he's identified you and is looking for us." It wasn't a question. She hesitated, and her dad caught on immediately. "*He's* the stalker you called about... isn't he?"

She nodded. "He probably has a Reaper cloak, which will allow to him appear invisible to you. He's collected souls, which might make him more powerful. He's partnered himself with a really dangerous Nephilim. There's no telling how strong he is."

He nodded, brows knit. Suddenly, he stood and walked back to her mom's office, returning a moment later with the family grimoire along with her mother's smaller one.

"Your mother has strong wards," he said as he sat and

started flipping through pages. "And those plants you think are extravagant actually have a dual purpose."

She frowned.

"Oh, yes." He chuckled. "Some will attack"—he tapped his finger on a page—"and others will shield. Some will trap and kill. Just depends on the plant."

She wanted to ask why her parents had such offensive plants scattered throughout the yard, what they were preparing for, but now wasn't the time. "I'm sorry I got you involved in this."

He paused his page flipping to stare at her. His eyes were solemn, serious, and he didn't blink. "Never apologize for doing the right thing."

"Even if it hurts people?"

He held her eyes. "That's when it's the hardest to do it."

She looked down but nodded. "Thanks, Dad," she murmured.

He grabbed her hand tight in his. Ever since her heart had gotten worse and there seemed to be an expiration date on her, being home had been stressful. Tense. Her mother had fretted and fluttered and hovered. It had only gotten worse after the replacement.

May knew it wasn't fair to them. They were just worried and afraid, but it was hard to live her life with them waiting for her to die.

Tonight, it finally felt like home again.

CHAPTER FORTY
FIRE AND BLOOD

May stared at her computer screen but wasn't seeing it. She'd spent the night with her parents. She told herself it was it was so she could make sure their wards were strong enough, as if she'd know, but really it was for her. She needed to be reassured that everything was fine. That it would *be* fine eventually. Her mom was convinced it was coincidence that Thormunt's car was in the area. At least her dad took her seriously. The threat was real. She just couldn't figure out why her mother didn't seem to think so.

Had she just been humoring her this whole time?

She dropped her head into her hand. Believing your daughter talked to Death was a lot to take in, but, she lifted her head with a huff, it wasn't like she was prone to dramatic storytelling.

It was just like her mom to not take her seriously.

May angrily shook her mouse to wake her computer up, only to grab her phone.

Me: Everything OK?

She waited, and the message went unread, so she set the phone aside. Maybe she was being paranoid. She had no reason to think Thormunt actually knew where her parents lived. If he did, he had to have figured out where she lived, so why would he go there and not after her?

Her phone dinged with a response from her dad.

> Pops: All good here.

She took a breath, relieved.

> Pops: Mom's at work

She nodded and set her phone down, then forced herself to turn to her reports, waking her computer up again. It took all her concentration to make it to lunch time.

She didn't know what Thormunt was doing, which made everything worse. She had heard nothing new from Ethan. Did that mean Thormunt was hiding? Or had he ditched his car? Would he know he needed to? Did he think he was caught?

Too many questions swirled in her mind. Too many unknowns.

She leaned against the counter in the small break room, a microwave lunch humming behind her, and slipped her phone from her pocket.

> Me: Still good?

Her foot tapped while she waited for a response.

> Pops: May
>
> You've got to stop

> You're going to drive yourself crazy

Her dad's texts came in quick succession.

> Me: I'm just worried.

> Pops: You sound like mom

Goddammit. She sighed and shoved her phone into her pocket.

"Fine," she muttered to herself as her lunch dinged in the microwave. Back at her desk, she continued writing and reviewing reports as she nibbled on her noodles. Glancing at the clock on her computer, she saw it was just after one. Her mom should be home soon. Today was her short day, with only office hours for the first half of the day.

She cleared her throat and pushed it out of her mind.

She'd almost emptied her email when her phone dinged with a message from her dad.

> Pops: What kinda car did you say this guy drives?

Her heart jumped into her throat.

> Me: Green Honda. Why?

No response came, and her breathing sped up.

> Me: WHY?

Finally, a text from her dad popped up.

> Pops: Yea, he's here.

"Oh my God," she muttered, heart pounding. "Oh my God."

She dialed Ethan's number.

He answered on the second ring.

"He's at my parents'," she said without greeting.

"Shit." His voice was stressed. "I'll send patrol. I'm on my way. Don't! Go over there."

"But they're my parents!"

"Don't!" he all but shouted. "Let the cops handle this."

"What are cops supposed to do against a zombie?" she hissed into the phone, already standing.

"Just..." He sighed and swore. "Wait for me. Don't rush in!"

She disconnected the call in an angry huff to see a text from her mom.

> Mother Dearest: Stay away.
>
> We'll fight him off.

She didn't hesitate.

Her heart was in her throat, mouth dry, and her hands shook as she sped toward her parents'.

The wards will hold. The wards will hold, she thought over and over as she ignored traffic lights and speed limits. Her car skidded to a stop in front of her home, tires squealing. She'd barely thrown it in park before she was out.

Above her in the trees, a raven cawed, loud and shrill. They were the messengers of change, and she feared for what she'd find in her home.

As she jogged up the sidewalk to the front of the house,

she saw plants that had once been lush and full, dead and limp. Several were uprooted. Dirt and leaves littered the front lawn as she cautiously approached the front door—the open door.

There were no wards.

Her breath stuttered, heart in her throat. She wanted to call out and shout for her dad, but a larger part of her wanted to be silent. Secret. If he was here, she didn't want him to know she was as well. She took a deep breath, and it caught in her throat as she slowly stepped into the house. Her breathing was too loud, but no matter how hard she tried to slow it down, she couldn't. Furniture was overturned everywhere she looked. Glass from the hallway mirror littered the floor, and spots of blood led to the kitchen.

"Dad?" she whispered, and crept farther into the house.

Slowly, she turned into the kitchen.

"Mom!"

She ran toward her mother lying on the floor but slipped on blood before reaching her. May moved awkwardly to her knees and crawled to her mother, who gasped and gurgled.

Her eyes were halfway closed, skin too pale.

"No, no, no, no," she muttered as she shakily tried to find where all the blood was coming from. There was too much blood. Too much.

Her shirt was soaked in it, thick and dark. Some was already clotting.

"Mom?" May shook her shoulders, and her mom's eyes fluttered, recognition filling them for a moment.

"May..." She took a rattling breath, and blood flecked her lips. "He's... here."

"Where? Where's Dad?"

Pain filled Janet's eyes, and they went cloudy, unfocused again.

"Mom?"

"You took her from me," a man's voice, seething with anger, came from the dining room.

May jerked and looked up, only to stare at James Thormunt. He glowered at her with a crazed look in his eyes.

"What?" she croaked, tears streaking down her face.

"You took my wife from me!" he shouted, and May flinched back. "You ruined everything. So now I'm taking something from you."

He turned to flee out the back door.

"No!" May shouted, and stood. *He can't get away. He can't!*

She ran after him, rage building in her chest, and took the corner to the dining room as he fled out the back door into the garden, but she managed to grab his arm. He spun, and, with an animalistic growl, tossed her aside like it was nothing. With a grunt, she slammed into the dining room wall. She pushed off again, but something grabbed her foot, and she fell, chin hitting the floor hard enough to rattle her brain, and stars exploded behind her eyelids. May yelped and scrambled away, only for her foot to be grabbed again.

She kicked at whatever held her, and twisted. Lifeless eyes stared at her, mouth gaping. She gasped and frantically looked around. Were there more? Had he brought others? In the kitchen, her mom still lay where she'd left her.

She kicked at the zombie again and scooted away, reading the fire in her blood. She glanced back after Thormunt, but he was gone. The zombie reached again for her, and she kicked its hands away.

Why was it crawling?

The thought came to her in slow motion as she realized it was missing a leg. Staring down, it moaned and growled, pulling itself toward her with its hands. His prosthetic was missing, and his other leg lay twisted unnaturally behind him, useless. May inched back until her back was against the wall as he slowly crept toward her, and she slowly realized what she was staring at.

She screamed until her voice broke.

Her father reached for her with pale hands, growling. The sound was raspy and breathy, and when he moved, May saw a large gash across his neck. It nearly spanned ear to ear.

"Nooooooo!" she screamed as he reached for and grabbed her other foot in a painfully tight grasp, an inhuman grip.

She screamed—a jagged, desperate sound—and kicked hard, her legs flailing as she tried to pull away from him, from the snap of those gnashing teeth. Panic surged through her, wild and cold. She kicked again. And again. Her voice cracked, breaking into a moaning cry—too heavy with sorrow to form a word. May broke one foot free and pulled herself to her feet, shaking off his grip.

"No," she moaned. Her breath was fast and raspy. The corners of her vision filled with spots as she hyperventilated.

"*I'm taking something from you,*" he'd said.

Fury filled her, so hot it made her blood burn and her skin flush.

This was worse. This was so much worse than anything she'd considered.

Her father's corpse reached her, his fingers grasping at her sneakers. Numbly, she inched away again, sliding along the wall.

"I'm going to kill you," she swore as the burning rage in her blood seemed to spill over.

With a pop and snap of power, something in her chest shifted.

Then exploded.

With a shriek, she sank to her knees as magic raced through her. She felt like she was on fire. Her skin burned, and heat scorched her face. The blood that had soaked her jeans and covered her hands and arms burned away, leaving soot and ash where they had been.

She watched in numb fascination as her parents' blood on her hands glowed as it sizzled and then was absorbed into her skin. It made her feel invigorated. Strong. Her breath came in harsh, fast gasps that had nothing to do with fear and sorrow.

An animalistic scream pierced the air, bringing May back to herself. Her father's corpse was ablaze, the screaming coming from him. She watched, numb and removed, as the flames spread through the dining room. They licked up the chairs, covering the table. The carpet turned black as it burned.

Eventually, the screams stopped, but the fire continued to spread. She watched it, not noticing the painful heat on her skin or the burning in her throat. It wasn't until she heard coughing from the kitchen that May was shaken from her stupor.

"Mom!" she shouted, and then coughed.

The smoke was thick and burned her mouth and throat. Dropping to her hands and knees, she crawled through the smoke back to the kitchen, to her mother. She tried to drag her toward the front door, but she was too heavy. Every time she stood, the smoke filled her lungs and her vision dimmed.

I will kill you.

"I will kill you!" she screamed it until her voice gave out.

CHAPTER FORTY-ONE
IT CALLED FOR BLOOD

"Dammit!" Shouting roused her.

Shouting and the sensation of being dragged.

"I told you to wait!"

May blinked her eyes, her burning, stinging eyes, and Ethan was dragging her down the sidewalk.

"No." She groaned and tried to stand. "Mom."

"Hey!" he shouted, and pulled her arm over his shoulder and hoisted her to her feet. "Fire's already got her. They're right behind us."

She glanced over her shoulder and saw two firemen, clad in their bulky gear, moving with her mother's limp body between them.

"Where's your dad?"

Tears rolled down her cheeks. "Gone," she whispered.

Then the coughing took over. She coughed so hard she gagged as the smoke and fire burned her throat and lungs. Ethan set her on the back of a fire truck and ran off while the paramedics put an oxygen mask over her mouth. Her mom was loaded into an ambulance, and it raced off, sirens screeching into the evening.

Firetrucks, with hoses and ladders stretched toward her parents' house, fought the blazing fire. She'd done that. It was all she could think as she watched the flames destroy her home.

May wasn't sure how long she sat there, people rushing around her, water seemingly everywhere. The bitter, chemical taste of house fire coated the back of her throat. Her fire. Her mistake. Her skin was tight and stung from the heat, and a few places were burned. She didn't notice it much. Later she would. But not now.

Eventually, the detectives came and talked to her. Numbly, she described what she saw when she'd entered the house. When she found her father... dead.

She left out the part where Thormunt had done the unthinkable.

They said her her mom was still alive but at a hospital. She'd seen the blood. She'd seen the injuries. She'd lost hope.

Ethan stepped in front of her, his face drawn and worried.

"Do you want to go to the hospital?"

She frowned and looked around.

"Your mom is there," he said when she didn't answer.

"No," she said, still watching the last of the flames and thick smoke rise from her home. "No, I won't be able to see her, anyway. She'll be in the ICU burn unit. They won't let me in."

She also acknowledged, slowly and pitifully to herself, that she couldn't face her mother lying in a hospital bed. She didn't want to face the tubes and wires, the machines surrounding her and keeping her alive. With a cold wash of dread, she realized that's what her mother faced every time she was in the hospital. That's what her mother dealt with for the weeks after her transplant. She had faced that, and May couldn't. She was stronger than May ever would be.

"Home?"

She blinked and finally looked at him. "Don't they need you here?"

He shook his head, and she noticed the ash smeared across his face. "The others have this."

She nodded, and he helped her to his car. The ride was silent, and for that, she was grateful. She needed the silence. Her father's face kept filling her vision, no matter how hard she shut her eyes. She tried to push the image away, but she felt the rage. The fury. It burned in her chest, and with it, that burning, simmering power in her chest grew again.

Panicked, she took a deep breath and pushed the magic down, she shifted in her seat. Ethan glanced at her from the corner of his eye but said nothing. Sorrow she didn't want to acknowledge, sat at the edge of her mind. She couldn't let herself think about what she'd lost. Not yet. It would break her, and she had something to do before that happened.

Suddenly, they were pulling into her apartment complex and Ethan was opening her door. She blinked at his hand as he held it out to her, waiting. Eventually, she roused herself enough to take it and let him pull her from the car and escort her up to her apartment. Inside, she slumped onto her couch, tears gathering in her throat again.

Loki climbed into her lap, purring and rumbling. May wrapped her arms around the protesting cat and hugged him, ignoring his meows at the tight grip. She buried her face in his fur and focused on his rumbling, vibrating purrs.

Ethan puttered around in her kitchen, but she didn't look to see what he was doing. It sounded like he was getting a drink, but she didn't care. Couldn't care.

She just nestled on Loki's back, tears clumping his fur.

A throat clearing and a clink of glass next to her had her lifting her head. Ethan set a mug on the coffee table and settled on the edge of the couch. His eyes were filled with pity and sadness, so she had to look away. She finally released her grip on Loki and leaned forward to sniff the tea.

"Chamomile?" Her voice croaked, and she swallowed around her dry mouth and ashy throat.

He shrugged. "Figured it couldn't hurt."

She smiled as she took the hot cup and sipped, and instantly, her throat felt better.

"So," Ethan asked gently, "what really happened?"

May stared into the mug and shivered. That rage, the burning, furious rage started to build again, and she had to take a deep breath to push it back.

"He went to my home. Killed my dad. My mom..." She took another deep breath, hands shaking. "He'd already turned my dad into a... a...." The rage rose in her throat, and suddenly, the tea in her mug was boiling. It sputtered and splashed on her hands.

With a yelp, she dropped the mug, and it shattered on the floor, scalding water going everywhere.

"Fuck," she breathed, and rubbed her hands on her face, pushing her hands through her hair.

Ethan jumped off the couch and rushed into the kitchen. He returned with paper towels and the dust bin. Silently, he cleaned up her mess and set it aside before settling next to her again.

She took another deep breath. "I saw him run out the back. I tried to chase him, tried to stop him, but he was so strong. He just *threw* me off like I was a toddler. And then... then my dad was grabbing me. I hadn't seen him yet. Thormunt got away while I was... dealing... with my dad. And then the fire... it just..."

"Shit," Ethan breathed.

May glanced at him, and he was running his own hands through his short hair.

"I had to." She insisted. "I couldn't let him go on like that. I had to." Her voice cracked and broke, tears falling again down her cheeks. "I had to."

Ethan reached over and pulled her into a hug, and May sobbed, loud and uncontrollably. "I had to. I had to. I had to."

"I know," he muttered, and let her scream into his chest.

She came back to herself, and her voice was sore, her eyes stung from all the salt, and even the burning rage had settled in her chest. Ethan patted her back softly but released her when she shifted. He kept his hands on her shoulders as she leaned back and looked at him.

"We're going to kill him," he declared. "Get your friend. We're ending this."

She sniffled. "Doesn't that go against your morality as a cop?"

"Nope," he said without hesitation. "Not this time. Not like I can keep him in prison anyway."

She nodded and sniffled again.

"We have to move fast. My unit's going to track him down eventually, and we need to do what we need to do before that happens."

"How are we going to find him?" She scrubbed her face and stood up with a jerk. "We couldn't find him when he went to kill my parents! How are we going to find him now?"

She paced the living room, growing more and more angry. More desperate. Her anger called for blood. *His* blood. Vengeance. Revenge. She wanted him to pay for everything he'd done.

"Hey, hey." Ethan held his hands out placatingly to her. "Calm down. Breathe."

She took long, slow breaths and steadied the raging fire in her. She wanted him to pay, but first, she needed to find him. And then... she would kill him.

CHAPTER FORTY-TWO
NOT EVEN FOR MAY

For the first time in Harper's memory, she did not want to collect a soul.

Steven Haines. His name had first appeared in her Book of Souls nearly thirty years ago when a bomb had taken his leg in a foreign desert. That strange thing, modern medicine, had stepped in again and given him more time. It had been a fleeting name back then. She'd hardly even noticed it, but now. Now that was a name she knew. It was a name she dreaded collecting.

Time froze around them, it was how she would be able to collect every soul herself. The scene was horror filled. Her stomach had knotted the second she saw the names flickering in her Book of Souls. She had hoped it would be peaceful, but the house around her was anything but.

Steve stared at her with a mixture of sadness, anger, and wonder. Thormunt, that damned Necromancer, knelt next to Steve's body, and she knew what he was about to do. The knowledge twisted in her gut.

"I've heard a lot about you."

Harper blinked at the man, who looked so much like May.

"My daughter says you like coffee."

Harper smiled, but it was filled with sorrow. "I like having coffee with your daughter."

He chuckled, a sad, hollow sound. "Yeah, she's like that. Makes friends with everyone."

Harper pulled her clock from her pocket. The window was closing. He would need to leave soon or be trapped here.

"You can't, undo this, can you?"

"No." The word was wrenched from her. "Though for the first time, I wish I could."

"Not even for May?" he begged.

A tear gathered in the corner of her eye. "No, not even for May."

He sighed, and it was filled with tears, a thick sound that got stuck in his throat. Steve walked around her and stared down at his wife's body. She lived still, barely. Harper checked her clock again. That window was also closing.

She prayed to the Fates she would not take them both now.

"Can I wait for her?" he asked softly.

Harper turned to Steve kneeling next to his wife. His ghost shimmered, and Harper could already see the Tether getting ready to set in place.

"If you do," she murmured, "you will linger here for all time."

"Like a haunted spirit?"

"Exactly like." Harper knelt close to him. "It is not an existence you wish for."

He gazed down at Janet. "But I can't leave her."

"Wait for her on the other side. But not here. Not like this."

He sobbed quietly. "When will she go?" He looked around Harper at Thormunt. "What will he do to her?"

"I do not know the future."

He shook his head, silent sobs shaking his ghostly frame. Harper held her hand out to him, and without looking away from Janet, he took her hand.

Steve released her hand as soon as they appeared in the Forgotten Forest. He looked around, surprise flickering in his face.

"So this is... what?"

She glanced around with him. "This is where you wait. Once you're ready, you move on. Or you don't. It is up to you."

"Janet will find me here? When it's her turn?"

She nodded, and with a defeated sigh, he walked away. She watched him go, hating, for perhaps the first time, that this was her life.

CHAPTER FORTY-THREE
POWER OF THE SOUL

The air shimmered and split, then Harper emerged from the glowing gap. Ethan swallowed and stepped back, looking pale. May stood, fingers twining together. Death's bright-orange eyes surveyed the room before settling on May.

They were filled with sorrow.

"Did you take him?" May blinked and fought back tears. When would she be done crying?

"If it eases your sorrow," Harper muttered, pale face framed by her raven-black hair, "know that I did not wish to."

The tears fell.

"It does not," she bit out, voice thick with venom and anger. "Where is he?"

Harper blinked. "He waits in the Forgotten Forest. He will not move on without her."

More tears fell. Angry tears. Grief-heavy tears that soaked her shirt. "You couldn't have saved him?"

Harper frowned and shook her head. "I told you, that is not within my ability."

"You're Death!" she yelled, and stepped close. "How is it not in your ability?"

"I do not choose who lives and wh—"

"You could've saved him!" she shouted, and shoved Harper's shoulders. The God of Death looked startled, eyes wide and mouth slack, as May pushed her again. "You could have!"

Her shoves turned into fists beating against Death. What was the point of being friends with Death if she couldn't even save the ones she loved?

"I would have!" She raged against Death, who let her fists beat against her. "I would've saved him if it were me!"

"But it is not," Harper said, sorrow making her voice soft. "And I cannot."

"Bullshit!" The crying was loud and ugly, snot and tears running down her face as she sobbed her anger into the God of Death.

Slowly, she noticed cold hands moving along her fists, her arms. They slowed her furious beating and settled on her shoulders, holding her still, before slowly curling around and holding. Gently. Hesitantly. Unsure. May sobbed into the cold chest as Death held her.

May took a shaking breath, throat thick with tears again, and straightened. Death's hands fell away like shrouds. Shaking her head, she cleared her throat and faced Death. Harper took a step closer, her face growing worried with her pinched brows. She brought a hand near May's collarbone, just above her skin.

"Something has changed with your magic."

"It doesn't matter," May snapped, and swatted Death's hand away.

Harper stared at her with wide, surprised eyes. She brought her hand over May's chest again, and this time, she felt a shimmer of magic brush against her own. Prodding. Testing.

She moved to swat the hand away again, but Harper caught her hand in a tight grip. "You've the anger to think you can order Death, and now the impatience to *swat* at me," she said, eyes moving over May's face.

May grumbled, tears cooling on her skin.

Harper's magic continued to prod against hers.

May's magic rose up against the intrusion, boiling in her blood. Her skin felt flushed, and Harper dropped May's hand in a small gasp. Harper looked at her own hand, as if it'd been in pain, and stepped back from May. Harper raised her hand again, sharp claws extended on her fingers, and pricked May just above her collarbone. She flinched at the unexpected sharpness. Harper drew her finger to her mouth, eyes never leaving May as she tasted the small drop of her blood.

Her eyes widened with shock, and maybe even horror, as her hand slowly lowered. "What have you done?"

May glared at her, even as fearful curiosity begged her to ask what the look meant. "I didn't do anything."

Harper stared at her, orange eyes pale and wide. May saw her long, thin throat swallow before she spoke. "You are a Blood Witch. The power must've been dormant in you, or you'd buried it, but it is not now."

Blood Witch. The words rang in her mind. *Blood magic. Evil magic.* Her mouth went dry. It would explain, a soft part of her mind said, why she was never very good at growing things. At Green Magic. Why her magic always seemed to resist her.

It was another way she'd failed her parents. She glanced at Ethan, who stood silent and still by the couch, watching with wide eyes.

"You must be careful," Harper warned, her voice low. "Blood magic is hard to control. It may very well be why your heart was so weak."

May's eyes snapped to Harper's pale face.

"Blood magic," Harper continued, "can burn you from the inside out if you do not control it. Yet more of your organs may slowly fail if you do not learn how to properly control it."

She cleared her throat. The coughing. She gasped. Her lungs. It wasn't the smoke. It was her magic. She shook aside the rising panic. That was for later. Right now, she needed revenge.

"Where is Thormunt?" she asked.

Harper watched her with an impassive face.

"Surely, you know?" May pressed. "Each soul. Surely, you know where they are."

May could see the conflict on Harper's face, and she pressed harder. "I'm not asking you to interfere. Just tell me where he is."

"This is a dangerously thin line I walk."

May raised her chin. "I'd do it for you."

It was low, she knew it, but she said it anyway. It wasn't a lie, at least. She couldn't save her dad, but she could avenge him. She wouldn't let Death stop her.

Harper blinked, and she knew she'd won.

"Fine."

May straightened, nerves making her breath flutter. Harper's eyes grew distant, vacant, and May exchanged silent glances with Ethan, who shrugged. Suddenly, Death straightened and held out her hand. May reached out and took Harper's cool and dry hand in her overheated one. She glanced at Ethan, not sure what would happen, and held her hand out to him.

The detective sent a cool side-eye at Death before sidling over and taking May's outstretched hand. Harper ignored Ethan's withering look and sliced the air with her claws. The air in front of them split, the edges glowing and bright. Harper glanced at May once before stepping through the opening in the world. May followed, taking and holding a deep breath as she did.

Her feet stepped down on dry grass and gravel. Her held breath puffed from her in a gasp as she looked up at Thormunt's house, the orange sun setting behind it.

"Son of a bitch," Ethan muttered to her right. He glanced at her. "I'm ignoring the teleportation stuff for now."

She smiled and turned her eyes back to the house looming on the hill. The new power in her blood simmered and burned, roiling. It wanted revenge. It rushed through her, made her feel energized and powerful. May stepped forward, only to be pulled back by Ethan.

"What?" she hissed at him.

"We're not rushing in there without a plan," he hissed back. "God or no God on our side."

Harper raised an eyebrow at the detective, but a shimmering split in the air paused whatever acrid words she had for him. Ethan gasped again and stepped back while May watched a Reaper she'd never seen before step through. Her wings were beautiful, like a downy woodpecker, black with white speckled throughout. The strange Reaper glanced dismissively at May and Ethan before turning worried eyes to Harper.

"Death." Her voice was light and soft, delicate. "Armeal and Kian are fighting."

Harper snapped her orange eyes to the Reaper.

"It is..." Her wings shifted nervously. "Escalating."

Harper turned to May with conflicted eyes. "I must go."

"I know. I understand."

Harper tilted her head and brought a cold hand to May's cheek. "I wish I did not need to."

She wished Harper didn't need to as well, but she wouldn't

say the words. She knew it would do nothing but make the God of Death feel worse.

"This revenge is mine."

Harper nodded. She hastily cut an opening in the air before disappearing through it with the other Reaper. May stood and turned to Ethan, who watched with a puzzled look on his face.

"You have some weird ass friends."

She huffed and ignored him. "So, what do we do, then?"

Ethan ran a shaky hand through his disheveled hair and glanced at the house.

"Will bullets kill a Necromancer?" he asked finally.

May shrugged. "Honestly, I don't know. My parents were skilled witches with strong wards and offensive abilities, and he walked out like he lived there."

She was going to burn him to ash anyway. Bullets or no.

"We know this is probably a trap, right?" he asked softly.

"Obviously."

"Okay, as long as we're all on the same page of stupid ideas." He swore and shook out his hands. "Follow me."

He ran up the property line again, hunched as he went. May followed, the dry grass and weeds loud as they rushed through it. As they neared the house, Ethan crouched more and slowed. He pulled his handgun from the holster, holding it low in his hands.

He glanced back at May, then nodded toward the house. Carefully, they crept toward the front of the house, ducking low beneath the front windows as they did. It was dark now, the sun finally having set, though the heat still radiated from the baked earth. They approached the porch slowly, cautiously, quietly.

Her heart pounded in her ears, and her new magic simmered in her blood. Ethan pressed his back against the house as he peered around at the door, then he turned back to her.

"Open door," he whispered, and she barely heard him.

They crept farther up the porch and into the house. It smelled the same, May noticed. Fallen crime scene tape littered the floor in the kitchen, and May suspected the surfaces would be covered with dark fingerprint dust if she could've seen it in the darkness.

A thump sounded down the hall, and they both jerked, dropping low. Ethan lifted his gun to point at the sound down the hallway. A glance to her, then he nodded. Together, they crept toward the master bedroom. May pulled the magic in her blood, and it easily responded. Small flames licked at her fingertips, itching to explode out. It burned to be let free, but she held it back.

Not yet.

As they got closer, the thumps got louder, and soon, they could hear muttering and swearing. Ethan paused at the half-closed door, room illuminated by the light inside, and took a deep breath. He looked at her and held her eyes before nodding once and standing.

He shouldered the door open as he shouted, "Police, don't move!"

May rushed in after him, her tongue bitter with adrenaline. Ethan pointed his firearm at James Thormunt.

"James Thormunt!" he shouted again.

May let flames circle her fist.

James turned on them with a snarl, spittle flying from his mouth. "Where is it?" he yelled.

May let her fire go, throwing it at the monster who'd ruined her life. It hit him in the shoulder, but he only flinched and swatted it away.

"You stole it!" More spittle flew from him as he lunged at her.

Loud bangs deafened May as Ethan fired several quick, consecutive shots into James's chest. He staggered with each shot, falling to his knee.

"Stay down," Ethan yelled, but the words were faint to May's ringing ears as she ducked away.

Thormunt heaved a breath, and it was wet sounding. He dragged his head up to stare at them, his eyes a sickly yellow. Then the bleeding slowly stopped in his chest and the wounds knit shut beneath his torn shirt.

Ethan took a step back, his gun slowly lowering. May's breath caught in her throat.

"They're stealing the power of the soul." Harper's words echoed back to her as she watched Thormunt stand on wobbly legs. She hadn't understood what that truly meant until now.

CHAPTER FORTY-FOUR
LOST HUMANITY

"Shit," May swore.

"Run!" Ethan shouted, and they fled down the hallway.

A growling, lumbering corpse, bones held together by leathery skin, snapped at them as they turned into the living room.

"Where the hell did that come from?" Ethan yelled as he fired off several more rounds at the zombie.

May summoned the fire in her blood and threw a fireball at the thing as she shouldered Ethan toward the kitchen in the back. "He's probably called them."

"Great!" he hollered as they spun into the kitchen and out the back door. The zombie's cries filled the night. He turned to May in the darkness, huffing and out of breath. "So, bullets *don't* do anything."

"He must be using the souls to bolster his own power." May huffed and turned back to the house as James stepped onto the small back porch.

"You ruined it!" James screamed at them.

"And what is it we've ruined?" Ethan asked, voice raised over the short distance.

May shot him a glare, and he waved her off.

"May as well try to get answers," he whispered at her. "Not like we know how to kill him yet."

"She said I could bring her back." James said as he stalked slowly toward them.

They stepped back, keeping the distance between them.

"Bring her back for real. All of her."

"Your wife," May said as they inched back. "You're talking about Victoria?"

"Don't say her name!" he roared—and as his voice tore through the air, the ground beneath their feet quaked.

May glanced down, terror slowly growing in her stomach.

"Ethan," she whispered as she froze.

"Yeah," he whispered back. "I felt that too."

Panicked, she looked around the dark field, trying to see in the night. Had he buried others here? How many? Where the fuck had he even gotten them?

"You wanted to bring your wife back." Ethan said gently, soothingly. "I get that. If I lost someone, I'd try anything to bring them back."

James Thormunt nodded, body haloed by the faint light from the house behind him. "But you ruined it. You took her from me." His voice was a whining, thin thing. "And you stole my scythe. *Her* scythe. Do you know how *angry* she'll be?"

May desperately pulled at her magic, the fire in her blood, but she knew it wouldn't be strong enough. Not against him. James flexed his hands and held them out from his body. The ground shifted, moved. And then hands were shooting up through the weeds and dirt.

"Shit," Ethan swore, and spun, seeing all the corpses pull themselves from the ground.

The first zombie pulled itself from the earth, a rotten smell filling the air in front of them. Ethan fired twice at it. Fast and without hesitation. The skull split as the shots found their mark, and the zombie dropped.

"So, the brain thing is real?" Ethan asked, voice too high, too breathless.

May had no words as she threw more fire at the next zombie. It burst into flames but managed several steps before finally falling in a screaming, screeching heap. Bile rose in her throat, and she fought the urge to vomit. Unconsciously, they moved closer, back to back, as they turned to face the quickly closing group of zombies.

Ethan's gun behind her fired several more times as she continued to send flames at the zombies before she heard a *click*.

"I'm out."

Shit, shit, shit, shit, shit.

How many were there? Eyes glowed in the starry sky, and the growls seemed to come from everywhere. To her left, a smoldering body, one she'd dropped early on, slowly pushed itself to its feet. It turned and lumbered toward them.

She gasped, too breathless to scream, and grabbed at Ethan.

On the porch, James laughed a crazed, maniacal laugh.

And then the world seemed to slow. May knew it didn't actually, but for her, it did. She heard his laugh. His glee in their impending doom. And fury filled her. Vaguely, she heard Ethan shout and jerk, but her focus was on the Necromancer laughing in the haloed light. And the blood that soaked his clothing.

"May!" Ethan screamed, and with a jerk and pop of sound, she came back to herself.

He grappled with one as it pulled him down, jaw snapping and drooling.

"No!" she screeched, and flung a hand out toward James's bloody clothing.

She pulled on the blood there. The power that was in the blood. She still wasn't sure what a Blood Witch was or what that meant for her, but she would not watch another person she cared about die.

And she was surrounded by blood.

Power filled her, sizzling and hot, and out of the corner of her eye, she saw James' blood burn and blacken on his clothing. She rushed to Ethan, wrapped her hands around the zombie's neck, and took that sizzling scorching power in her veins and *burned* it. She took the fire that always came so naturally to her, fueled by this new blood power, and forced it through her hands to the corpse.

It burned white hot, flaring instantly and dropping in a pile of smoking ash.

Ethan shot to his feet, dusting the smoking bits off as May gulped down air, lungs not working fast enough. Her throat burned, but she didn't notice the smell of burning flesh anymore or taste the ash on her tongue.

A hand scratched at her arm and back as another reached them.

"Enough!" she screamed, and flared hot again.

It dropped in another pile.

Her vision blinked in and out, her breath coming too fast, too shallow. The power danced in her veins as her heart thumped a manic pace in her chest. Gulping down rancid air, she turned to James; he'd stopped laughing.

"Kill them!" he screeched, pointing a shaking hand at them.

But the dead were slow. And she was fueled by rage.

She ran, dodging through hands and past clamoring bodies. She didn't know how many were actually after them. Her only focus was Thormunt. She reached him, hands outstretched, her lips pulled back in a feral snarl. Her fingers touched his shirt as she scrambled for him. He threw her off with a flail of his arm, and punched with his other. The blow hit her clumsily in the shoulder, but the strength behind it was unnatural and threw her off her feet. Numbly, she felt the pain in her arm as she fell in the dirt.

May ignored it and jumped back to her feet, rushing for him again, but a corpse grabbed at her leg and pulled her again to the ground. Her face hit the dirt, and she tasted blood as she bit her tongue. She turned to kick the thing, and Ethan slammed into it in a flying tackle. They both rolled to the ground, and he clamored free of its flailing hands.

"Go!"

Her eyes landed on Thormunt again, and this time, he was the one to turn and run.

She reached for him with her magic, her desperation, her rage. She reached for the blood in his veins with the power in hers. The knot of magic in her chest flared, expanded, and popped.

May felt the moment her magic touched his blood. It felt solid in her hand. Real as she held it. Held *him* still.

He screamed in her grasp as she walked over to him. Around them, the zombies had also frozen. If she focused, she could feel them as a faint extension in his blood. Like threads of a spiderweb. He thrashed against her grip, and she squeezed her hand against it.

Thormunt stared at her with wide, sickly eyes. The rage burned in her, and whatever was in her eyes, made him go pale.

She burned the blood in her mouth and felt the sizzling

power in her veins again. May slid her hand along his neck. It was gentle, almost a lover's hand.

"You're going to burn."

She saw her father's face. His smiling face and gentle laugh. She heard his encouragement and felt his arm across her shoulders when she struggled with her magic. She'd never have that again. Her mother, lying in a hospital bed, robbed of her soulmate. They'd never have the peace of *before* ever again. It was gone. He'd robbed them of that. In the back of her mind, she wondered, if this would cost her, her humanity, if this was the last step down the slippery slope she'd been struggling against. She released her magic and smiled as he screamed.

She found she didn't care.

CHAPTER FORTY-FIVE
HISTORY REPEATS

The echoes of barking and howling filled the air. The usual silence broke with the hounds' growls—deep, furious, and filled with a promise of blood. Harper rushed through the snowy trees, Nerwen at her back, as the sounds of fighting slowly overcame the sounds of her hounds. She burst through the tree line and into the clearing. The Maw glowed green, the souls of the damned rushing and pressing against the boundary, but what held her attention this time was the crowd of Nephilim.

They pressed against each other. Some had thrown off their cloaks, a sight that made Harper's blood boil and teeth clench. They pressed against each other, teeth bared and hands clenched. More than a couple lunged and swiped at each other. At the center of the mob, stood Armeal and Kian. Blood coated both from a myriad of injuries and cuts. Armeal had Kian's wings in his fist, pulled painfully tight behind him, as Kian snarled like a rabid animal.

"What is this?" she bellowed.

The Nephilim froze at her words reverberating about them.

Even her hounds paused as her shout shook the ground. The Nephilim parted, some more reluctantly than others, until the brawl between Armeal and Kian lay before her. They were the only two that seemed unaffected by her shout, so she stalked toward them.

Luras caught her eye in the crowd, and the tense set of his shoulders, his wings held tight, and fist clenched around his scythe, made her pause. What had brought this on?

"What is this?" she asked again as she stopped before the two.

Armeal held Kian to the ground, his knee pressed into the other Nephilim's back as he wrenched his wings back. Blood trickled down from finger spaced gouges in Armeal's cheek.

"He is a traitor," Armeal growled, his furious eyes never leaving Kian's back.

"Then why is he still here?" she asked Armeal. Then to Kian she asked, "Why did you not leave with the others?"

Kian grimaced, his face contorted in an angry mix of pain and rage.

"He spied," Armeal said, and wrenched Kian's wings farther, "for Yrien."

The crowd surrounding them riled. They hissed and growled, pressing in on them.

Luras and Nerwen flared their wings to try to push them back, but the crowd didn't listen, and still, they pressed in.

"And how helpful my loyal kin was."

Harper turned sharply toward the voice, her angelic voice, and saw the figure standing farther down the Maw. She kept to the edge of the gaping hole, almost like a taunt; almost as if to say *See? It doesn't scare me.* Her wings were healed, though one hung the littlest bit lower than the other.

So, history really does repeat.

Yrien stalked toward them, and the Reapers shuffled away.

A scar now marred that beautiful face as it cut from the corner of her right eye to the tip of her chiseled chin. Yrien smiled at her, though there was no warmth in her gaze.

Harper bared her teeth at the Yrien, and her hounds growled, a low vibrating sound she felt in her feet.

"How dare you show your face here."

Yrien tilted her head, looking at Armeal pinning Kian, and with a flick of her fingers, green threads of magic threw him back. Harper groaned as she felt the Soul Magic pull from her, a painful, drawn feeling. The Nephilim gasped around them, and Kian slowly, stiffly pushed himself to his feet to stand at Yrien's right.

"How dare you," Harper growled. "The magic of the death is *forbidden*!"

"Only because you say it is!" she shouted back. She smoothed her hair back from her face, like she could smooth her anger away, and shook out her lopsided wings. "See, I need it now." Her fingers danced across her sternum. "And I'm tired of taking scraps."

"Souls," Harper said, her voice dangerously low as she stepped forward, claws out, "are not *scraps*! They do not exist to keep you alive!"

She surged forward, only to be stopped by a wall of Nephilim—Yrien's Nephilim. Luras growled and pushed through, but he was soon held down by more of Yrien's supporters. Nerwen was silent, and Harper couldn't spot her beautiful wings in the crowd. Armeal still hadn't risen from the attack Yrien had thrown on him. She stared in shock at the Nephilim blocking her way. Yrien grinned at her with arrogance and malice.

"So," she said slowly as she eyed the Nephilim, "not all of you left when you were given the chance."

"Leave?" Yrien asked as she slowly stepped forward, and

her followers parted for her. "Why would they leave their home?"

Harper flexed her claws. The hellhounds growled, a sharp, angry contrast to her delicate voice. Harper summoned *her* scythe into her hand. The gleaming, black blade arched above her head as the thick staff settled in her grip. Yrien only smiled wider.

Armeal stepped next to her, breathing heavily, with fresh blood running from a gash in his hairline.

"If you are loyal to me," Harper said, adjusting her grip on her scythe, "you will flee to the woods."

She noticed hesitant movement around her, and that hesitancy was all it took. It was too late for them to flee before chaos erupted.

Yrien dove for her, her claws extended and teeth bared.

Attack! she commanded her hounds as she met Yrien's attack, Harper's scythe swinging down on her. Yrien caught it, and again they tugged against each other as they spun. Around them, Nephilim fought Nephilim. She caught Armeal's white wings to her right as he threw Nephilim aside, and the sound of screams echoed painfully in her ears at her hounds tasting Nephilim flesh again.

"You're so easily distracted," Yrien whispered, and she pulled Harper close. "First with the Necromancer and his silly wish for his wife, then your little witch, and then again..."

Yrien looked slowly, meaningfully toward the Maw. Harper's blood ran cold as she followed Yrien's gaze. She saw Kian, scythe raised, swinging it for the Maw's boundary.

Her chest exploded in pain when the blade broke the magic holding back the damned. She dropped her scythe in a gasp and fell to her knees at the unexpected agony as her soul threatened to be ripped from her. A sound so loud, so evil, when it broke through the Underworld, it caused the ground to shake. Her hounds went wild, and even the Reapers scattered. Harper stretched her magic for the Maw, green threads twisting from her clawed hands as she struggled to hold the barrier together.

"And you're too arrogant." Armeal's voice sounded above her, followed by a squelching sound.

She chanced a glance up and saw Armeal's scythe blade protruding from Yrien's chest, blood soaking the front of her robes nearly black.

The Maw's boundary heaved, the souls of the damned pressing against it as it threatened to fail, and Harper turned her attention back to it. Frantically, desperately, Harper flared every bit of her magic, her very soul, to hold the threads together. To keep the damned in. It didn't matter if her Nephilim won this fight, if Yrien fled or killed them all. If the Maw broke open, if the damned escaped...

It would trigger the End of Days. It would call the Horsemen to ride.

Her focus narrowed to the Maw. Sounds grew muted, her vision narrowed, and her magic flew from her to repair the broken boundary. Harper groaned as she physically reached for the fraying threads. Spirits and ghosts slipped through the opening, and her hounds growled and tensed behind her. Those that strayed close enough to the ground were set upon by her sleek, deadly hounds. She pulled for the strength of the dead, the souls wandering the Forgotten Forest, but it wasn't enough.

Armeal knelt beside her and smelled of iron. "What do you need?"

She couldn't speak. She was aware, peripherally, of fighting happening around her. The screams and growls were muted to her ears, unimportant.

All her strength went to knitting the magic that held back

the End of Days. Harper could see greater demons rising from the depths, aiming for their chance at escape. She had to close it before they reached it. She put every last bit of herself into the magic. Her vision went dark at the edges. Suddenly, a burst of energy, of magic had her sitting upright, her vision clearing, her breathing easier.

She glanced at Armeal, who now hunched in pain, face ashen gray and wings withering, as he leant her his strength, his life.

No, she thought, and started to block the connection, but he cut his eyes to her in a harsh glare.

"But your wings," she muttered, glancing again at his wings fading faster and faster.

"It does not matter," he grunted. "It is my duty."

His duty...

As this was hers.

With his help, Harper sealed the boundary, and with a gasp and grunt of pain, fell to the side as it settled back into place. They each lay in the snow, panting, gasping until slowly, hesitantly, Reapers approached and helped them to their feet.

No one spoke. No one dared breathe.

She looked at Armeal and felt true sorrow at his black wings. Gold veined through the feathers in way a she thought beautiful, but she knew he would not. For their beautiful white was gone. He did not look at them, but he did not lower his eyes as he met hers.

"Yrien?" she asked softly.

"Disappeared. The coward fled after I wounded her; took her followers with her." Armeal grunted, his face withdrawn. "How does she survive?"

"The dead," she said, and started walking the carnage left behind. "She's using the souls to sustain her life."

She found Kian lying near the edge of the Maw, scythe still

in his hand from where he'd cut into the boundary. The burst of magic had killed him, most of him burned and blacked from the power. Yrien would've known releasing such power would claim whoever was stupid enough to try. She'd sent this Nephilim to his death for nothing. She'd wasted a life simply to injure her.

She sighed, too tired to feel anger and too betrayed to feel sorrow for his death, and turned in a slow circle, noting the numbers of those remaining. Many lay dead on the snow-covered plane. She walked among them, but she stopped when she saw the small body in a too-large Reaper cloak. She knelt next to the body of Serenity, the quiet, timid Reaper who had seen too much of war.

Sorrow filled her. She had told Serenity she would protect them. Protect her. And she had failed. Those that had stayed, those that were loyal, she had still failed them.

Nerwen and Luras slowly came to stand with Armeal, and Harper forced her sorrow back. Death could not weep for the dead.

"Gather our dead," she said as she stood. "Armeal will show you where they may rest. Leave the bodies of the traitors for the hounds."

She locked eyes with him until his widened with understanding, and he nodded. He would show them to the cavern for the fallen. He would know what to do with the scythes.

"And you, Death?" he asked.

She looked over the Maw, calm and guarded once again. Her fingers pressed to her sternum. How? How had May done it? Was that why the ghosts sought her out? Was this why she could touch the Tethers?

"I must speak with the Fates."

She stood in the swirling, darkness of their world and felt an exhaustion she'd never felt before. It was more than the loss of the magic, of repairing the Maw. It was the loss of Serenity. The loss of those that had stayed.

"She brings death with her," the Crone's harsh voice broke into her reprieve. "Many threads ended this day."

She snapped tired eyes to the Fate. "I have a question."

"Oh," the Crone sang in her crackly voice, "let us see if this is the right question."

"She has struggled," the Maiden said, her voice gentle and young, "to find the right one before."

Harper took a deep breath. "I think I've found it now."

The Mother, crow's feet at her white eyes, smiled softly. "Have you?"

"I tasted something in the witches blood. Something... I didn't think possible."

The three stood shoulder to shoulder, their sightless eyes boring into her. "Ask," they said.

"You said May and I are bound together. Our threads interweave."

They nodded, and Harper could sense their apprehension. She could feel it in the air, like lightning before it struck.

"Is that because—" Harper swallowed, her mouth suddenly dry. "Because May has bound a piece of my soul to hers?"

The Crone smiled, her broken teeth showing in her wide grin. "Finally, she asks."

"How?"

The Maiden spun webs, a multitude appearing in her hands and she stretched them wide. In them, a scene was woven in the silver and blue strands. The Mother stepped forward, her hand pointing delicately to the threads. It was a scene Harper remembered but had once forgotten. May lay on the floor of her apartment. She'd been so close to death that time; the window had been so narrow. Harper had watched the witch struggle to breathe, struggle to fight through a heart that had failed her. But Harper had forgotten that sharp pain she'd felt right before May had won the battle with her death. It had been sharp and quick.

She'd forgotten the *wanting* feeling, the aching. The missing.

"The Blood Witch did the unthinkable," the Crone rasped, pointing her shears at the scene. "She stole a piece Death to ward off her own."

"But there is one more question." The Mother turned her white eyes to Harper.

Harper swallowed, her eyes going again to the scene where May had taken a piece of her. "What does that mean for me?"

They laughed. "It means," the three said, their voices overlapping and echoing around them, "Death no longer walks alone."

CHAPTER FORTY-SIX
EVERYTHING ENDS

The heat of the fire barely registered in May's mind as she watched Thormunt's body burn. The white-hot heat, hotter than any normal fire, made quick work, and soon he was a pile of ash and bone. Around her, the last of the zombies burned, their screams and moans soft in the night air.

Ethan stood at her shoulder, breathing heavily, soot smeared across his face and in his hair.

"We need to go," he said.

May couldn't look away from the burning piles.

"May!" He shook her shoulders, and her eyes snapped to his finally. "We need to leave. The cops are going to be here any minute. Same with Fire. There's no way the neighbors didn't see the bonfire you just made."

Shaking herself, she finally *saw* the carnage around her.

Shit, she thought, panic rising. *Shit, shit, shit.*

There were too many bodies. Even burned to ash, many piles were too big. There would still be bones. Enough for the police to notice. Notice and ask far too many questions. She could already hear, in the far distance, the faint sounds of sirens. Kneeling, May placed her hands onto the dry earth and yellow grass. She pulled on the fire in her blood, it came quick and easily now, and she felt her body warm. Her chest burned, and coughs rose in her throat. Racking coughs shook her as she pushed her fire through the grass.

"May!?" Ethan shouted over the growing roar of flames. "May, what are you doing?"

She stood, wobbled, and bent over with another fit of coughs before she could answer. "The cops can't find the zombies. But him"—she pointed at the pile that was James Thormunt—"they can find."

Ethan nodded slowly. "They'll think he tried to burn the place down. Cover up for what he did to his wife."

"Hopefully," May rasped, and pulled Ethan's arm. "We should go now."

Carefully, they ran through the far edge of Thormunt's property. Away from the flames and smoke. The smell of burned flesh. The sirens were loud in the air now, and there was a growing crowd of neighbors on the street. They continued along the road, away from the house.

"Do you know where we're going?" May asked once the heat of the flames no longer touched her shoulders and the sounds of firemen shouting was a distant whisper.

"Yeah," Ethan muttered. "This road eventually connects to another. We can follow it down to the main thoroughfare. Maybe call an Uber."

May looked down at their clothes, covered in soot and smelling of smoke and bad barbecue. She wasn't so sure about the Uber, but she was too tired to think of a different plan. So, they walked in silence in the dark, until slowly, they entered a newer part of the neighborhood. Streetlights started dotting the road, and soon there were the sounds of traffic and nightlife. May followed Ethan blindly, wheezing and coughing as they went, until eventually, he deemed it safe to try for an Uber.

Surprisingly, only one driver turned them away.

"Your rating is really going to take a hit after this," May muttered as they dragged themselves from the car and toward her apartment.

Inside, they stood there. Silent. Confused. Maybe a bit broken. Ethan finally took a deep breath and pushed her toward the bathroom. They each took their turns showering, and then they were back on the couch; Ethan in his again borrowed military sweats. May stared at them and remembered her dad. Remembered it all. The sobs burst from her without warning. She curled in on herself, knees to her chest as she wished the world would swallow her whole.

Her father was dead, her mom was... barely clinging to life. Her childhood home was gone. She'd burned her father's corpse. The horror kept rising to the surface, the smell, the sounds. The screams. She tried to tell herself she'd killed the man responsible, burned him to nothing but ash, but that didn't settle her soul. It didn't ease her broken heart. She only thought, through the tears and fear and sorrow, that she had killed him and liked it.

Ethan's arms wrapped around her shaking shoulders, and he hugged her tight as she cried.

The sharp, piercing sound of a phone ringing jerked them both awake with a gasp and grunt an unknown amount of time later. It must've been soon after they'd finally fallen sleep. Ethan grunted and rolled off the couch as he flailed for the phone on the coffee table. He thudded to the floor on his knees with a grunt and a curse. May's heart pounded in her throat as she tried to catch her breath.

"Hello?" Ethan muttered into his phone, only to frown when the ringing continued. "Shit, I think it's yours."

May looked around the apartment for the sound, unable to remember where she'd dropped her phone.

"Kitchen," Ethan muttered, and he pushed himself standing. He stumbled to the kitchen, then handed her the ringing phone.

She squinted at the screen, and her heart stopped when she saw the name of the hospital.

"Hello?" she said trepidatiously.

She listened, growing increasingly numb as the chaplain on the other end of the line talked. They were kind and soft-spoken. At least she thought they were. She nodded, then remembered and muttered a "Thank you" and hung up the line.

"What?" Ethan asked, still standing and staring down at her. "What happened?"

"My mom's dead," she whispered.

She remembered something about too much blood loss. And an infection from the burns. Something like that.

Distantly, she noticed Ethan sitting, wrapping an arm around her. Talking.

But all she could think was how unfair it seemed. She'd killed him. She'd burned him alive. And he'd still managed to take everything from her.

May stumbled numbly through the mortuary planning and organizing. It helped, she told herself macabrely, that the house had burned to the ground. It made going through their things easy. The days following her parents' deaths, life began to feel rote. But rote was good. Rote was human. Grief was normal. It wasn't supernatural. Ethan told her the police had closed the case into James Thormunt. His remains had been located and identified. And the killings stopped. May tried to find solace in that. Peace. Some form of justice.

Her phone was never silent; text messages and calls from her coworkers offering condolences. Her father's remains and her mother's body went to her office for their autopsies. Her coworkers would've known what happened as soon as they'd shown up on their tables. She couldn't bring herself to respond to the messages. It was too much.

Most days, it didn't work, but she tried.

Lady Death was absent, and the one time she'd whispered into the compact for Armeal, it had gone unanswered. She didn't know what that meant, but she was too preoccupied with her human grief to put much thought into it now. Later, maybe. But not now.

She returned to work, eventually, to the routine it offered. Her coworkers were awkward around her, but eventually, even that faded back to normal. The ghosts were still a thing. Though, now, they didn't bother her or demand her attention. They just... were. Some seemed to notice her. Most didn't. Her life slowly returned to normal. And that, even with the occasional ghost, was all she wanted.

ABOUT THE AUTHOR

Award winning fantasy author Natalie Johanson lives in the beautiful mountain valley of Utah with her two cats, Watson and Holmes, and her adorable wife. She spends far too much time staring out of windows, drinking tea, and buying books she'll never have the time to read.

Her debut novel, Shadow's Voice, became an award-winning book, followed quickly by Shadow's Past. The award-winning series *The Shadowstalker* continues to grow and monopolize much of her time and focus; not that she had much to begin with.

www.ingramcontent.com/pod-product-compliance
Lightning Source LLC
LaVergne TN
LVHW041655060526
838201LV00043B/441